DJ TEES

DJ TEES

JOHN NICHOLSON
Nick Guymer Series
No.4

HEAD
PUBLISHING

http://www.johnnicholsonwriter.com

Thanks to Robert, Janet & Sarah for their editorial talents, insights and inspiration.

Cheers to Dawn, Alan, Andy, Daniel and all my readers for their support and encouragement.

And, as ever, this is dedicated to the Teesside diaspora, wherever they may be.

*"Listening
to women
made a
man
of me"*

CHAPTER 1

'Do you know there's a tattooed, naked woman drinking wine in your stock room, Jeff?' said Nick Guymer, pointing to the back of the shop. 'I just walked in on her.'

'Was she totally naked?'

'Well, she was down to rather minimal underwear.'

'Got a good look, did you?'

'The merest brief glimpse. I'm too much of a gentleman to stand there with my tongue out for long. Impressive ink work though. Do you know her, or is she part of the evening's entertainment?'

'Yeah, it's Janice. She came straight up from work for this party. She's just changing.'

'Janice? *The* Janice?'

'My girlfriend Janice. Yes. Don't look so shocked. As you have seen, she is a human female and not some sort of shaved gibbon.'

Nick laughed. 'No man, I'm not shocked. I just didn't know she was coming up for the big new shop opening.'

'Big new shop? It's hardly a Virgin Megastore, is it?'

'No, but all the same, it's a big thing man; opening a brand new shop on Stockton High Street. I'm proud of you.' He slapped him on the arm.

'Aye well, someone has to resurrect Stockton, don't they? Why not do it through the sale of old vinyl records to the socially dysfunctional? That should increase the town's GDP by about 185 quid per annum.'

'Hey it's a big stock room you've got in there, though. This place is quite a size really, isn't it?'

'Yeah it's three times as big as the Harrogate shop, but somehow I've already managed to fill it full of boxes of albums. I like it though. It's quite classy. And talking of classy, here's your Jules.'

Julie Wells walked into the store in a blue denim jacket, white jeans, white t-shirt and baseball boots. She stood for moment resting her weight on one hip, scratched her centre-parting, pushed her loosely curled blonde hair behind her ears and looked around.

'Hey it's class this, Jeff, man,' she said, in a broad Teesside accent. 'I like all the posters on the walls and that. Smart, like.' She flashed her turquoise blues eyes at him and slapped him on the back. 'How brilliant is this, eh? A shop on Stockton High Street. It's mint, I reckon.'

'Aye. It is like. Thanks Jules.'

She bounced on her toes, excitedly. 'So pleased you're doing this, man. Stockton needs somewhere for all the weird blokes to go.' She laughed and patted him on the back again.

He looked at his watch and tugged at his big greying beard. 'We've got about ten minutes before people turn up. I've got all sorts coming, including your mam, Jules. I'd better see what Janice is up to, can't have her comatose on cheap Cava just yet.'

He went into the back room.

'Janice?' said Julie, in a conspiratorial whisper, 'Is that his girlfriend?'

'Yeah it is.'

'What's she like, do you know?' She grinned at him.

'I've not actually met her yet. I've only seen her in the back getting changed. She was wearing the sort of underwear the *Daily Mail* would definitely call skimpy.'

'She laughed. 'Skimpy? Really? Women don't normally show you their knickers so quickly.'

'You did.'

'Aye, but I've always been a bit loose, me, like.' She laughed and thrust her groin at him.

'She's got loads of tattoos up her arms and legs - big roses and some sort of mermaid, plus the usual tribal stuff.'

'So you stood there for five minutes and got a good eye full, did you?' She raised her blonde arched eyebrows at him quizzically.

'No, I'm just very observant and she did have a lot of flesh on display. I just apologized and walked back out. That's all, honest.' She let out a bark of laughter.

'Well you've got to make the most of a naked freebie like that, especially at your advanced age, ya auld get.' She tapped him on the belly with the back of her hand.

'She's a well-built woman, like. All breasts and wrestler's thighs.'

'Hey, don't be rude. We're all very sensitive about our thighs.'

'Did I say it was a bad thing? Actually, I think she's great for Jeff. A proper biker lass. Just what he needs.'

'Well he's lost such a lot of weight since his heart attack and he looks in rude health these days. It's nice that he's got a lass. I don't think I've ever known him have a girlfriend.'

'He's quite the businessman now, our Jeff. Quite a catch. He's a man with two shops, albeit two shops filled with old records by Gary Numan and China Crisis and populated largely by middle-aged men with poor personal hygiene.'

She jammed her hands into her jeans pocket and shivered.

'God, I'm dead cold, me. I thought because the sun was out today it was going to be one of those a nice mild early Spring days, but it's bollock freezing - if I had any bollocks to freeze, that is.'

'What's the female equivalent of that then?'

'Of bollock freezing? It's got to be fanny freezing, hasn't it? Or maybe clit cold. Oh no, that's not right at all. I never said that, right?' She shivered and shook her head.

'Whatever it is, it's still only late February on Teesside Jules, we don't take off the thermal underwear until July, you know that.'

She pulled at the waistband of her jeans. 'I forgot I was wearing long johns, must be why these feel so tight on us. So when is the big celebrity due to arrive?' she said, picking up a copy of Joni Mitchell's *Miles Of Aisles* album and opening up the gatefold sleeve. 'Love this. How gorgeous is Robben Ford in that photo?' She showed it to Nick, pointing to the guitarist featured on the live record. He grinned. She constantly surprised him with her rock knowledge gleaned from living around his huge record collection.

'Celebrity might be too big a word for Mr DJ Tees. Tees Digital's most popular presenter.'

She put the record back in the rack. 'Well he's big on Teesside. Everyone knows Alan Armstrong. Even I know him and I don't even listen to the football phone-in that you do with him. I like his drive-time show though. I always listen to it on the way home.'

'He's due any time now,' said Jeff, coming up behind them with a glass of wine for Julie and a bottle of water for Nick.

'Cheers, Jeff,' she said. 'Good luck with the new shop. I'm sure you'll be dead successful.' She clinked his glass in a toast.

'Well I had a go at being dead and that didn't suit me. So I'm aiming for successful,' he said, rolling his eyes up into the top of his head.

As he talked, a tall woman emerged from the back room in a black jumper and jeans. She had cropped greying hair and a nose that looked like it had melted slightly.

'Hiya. I'm Janice,' she said in a pronounced West Yorkshire accent.

Nick saluted her. 'Is this your first time up on Teesside?'

'Yeah. I've never been up here before.'

'Where are you from, like?' said Julie.

'I live in Harrogate on Claro Road, but I were brought up in Castleford.'

'OK. So you know glamour when you see it then,' said Nick, gesturing around him.

She laughed. 'Yeah. I like what I've seen so far though.'

'I love Stockton, me,' said Julie, stamping her cold feet to get them warm. 'I know it's a bit knackered, but somehow, that sort of suits it. I can't imagine it all done up and posh. It'd be wrong. If we could just attract some proper long-term investment to match our faith in the place, it'd be a lot better off. It's got so much to offer, I reckon. The countryside around here is really lovely.'

'That Davey James should get you on his team to do PR for the area,' said Jeff, handing Janice a glass of sparkling wine.

'Who's that?' asked Janice, sipping at the wine and then wincing.

'Oh god Jeff, that's absolutely minging that is.'

'Aye, some of the bottles are past their sell-by date by a mere year. I'll open another for you, might get a better one.'

'Davey James? He's the big hero around here these days. He heads up this...what's it called Jules?' said Nick.

'The Urban Renewal Organisation,' she said, pinching her nose and sipping the wine melodramatically. 'Jeff man, this stuff isn't wine, it's a heady mix of piss and vinegar!' They all laughed.

'Yeah, that's it. The URO,' said Nick. 'He campaigned to get public money to support the building of low-cost housing schemes and other social rejuvenation projects on Teesside. He's a Boro lad who made a packet in property development over in Spain, came back here and set up this URO thing with his own money. He's building all the houses though, so he's coining it in, big time.'

Janice nodded and took a fresh glass from Jeff. 'Ah that's better. Thanks.'

'Aye, everyone loves Davey,' said Jeff. 'All the politicians want a photo op with him. Mind, to be fair, he's sorted out a lot of stuff that's needed sorting out for a long time. You know that new estate he built on Darlington Back Lane, you can rent a two-bed semi there for only £300 a month. Low-cost housing that isn't a bloody hovel is the least any town should be able to offer its citizens, I reckon. Especially when people are expected to work 40 hours a week for a minimum wage so low that you can't actually live on it.'

'Amen comrade,' said Nick, hi-fiving Jeff.

'He sounds proper good, him,' said Janice. 'We need a bit of that in Castleford.'

Julie smiled and waved over Nick's shoulder at someone behind him. He spun around to see an old school friend, Paul Trent.

'Alright Paul.'

'Alright Nick. 'Hiya Julie.'

She grinned at him. 'Ey up Paul. How are you then?'

'I'm alright me, like. Sick of the Boro being shit.'

'Aye, we are rubbish, like. Championship next season, I reckon,' she said.

Paul turned to Jeff. 'Gorr any new wave singles, Jeff?'

He nodded. 'Yup, but they're not unpacked yet. Come back later in the week Paul, I'll have 'em all out by then. Do you want a drink?' Jeff offered him a glass of the Cava.

'Oh ta like. I'll just 'ave a look at them singles there, while I'm 'ere like. Hey that's nice that. Is it wine? Tastes like cider to me, that, like. I love cider, me.'

He found his way to a big box of seven-inch vinyl and slowly and methodically began to look through them.

'Never happier than when looking at old singles, that lad. He was just the same at school 30-odd years ago,' said Jeff, affectionately.

Julie turned to Janice. 'They were all at the same school together y'see. I was an' all, but I was a few years behind them. We call him Daft Paul. He's not daft really...just a bit different. Lovely lad. Loves the Boro and records and drink and parmos. And that's it. It's the simple life for Paul.'

'Aw bless 'im,' said Janice.

'I like these tattoos,' said Julie pointing to a winding vine of roses up Janice's arm.

'Cheers. Aye, that's a new one. Have you got any tatts Jules?'

Nick laughed.

'What are you laughing at?' said Julie.

'Nowt. You tell her,' he said.

Julie blinked slowly and witheringly at him. 'I do. Well, a little bit of one. I was supposed to get 'Boro' tattooed on the small of my back, but they did the B and then I passed out...'

'...due to being utterly pissed,' added Nick

'...due to being shit-faced, aye. This was about 15 years ago. So I was supposed to go back and get it finished, but I never did so I'm left with one red B...which is a bit odd really. Ruined my small of the back modelling career.'

As she talked, a man with collar-length, shaggy dark hair, wearing a black jacket and ecru chinos looked around the door.

Nick waved at him.

'Here's the star of the show, come in Al.'

'Now then young Nick,' he said, shaking his hand and looking around.

'Young? Are you sure?' said Julie, shaking the DJ's hand. 'Nice to meet you Mr DJ Tees. I'm Julie. We've not met before have we?'

'No, I don't think so. You were at Ian Ramsey though, weren't you?'

'Aye. That's right. I was three years below these two though.' She pointed at Nick and Jeff, who busied himself with wine.

'Al was in the fourth year when we were in the fifth,' said Nick. 'It was the fourth year you came to the school wasn't it?'

'Yeah that's right. Came up from York. My dad got a job at ICI. I remember you though, Julie. You've not changed at all.' He smiled warmly at her.

'See Nick, Mr DJ Tees remembers me at school, how come you don't?'

'Oh well, my life was wall-to-wall glamorous blonde lasses back then. I was fighting them off with a stick. So you all blend into one in my mind,' he said with a shrug. She laughed.

'Scaring them off with obscure prog rock albums, more like,' she said.

Nick turned to Jeff. 'Quick Jeff, which progressive rock record is best for repelling women with?'

Without missing a beat, the big man replied. 'ELP's *Brain Salad Surgery*. No woman has ever liked any ELP album. It's a passion killer.'

'Ha, that's where you're wrong. I like the first side of *Pictures At An Exhibition*,' said Julie.

Jeff laughed. 'You might have to check to see if you're actually female, Jules. Maybe there was some sort of mix-up at the hospital.' She laughed and punched him on the arm. Alan Armstrong smiled and nodded.

'Well it's good to meet you Julie. Yeah, that whole DJ Tees thing seems to have stuck with me now. I feel a bit embarrassed by it. Makes me seem like I'm a bit of a Billy Big Bollocks.' He looked around the shop. 'This place takes me back, it's like Alan Fearnley's old place used to be in the 70s. Wall-to-wall albums. It's like going back in time.'

'Yup, that's the idea. It's my gaff by the way, I'm Jeff, if you remember me from school? Thanks for coming Alan.' They shook hands.

'Alright Jeff. This place looks great for men of a certain age. I'll have to get my old turntable out of the loft. I must've put it up there in 1990.'

'Any old vinyl that you don't want, bring it in for me, especially if it's 60s or 70s rock,' said Jeff.

'I might have some Dire Straits records somewhere.'

'Ah...well...don't bother with those, I've got about four copies of every one of their records already, but if you've any obscure psychedelic folk music from 1971, I'm yer man.'

Jeff gave him a drink and began circulating the room as his guests began to arrive.

'Thanks for doing this for me, Al,' said Nick. 'It'll really help Jeff get a bit of publicity. The *Gazette* is sending someone down and *Tyne Tees* are sending a camera because you're here.'

'No problem. Always happy to help out a local business. God knows, it's going to be hard making it work in the teeth of this recession. There's not much money around is there? I know I'm skint.'

'Yeah, we're totally borassic as well. So, no there isn't, not on the High Street, nor at the Boro for that matter. Fans are growing restless with our form aren't they? We'll get more angry punters calling in this week if we don't beat Wigan.'

Alan made a flat grimace and shook his head.

'I don't understand some fans, they seem to think Steve Gibson should keep getting further in debt just to buy some over-priced players. Between you and me, the sooner we go down, clear out all of the players on silly wages and get the club back on an even keel, the better it'll be. We've been living above our means for too long and eventually you've got to wake up and realise the party is over. Eindhoven already seems like a long time ago.'

'Well I think relegation is odds on. We can't score a goal to save our lives right now,' said Nick, looking around. The room was filling up quickly. It was a big turnout. Amazing what a crowd free booze and snacks could draw, even early on a Tuesday evening in February. He didn't recognize any of them, but then Jeff always did have a big social circle on Teesside and had kept in touch with a lot of people that they'd gone to school with.

'Oh hey, did you manage to find those old programmes for me?' asked Alan.

'Yeah. They're in the car. They're mostly from the mid 70s. I only collected them for about two years, then I moved on to vinyl to scratch my collecting itch.'

'Great. I really love them as historical documents. The way they look, the photos, the type of fonts used, they always reflect the era they're from,' said Alan. Nick nodded.

'Totally, yeah, that's what I like about records as well. People think I'm mad for liking how a record label looks - the way the text is laid out on it and all of that. It's art and history and music all rolled into one.'

He turned around. The place had really filled up now. Jeff had disappeared somewhere, Julie was preoccupied with getting her newly arrived mother and auntie a drink.

'I'll just go and get them for you or I'll forget. Don't know if you know anyone else here, Al?'

He looked around. 'Nobody I recognize. Not to worry. Does Jeff have a toilet in here?'

'Yeah it's in the stock room. Just go through that plywood door and it's the room right at the back.'

'Cheers mate.'

Nick walked out of the store, pushed past some people who had spilled out onto the pavement and strolled down to nearby Silver Street, where he was parked outside of The Stag pub. The skies had cleared and it was set to be a frosty evening as he opened up the old BMW and took out the Tesco carrier bag of programmes. He took his time walking back. Parties weren't his sort of thing really. He found being in large groups of people all talking loudly at each other, both exhausting and quite inhibiting, so he didn't hurry back. As he approached, there was a crowd of people milling around the entrance to the shop, drinking the cheap, nasty Cava, smoking, laughing and generally being northern and noisy.

As he entered, someone pushed past him and went out, making a little more room. A man in a black roll-neck sweater and jeans turned to look at him with a funny, nervous look in his eye. Nick didn't have a clue who he was and gave him a perfunctory smile and nod. Teesside was full of people who looked familiar. It was a small area really and you were rarely far from someone you knew or someone who knew you. As he got inside the shop, Julie was standing on top of some record boxes in the corner of the room with her camera held aloft, taking photos. She'd put a new fish-eye lens on so she could capture the whole room in a single shot. A long time fan of photography, she especially liked photographing wildlife around their home in the countryside, south of Yarm. This was a different kind of wildlife though.

'Everybody say penguin!' she shouted, as he got into the room. There was a ripple of laughter as people shouted the silly word and raised glasses. She took a short burst of photos on an automatic setting, then paused to look at the results. Nick picked up a small bottle of fizzy water from the counter and held it up to toast the occasion. Where was Jeff? He should be in these pictures, but he couldn't see him as Julie took another burst of shots on a rapid automatic setting, checking the results once more.

'One more time with feeling!' called out Julie '...and say cheesy peas!' They all did so as she took a final collection of shots.

Jeff came out of the back room, picked up a Cava bottle and began circulating, topping up glasses and chatting. Nick saw him, but couldn't get through the crowd to tell him he'd missed the photos before he felt his arm being tugged on. It was Julie's mother, Jackie; a small, wizened woman in her late 60s who seemed largely held together by the tar from a million cigarettes. She was only too keen to turn up anywhere there was free drink. She'd come with her sister, Julie's aunt Sandra, a formidable 65-year-old Hardwick woman with hair dyed jet black and a face set in a permanent look of indignation.

'Still not drinking, Nick?' Jackie said, gesturing at his bottle of water.

'Nah. It doesn't sit right in my head.'

'You don't drink, you don't smoke, what do you do for fun then?'

'I have it off with your daughter, Jackie,' he said with a grin. She let out a rasping laugh.

'You dirty sod. She was a virgin before she met you, you know that?' She let out another cackle full of tar and phlegm. Sandra did likewise. 'And if you believe that, you'll believe anything.'

'Is mam being arsy with you?' said Julie, getting off the boxes in the corner and peering over his shoulder.

'Hey, I'm nowt but sweetness and light me, Jules, you know that. I was just saying how you'd never been kissed before you met Nick.'

'Don't try and stir it, mam,' said Julie, jabbing a finger at her mother.

'Me? I'm doing nowt, me.' She looked around her innocently. 'Mind, white jeans at a party Jules, what are you thinking? You're only one wet fart away from trouble in those.' Sandra cackled another laugh and swilled down the rancid Cava. 'And they're a bit tight aren't they, considering your age, like. They're right up your doo-dah, those. Are you not wearing any knickers? It's not that sort of party is it?'

Julie pursed her lips together and looked away from her mother in annoyance, turning back to her to say,

'Don't be vulgar, mam. It's not clever. You know nothing about clothes anyway.'

'I know you've got summat on them already.' Jackie pointed at a smut on Julie's leg. 'And that white's out of fashion this year.'

Julie set her jaw against Jackie and looked at her scornfully. 'You're giving me fashion advice, mam? You? You've still got a purple shell suit at home.' When arguing with her mother, she often lapsed into her old Hardwick accent, pronouncing purple as 'pearpull'. 'Anyway I thought you might have put your good Marksies jacket on instead of that cheapy turquoise thing off the market.'

'Cheeky sod. This *is* my good Marksies jacket,' said Jackie, annoyed. 'Now, to apologize for that, you can top my glass up with big Jeff's fizzy stuff.'

They seemed genetically programmed to antagonize each other. The way they went on often put Nick in mind of Dora Bryan and Rita Tushingham in the film *A Taste Of Honey* from the early 60s. Underneath it all, they loved each other after a fashion, but neither would give an inch to the other. He got hold of one of the nasty bottles and topped up her glass. 'Do you actually like this stuff, Jackie?' he said.

'Aye. It's a nice drop, like. Tastes like cheap pop to me.'

'Good grief, your taste buds must be destroyed after 50 years of smoking 60 fags a day mam,' said Julie, shaking her head and walking away. Her mother pulled a face and stuck two fingers up at her daughter behind her back and then laughed.

Nick looked around for Alan to give him the programmes, but couldn't see him. Jeff was still topping up glasses and chatting with prospective customers. He was pleased for his oldest and best mate; pleased he'd got his health back after the heart attack, lost four stone off his sizeable frame, got a girlfriend for the first time in years and done well enough with his shop in Harrogate to warrant opening another in his home town of Stockton-on-Tees. He deserved some good times.

The new shop was situated on the corner next to Stockton Parish church, along from the Royal Oak, a veritable institution of a pub that he and Jeff had drank in since they were 15 years old, just set back a little from the High Street. It had been a restaurant or café in the 1970s when they were kids, but had recently been a computer store. It was a good-sized space, probably three times as big as the Harrogate store and it needed filling with thousands of records if it wasn't to look empty. Jeff had installed some record bins around the perimeter and then planned to put more boxes on tables up the centre of the shop floor. A new big red sign above the door declared, accurately enough, 'Jeff's Records'. With the recession in full swing, it probably wasn't the best time to open a new shop, but then Stockton was always in recession and seemed to have been so since about 1977. The latest one had hit the place hard, but it had been hit hard by the previous 30 years. There were few if any economic boom times on Teesside; just getting by was a way of life for most people.

A middle-aged man in a parka, rucksack on his back, knelt on the floor and went through a 50p box of albums emerging with two ELO records.

'Who do I pay for these?' the man said, proffering a pound coin towards Nick who waved it away.

'Nah. Take 'em man. Opening night freebie,' he said knowing that Jeff had seen enough copies of *Out Of The Blue* and *Eldorado* to last him a lifetime and would just be happy to get rid of them. Vinyl retailing was as much about getting shot of the unwanted worthless stuff as selling the rare records.

The delight on the man's face was out of all proportion to the largesse that was being bestowed upon him. Maybe just getting something for free was a small victory in a cruel world.

Where was Alan? He still couldn't see him. He'd started working on Alan's football phone-in show at the start of the season and it had gone so well and become so popular after an initial run of three that he'd been invited back for the whole season. There was not much money in it, but it was funny, often unintentionally so, and as he'd been friends on and off with Alan since school days, it was no effort to do.

Julie came up behind him and held him around the waist briefly.

'How are you doing?' she said in his ear.

'Fine. Have you seen Alan?'

A middle-aged, dark-haired woman with dark, panda-like rings around her eyes squeezed past him and went out of the door. Who were all these people?

'No, I haven't. Mam is driving me spare. This place is packed, I don't think you could get any more in here.' She looked around her and took a sip of wine. 'Do I really look alright in these jeans? Mam's been going on and on at me about them being too tight and too young for me because they're cut low on my hips.'

'You look great man. Honest. She's just winding you up.'

'I know. I'd hate to be mutton dressed as lamb, though. You can't see my knickers through them can you?' She quickly turned around and he glanced at her backside.

'No you can't. I assumed you weren't wearing any.'

'Your mind lives in the gutter.'

'Aye, right next to yours. You look great and if anyone said you didn't, your mam would, ironically enough, be the first to kick them in the teeth. Just laugh her off.'

She pecked him on the lips. 'You're right. I will. I don't know why she still gets to me after 44 years.'

'Because she's your mam and she knows to how to press your buttons.'

'Aye well, I'll have to get a cab for her soon, she'll drink the place dry given half a chance. Do you know many of the people here?'

'Not really. Some semi-familiar faces.'

'I took loads of photos as keepsakes. This is such a big day for Jeff. I know it sounds daft, but in my mind, having a shop on Stockton High Street is just dead big and important.'

'That's because we grew up when it was big and important. Sadly, it's not like that any more, is it?'

'No, but even so, it's still a big thing, I reckon.'

The AA Show producer, Amy Jones, came over to chat. Jeff came after her.

'Have you seen Alan, Amy? I want him in a photo,' said Jeff. She shook her head.

Nick looked around the room. 'I don't know where he's gone. I went and got this bag of programmes for him and I've not seen him since. He was going to the toilet,' said Nick.

Jeff frowned and scratched his beard. 'I'll go and see if he's still back there.'

Amy's face was a picture of puzzlement. 'I wonder where he's gone?'

'Maybe he got called away,' said Nick.

But within 30 seconds, Jeff was back and in a hurry. By the look of shock on his face, Nick knew something was wrong immediately.

Jeff grabbed him by the shoulder.

'What's wrong?'

'Some bad shit has happened. This way...'

He led him into the back room through the piles of boxes and pointed to the open toilet door. Inside, slumped face down on the floor, was Alan Armstrong. Motionless. Lifeless. Dead. Very dead.

CHAPTER 2

'Bloody hell...Alan...Alan...can you hear me?' said Nick, squatting to one side of the prone body.

'He's dead,' said Jeff, dialling 999 on his phone.

'Shit...shit...how did this...has he had a heart attack or something? Alan...Alan...wake up mate...' He shook him by the shoulder, but it was pointless, he obviously wasn't alive. It was then that he noticed a trickle of blood emerging from underneath the body, released by his shaking of the corpse.

'He's bleeding Jeff, look! You don't bleed like that if you've had a heart attack.'

'Hello. I've got a dead body in my shop, I need police and ambulance. He might have had an accident or someone's attacked him...I don't know...I can't tell.' Jeff gave the emergency services the address.

'What's going on in here then...?' said Julie, putting her head around the door and walking in. 'What's wrong? Eeee fizzin' hell...what's up with him? Is he drunk?'

'He's dead, Jules,' said Nick, standing up, feeling shell-shocked to the point of numbness.

'Eh? Dead?!' She looked at him with her blue eyes blank with incomprehension. 'How's he dead, like?' She bent over him. 'Oh my god, he's bleeding...look...are you sure he's dead?' She lay a hand on his back and then got down onto her hands and knees and tried to look in his eyes, but he was face down, staring but not seeing. 'But he feels warm...we should cover him with something. Get your coat Jeff. He might not be dead. Not...you know...technically or something...oh my god...you poor man.' She patted him on the back instinctively, as though to comfort him.

Nick threw Jeff's big parka to her and she lay it over him. He looked around the large room. Jeff had filled it with plastic boxes of albums still to be sorted; stock he'd accumulated for the new venture. There was no way out of the room except through the shop.

'Poor fucker,' said Jeff, shaking his head looking at the body as he rang off the phone. 'Christ, I don't know what to say, or do, or think. He was just alive in there and now he's gone. I can't grasp it...it's...it's fucking mental.'

Julie stood up. 'He's bleeding really heavily, you know. It's soaking into his shirt and jacket, but it's pouring out of him. God, I feel sick.' She held her hand over her mouth. 'Unless he fell on something sharp, I think he's been stabbed or shot or something. Eeee poor fella. Eeee god, this is awful Jeff and on your big day an' all.'

'A big day for me, a lot bigger for chummy here, as it turns out.' Jeff's curtain of long hair fell across his face.

'If you're right, Jules, we shouldn't touch anything. This might actually be a crime scene, though I don't know how anyone could have done this while we were all through there,' said Nick. 'Does this place look how you left it, Jeff? Has anything been moved, anything been robbed?'

Jeff pushed his long hair over his shoulders and stroked his beard and he looked around.

'It's all just boxes of albums, isn't it? A desk with some invoices on, a kettle, jar of coffee, two mugs and a sink that has seen better days...nope, this is how I left it earlier. I just piled all the plastic storage boxes up so there was a pathway to the bog.'

Nick stood by the door. It was a bit of a maze.

'You've got a hell of a lot of stuff in here, Jeff. '

'Aye, some of those boxes are empty though. I just stacked them up as high as possible so they'd not take up too much room. But you're right like, there's about five thousand albums in here to sort and price up. It's a bloody nightmare job.'

As he talked, sirens blared out, coming along the High Street.

'What am I going to do with everyone? We can't exactly keep the party going with a stiff here in the back can we?' said Jeff. 'I better tell them it's all over. We've still got some of that terrible wine left too.'

'Watch your mouth Jeff, don't be heartless, man,' said Julie, her hand still over her lips.

'Cops will want everyone to stay put won't they? Suspicious death and that...' said Nick.

A familiar face looked through the door. The tall, sharp and neat Detective Inspector of Cleveland Police, Colin Harcombe; a man with a severe side parting, beak-like nose and granite jaw. They all knew him well.

'I thought this was your new place, Jeff,' he said, coming in and holding out his hand. 'I got your email invite, but I couldn't come. I was working. Working here as it turns out. Nick, Julie...the whole gang's here eh? Now, what on earth happened?'

A second officer followed his boss into the room. Nick pointed at the body.

'It's Alan Armstrong, Mr DJ Tees, y'know, the Tees Digital DJ.'

'I found him lying here,' said Jeff. 'He's been bleeding heavily.' He pointed at the trail leaking from the body.

Julie stood, arms folded across her chest, chin resting on her hand, quietly shaking her head. 'I think he's been shot or something, Colin.'

The DI went over to the body, inspected him closely and squatted down next to him, placing his head flat on the ground. He pushed the body up a little while he looked under him. He made a noise of surprise and let out a low whistle as he did so. 'He's been stabbed in the stomach. The knife is still in him, right up to the top of the handle. Nasty.'

Julie let out a cry of shock. The policeman went quickly into official mode.

'Right, I need you all out of this room. This is now a crime scene,' said Colin Harcombe with a natural authority. He instructed his fellow officer to stop anyone from leaving. 'Get the music off, start taking names and addresses. No-one leaves.'

'Oh God, I feel sick,' said Julie, turning away. Nick put his arm around her shoulder and pulled her into him.

'Who'd want to do that to Alan? He's just a fella from the radio.

I've known him for over 30 years. No-one hates Alan,' said Nick. 'He's one of the good guys. A nice man.'

'Well, he didn't fall onto the knife. Someone's done for him,' said Harcombe in his distinctive, clipped, almost 1950s style of speaking. 'Bad business. Very bad. I'll need a list of everyone you invited here, Jeff. '

He nodded. 'Yeah, of course. I can't believe anyone has come here and killed him though. I mean, murder? Really?'

They all stood behind the counter in the shop looking at each other in shock as the paramedics arrived. There were shrieks of emotion as people heard the news. More police cars arrived. No-one was allowed to leave as the place was locked down. Names, addresses and statements were taken from everyone present by a huge team of police officers. TV cameras arrived and lights from live reports for local TV shone brightly into the dark Stockton night. After an hour or so, Nick spoke to Harcombe in the back room.

'Col, I was just thinking, I was probably the last person he spoke to...' As he entered, the paramedics where sliding the body into a black zip-up bag to take for a post-mortem. The large, chunky black knife handle was now quite clear. It was stuck into the top of his stomach at an angle, about five o'clock, as though it had been jammed into him with an uppercut. No blade was visible, only the handle. It must have gone right up into his heart. He felt ice cold at witnessing the evidence of such a profound and simple act of brutality. Why would anyone do that? He was one of life's gentle souls. Even the usual passion and bluster that the football phone-in generated was somewhat diffused by his good nature and reasonableness. He wasn't a shock jock with instructions to wind up the listeners in order to get them to phone in and shout loudly about things they knew very little about. That wasn't his gig at all. He was reason itself. Always giving people a chance to talk. No-one could dislike him enough to have a harsh word about him, let alone to want to kill him.

'Maybe it was a robbery gone wrong,' said Jeff, eventually, after everyone had been interviewed by the police and allowed to leave and the deceased had been taken away. 'Maybe someone thought there was money in the back, sneaked in, Alan tries to stop him and boom.'

Julie shook her head. 'No,' she said, with certainty.

'How can you be so sure?' said Jeff.

'Because of where he fell.'

She walked into the toilet, now cleaned of his blood.

'He was stabbed in here. Someone was waiting for him.'

'She's right Jeff,' said Nick. 'They've hidden in there, Alan's come to use the toilet, and they've knifed him in the guts. He wasn't, y'know, undressed in any way, so we know he hadn't started to use the toilet. So he was stabbed like this...' He swung his right arm upwards, clutching an imaginary knife. 'I think he died right away – that knife would have gone right up into his heart, so he's slumped forward onto the floor, maybe slumped onto the killer. And then whoever did it must have walked right back into the crowd of people in the shop. Whoever did it, we absolutely must have seen them.'

Jeff scratched his head and looked awkward and uncomfortable.

'Yeah OK I can see that, like, but how did they know when he was going to need a piss? You can't just hide out in a toilet on the off chance. You might be there for hours and other people would keep coming in to use it. It doesn't make any sense, that. They must have followed him in, got round in front of him and stabbed him. I don't think anyone just stood in there on the off chance.'

Colin Harcombe came back. 'Right, we're done here now. Are you two still at the farmhouse outside of Yarm?'

'Yeah. Jeff's actually staying with us while he gets the new shop up and running.'

'Ah, good. Right. I shall be in touch.' He took a look around and shook his head. 'Bad business this. I will *not* be tolerating knife crime on my patch. That much I can assure you of.'

After he'd gone, Jeff mimicked the tone of the policeman's voice. '"Bad business this." He's like *Dixon of Dock Green* that bloke. Speaks like it's still 1952.' He rubbed his face with his hands.

'Come on, we might as well get home,' said Nick. 'Where did Janice go?'

'Oh...err...she got off home to Harrogate. No point in her hanging around.'

'She could have stayed with you at ours,' said Julie.

'Thanks Jules. She's got work in the morning anyway, so...what did you make of her?'

'She was nice, Jeff. Down to earth,' said Julie

'Yeah she's that, alright. This will probably put her off though.'

'Nah man, not unless you actually murdered Alan,' said Nick.

'Then again, women love a jail bird though, don't they? Those death row inmates get loads of female attention,' said Jeff.

They turned out the lights and locked up the shop. It was after 10.30pm and quiet now. A lone 17 bus to Ingleby Barwick pulled up at a stop and an old man got off.

'I'm not sure I'll want to go back in there on my own. The place is imbued with the stench of death,' said Jeff as he pulled the shutter down and fastened the padlock. 'I might get Lukey to come up and help me and to give me a bit of company. I'll let him ride my bike up here. He's always on at me to give him a go on it.'

Nick drove them in his old BMW to their house in the countryside, south of Yarm. Jeff followed in his van.

'I forgot how nice it is here. It's peaceful, isn't it? Listen to that, not a sound...not even the cry of a drunk dropping his kebab,' said Jeff as they stood on the doorstep.

Nick laughed then felt guilty for laughing so soon after Alan's death. Later that evening, he sat in bed as Julie brushed her teeth.

'Are you alright, luv?' she said, standing at the end of the bed, toothpaste foam on her lips.

'Alright?'

'About Alan and that. There was nothing we could do for him, was there?'

'No. I just find it hard to believe this happened to him at all and at Jeff's too. Why Alan and why at Jeff's?'

'I can't imagine,' she said and went to spit out the toothpaste. Back into the bedroom she pulled off her white jeans and t-shirt.

'Oh god, it's good to get them off. They were cutting the blood off to my legs.' She rubbed at the red mark the tight waistband had left around her hips. 'I hate to say it, but I think mam was right about them, they were too tight. I'm sure they didn't used to be. Maybe I've put on weight.'

He looked her up and down, standing in front of him in a white bra and a small pair of white knickers, her hands on her hips.

'There's nowt on you, man. You don't look any different to how you've looked for the last three years and anyway, I like you in those white jeans and t-shirt.'

'Yeah, but you're a bit pervy about white pants and underwear aren't you? You always have been. I don't mind, but it clouds your judgement. Ha ha. Was I not supposed to say that? Did you think I didn't know? It's not hard to tell. Look at you, giving me the once over. Your eyes are like saucers.'

'I don't know what you mean, Jules,' he said, innocently.

'It's alright, your dirty secret is safe with me, lad. Here...here's a treat for you...' She took off her underwear and threw it at him, laughing again.

'I'm not sure these will fit me,' he said, holding her knickers up.

'Oh aye, well I'm sure you'll have fun finding out,' she said, pulling on her pyjamas and getting in alongside him, peering at him under the sheets as she did so. 'Ah ha. Look at the state of you. Thought so. Total perv.' She made a silly grin at him.

'This is all very embarrassing,' he said, putting his hand over his groin.

'I know. Ha ha. You've actually blushed. Aw, that's cute. Its funny that you're so easy to turn on. I like it.' She kissed him on the cheek and flopped down on her back and let out a big sigh. 'Right, OK, change of subject to more serious things. I think there has to be more to Alan than you knew. I mean, he wasn't a close friend was he? You don't really know much about his private life.'

He threw the underwear into the wash basket.

'What? You think he's a drug smuggler or something? A gangster? And that's what has got him killed?'

'Not necessarily, but maybe he did something, a business deal perhaps and it went wrong and he pissed off someone badly. You don't know. It's easy to think someone who is apparently respectable can have another life all together. They see that all the time at the Teesside Women Centre.'

Julie had been volunteering at a Stockton-based women's drop-in centre since before Christmas, doing admin and answering the phones. 'You get these blokes who are evil wankers and y'know, they torture their wives and behave like animals behind closed doors, but everyone else thinks they're all sweetness and light. They can't imagine that he's a total bastard, so they blame the woman for making it all up.'

He turned out the light and she lay on her side, putting the flat of her palm on his chest.

'They run this thing called the Freedom Programme that tries to educate women about what domestic abuse is 'cos a lot of women don't even realise that what might seem normal in their relationship is actually abusive. They tolerate so much that they shouldn't have to tolerate, so it shows them what to look out for and to question what they're putting up with day-to-day. It's really good. Very supportive, like. And it helps them spot a wrong 'un in the future. A lot of women get really isolated by these men. It's terrible.'

Nick sighed. 'Men are twats. We cause so much trouble. When we're not beating each other up, we're beating women up.'

She pulled gently at the hairs on his chest.

'Aye, there's some truth in that, but there are decent blokes out there as well. You've got to remember that. Your trouble has always been your depressions, but your moods have been better for ages now, especially since quitting drink and sugar. So I don't want you getting really down about this Alan business. I know it's horrible, but being miserable won't change anything.'

'Yeah. I know.' He sighed again.

It was true, but it was still really hard work for him not to get depressed. He didn't talk to her much about it because who wants to hear someone going on about themselves all the time? But every day was a struggle to a greater or lesser degree; a struggle to keep the dark thoughts and the emotional void at bay. He was never ever free of it, not for one second. Fighting it had become a default part of his daily existence. He'd learned to manage it better and his ongoing talking therapy worked as a bit of a pressure valve, but he still couldn't even say he was that happy most of the time. Instead he aimed to be content, because it seemed much more achievable. He used to think that one day, somehow, he'd be fixed, that he'd be better and his depressive episodes would be a thing of the past, but now he knew that wasn't going to happen. This was who he was, it was who he'd always been and there was no altering that basic fact. He put his hand on Julie's as she talked.

'I don't know how the support workers down there do it without just breaking down every day. They see and hear some awful things. I just hear bits and pieces because I'm around the office...'

'...and I bet they get paid sod all.'

'Nowt at all really, I'm sure.'

'It's always the way, isn't it? It's like people's good nature is exploited, so if you do a socially responsible and useful job, you get nothing, meanwhile evil sods get rich by being fucking people over.'

' "Life is unfair and then you die," that was one of mam's favourite expressions when we were growing up.'

'Alan went for a piss and didn't come back. Just like that. He was gone. That was certainly unfair.'

He hugged her to him tightly, still fretting over Alan's death and eventually fell asleep.

It was a bright, cold morning. Nick was awake early as usual and took a walk around a route he regularly followed out of the back of the farmhouse, in a loop along the side of a ploughed field, down to a fast-running beck and back around through a copse of trees. The Cleveland Hills were a purple strip on the skyline with crumbs of white clouds scattered above them against the azure sky. As often happened, a robin skipped alongside him, flitting through the hedgerow as though hoping he might be able to feed it. Fancifully, he thought it was the same robin every day. A morning walk helped him keep his mood up. Maybe it was the connection to the natural world. By the time he got back, Julie was up and frying bacon and eggs.

'Nice walk?' she said with a bright smile as he walked in the kitchen.

'Yeah, the robin followed me again. I'm like a pied piper for robins, me.'

'I love a robin. Smart bird. When I was digging up the carrot bed, one was sitting and watching me the whole time. I could've reached out and touched it. They're dead tame. Give Jeff a shout will you, I'm almost done.'

'Jeff! Breakfast!' he shouted, but the big man was already on his way and appeared at the top of the stairs in a tie-dyed t-shirt and jeans.

'I love staying here, man. The smell of hot lard in a morning and a woman in the kitchen wielding a fish slice. Perfect.'

He grinned at them both.

'Is it not as good if I wield the fish slice, then?' said Nick.

'Well, to be fair son, you're not as good looking are you?'

'Eeee, you're being nice. You must be in love,' laughed Julie, putting a plate of bacon, eggs, a slice of black pudding and a fried tomato in front of him.

'Look at this. A feast!' he said, drumming on the table with his knife and fork.

Nick made coffee, filling the kitchen with the aroma of roasted Java.

'You're still low carb then?' said Nick.

'I've lost 70 pounds on it, so why wouldn't I be? It's high fat low carb, to be precise. Straight out of your cookbook, Mr Guymer.'

'I bet your doctor hates you for it.'

Jeff nodded. 'Told me off for eating lots of butter. I told him straight, I was 20 stone because I drank loads of beer, ate loads of carbs, especially bread and potatoes, so if I stopped doing that, it seemed logical I'd lose weight. And I did. Mind, the thing that really pissed him off was that my cholesterol has halved on the new regime. I think he reckons I'm cheating his blood tests, somehow.' He grinned at the thought. 'I get the feeling he knows sod all about any of it. Just wants to prescribe drugs and get me to fuck off.'

'Well we're both dead proud of you,' said Julie. 'You look amazing. Ten years younger.'

Jeff held up a forefinger. 'That's nice of you to say Jules, but err, no I don't. One, I'm still an ugly hairy bastard and two, I'm still a fat sod; just a much less fat sod. I need to get rid of another two stone yet. But I'll do it. I'm all about pure food these days. No crap. Never felt better.'

'Well you look great on it,' she said, sitting down to eat. 'This is organic bacon and eggs, mind. So I hope you can feel it doing you good.'

'Delicious. I've started going to the gym as well.'

'You've not, have you?' Nick said.

'Aye. Resistance training they call it, probably because everyone resists doing it.'

'Weights and that?' said Julie.

'Yup. I'm lifting 30 kilos.' He flexed a bicep.

'You're like the Teesside Incredible Hulk,' said Nick.

'I'm built like a brick shit house now, me.'

'His Lordship here does that as well, don't you?' said Julie. 'He's got a load of weights in the spare room if you want to use them. You'll be getting a six pack, next,' said Julie, pouring coffee.

'There's one under there somewhere, like. I'm just pleased to be able to see my bollocks again. It's been a long time.'

'Yeah, we're eating Jeff. No bollock talk at the breakfast table, please,' said Nick, holding up a hand.

26

'It's not like we're eating sausages.'

'All the same...'

Julie chuckled to herself. 'I'd never have thought you'd change your life around so much, Jeff. It's really amazing, especially quitting drinking lager. You bloody loved lager.'

'Yeah well, if nearly dying doesn't make you wake up and smell the embalming fluid then nothing will. I can't be dying yet, not until I've completed my collection of non-European Jethro Tull releases, anyway. Life or lager isn't a difficult choice. It's one poor old Alan Armstrong would like to still be able to make.'

'Aye. Amen to that,' said Nick.

'Are you not eating Jules?' said Nick, seeing she was just having coffee.

'No. I feel a bit sickly. Not sure I'd keep it down. I'll be alright.'

Jeff pushed his empty plate away. 'That was fantastic, thanks Jules. I texted Luke last night. He's coming up as we speak. I want him to help me to go through all the new stock and get it priced up, assuming they let me into the crime scene. Death or no death, I need to start earning some dosh and I don't want to have to be in there on my own with the ghost of Alan Armstrong haunting me.'

'That's right enough. You've got to be practical,' said Julie, rubbing her stomach. She looked a bit pale and drawn.

'What are you two doing today?' Jeff asked, finishing his black coffee.

'I'm writing my thesis on Romano-British administration in the first century, for my MA, like, then I'm going into the Teesside Women office to do some admin, or at least I will if I feel up to it,' said Julie.

'I'm writing a column about why Middlesbrough being relegated wouldn't be the end of the world,' said Nick. 'I'll come over at dinner time and we'll go and have a steak if you like. I'll buy.'

Jeff pointed at him. 'You're on, pretty boy. I shall have seen enough Jim Reeves records by then to drive any sane man loopy.'

'Why are there so many Jim Reeves albums in second-hand record shops?' said Julie, putting dishes into the dishwasher.

'Because he sold millions in the 50s and 60s, everyone who bought them is now dead and no-one, not one person left on earth wants to play them. Thus they all got dumped on innocent record dealers like me. It's a little known fact that 18 percent of all land fill on earth comprises of Jim Reeves records. Another 8 percent is Phil Collins solo records.'

'I liked Phil Collins in Genesis,' said Julie. 'He was such a brilliant drummer. What's that one I love on the live album, Nick?'

'Dance On a Volcano.'

'Aye, that one. Du-du-du-du-du-du-du-du-du-du,' she said, doing an approximation of Collin's classic tom-tom style.

'Everybody liked Phil Collins in Genesis,' said Jeff, '...but singing Motown? That, quite genuinely, should be illegal,' he laughed, hitching up his jeans. 'But I fancy a bit of early Genesis. *Selling England By The Pound* will be the first thing on the turntable this morning, We're bound to have a copy of it somewhere in the shop.'

Julie opened her laptop and read the *Evening Gazette* web site headline as Jeff got his stuff together.

' "DJ Tees Found Dead. Unexplained Death In New Stockton Shop". So they're not actually calling it murder yet. Interesting.'

'It has to be murder, doesn't it?' said Nick, handing Julie the plates.

'The poor sod didn't stab himself, did he?' said Jeff, putting his laptop in a bag along with some magazines and a notepad.

'I don't think he could have, not given the angle of the knife,' said Nick.

'Could have been manslaughter. Maybe someone accidentally knifed him,' said Julie, reading the report.

'No way, man. Nobody gets a knife in the guts like that accidentally. Not unless you're in a knife throwing circus act and even then it's not likely,' said Jeff. 'I bet he had a secret life. Everyone thinks he's this nice guy, but on the quiet he's been up to all sorts, eventually he pisses someone off and gets filleted like a kipper.'

Julie made a groaning noise of protest at his language.

Nick rubbed his forehead. He'd been thinking the same thing, but you didn't like to think badly of anyone you'd got on well with for so long. He was an apparently plain, middle-aged man with a wife and grown-up kids who lived the semi-detached suburban life in leafy Hartburn, one of Stockton's nicest suburbs. There wasn't even the smallest hint of a life other than that.

He tried all morning to settle into writing but couldn't. His mind was restless and he couldn't get the image of Alan Armstrong's lifeless body out of his mind. All he could see was him lying face down on the toilet floor. He kept trying to analyse what Alan had said to him before going to the toilet to see if there was anything significant, but it had all been so innocuous. He'd asked where the toilet was, so obviously he didn't know beforehand, so it seemed highly unlikely he'd arranged to meet the person who had killed him in there. It had to be a random act of violence by a lunatic.

As walked up the High Street to Jeff's after parking in the Castlegate shopping centre, there were three police cars outside the shop. Two officers stood in front of the door.

'Hiya. I'm Nick Guymer, Jeff Evans who owns this fine store is my mate, is he inside?'

'No-one's allowed entrance to inside, sir,' said the uniformed officer in the awkward, studied manner of all police officers. No entrance to inside? Did he think he wanted entrance to outside?

Nick took out his phone and called Jeff.

'Nick?'

'Jeff man, I'm outside your store but they won't let me in.'

'Aye, they've got forensics in here with me and Lukey dusting for prints and DNA and looking for low numbered copies of *The White Album*. They could probably find the residue of a lot of drugs on half the records in here. Hang on there, we'll come out. Can't get much work done anyway.'

Nick stood and looked up and down the familiar High Street. It was now an overcast early Wednesday afternoon, the early morning brightness covered by a grey blanket of cloud.

Wednesday was market day, the biggest day of the week when he was a kid. The market used to spread the length and breadth of the High Street. Pub opening hours were even extended on Wednesdays to accommodate the traders. It was one of those old laws that stretched back to god knows when. Now, with more liberal licensing laws, that sort of specialness had gone. You could be drunk at 4.00pm on any weekday afternoon instead of just Wednesdays in the White Hart, which had been a routine he enjoyed aged 17, often leaving school and going straight down there. It didn't seem much like progress.

The market used to be packed out, mostly with women buying things that only seemed to be available on market stalls, such as elastic or bias binding or long green wool army socks. Now it still happened, but it was unrecognisable from what it had been, because the unpalatable truth was that not enough people wanted to buy what people who had market stalls had to sell, and most of what they did have to sell you could get elsewhere. That wasn't the case in the 1970s. No matter how much everyone wanted to pretend it wasn't so, that was, quite obviously, the truth. The market continued and it was still popular, but its glory days and its unique selling points were well in the past now. But at least they were trying hard to make Stockton viable again, trying to get things moving and not surrender to the industrial and economic decline that had seemed to be its destiny since the late 1970s. But by god it was a tough fight and one that they were by no means certain to win.

There were loose groups of unemployed young lads from the economic underclass hanging around, doing not much. With ravaged skin and dressed in a uniform of baggy-arsed tracksuits, hoodies and trainers, they pulled on fags and had their hands stuffed down the front of their pants, playing with themselves, presumably to distract their minds from their meaningless, work-less existence. It didn't bode well for the future. They didn't look like a useful workforce waiting to be employed, they looked more like they were waiting for the Pound Pub to open. All their youthful energy being drowned in cheap lager and strong cider. What a bloody waste. Yet despite being skint and stuck in, what looked like a spiral of economic decline, judging by the numbers of pregnant girlfriends they had around, they seemed to be involved in an intensive breeding programme; one which the rest of society was going to have to pick up the tab for at some point. Had society let them down, or were they letting down society? Maybe both. In one way he felt sorry for them, because life didn't seem to offer them much, but then they didn't seem to be helping themselves much either, probably because they were depressed, drunk, stoned or all three. Surely no-one wanted to live such a fruitless, aimless life, but they seemed beyond help. Nick let out a big sigh. Was he wrong to think there was a permanent air of melancholy to the place these days? Maybe it was just him and his state of mind.

Jeff emerged from the shop with Luke, the lad who he employed to help him out in the Harrogate store. 24, thin, with long, lank greasy hair and dressed in an old hoodie and worn out skinny jeans, he was an inheritor of the great unwashed, slightly dysfunctional record collector tradition. Meet the new generation, same as the old generation.

'Hey Luke,' said Nick, holding out a hand.

'Now then,' said Luke, in a broad West Yorkshire voice.

'You've spent all morning with the police around the shop?'

Jeff nodded. 'Aye, they were waiting for us when we turned up. Asked all sorts of questions.'

'I said to him, I reckon they think we've done away with that bloke,' said Luke. 'Just as well I've got an alibi for last night.'

They walked along to a restaurant called 'The Meating Place'.

'Lukey's come up with a good theory though, haven't you Lukey?' said Jeff as they sat down to order.

'Oh aye. What's that?' said Nick.

They ordered a sirloin steak each. Luke picked up his knife and began gesturing with it.

'Well. The way I look at it is this. Your blokey, Alan Armstrong, he's gone for a slash, right? Now, he's been stabbed in the front, so the stabbee must have been in the toilet, facing out, in order to be able to do that, right? He's gone, boom, right up him...' he gestured an upwards motion with the knife '...Armstrong has fallen forwards, probably onto the killer who has then had to let him fall to the ground with the knife still in him. Rather than try and get the knife back, he's panicked and legged it...but here's what I think, right. I think the stabber wasn't there to kill Mister DJ Tees, he was there for another reason and Armstrong just unluckily walked in on him and got it in the guts.'

Nick stared at the lad, his curtain of lank hair hanging below his shoulder. He was right. Why hadn't that occurred to him before?

'You son, are a clever sod,' said Nick, 'I never even thought of that. That's why it seems so odd that Alan was killed; a nice bloke like him who hasn't got any enemies. It made no sense, because there was no sense behind it, he was just unlucky. It wasn't personal, it was a mistake.'

'Exactly. Aye,' said Luke.

'I only employ the north's finest intellects, you know,' said Jeff, rubbing his neck and looking away from Nick.

'Are you alright, Jeff?' he said

'Why?'

'You've gone pink in the cheeks.'

'Shut up, I'm having a hot flush. It's the menopause.'

Nick rubbed his chin as the waiter brought them coffee. 'Trouble is, if we think that's the truth, what was the killer supposed to be doing in there? Was he waiting for someone or was he there for another reason?'

Jeff raised his forefinger to make a point, a habit he had. Nick pointed at it. 'You've even lost weight off your fingers.'

Luke burst out laughing. ' 'e 'as like. 'ow did you do that Jeff?'

Jeff looked at his hands. 'I wish I knew. It's not like I've been exercising my fingers more than usual.' He raised the finger again '...but I tell you what I don't like...if our killer was in the back room, they had to be looking for something. Something hidden there maybe, or some information. Alan just interrupted them. And if they didn't find what they were after, they'll be back again and next time it might be me who says hello to Mack The Knife.'

'We should keep a weapon back there,' said Luke. 'A big fuck off bat or a meat cleaver or summat.'

'Hold on hold on...what could be in the back of an old shop that's of any interest at all to anyone?' said Nick. 'Who had the shop before you?'

'It was a computer store. Sold hard drives and stuff. But he went bust,' said Jeff, tugging at his beard.

'There you go then. Whoever did it wanted a hard drive he'd brought in. Maybe it had porn on it or something incriminating,' said Luke.

'He's right y'know. That might be it,' said Nick

'There's nowt there. I looked. There's just one old empty cupboard,' said Jeff. 'I even looked in the toilet to see if anything had been strapped inside the tank like in the movies when they tape a gun in there. But there was nothing.'

'Aye, but it could be an SD card, couldn't it. A small bit of plastic is easy to miss. It could be hidden in a crack in the brick work,' said Nick.

Jeff pointed at him. 'Good call my bony-arsed friend. But you'd hope the coppers would find it all the same. That's their job, after all.'

Luke snorted. 'Aye, but how much confidence would you 'ave in your standard issue copper to even manage to see 'is 'and in front of 'is face? Bloody thick as two short planks, coppers. Most of 'em, anyway.'

Nick was inclined to agree, but then looking closely didn't involve any actual intelligence, did it?

The steaks arrived and they tucked in hungrily.

'How many people did you invite, Jeff?' said Nick

'I emailed 63 and said they could bring someone if they wanted.'

'Any idea how many turned up?'

Jeff shook his head. 'Hard to tell wasn't it? You were there. How many do you reckon?'

'The shop was full. You couldn't move in there. That space must hold 30 at most. 25 maybe. But then there were people drinking outside as well. So that was probably another 15 or so. I suppose there were 50 people there at the peak of it. '

'Well I saw two blokes who looked like they'd walked out of the Royal Oak and just come in for the free wine, but I thought, sod it, I don't blame them. They were just gadgees - y'know, typical Teesside booze-hounds,' said Jeff.

'Did you know everyone else then?' said Luke, scraping mustard out of a jar.

'I knew most of them, but not all by any means. I mean, Julie's mam was there with someone, I dunno who she was.'

'That was her sister, Sandra. Classic free drink scammers them two,' said Nick. 'How did you invite Jackie, anyway?'

'I emailed her cos' I knew you and Jules would be there and...'

'She's on email?'

'Yes granddad, even the old 'uns are online these days. Haven't you heard?'

'Bloody hell, I'm pretty sure we don't have her email address.'

'Aye you do. Jules gave us it.'

'Oh. Right. Why did you invite her though?'

'I'll tell you why. Because old birds like Jackie Wells know everyone. They're like a portable advertising hoarding. Get 'em on your side, get 'em pissed up and they tell everyone about your shop and where it is. You can't buy that sort of word of mouth publicity.'

'Well, you can, with corked white wine, apparently,' said Nick.

'I'm telling you, it pays to be talked about. Mind you, we'll not be short of interest now we've had our first murder.'

'We'll probably get a lot of Death Metallers in looking for blood stains,' said Luke. 'Bloody mad lot, them.'

'As long as they buy something, I don't care. I need to get that place pulling some cash in,' said Jeff.

'Have they given you an idea when you can do anything?' said

Nick.

'They said they'd be done, just for now, this afternoon. So if they clear off, I'll stay open till 9pm. I was saying to Lukey, I might open it 2pm till 10pm. Might as well be open in the evening when people are actually able to buy stuff. I don't know why shops open when everyone who has any money is at work and close just as they knock off. It's just a hangover from the past.'

The steak was a bit tough and over-cooked, the side salad a bit limp and the coffee weak. Nick found himself wanting to excuse the poor quality of it just because it was in Stockton. If it had been anywhere else, he'd not have hesitated to be critical, but somehow, slagging off a Stockton restaurant felt like being disloyal or unfaithful - kicking someone when they're down, almost. Stupid really.

Luke pushed his plate away. 'I'm glad you're paying for that an' not me. Bloody terrible,' he said, with a sneer.

'I've had better, like,' said Jeff. 'But I've had worse. Probably.'

Nick's phone rang. He looked at the screen. It was Malcolm Pallister, Tees Digital's boss.

'Alright Pally.'

'Nick. How are you?'

'I'm alright. Shocked, of course.'

'Yeah, yeah. It's a shocker, no doubt about that. And you were there, is that right?'

Nick explained the circumstances.

'Well I'm calling you because I'm putting together a tribute show for Alan and I want you to come in and record a few memories.'

'Oh, of course, yeah.'

'This afternoon OK? It'll only take an hour or less.'

'Who's going to do the Saturday football phone-in?'

'I've got an idea about that. I'll talk to you later.'

Jeff made an enquiring face at him. Nick explained who it was.

'What's he like then?' said Jeff.

'I don't like him.'

'No?'

'Nah. He's a bit of a twat. One of those blokes who thinks they're a big man, when in reality all he does is run a small regional digital radio station. It's not like he's Tom Donahue or something.'

'Very good classic rock radio reference,' said Jeff, his right index finger on his nose his left pointing at Nick.

'Who's Tom thing?' said Luke.

'He was one of the first FM rock jocks in the States in the late 60s,' said Nick.

'How the 'ell do you know that?'

Nick looked at Jeff who pulled a mad face.

'How *do* we know that, Jeff?'

'Osmosis. Rock 'n' roll osmosis. Who knows where the info comes from? We just soak it up. I'll tell you another thing, he started a label called Autumn Records...'

'...bloody 'ell,' laughed Luke.

'...and talking of obscure labels, I've got something for you in the shop, Mr Guymer...'

'Oh yeah?'

'Yeah. A single on the Fillmore label...'

'Oh yes...nice work Jeff.'

'...one side is the Grateful Dead, the other is the Elvin Bishop Group...'

'Beautiful. Oh, is it that one that was released from the *Last Days Of The Fillmore*, triple live box set?

'Yup that's it. Both live tracks. The penultimate release on Fillmore.'

'That's made my day, that has. I think only 17 records came out on Fillmore. I've got two albums and four singles.'

'Fillmore? The old venue in America?' said Luke.

'The bloke who set them up, Bill Graham, had a label for three years, 69 to 72. Nick collects them. They're US only and hard to find, but it's do-able with a bit of effort. A classic bit of collecting,' said Jeff, approvingly nodding. 'Just pick it up when you want. I don't want any money. Have it towards my bed and board.'

Nick put his thumb up and wiped his mouth with a napkin. 'I'd better get over to the Boro to record this Tees Digital thing then. I might look in on you later if you're staying open late.'

CHAPTER 3

A scattering of crocuses had been planted along a verge as Nick drove down Newport Road. They made an irregular carpet of purple and white against the green. He didn't remember anything quite so colourful or natural when he'd taken the same route as a teenager in the 1970s. As he went past the building which had housed The Rock Garden from 1976 to 1981, it didn't seem that long ago since he stood in line to get in to see Penetration, the only punk band he'd ever really liked, unusually fronted by a woman, Pauline Murray. It was astonishing how 30 or more years could just pass like that. He'd been 17 when he'd seen Penetration, now he was 48. Forty bloody eight. Bearing in mind Alan Armstrong's fate, maybe rather than feeling nostalgic and old, he should just feel damn grateful to still be alive.

The radio station was little more than two studios, a reception and a waiting area, set into an old Victorian building in the centre of Middlesbrough. Nick had just found a parking space when his phone rang.

'Hey Jules?'

'Hiya. Where are you?'

'I'm in the Boro. Tees Digital called. They want me to record some bits for a tribute show to Alan.'

'Oh. Right. How long will that take?'

'An hour they reckon. Why?'

'The fuel pump has gone on my Peugeot. I can fix it, but I'll need to get the parts from Sid's garage and they've had to order it in, so it won't be here till tomorrow. I was hoping you could pick me up.'

'Yeah. No worries. Are you at the TW office?'

'Yup. I'm done at 4.30.'

He looked at his watch. 2.45pm. 'I'll pick you up later then. If I get delayed I'll call you.'

'Thanks, luv,' she said, cheerful as ever. He got out the car, smiling to himself. The irony of her old 205 breaking down was that she'd actually love to fix it. She'd kept it going for 15 years now, stripped and serviced it herself every year or so. She could even make sense of a Haynes manual.

'Now then Nick,' said Malcolm Pallister, extending a long arm towards him. He was at least six foot and built like a wardrobe; albeit a wardrobe in a blue V-neck lambswool Pringle sweater and black slacks, looking like he was dressed for an edition of A Question Of Sport in 1982. He was about the same age as Nick, but looked much older with what remained of his grey hair cropped short. 'Terrible thing to happen to Alan...to anyone...everyone is still in shock. But I thought we should do something as a tribute to him.'

'Yeah, of course. I'm still a bit numbed by it, especially as it happened on the other side of the wall from where I was standing.'

'But you didn't see anyone?'

'Well not running out with blood on their hands, but whoever did it must have passed through the room. That's the freaky thing about it.'

'Pity there's no CCTV footage.'

As Malcolm he spoke, Nick suddenly, shockingly, remembered something. Julie had taken those photos of the room full of people. They'd both forgotten that in the shock of what had happened. Maybe she had taken a photo of the killer? Bloody hell. Maybe he should just get off home and look, the police might need the evidence to catch them quickly. Then again, how would they know which person in the photo had done it?

'At the risk of being crass, this programme will be a big ratings winner for us, so we're doing a full hour. Greatest AA Hits and all that, OK? All I need you to do is a couple of recollections and some sound-bites.'

He showed Nick into the studio they used for the phone-in on Saturday evenings. He'd thought about what to say on the way over. One anecdote about his affection for Middlesbrough legend, John Hickton and his improbably long run up when taking penalties and another about how he'd handled a caller who was so furious with Gareth Southgate's management of the Boro that season that, live on air, he called him a 'big-nosed arse.' Alan had said that was anatomically impossible, much to everyone's amusement. Handling aggressive and sweary callers was always tricky and Alan had been very good at responding to them, but not stoking their anger any further, as some in the profession did. Nick finished his recordings by saying, 'Alan was just a regular guy. He wasn't born here, but he was very much one of our own. I'll really miss him.'

'Great stuff, Nick,' said Malcolm, listening back to what he'd recorded. He seemed cheerful, happy even. It would make a good programme and it seemed that's all Malcolm was really bothered about.

'Now we've got that out of the way...' he said, guiding Nick out of the studio with a hand on the small of his back, '...how do you feel about doing the phone-in on Saturday?'

'Me? Who with?'

'With no-one. I'm suggesting you do it on your own. I'll get Amy to produce it for you. All you'll have to do is press one or two buttons. She'll do the rest. Don't worry about the technical side.'

Nick shrugged. It felt a bit like jumping into someone's grave. He was less than 24 hours dead and here was Malcolm planning Alan's replacement. It didn't feel right. Not yet.

'Can I get back to you about it?'

Malcolm pulled face, seeming to take that as a bit of an insult. To him this was a big gig and not something anyone with any sense would turn down.

'Well...OK...but I'll need to know by this time tomorrow. I've got to fill the airwaves somehow.'

Well, no, you don't really. Or rather, if he didn't, no-one would really mind for a week or two. It wasn't as though Alan had been Wolfman Jack producing an essential new art form. His passing wouldn't leave a cultural void that needed to be filled quickly. It was just football chat and as such, not actually important at all.

'Sorry, I'm a bit late, I'm on my way now, Jules,' he said, as he crossed Bridge Road over the Tees and turned onto Yarm Lane. It was already 4.30.

'Alright. I'm running late anyway. Just come into the reception area. I'll see you there.'

He went down Oxbridge Lane, passed the Oxbridge chippy, a place he'd frequented post-pub most nights as a teenager 30 years ago, crossed over Hartburn Road and drove down to Greens Lane which ran past Ian Ramsey, his old school. Even a brief sight of the place still had the ability to make his stomach turn a little knot of angst. Some part of him was stuck in there, still trying to avoid having the snot kicked out of him and still trying to pluck up the courage to talk to girls he fancied. One way or another, it was five years of ceaseless, hormonally-driven, emotional trauma. Did anyone ever really enjoy school?

The Teesside Women Centre was in an old Victorian mansion at the bottom of Greens Lane. He'd walked past it almost every night when he was 16 and 17 on his way from his home in Fairfield to his regular drinking haunt, The Stockton Arms, where he'd meet Jeff to swill down pints of Stones Best Bitter and talk about rock 'n' roll. Back then it had been some sort of youth centre.

Pulling into a dark car park under some old trees, next to Julie's stricken car, he walked into the reception area. He felt awkward because he was a bloke and here blokes were nothing but a problem. All the tears, the torture and the bruises were all caused by men. And whatever else he was, he was definitely a man and thus, he felt, rightly to be seen as a potential problem.

He could see Julie through an internal window. She was sitting behind a computer in an office with her back to him. The walls were covered with posters detailing help for everything from rape to child abuse and sexually transmitted diseases. Other notices about escaping abusive relationships and reporting violent behaviour really brought home what the place was all about. From here they organized accommodation for women who needed to get away from abusive partners and husbands. It was also a drop-in centre for dispensing advice and education, or just a safe place for women to get a cup of coffee and some sympathy.

It was both depressing and yet also heartening. Depressing, because it told so many stories of physical and mental torture, but heartening because here, women were welcomed, understood and helped by other women who, as far as he'd been able to see, were selfless, strong and empathetic. This was not easy work and it paid relatively meagre wages, which in itself seemed to reveal a remarkably misplaced set of ideals and values. Why did the people doing valuable jobs out of a sense of duty and compassion get their labour exploited for so little financial reward, while others in the corporate grind-core machine were paid handsomely for far less worthy work?

He ran his hand through his hair a little nervously and tried to get Julie's attention.

'Yes. Can I help?' said a voice behind him.

He turned around to see a tall woman with wiry grey hair, arms folded across her lime green cardigan. He found himself speaking in a higher voice than normal, almost to make himself seem less male and thus less of a problem. Idiot.

'Hi there. I'm just here to give my g-g-girl...err...to give Julie Wells a lift,' he said, his voice squeaking a bit at the end of the sentence. Girlfriend suddenly didn't sound right. It sounded sexist. Or did it? He wasn't sure. She *was* a girl. No she wasn't, she was a woman. Oh god.

He genuinely felt he wasn't some sexist pig idiot, but how did you show this to a stranger who, understandably enough, might think you were. He didn't want her to think he was some mad bloke trying to retrieve his wife from what he would undoubtedly see as the clutches of PC obsessed, lesbian feminists.

Fortunately, Julie heard his voice and looked around, waved at him and smiled. She collected her bag and coat.

'Hiya,' she said, a little laugh in her voice as she read the look in his eyes.

'Martha, this is Nick. Martha is the team leader here.'

He made a weak smile and nodded. Another woman came out of an office with a yellow folder under her arm. Seeing Julie, she stopped and came over.

'Jules, are you coming to the party at the Penny Black on Saturday?'

'I am, aye,' she said.

'Good good. We need someone who can actually sing.'

'Jules can't sing. She makes a noise like a wounded animal,' said Nick, thinking he was making a joke, but realising, as it came out of his mouth, that it actually sounded like he was putting her down in front of colleagues - a classic bullying tactic. Shit. He immediately wanted to say something to make this right. 'That being said, I'm a big fan of animalistic, atonal wailing.' Was that any good? No. Fortunately, Julie laughed and agreed with him.

'That is true like, you'll need to bring some ear plugs if I open my lungs up. I've been known to break wine glasses. I make noises only canines can hear.'

He was about to make a quip about the party attracting a lot of dogs if she sang, but thankfully stopped himself.

'And don't expect me to dance, either. People having seizures have more rhythm than me.'

The two women laughed a little at her jokes.

'Right, come on then, I'm ready,' said Julie, patting him on the back. 'See you on Saturday.'

'Ta ra Jules, see you, Nick,' said Martha walking off with a wave.

As they got outside he let out a breath.

'What's the matter with you?' she said.

'Nowt. It's just I feel so tense in there.'

'Because of your penis?'

'Eh?'

'You feel nervous because of that thing between your legs.'

'Well yeah. Being male just seems...I dunno...bad, I guess.'

'Don't be bloody daft. That's all in your head,' she said, opening up the passenger seat door.

'Yeah, you're probably right.'

He got in and turned on the headlights. 'I just feel like I should just say sorry when I'm there.'

'What? You're apologising for all men everywhere? Who are you to do that, like?'

'Well, sort of. I dunno. I just feel this urge to say, it's OK, I'm not one of the evil sods you hear about every day of the week.'

'Aye, but plenty of the evil sods would make exactly that claim. A lot of abusers think they're in the right, so even if you did say that, it wouldn't help would it?'

He groaned a little. 'Yeah, I suppose so.'

She patted him on the arm. 'Just be yourself. This lot judge people by what they do more than just by words, anyway. Words are cheap. Anyone can learn the right things to say and then behave badly, can't they?'

'I suppose so, but I'd like to think I could spot a bloke who was dodgy by his choice of words.'

'That's because you're a writer isn't it? You're all about words. Here they're more about actions. Not that the words we use aren't important. They are. Words can hurt and be oppressive. But equally someone can say nice things to you while hitting you in the face, can't they? Come on, let's get going mister, I'm starving. I put a beef stew in the slow cooker before I left.'

He turned to look at her and smiled. 'That was a typically nice thing to do. Thanks Jules.'

'I know. I'm an angel. Albeit an angel with shocking wind from the broccoli I had for dinner.' She wound the window down. He laughed and kissed her on her cold cheek. 'You're a daft bugger, you. Worrying about being thought of as too blokey. And why were you talking in that high voice? Ha ha. Trying to make out you've been castrated?'

'He'd be a lot less threatening, a castrato, wouldn't he?'

'I dunno, I've never met one. I did once date a farm lad with such a small willy, I did briefly think it must have been cut off...'

'...in a threshing machine accident, maybe?'

'...or bitten off by an angry hen...or whatever. Ha ha. Poor kid. He was so paranoid about it. Felt sorry for him.'

'A man does not need his genitals pitying. Trust me.'

She laughed. 'No, I'd hate someone to pity my fanny. Fanny pity is no good at all.'

'I would never pity your fanny, Jules, except perhaps when I'm doing something in it with a very swollen part of my anatomy.'

She gurgled a laugh. 'Nooo...no need, that's when it's having the most fun, man.'

It was only just over five miles to get home. He took Darlington Road to Hartburn Avenue and then south toward their old farmhouse in the countryside, just outside of the well-to-do market town of Yarm.

They both laughed as they sat at lights outside of Eaglescliffe.

'What was going on at the radio station then?' she said, drumming out the beat from Steely Dan's song 'FM' on her thighs, as it played on the radio.

He explained what he'd done.

'It was really weird, talking about him like that. I've not even got used to the idea of what's happened to him yet. The station boss wasn't exactly in a mood to mourn Alan's loss. He was all for moving on already.'

'You should talk to Marc Lewis about it when you have your next therapy session. Work it out of your system.'

Nick had been seeing his therapist for a couple of years now. He only went once or twice a month these days and although Marc Lewis wasn't his favourite person in the world, he'd been forced to admit a long time ago that talking about his mental problems was a helpful thing and one which had, to some degree, helped keep him healthier.

'Did I ever actually meet Alan before yesterday?'

'No I don't think so, not unless you met him at school. When I was working on the Northern Echo in the early 80s he was a sports reporter and we'd go out for a pint. It's funny, we were never really big mates, but we knew each other for over 30 years and were always friendly enough. I always felt he was a nice bloke, but a bit too pipe and slippers to be a close mate.'

'Too settled down, like?'

'Sort of. He was always off home to the wife and young kids. He had a mortgage for a new house when he was 21. He seemed so grown up and much older than me, even though he was a year younger. I was going to gigs and out on the piss, while he was at home watching the TV and feeding the bairns rusks.'

'Some people are like that though aren't they? It's like they're born middle-aged.'

'Since we'd been doing that phone-in, I'd felt a bit closer to him. Maybe because I've caught up with his middle-agedness.'

'Well now you're living with me, you've gone all pipe and slippers as well. Not that you have either a pipe or any slippers. But you know what I mean.'

'They'd better catch the bastard that killed him. Hey talking of that, I remembered something earlier. You took those photos of the shop full of people. We've not looked at them yet, you might have got a photo of the killer!'

She let out a squeak. 'Eeee god, fizzin' hell. I totally forgot. That could be crucial evidence. I took loads of pictures on that automatic setting. Most people were looking up at the camera, but some of them weren't interested. Mind, it's not like we'll see someone walking through the shop with a bloody knife in their hand, is it?'

'No, but they could easily have had blood on them. Alan must have slumped forward onto his assailant after being stabbed before he hit the deck.'

As soon as he opened the front door, the whole house was filled with the smell of slow-cooked beef stew, both welcoming and comforting. They sat down to eat right away. Afterwards, Julie poured herself a glass of red wine while he made himself his favourite Sencha green tea.

She sat down on their huge old leather sofa, loaded her camera SD card into a card reader and plugged it into her laptop. Nick sat alongside her.

'OK, let's have a look then,' he said.

'Here we go. The first one was taken at 5.43pm.' She pointed at the time and date embedded into the image. The fish eye lens gave the image an oddly bent, warped look, but took in the whole room from the entrance to the back wall into which the stock room door was set.

'I think I must have been coming back from my car after getting those programmes for Alan. I was just outside when you started shooting. Look, I'm definitely not in these first ones.'

She squinted. 'Can we put this on the big telly so we can see it more clearly?'

He hooked up the laptop to the screen with a USB cable. The image was huge on the big flat-screen TV that hung on their wall, a gift from Julie's brother Ricky, courtesy, almost certainly, of criminal activity.

'That's much better. Hmm, you're certainly not in these...and I can't see Alan either...and I can't see Jeff.'

'Let's think back. I was talking to him about the programmes and I said I'd go and get them. He said where's the toilet? I told him, then turned to go. I was away from maybe five minutes or a bit longer. When I came back in you'd started taking photos.'

'So you must have left at about 5.38 or so...' She looked at the images taken one after the other about eight seconds apart. 'Ah now, here you are, you've just come in on this one. It's 5.44 now. You look dead gormless, your gob is open.' She laughed a little at how he'd been captured.

Nick stroked his stubble, then pointed at the screen and walked up to it, pointing. 'See this bloke here right in front of me as I came in, cropped hair and wearing a black roll-neck jumper, he looked at me right in the eyes. I thought he must know me, so I nodded at him. He gave me a funny look.'

'A funny look?'

'Yeah. Like he was surprised to see me. You know how you look at someone you didn't expect to see?'

'But you don't know him?'

'Nope.' He stared at the photo again. 'It's odd that Jeff isn't on these pictures at all yet. Where's he gone? Skim through all of them.'

She clicked through all the images. The very last one was the only photo to show Jeff. He seemed to be coming out of the back room. He was a little blurred so must have been moving. She pointed at him. 'If he was coming out of that back room after Alan was killed, he would have seen Alan lying there wouldn't he?'

'You'd have thought so wouldn't you? There were a lot of boxes in the way. But it's not just that, is it? If Alan was in there, so, at some point, was his murderer. So why didn't Jeff see them if he was in there?'

'But he has to have been coming out of there because he's not in any of the other shots and there's nowhere else for him to have gone. If he'd been out front, we'd have seen him on a photo, but he's not, he's missing,' said Julie. 'So he's been in there for the whole time I was taking photos.'

'It's odd. We'll ask him later. Let's just work out a chronology of events here. I left Alan to get the programmes at approximately 5.38. He turned away from me to go into the back room toilet as I left. You took the first photo at 5.43 and neither Alan nor Jeff are in them. So they must both be in the back room. There's nowhere else for them to be. This is really bloody weird, Jules.'

'When did Jeff find him dead?'

'It wasn't that long after, but I'm not sure, really. You'd finished taking photos and then you and your mam were having a go at each other and we were chatting for a bit, before Jeff came over and asked where Al was, then he went into the back and found him. Judging the passing of time from memory is impossible. I'd have thought it was a few minutes.'

'Actually, when I think about it, I know I looked in on you at a bit after ten to. I know that because when Jeff came and got you, I looked at my watch and I thought I'll give mam ten more minutes and then I'll get her a cab at six, because she was drinking really heavily. How long had you been in there before I came in?'

'I went in, saw Al on the floor, I squatted down beside him while Jeff called the cops. That can't have taken more than 90 seconds or two minutes at most. You came in right at that moment. So it must have been 5.50 or so when he got me and took me in the back. So he found him 5.48-ish.'

'My last photo, the one with Jeff in, is timed at 5.46 and 44 seconds. Alan has to have died sometime between 5.38 when he left you and when Jeff found him at about 5.48. But Jeff was in that back room until nearly 5.47 which just leaves a minute or less for Alan to come back in, go past us to the back, get stabbed and for the killer to get away. That's not possible. We'd have seen Alan because we were looking for him and there's just not enough time for it all to fit. Yet if he was already dead, killed at 5.38, why didn't Jeff at least see the body in there?'

He pulled on his bottom lip in contemplation while she went back through them. 'Look for anyone coming out of the back room or hanging around there,' she said.

There were 36 photos in total, but only the last one showed anyone near the back room door and that was Jeff. Nick counted the people in the first shot. No-one seemed to enter or leave with the exception of him and Jeff. In every photo there was 26 people, 27 in the last one, the additional person being Jeff. But no-one had gone into the back and only Jeff was coming out of the back.

'What about the man who looked at you funny? Was he feeling nervous or guilty or something?' said Julie, pointing at the man in the black roll-neck sweater.

'He might have been yeah. Let's focus on him. Start at the first photo and let's see what he does.'

The first few showed him standing near the door holding a wine glass. He seemed to be talking to another man in front of him. He turned to look at the camera, then as Nick came in, turned to look at him. They were only two feet apart at one point, the point at which he'd stared into Nick's eyes. In three pictures he seemed to be talking to Julie's mother, or at least standing next to her. By the last shot, he'd turned his back to her and remained there until the last photo.

'I probably read his look wrong. I'm not good at that sort of thing at the best of times,' said Nick. 'Maybe he wasn't suspicious at all.'

Julie poured herself another glass of wine and sat back on the sofa, mulling it over.

'This will sound mad, but if I was the police looking at this, I'd think Jeff was the prime suspect. He wasn't in the room when Al was stabbed and he seems to be coming out of the back room shortly after he'd been killed. He's the one who finds the body. In fact, if we show the police these photos, that's exactly what they will think. They'll think Jeff murdered Alan.'

He looked at her incredulously. 'Jules, man. Jeff hasn't killed him. You know that.'

She nodded. 'I...I know...but I'm just saying how it looks. There's no point in me not saying how it looks because soon enough the coppers will make the same conclusion.' She bit her lip a little. 'Anyway, one thing working at TW has shown me is that even the nicest blokes can, behind closed doors, behave appallingly. People who no-one would think was an abusive husband turn out to be exactly that.'

Nick folded his arms and sat back. 'Aye, I know, but we're talking murder here. I've known him since 1976. He's not a killer, Jules. He's...he's not.'

'I'm just saying, that's all...appearances can be deceptive,' said Julie, her arched eyebrows raised.

'Jeff didn't even know Alan.'

'Alright, alright, but you can't tell me it doesn't look dodgy, Nick. It bloody does. You know it and I know it. If we show these to the police, they'll haul him in. God help him if he doesn't have a rock-solid alibi as to what he was doing in there and frankly, I can't see that he does.'

'Actually, now that I think about it, he was looking a bit odd this lunchtime. He was red-faced, blushing almost, when we were talking about how the murder was done. Come on, let's go down to the shop now and have a look around that back room.'

'And we need to ask him what he was doing in that 5.38 to 5.46 time frame. No-one else went in there. He *was* in there and yet he didn't see the killer or the body. Something is damn well wrong with that. He's lied to us. He must have,' said Julie, knocking back the last of her wine.

'Well I'm not going to dress it up for him. I'll tell him straight. He'll have an answer. Obviously, he wasn't killing Alan, so he must have been doing something else.'

'Right. Come on then. You'll have to drive. I'm a bit pissed.'

As he drove back to Stockton High Street, Julie said, 'I know I'm being daft, I'm sure it's nothing to do with Jeff. I mean, I've known him for years as well and he's never been violent.'

'He can be intimidating. He's six foot four and even with the weight loss, he is still a huge bloke.'

He parked up on Silver Street again and they walked around to the store. The big glass window was now well lit and they'd already decorated it with album sleeves and an old record player. If records were your thing, it looked really inviting.

Inside Luke and Jeff sat either side of a counter with piles of records beside them, pricing them up.

'Alright you two,' said Nick. Jeff looked up.

'Now then.' He reached to one side and produced the Fillmore Records single. 'Here you go.'

Nick took it and looked at the distinctive yellow and orange label. 'Cheers, man. Have you had many punters in?'

'Yeah it's been quite busy,' said Jeff

'Busy? We've already taken £210!' exclaimed Luke.

That didn't sound that much, but they both seemed happy with it.

'So what happened to the police?'

'They sodded off at about three promising to return at some point unspecified,' said Luke, looking up the value of a Black Sabbath album in the Record Collector price guide.

'Ah, right. We've been doing a bit of investigation ourselves, haven't we Jules?'

'Yup. I took some photos last night just before you found Alan Armstrong.'

Luke looked up. 'Hey that could be crucial. Was anything on them?'

She pushed her hands into her jeans pockets and hunched up. 'Nothing obvious.'

'Are you sure there's no other way to get to the back room other than through that door?' said Nick, pointing to the plywood door behind the counter.

'Deffo,' said Jeff. 'There was a back door at some point, but it's been bricked up, probably 20-odd years ago. For security, like, I should think.'

'Can I have a look?' he said.

'Be my guest,' said Jeff.

Nick pushed open the unpainted plywood door. The floor was covered in scuffed and scratched old red lino, dating back at least 30 years. It was breaking up at the edges revealing the original oak floor boards underneath. There were still lots of big storage boxes full of records stacked against the outside wall. The empty boxes formed a wall between the door and the toilet.

Julie walked in behind him and looked around. 'There's nowhere for anyone to hide, is there?'

He shook his head. 'No, that's what I was thinking. There's no window in here to escape from.'

She lowered her voice. 'If Jeff was in here with the killer, he'd have seen them clearly and he'd have seen the body.'

'Yes. Jeff would,' said Jeff, looming up behind her. She visibly jumped, shocked by his presence and let out a squeak and patted her self on the heart. 'Shit, you made me jump, Jeff.'

'See, this is the problem, big man,' said Nick. He explained what Julie's last photo showed. 'So you see, it looks like you were in here, either while he was being killed, or just after he'd been killed, but you reckon you didn't see anything. How does that work?'

Jeff looked slowly from him to Julie and back to him. 'No. What you're really saying is I killed him. That's what you're saying. I'm the only one who could have done it. You all but said that. Well thanks a bloody bunch. I thought you were my mates.'

'Don't get crazy, Jeff. We don't think you did it, we're just worried that if the police saw the photos, they really would. No-one goes in or out of there except you and it's you that finds the body. You can see how it looks. It bloody does look like you killed him. Have you got an alibi?' said Nick.

'I never touched him, so I don't need an alibi,' he said, his voice full of indignation.

'I know, but you were coming out of here...' began Julie, but Jeff had his finger aloft to stop her.

'Err...no. What that photo shows is me by the door. I wasn't coming out of there at all. What I did was open it and then close it again. I thought there was a case of wine in there and was about to go and get it, but then I saw it under the counter, so I didn't.'

'Ah right, right,' said Nick, nodding, wanting to believe him. 'So you went up to the door and took a look and then spotted the wine?'

'Yeah. That's it.'

Immediately, Nick knew something wasn't right about that. 'So why aren't you on the other earlier photos then? You would be, but you're only on the last one.'

'Fuck you!' He yelled. 'You can fuck right off!'

'Jeff man, don't get a cob on,' said Julie. 'We're just trying to work it out.'

'You think I fucking well killed him don't you? You do. I can see it in your eyes. Me? A killer? It's fucking disgusting.'

Luke came in, on hearing the raised voices.

'What's up?' he said.

'These pricks think I'm a murderer.'

Luke snorted a laugh, but then realised he was serious. 'Eh? Why would you think that?'

'We don't. He's just over-reacting. All we're trying to do is work out where everyone was, where the killer was and how they got away with it,' said Nick, annoyed. 'So calm yourself down Jeff and stop trying to play the wounded soldier. A mate of mine was butchered in here, in case you've forgotten and I owe it to him to find out who did it, even if it means treading on your sensitive bloody toes, so shut it, stop being a stroppy kid about this and help us find out what happened. I never said you'd done it, you're just being a sodding drama queen and you're obviously hiding something. You're obviously lying to us for some reason, so spit it out...oweee man...don't be a big fucking pussy and don't look at me like that, you're 48, not eight years old.'

He stood, hands outstretched, gesturing to him. 'Come on, cough it up. We're your mates.'

CHAPTER 4

Jeff ran his hand across his mouth and shook his head. 'Alright. Alright. I'm sorry.'

'I should bloody think so,' said Nick. 'So what were you doing and where were you doing it?'

Jeff let out a sigh. 'I was in here with...with a woman.'

'With Janice?' said Julie.

He shook his head. 'Nope. With Rita Walker.' He rubbed his neck with his right hand and looked awkward. 'You know her, Nick.'

'I do know Rita, aye. I mean, I know the name. We went to school with her. She was really nice.'

'Hold on. You weren't shagging her in here were you?' laughed Luke.

Jeff nodded solemnly. 'Aye, well...I'd been chatting on Facebook with her. I'd always fancied her. I told her I was opening this place, I met her a couple of times last week and one thing led to another, didn't it? I was so amazed she was interested, I couldn't resist. But I thought it might be a bit hasty to dump Janice. Like I say, I'd met her last week a couple of times and then she just turned up last night out of the blue.'

'I'm sorry Jeff, I'm as much a woman of the world as you'll find anywhere from Hartlepool to Darlo, but are you seriously telling me she turned up, said "come on big man, give it to me now" and right under your girlfriend's nose you took her in the back, closed the door and got down to it on the floor?'

'...standing up against that table actually. But, yeah. That is exactly what happened, Jules. Honest.'

'Really? Bloody hell. She must have been pretty bloody hot to trot.'

He shrugged. 'I didn't psycho-analyse her as to why she was so horny, I just did what most blokes would do...I just filled my boots, didn't I? Feel a bit bad about it really. For Janice and that...y'know...but...' He shrugged again.

'Hang on, let me get this right. You were in here having a quickie while Alan was in the toilet meeting his maker?' said Julie, still incredulous.

He nodded, not meeting her eye. 'I didn't know anyone was in there did I? I never saw anyone, I never heard a thing. I didn't want to admit it to the coppers when Janice was here. Rita didn't stay long. She just nipped in, we did the business in here and she left again. I saw her go past you, actually. Dark hair and eyes.'

Nick slapped his leg. 'Yes, I noticed her. I thought she looked vaguely familiar, but lots of people on Teesside look vaguely familiar to me.'

'Let's get the timings on this right. What time did you come in here with Rita Walker?'

'I haven't a clue. Just no idea.'

'OK let's count back then. How long where you in here with Rita?' said Julie.

'About five minutes, at most six,' he said sheepishly.

Luke cheered. 'Bloody hell Jeff, you must have got it out, got it up and blobbed it almost immediately.'

Julie groaned in displeasure at his language.

'It was really exciting,' said Jeff. 'That sort of thing has never happened to me in my life. Not ever. It was like a fantasy come true. She just wanted to...to...like, pleasure us, like.' He was positively bashful.

'Well, well, well, this is a turn up for the books, isn't it?' said Nick. 'I think I'd have had you down as a killer before I had you down as a shagger.'

'I don't know whether to be insulted or flattered.'

'OK, OK, so in the light of this revelation, let's just go over events,' said Julie.

'Alright, but can we do it in the pub? I feel bad talking in here,' said Jeff.

Ten minutes later they had locked up the shop and were sitting in the Royal Oak. Julie got lager for Luke, white wine for her and

Jeff and water for Nick.

She leaned forward. 'Right. So let's recap. When I took the photos you were in the back room with this Rita Walker. When did she arrive?'

'Not long before. She turned up, gave me the nod. We were in the back by the time you were taking those shots because I heard everyone shouting penguin. So she'd arrived just before you even started the photos.'

'But Al left me at about 5.38 to go to the toilet. He's not on the photos. So you must have just missed him. He must have gone in for a piss, got killed and then you've then gone in with Rita...'

'...a couple of minutes later the big man 'ere 'as shot 'is load. Then what did you do?' asked Luke.

'I went back into the shop. Which is when you photographed me. Rita came out just after me and went home, but it must have been after you took the last photo,' said Jeff.

'Tell me exactly what you did after that?' said Nick.

'I went into the shop, had a drink of wine, topped up a couple of glasses for a few minutes. I circulated a bit then I remembered the *Gazette* were sending a photographer and they'd want one of me shaking Alan's hand. That's when I asked you where he was, went in the back and found him.'

'So the toilet door was open then?'

'Yeah.'

'But it can't have been when you were with Rita,' said Luke.

'No. At least, I don't think so.'

'You don't think so? You'd have noticed if there was a bloke slumped there wouldn't you?' said Nick.

'I would if the light had been on, but I'd turned it out when we went in.'

'Why did you do that?' said Luke, astonished.

'I dunno, do I? Modesty, maybe. I probably thought if Janice walked in, at least she'd not see us right away. It's pitch black in there. There are no windows, so there's no light at all. And we were up against the table in the corner, so that pile of empty boxes was between us and the toilet. But honestly, there was no noise and nothing to indicate anyone was there. If he'd been in there and alive he'd have shouted, hey, put the light on, wouldn't he?'

Julie took a long drink of wine. 'Bugger. So we're back to square one. He actually could have been lying there dead and you'd not have been able to see him.'

'Oh shit. Don't say that. That's fucked up - him just lying there,' said Jeff shuddering.

'Aye, that's right. And I'll tell you what. The killer was in the room while you were shagging this Rita. He has to have gone in earlier than Julie's photos and done the job,' said Luke.

Jeff let out a groan and put on his best Graham Taylor voice. 'Do I not like this?'

'It might not be a he,' said Julie. 'It might be a she. Just a point of detail we shouldn't ignore.'

'Whatever. So it goes like this...' Luke picked up the beer mats and laid them out. 'Killer goes in there just after Alan has left Nick - 5.38 or 5.39. He knifes Alan as he comes in for a piss, but before he can get away Jeff and Rita follow him in and do their business from about 5.40 to 5.46. He lies doggo. Meanwhile, you start taking photos. Jeff finishes and comes out, just as you finish taking snaps. Rita comes out right after him and then finally our killer emerges at about 5.47 or 5.48 just as Jeff goes back in, puts on the light and finds the body. So there are no photos of the killer or of Rita. There's no time spare for it to have happened any other way than that.'

It sounded like a foolproof theory.

'I like how that works,' said Jeff. 'The only thing I'd say though is that I'm sure I was out of the back room for longer than a minute or two. I didn't do much, but I'd have said it was longer than that.'

'You can't 'ave been' said Luke. 'Must've just felt like longer.'

'The killer couldn't have planned it though could they? They had to be in the room, waiting for Al to go to the toilet and then followed him in. If he'd held onto his bladder, he'd never have been killed,' said Nick.

'But we still have no motive for the murder,' said Nick.

'He'll have had a secret life. Mark my words,' said Jeff, his index finger aloft again.

'So do we tell Col Harcombe all this?' said Nick. 'Are you OK with that, Jeff? We can't hold info back from the cops, can we?'

Jeff nodded. 'We'd better tell him.'

'Has this Rita woman been in touch with you since?'

'Aye. She texted me. She was shocked, but I don't think she realises how close to this we'd been because obviously she was gone before I found him.'

'I'll tell Colin tomorrow then,' said Julie.

They all went quiet for a bit.

'Sorry again for losing my rag earlier,' said Jeff.

'It's alright. It's the stress, isn't it?' said Nick.

'Aye. It's the deception. I'd be a terrible polygamist.'

'Where are you staying, Luke?' said Nick.

'Ah I forgot to say, he's staying up here so he needs a doss,' said Jeff. 'Just on the sofa or in a bin.'

'Is that alright? Just for one night while we sort this stock out. I need to get back to Harrogate tomorrow night,' said Luke.

'As long as you don't mind sleeping on cushions,' said Julie.

'I can sleep standing up, me,' said Luke.

Later that night, Julie and Nick lay in bed talking in the darkness of the countryside night.

'I'd never have thought Jeff was up to all that shagging shenanigans, would you?' said Julie.

'Never. Honestly, that has really shocked me.'

'Me too. You think you know someone.'

'I know. You're right.'

'Words are just words, like I said. It's actions that really show you what someone is like.'

'Especially if the action is a fatal stabbing. I can't help but wonder what terrible thing Alan had done to provoke that. I'm not saying he deserved it or anything, but there has to be a reason, surely.'

'Maybe Colin has found something out about his private life that'll give them a lead.'

'I'm sure they'll be digging into it and looking at the forensics as well.'

As was often the case, if they hadn't made love, Nick found it hard to fall to sleep and long after Julie had dropped off, breathing slowly and quietly beside him, he lay on his back, his mind whirring at a furious rate. Without the serotonin calm that sex endorphins released, it sometimes seemed as if he was actually more wide awake at night than he was during the day. When he was younger it used to frustrate him, but these days he was so used to it that in some ways, he rather liked it, especially since moving to the countryside where the night was so quiet.

Their sex life had calmed down after their early months of moving back in together when they'd been unable to keep their hands off each other for more than a few hours. For the last nine months, after a lot of discussion, they'd stopped using any contraception in the hope that Julie might get pregnant. It had been a huge decision to make, but nothing had happened and that was always going to be the likely outcome, not least because the doctor had said the odds on conceiving at 44 were under two percent. They'd simply left it too late and lately, it had really started to trouble him, especially in the middle of the night.

Having kids was never something he was interested in, right into his mid 40s, quite the opposite, in fact. The idea of being responsible for children had been frightening and intimidating. So he'd never really seen the attraction at all, especially as someone who suffered from low moods, introspection and outright depression. He had always worried it might be a terrible genetic thing he would pass on and curse an innocent life with. But in the past year, that had been replaced by a rising need to give, what Marc Lewis, his therapist, had described as, unconditional love. He feared that a life without your own kids to love might be a self-indulgent and far colder life. But there was no getting away from the fact that it was too late. He'd just have to find a way to get used to that reality.

Eventually, the warm blanket of sleep begin to wrap itself around him. When he emerged back to consciousness from a strange dream where he was a DJ playing vinyl records, not of music, but of footballers talking, Julie had got dressed in old blue jeans and a grey hoodie. She leaned over and kissed him on the forehead.

'Morning, sleepy head. It's after eight already. I'd better get some food on the go for the lads.'

He sat up and yawned. 'I'll do that, Jules. They'll think you're playing at the little wife and you hate that.'

She sat on the side of the bed and pushed his messy hair off his forehead.

'That's true, like. It's one of those sexist bullshit defaults - the woman in the kitchen feeding men. But then I don't mind cooking food for people, I quite like it, even though you're much better at it than I am.'

'Just give me a minute to get my shit together and I'll do the bacon and coffee. You do the other stuff.'

'OK, cool.' She was about to go downstairs, stopped and looked back at him.

'What?' he said.

'Thanks for thinking of that.'

'Of what?'

'Men expecting women to cook for them.'

'Aye, well, I've been thinking a lot about that stuff...mostly since you've been volunteering...that sort of attitude is everywhere and about almost everything when you start to notice it. Things only men do, things only women do, or are expected to do and then we all get judged weirdly because of it. It's fucked up.'

She laughed gently. 'Are you trying to get in my knickers by coming on all feminist?'

'No, I would never come on a feminist, Jules. Not unless she specifically requested me to.'

She laughed, picked up a jumper from the bedroom chair and

threw it at him. 'You're a dirty dog, you are.'

'Takes one to know one.'

'Aye, and you can stop thinking about doing that that as well, not when we've got guests in the house. You know what we're like. It'd be embarrassing for them.' She winked at him and went downstairs.

He loved her flirting with him, even though it was often a bit juvenile. He rolled over into her still-warm side of the bed and inhaled her smell.

By the time he'd got downstairs, Luke was already up and about, talking to Julie in the kitchen.

'Now then, kidda,' said Nick.

'Eh up, Nick,' he said, all messy long hair and unpleasant baggy-arsed, but tight-legged jeans. It was the privilege, or even the duty, of the younger generation to annoy men his age with their clothes, but even so, these were sodding horrible. It made him look like he was wearing a nappy, or some sort of incontinence bag under the jeans.

He got a packet of bacon out of the fridge while Julie cracked eggs into a bowl.

'I never normally 'ave a breakfast. This'll be a bit of a treat. Like bloody Xmas at me mam's.'

'We eat huge breakfasts here, don't we, Jules?'

'Massive. All done with lard and butter. Proper, like. Mind, we don't eat wheat...or any grains really, so you'll have to make do without them, Luke.'

'Jeff's the same these days. Weird innit? He started eating loads of fat and butter and he lost all that weight. It's err...what's the word...counter-intuitive, aye, that's it.'

'Well, the doctors and everyone got all that diet stuff wrong, didn't they?' said Julie. 'It's sugar and carbs that make you fat. I wish I'd learned that years ago.'

'You look crackin' on it Jules,' said Luke. 'You've got a great figure, for your age, like.'

She looked at him out of the top of her eyes as she beat the eggs. 'For my age?! You'd think I was 78. I'm only 44, how old are you?'

'24.'

'Oh god. Stop making me feel old.'

'Sorry. I feel like a right old git, if it makes you feel any better.' He sat down at their big pine kitchen table as Nick began frying bacon and tomatoes.

Jeff came down the stairs and looked around the kitchen door. 'Ah I see you're playing mother, Nick. Good man.'

'Nope. Actually, I'm playing father. Not mother,' he said. Julie grinned to herself. Jeff didn't even mean it, he was just saying it, but it was through such default expressions that attitudes got entrenched and became self-perpetuating.

Everyone quickly cleaned their plates, except Julie, who had a bit of bacon but couldn't face anything else. Sometimes it seemed to take so long to prepare food and yet so little time to eat it. Jeff and Luke had just left in Jeff's van when the phone rang.

'Nick? It is Colin Harcombe here. Can I come and see you?'

There was no need to introduce himself, that stern, serious, respectable voice was unmistakeable.

'Funnily enough, I was going to call you today. We remembered Jules took some photos at the party in Jeff's shop. They might be of interest to you.'

'Really? Well well. Yes. I see. Yes indeed. Well perhaps I could come over now if it is convenient.'

Half an hour later, the policeman's car pulled up outside of the house and Colin Harcombe's angular body emerged from it like a stick insect. Nick greeted him at the door while Julie made them coffee.

'Nice to be here again,' he said, looking around. 'Splendid place to live and the smell of bacon and coffee in the air too. Very homely. So tell me about these photographs.'

Nick put them on the TV screen, explaining what Jeff had been up to in the back room with the light off. Harcombe was not at all pleased to hear this news. His face was set in a deep frown which over the years had left deep scars in his forehead and around his eyes.

'He should have told my men this in his interviews. Very bad form not to. Illegal in fact. Withholding evidence from the police is not something that I like to think innocent members of the public would ever want to do, especially in a case of murder. This...this concerns me greatly.' His disapproval was absolute.

'To be fair, I think he was just embarrassed by what he'd been up to,' said Julie, hands cupped around a coffee mug.

'Even so. He lied to officers. Not good at all. Bad business...I shall have words...'

It was his favourite phrase, 'bad business'; everything from petty shop lifting to murder was a bad business to Colin Harcombe.

'...however, I shall put it to one side for now. These photographs are very useful, thank you. Straight away I can tell you, this man here...he is known to us.' He stood up and tapped at the screen with a forefinger. 'That is Jimmy Butcher. Well named, too. A violent man. Has done two stretches for assault, one with a knife, if my memory serves me well. Hmm. Yes. Very, very interesting indeed. He was not there when we took names and addresses. He must have left by then.'

He was pointing at the man in the black-roll neck sweater. Nick stood up and looked at the TV screen and pointed.

'Him? That's Jimmy Butcher? I went to school with him. He was in my year. He actually looked at me weirdly when I came back in. See here, on this shot, I've just walked in and he turned to look at me right in the eyes. At the time I thought he was looking at me in a funny way, but I'm not that good at discerning what expressions mean, so I ignored it. I didn't know it was him. It never occurred to me I might know him.'

'Describe his reaction,' said Harcombe.

He closed his eyes to try and remember. ' If I had to call it anything I'd say it was the look someone gives you when they didn't expect to see you. A sort of "oh, I didn't expect to see you here" look, but I can't be sure.'

'Reading people's faces really isn't Nick's strong point, so in fairness, I'd not rely on his interpretation,' said Julie, '...and anyway, he might have just recognized you from school. Didn't you recognize him at all?'

Nick shook his head. 'No. He doesn't look anything like I remember. He's changed a lot since he was 16.'

Harcombe nodded sagely. 'Could you make a copy of these photos onto a CD for me?'

'Sure,' said Julie and began copying the files.

'Thank you. I actually had wanted to speak to you this morning because something else has come to light.'

He placed his fingertips together and looked at Nick with stern eyes.

'I don't wish to worry you unduly, but has it occurred to you that you and Alan Armstrong are not dissimilar in appearance?'

'Me and Al?' Are we?'

The policeman nodded. 'Superficially anyway.'

'What are you saying that for?' said Julie.

'Well, this is only a theory we're working on, but as of yet and we're less than 48 hours into it, but we cannot find a single thing in Alan's life that would suggest why he might have met his death in this way. He was, in every way, a decent family man. As a consequence, it is being suggested that perhaps this was a case of mistaken identity...'

'Christ, you think they meant to kill me?' said Nick.

'It is just a theory. He had shoulder length dark brown hair like you. He was the same height and roughly the same build.'

'Nick is broader and more muscular than Alan was, surely,' said Julie. 'Wasn't he quite flabby?'

'He was. I'm not saying he was identical to you, only similar. You two worked together, so it's a connection I'd like to explore. Did you have any regular phone-in callers?'

'Yeah, plenty.'

'Any really odd ones? Or threatening?'

'Not that I know of. You'd have to ask Amy, she's the producer, she'll have screened out any of the obvious loonies.'

The policeman made a note of that. 'And have you had any reason to believe you had an enemy or someone who would wish you ill?'

Nick shook his head. 'No, of course not. Not at all.'

Harcombe jotted a note down and then looked up at them.

'Alan Armstrong was killed with a Bowie knife. Do you know what one of those is?'

'It's a hunting knife, isn't it? A big thing,' said Nick.

'Yes. Yes indeed. Not the sort of thing we see every day here on Teesside. Do you know of anyone who might have a knife like that? Someone who is into hunting, shooting and fishing perhaps?'

'Nope. We don't know that sort of person,' said Nick. 'Am I in danger, Colin?'

He shook his head firmly in a reassuring way. 'No. We have no reason to believe you're under threat in any way whatsoever. I'm just exploring ideas at the moment. Did Jeff invite Jimmy Butcher, do you know?'

'I don't know, but I can ask him.' He took out his phone and called him.

'Jeff? I've got Colin here. Do you know a man called Jimmy Butcher?'

'Of course, don't you remember him? He went to our school man, to Ian Ramsey. He was expelled for beating some kid up in the fifth year. Him and his brother. We were shit scared of them. You must remember.'

'I do remember him, but I'd not seen him since school. Did you invite him to your do?'

'Butch? Of course not. I don't even know him to talk to.'

'Well, he was there.'

'He wasn't, was he? I'm not sure I know what he even looks like now.'

'He was certainly there while Jules was taking the photos.'

'I pretty sure he wouldn't have remembered me. Last he'd have known, I was just a long-haired kid over-fixated on Uriah Heep records. I never even spoke to him at school. He was one of those idiots you were glad not to have to deal with once you got to sixth form. Is he the killer? He always was a nutter.'

'I don't think he can be. He was in the shop all the time you were in the back and then he left before the police came. OK, I'll talk to you later.'

He told Colin what Jeff had said.

'All the same, I think we'd better have a word with Mr Butcher. See what he's got to say for himself. Him being there...I don't like it at all. Not one tiny bit. The fact he didn't hang around only makes me feel he's guilty of something.'

'Maybe he was just there for the free drink,' said Julie. 'Jeff said a couple of gadgees came in from the Royal Oak.'

The policeman stood up and took the CD.

'OK. Thank you for your help. I shall be in touch. This Butcher development, I think, will prove significant.'

After Colin Harcombe had left, Nick put the photos back on the TV and looked at Jimmy Butcher. He wasn't doing anything. Just standing there, looking one way, then turning around and looking the other.

'He's right beside your mam at one point. Would she know him?'

'Mam knows everyone. If she doesn't, Kev and Ricky or Terry certainly will. If he's been inside, they'll know him. I don't really remember him from Ian Ramsey.'

'Might be worth asking her if she talked to him then.'

'OK, but he can't have killed Alan. We know that for sure. He's in all the photos I took and we know - or suspect - that the killer went in there before I took photos and came out after I'd stopped. There wasn't any time for him to do it before that.'

'Hey, when are you picking up that fuel pump from Sid's?'

She looked at her watch. 'Oh shit. I was supposed to be there at 10.30. Can you run me down there, then onto to the TW house in Hartburn so I can fix the Peugeot?'

'Sure thing.'

She got her tool box and put a pair of navy blue overalls on so she didn't get grease and muck on her regular clothes, fastened her hair into a pony tail and put on a baseball cap.

'Right. I'm ready. Do you want to look in on mam once we've been to Sid's?'

'Yeah, just a quick visit to ask her about Butcher.'

'Alright, but I'm going to say I've got to go after ten minutes - I've got to get to work - right? I'll have had a gut full of her bitching by then. You watch, I bet she says I look like a lesbian because I've got my overalls on.'

They stopped off at a small garage on Durham Road to pick up the new fuel pump. She came back holding cylindrical device made of white plastic. It looked complicated.

'How do you know what the hell to do with that?' he said as she held it up at him with a grin.

'It's easy. This is the low pressure pump, it goes in the fuel tank. That 206 has two fuel pumps...'

'Mmm, suddenly feeling sleepy,' said, Nick, closing his eyes.

'Why doesn't this interest you? Don't you know that you're not a *real* man if you're not interested in cars?'

'Aye. I'd worked that out by the time I was 15. Made me determined to read even more poetry.'

She laughed. 'Poetry, like? Are you a puff or what?' she said, in as broad a Teesside accent as she could muster. They drove away, turning off left onto Hardwick Road to Jackie Wells's house on the Hardwick Estate.

'Ten minutes. No longer. Right?' she said as they walked towards her front door.

'Mam! It's me and Nick,' she called out, knocking on the door, opening it and walking in.

Bessie, the old black-and-white mongrel, came trotting out the kitchen with a bark.

'Hello Bessie, darlin',' said Julie, tickling her ears.

'What are you doing here?' said Jackie, following the dog, a fag hanging out of her mouth. 'What's wrong?'

'Hello mam. Nice to see you, too.'

'I only saw you the other day. It's not like you're my long-lost daughter is it?'

'God no. I'd hate to think I was special, mam. I just dropped in because we wanted to ask you something.'

'What are you dressed like that for? You look bloody awful, our Jules. You've got a nice figure, why don't you show it off instead of hiding it under those overalls. She looks like a bloke, doesn't she, Nick?'

'No. She looks like Jules to me, Jackie.'

'Like a bloody les...'

'...lesbian, yes mam, I know. How very predictable. I'm just dressed like this to do some work on my car. I just picked up a fuel pump. Should I dress in my Armani suit to do that?'

'I'm just saying. You've got to look nice for your fella or he'll be looking elsewhere.'

'Mam! Stop it. You're just saying shit like that to annoy me. Why can't you be nice?'

'I'm just saying...'

'...well don't.'

Jackie made a zipping gesture across her lips.

'Jackie - do you know a bloke called Jimmy Butcher? He was standing by you at Jeff's shop party thing the other night,' said Nick.

She lit up another Silk Cut. 'Am I allowed to speak now?'

Julie pursed her lips together and narrowed her eyes at her mother, silently scolding her sarcasm.

'Aye, as it happens I had a word with him. I was wondering what he was doing there. He's wrong 'un, that fella. I mean god knows, your brothers are no angels, but they never knifed anyone.'

'Mam, Kev was done for aggravated burglary because he carried a weapon. Let's not pretend, eh. Ricky and Kev are violent...or they have been in the past.'

'Aye, but they never used a knife, did they?' she said as though this meant they were innocent. Julie turned her back on her and walked towards the door.

'So what did you say to him the other night?' said Nick.

Jackie pulled on the cigarette and let the smoke drift into her eyes. How didn't it make her eyes water? She must have grown a special inner eyelid. He'd always thought smoke seemed to be like food for her.

'I said, well well, they let you out of jail, did they?'

'What did he say to that?'

'Not much. He just said, hello Jackie you old c.u.n.t. I said, well that's nice. Are you going to knife me? Taking the piss, like. I wasn't to know that was what was going on in that back room was I? Eeee, god, terrible.'

'Was he with anyone?'

'No. He was on his own.'

'Did you tell the police this?' said Nick. Stupid question.

'I told the police nowt about nowt,' she said, indignant at the very suggestion. 'I thought Big Jeff must have invited him.'

'No he didn't. He just turned up and, given his predilection for knifing people, the cops are naturally interested in what he was doing while Alan Armstrong was getting killed,' said Julie. 'You should've mentioned it, mam.'

She coughed a loose, catarrh cough. 'I didn't take notice of when he arrived or when he went; it doesn't mean he knifed that bloke though, does it?'

'I'm surprised you can remember even being there mam, you'd had at least six glasses of Cava in an hour.'

'They were only small. I was only being polite. It was cheap rubbish, anyway.'

Julie shook her head and sighed.

'Any idea where he might live now?' said Nick.

'Haven't a clue. His mother died years ago. His brother is still in jail, I think. He's got family in Roseworth though, I reckon.'

'Did you, at any time, see him move towards that back room door - the one behind the counter?'

She shook her head and inhaled deeply again.

'Nah. Sorry Nick...Jules is right, I was as pissed as a fart. I'd had a few in the club with Sandra before I arrived, so I was well gone.'

Julie looked up at her, astonished.

'Mam, you just said I was right. Are you feeling OK? You never say I'm right. Not about anything. Like, ever.'

'Don't go getting a big head about it, our Jules. I'm just saying I was pissed. You still look like a lesbian in those overalls. A woman shouldn't be fixing cars, it's man's work.'

Nick saw Julie was about to advance on her mother and give her a piece of her mind so he put up both hands and guided her towards the door.

'Thanks Jackie. We've got to get going. Julie's got to be at work.'

'Work? At that place in Hartburn? You want to watch yourself there Jules, they'll all be fancying you!'

He hustled her out of the door before another row began.

'That bloody woman. Oooh I could scream. Cow,' she hissed. 'She's just doing it to annoy me, I know...but it...it really bloody annoys me. Still spewing out this "men's work" thing. It's pathetic. She's always done that. She used to go on about me 'catching' a man, even when I was 16. Like your life was nothing if it didn't involve a man. Then there was all the "you'll be on the shelf" business when I was in my late 20s and early 30s. Like I was a can of beans about to go off. She was always so male-centric. She's even like that with you. She flirts with you...'

'...she doesn't, does she?'

'You must have noticed.'

'Not really. She tries to be nice to me in order to get at you. I've noticed that.'

'Well, she does. She's like that because she thinks that's how women 'get' men. She genuinely thinks that if I don't make myself pretty for you, you'll go and shag someone else and I'll deserve it. That's how she thinks.'

'Well, she's old school. She's 68, Jules.'

'I don't care, she should've learned by now that women don't need men in their life. Or not the wrong bloody men, anyway. And she should know. She married a bad 'un: a violent drunk. It negates my individuality and really, it's just another sort of objectification, saying it's all about how you look and not who you are. I fucking hate that. I really do. It's about my brain, not about my tits and arse.'

They drove down Durham Road to the roundabout, taking Bishopton Avenue to Oxbridge Lane and then onto Greens Lane. It was a quiet drive, without a lot of traffic on the road. Julie was still chewing over her mother's comments.

'What upsets me most is that it's people like mam saying stuff about wearing overalls and fixing cars that makes it hard for women to get into being a mechanic or whatever. It makes it culturally much more difficult. It boxes things off. I mean, it happens to blokes as well to some degree, but mostly it's used as a way to put women down. That's not for youse lot darlin' - put a bit of lippy on and do the housework pet, eh. Leave it to the men folk. She's always been like that with me. It was always like I wasn't as important as the lads. They could do what they wanted, but I had to get my tits out for the boys first and foremost because you're nowt without a man. God forbid you might use your mind. I mean, I sort of grew up feeling that I always had to have a boyfriend. And I'm sure it's why I was so promiscuous when I was younger. Subconsciously, I think I thought you could only get men to love you through your vagina. Mam had driven that sort of shit into my brain. If I hadn't fallen in love with you, I'd have gone through life single, I reckon and it wouldn't have been so bad, not the end of the world and certainly better than being with the wrong bloke. This obsession with pairing up that mam has always had, its really destructive.'

'Yeah, I think this is where men have it easy. We're not judged like that. Trouble is, it's hard to know what to do about it. It's all so culturally ingrained. I have to confess that one of the main motivations for me trying to be a more sensitive bloke was partly because I thought it'd get me more women.'

'And it did?'

'No. I think I'd have been much more successful if I'd just been normal. Turned out a lot of women actually wanted a regular, macho bloke and not some scruffy, dysfunctional git who liked poetry. Mind you, I'd say the ones I did go out with were really good fun. So I made up in quality for what I lacked in volume.'

'You and normal have never gone together,' she said and made a big wet farting raspberry, sticking her tongue out. 'There, that's what I think of it all.' She did it again and laughed. 'That feels better, actually.'

'Ha ha. Well, that's as perfect an expression of feminist rage as I've ever heard. Being puerile is much under-rated,' he said. She did it for a third time as he pulled into the TW house grounds and parked next to the broken Peugeot.

'If any bloke comes up to me and says, "eeee you can fix my car if you want, darlin'" or some other witticism I'm going to insert a faulty fuel pump up his arse and he'll have to pull his bollocks out of his pelvis.' She got out her toolbox from the boot of his BMW, popped the bonnet and got to work.

Nick rested on the side of the BMW and watched her work. It was amazing to him that anyone could understand the workings of a car, or indeed of anything mechanical. It wasn't a choice he'd made. He just couldn't do it. Even as kid he'd been unable to make sense anything that involved practical skills and his old metalwork teacher had actually hit him for being so useless at making a copper pendant.

'Come on you bloody bugger,' she cursed, hitting at some recalcitrant connection with a hammer. 'Sod it, I need some brute force. Here...' She handed him the hammer and a spanner. '...put that on there and hit it until it comes loose.'

He did as he was told. The nut shifted with two good blows.

'See. I am a proper man after all,' he said, handing her the tools, flexing a bicep.

'Don't go getting all alpha male on me. I must have loosened it for you.'

As he laughed, a car pulled in.

'Hello Julie. I didn't know you were good with cars.'

She looked up from the engine. 'Hello Martha, yeah I learned it all on the estate when I was a kid because people were always messing around with cars. I'm fixing the fuel pump.'

'Gosh. Impressive stuff. Hello again, Nick.'

He nodded and smiled. 'Hi there. I love watching her work on cars. It's a Byzantine mystery to me. I always preferred poetry to cars when I was growing up,' he said, hoping this would make him seem somehow a more acceptable version of male. Stupid. She didn't seem impressed. Why should she?

'Would you like some coffee?' said Martha.

'Ooh yes please,' said Julie.

'I'll put the kettle on then,' she said. 'If you could come and pick it up, Nick?'

'Sure.' He nodded and smiled. She was a stern-looking woman in the manner of a strict teacher, but one you wanted to please, as though her praise was doled out sparingly, so when you got any, it felt extra special.

As he waited, another car pulled in - a top-of-the-range Lexus - and an expensively dressed, rather glamorous woman in a black suit got out and went into the house. As the Lexus turned around, the driver looked right at him. He was a middle-aged bloke in a denim shirt with messy shoulder length hair pushed behind his ears. It pulled away and went back up Greens Lane. Julie turned to look at her as she went in.

'That was a top-notch motor. 80 grand's worth of Lexus there,' she said. 'I've seen her here quite a bit in recent weeks. She looks a bit like a movie star doesn't she?'

'Aye, who is she?'

Julie shrugged. 'I don't know. Not my place to ask. I think she's come for the Freedom Programme. Do you want to go in and get that coffee, my hands are bloody freezing.'

There was a cool wind blowing as he went into the house.

'The kettle's just boiled in the office,' said Martha as he entered the foyer. She was standing outside of another room, propping open the door with her foot, talking to the well-dressed woman who had got out of the Lexus.

He went in and poured the hot water onto some instant coffee and took them outside. As he passed by the two women, he heard Martha say, 'You shouldn't have to put up with that, Deirdre,' and the woman say back, 'I know that now, but I wish I'd known it a long time ago...'

'I'm just about done,' said Julie as he returned with the mugs. 'Just need to tighten it up and it should be fine. Turn it over for me.'

He turned the ignition key and it started first time, ticking over with a satisfyingly regular purr. He cheered. She grinned through the windscreen at him and put her thumbs up.

'Who's a clever girl then?' he said getting out. 'Or rather, who's a clever woman. It just feels wrong saying girl here.'

'I told you, don't be paranoid.'

'Sorry. I always feel like I'm a sexual politics faux pas waiting to happen when I'm here.'

'I don't know why. I keep telling you to stop trying to do the right thing and just be yourself.'

'Aye. Right.' He took a drink of coffee. 'That woman who got out the Lexus is called Deirdre, she was talking to Martha in there...'

'Yeah? Well, Martha runs that Freedom Programme I was telling you about. There's a class on.'

She slammed the bonnet down and wiped oil off her hands on an old rag.

'Right, that's all done. I need to do the spark plug gaps soon, but I'm too cold to bother just now.' She gripped the mug and held it to her nose which had gone pink with the cold breeze. 'Do you think we'll beat Wigan on Saturday then?'

'No. But then I never expect the Boro to win.'

'Defeatist. Actually, I don't mind if we do go down. Premier League is over-rated. I'd rather win more in a lower league.'

'Totally, aye. But all the younger fans are pissed off because all they've ever known is top flight success. They're all depressed, whereas us old timers see it as part of the natural state of things.'

'Even so, only one goal and one point in eight league games is pretty diabolical, even by our historical standards.'

'The club's run out of money though, hasn't it? Or rather, Gibbo isn't prepared to put us further into the red than we already are. Seems sensible, really. Relegation isn't the end of the world. Survival of the club is far more important.'

'Are you going to do that phone-in after Saturday's game?'

'I dunno. What do you think?'

'I think you should. Alan would have said to. Life and the Boro go on...'

'...aye, long after the thrill of living is gone.'

She smirked. 'You quote that far too much, you know. John bloody Cougar bloody Mellencamp,' she laughed a little. 'Poor man's Springsteen, if you ask me. 'Jack and Diane', it's no 'Racing In The Streets', is it?'

'No. You've got that right, like. So you think it'd be OK?'

'Yeah. As long as you think you can do it.'

'I could definitely do it. Amy will just handle the technical side. I just have to take the calls and try not to insult people. '

'Well, it'd bring a bit of money in and we need every penny we can get right now. My Durham Uni fees cost a fortune.'

'True. OK, I'll let Pally know this afternoon.'

'I'll just take these mugs in and wash my hands. You can get off home if you want,' she said.

'I'm just going to look in on Jeff briefly. I forgot to bring home that Fillmore Records seven-incher yesterday.'

She nodded. 'OK. Why do I always feel like I should make a seven-incher joke? I should have got over that by the time I was 16.'

'It's because you've got a dirty mind.'

'That must be it. Dirty mind and dirty hands.'

He kissed her on her cold lips.

'Alright, dirty lady. I'll see you in a bit.'

CHAPTER 5

Nick parked in the Castlegate Centre and walked up the High Street to Jeff's shop. It was a properly cutting wind now, a typical February north-easterly, sharp enough to remove your kidneys. Thursday afternoon on the High Street was pretty quiet. Jeff was actually standing in the window of the shop, pinning some album sleeves to the side wall as he arrived.

'Eh up Nick,' said Luke as he walked in.

'Is Jeff supposed to be part of the window dressing?' said Nick, gesturing at him.

'He wanted to stand in there naked.'

'Well, unlike my missus, I'm not going to make any seven-incher jokes. I'm a bigger man than that,' said Nick.

'Aye. So I've heard,' said Luke, dryly.

'I just came to pick up that Fillmore Records single. Any more police action?'

'No. Nothing.' He looked under the counter and found the record for Nick. 'We're still pricing up all the stock. He's been a bit squeamish about going in the back.' He nodded at the window.

'Jeff? Has he?'

'Aye.'

'Doesn't it bother you, Luke?'

'Me? Nah. I grew up in West Yorkshire. People dying a bloody death is normal there, innit?'

Jeff emerged from the window.

'It's not the blood per se...it's the fact that someone's life ended in there,' he said, pushing his long, greying hair behind his ears.

'Aye, but look at it like this. This building has been here for over 200 years, loads of people have probably pegged it in here,' said Luke. 'You're not worried about all of them, are you?'

'I didn't say it made any sense, did I? I daresay I'll get over it. You staying for a brew?'

'Nah, I've just had one with Jules, thanks. Just came to get that single. Any decent sales today?'

'Been quiet. No-one around.'

'You said that bloke who spends good money is due in this arvo,' said Luke. 'Matt Little.'

'Matt Little? Is that Big Little? From school?' said Nick.

'The very same. Still loves his West Coast psychedelic stuff. I've got some Doors UK first pressings for him on orange Elektra,' said Jeff.

'Nice. I love all that early Elektra label stuff.'

'Is he tall or small then?' said Luke.

'Nope. Neither. Just regular. School nicknames are rubbish,' said Jeff.

'What was your nickname then?'

'Mine?' Jeff pointed to himself. 'Unimaginatively, mine was Big Jeff.'

'Mine was Nick,' said Nick. 'So what's Big Little been doing all these years? I've not seen him since sixth form.'

'Worked in Canada as some sort of music producer in the movies. Not big time Hollywood stuff, just independents. He did really well in the property market over there and made a small fortune. Came back home a couple of years ago. He's still a big collector. He emailed me 18 months ago. He's been down to the Harrogate shop a few times because he lives near Easingwold in North Yorkshire. Still a really nice bloke. Very laid back, as befits a man who enjoys long, meandering psychedelic guitar solos.'

'Yeah, I remember he played me the first Quicksilver Messenger Service record in sixth form. Great album, that.'

'Yeah, that's him all over. Apparently, he's invested in companies up here and that's why he's around a bit more often. He's the sort of punter I want to make into a regular. I'm hoping to tap into all those old lads from school and sixth form who we used to knock around with. Most of them probably still collect records.'

'Makes sense, aye. Right, I'll see you at home later. Are you off down south tonight, Luke?'

'Aye. I've got to open the Harrogate shop tomorrow. Friday

afternoons and weekends are our busiest days.'

'OK man. Nice to have seen you.'

'Aye, thanks for the kip down and say ta to Julie for cooking the food an' that.'

There it was again. He'd done the cooking as well, but in Luke's mind it had defaulted to the woman of the house, cooking being women's work. He didn't mean any harm by it, but it was annoying all the same.

As he was walking out, a man in a brown leather coat was walking in and they almost bumped into each other. 'Sorry mate,' said Nick, side stepping him.

'No, I'm sorry...oh...is it...is it Nick? It is isn't it? God, you've not changed at all.'

Nick focused on him. He looked only vaguely familiar.

'Sorry. Do I know you? I'm terrible with names and with faces for that matter.'

'Matt Little. Big Little, as was, from school.' Nick squinted at him. He had messy shoulder length hair, soft, wide apart brown eyes, thin pink lips and a broad face. He was a bit taller than Nick and was well upholstered with middle-aged spread. Heavy lines were etched into his forehead, his skin leathery and dry. He was the sort of man who looked tired even when he wasn't, but also the sort of man who, when he smiled, lost 20 years of age.

He held out his hand. He'd changed a lot since his teenage years and yet somehow he did look familiar. As Nick shook hands and looked in his eyes, he suddenly realised exactly why. He was the man who had just been driving the Lexus at the TW centre. Dark blue denim shirt and messy hair. Yes.

'Wow that's weird, we were just talking about you,' said Nick.

'Ah, I thought my ears were burning. Jeff's email said you were living back up here as well. Funny how we've all sort of come home, isn't it? It's great to see you again. You've aged well, Nick.'

'Thanks mate. It only seems like a year or two since we were all in the sixth form, drinking downstairs in the Talbot, remember?'

'I loved the Talbot. Their jukebox was an education. Tragic that

79

it no longer exists.'

'Yeah, like our teenage years, it's long gone.'

'So where do you live then, Nick?'

'We rent an old farmhouse south of Yarm, off the A1264, y'know? Down a track, just near Saltergill Wood. It's all on its own and set well back from the road. It's very quiet and a bit run down, but we love it, like.'

'Oh yeah I know. It's beautiful out there,' said Matt. 'You'd not think you were on Teesside, it's that nice. Ha ha. I live in the country as well as it happens, just outside of Easingwold, down the A19 to York. It's all huntin' 'n' shootin' 'n' fishin' around me, but I'm up on Teesside a lot, so I think I'll get a place up here soon.'

'It's lovely in North Yorkshire. I lived in Harrogate for years. Do you live on your own down there?'

'Yeah. Long time divorced now. Kids are in their 20s. Both working in America on the west coast. I always tell them it must have been all the Grateful Dead records I played them when they were little that influenced where they ended up living.'

'I was just saying how you turned me on to Quicksilver in sixth form.'

'I still love them. Trying to get hold of UK copies of their singles. Not having much luck though.'

'You can get them on GEMM or some other online store.'

'I don't like to buy stuff online. To me, it just feels like cheating.'

Nick laughed and nodded. That was his own view too. You had to put in some effort. Collecting was about the random chance of just happening upon records as much as it was about owning them.

'Well, Jeff's got some west coast stuff for you.'

'So you're still a vinyl man?' said Matt Little.

'Yeah, I've got a lot of stuff...nearly 10,000 items now across albums, singles and CDs.'

'Wow. You must be a single man then!' He laughed at his own joke.

'I was until a couple of years ago, but I managed to find a woman who understood. Eventually, like. Julie. Julie Wells. You remember the Wells brothers, don't you?'

The look of horror on his face was enough to tell him all he needed to know.

'Aye, those lads. Jules is their sister.'

'Wow. That's some in-laws to have. They had a terrible reputation...oh...err...if you don't mind me saying so. No offence.'

'None taken. You're right. They did and rightly so. Nice to have on your side, but not so nice to have them as enemies, though they're much better these days. Well...that's all relative, obviously.'

Jeff greeted him. 'Alright, Matt. I see you've met Nick...did I hear something about the Wells brothers?'

'Nick was just saying he lives with their sister.'

'Aye. He does. She's too nice for him, though I reckon she's harder than her brothers...oh...in a good way, like. Don't hit us, Nick, son.' He mugged a face at him.

Nick aimed a mock punch at Jeff's chin.

Matt laughed. 'Hey look, I'm sorry I couldn't make it the other night for the opening. Something came up at the last minute.' He ran his hands through his messy hair a little nervously. 'Sounds like I missed being at the centre of the big news story. Terrible thing to have happened.'

'Nice bloke as well, Alan Armstrong,' said Nick.

'Actually, I knew him a little bit and his boss, Malcolm Pallister. I invested in the Tees Digital company. Have the police got any idea who did it?'

'If they have, they'd not tell us,' said Jeff, pulling out some records from a box. 'We're not even allowed to use our own toilet yet in case their forensics want to go over it again. It's all taped off.'

'And you had no idea it had happened? No screams or anything?'

'Nothing. At first we thought he'd had a heart attack or

something,' said Nick. 'But when they lifted up the body, he had a bloody big knife right in him.' He patted at his breast bone.

'Aye, a big hunting knife,' said Nick.

'A Bowie knife they call it, I think,' said Jeff. 'Presumably because only a lad insane would use one...see what I did there? Even in death there is rock-based humour.'

Matt Little looked concerned and shook his head. 'Err...are those the ones with a big handle?' He mimed the size of it.

'Yeah, evil looking things,' said Luke. 'Brilliant killing tool.'

'That's really just terrible. I know what those hunting knives are like. There's a shop in Easingwold sells them. Eeee, well, it's a bad world, isn't it? It's a worry to think of someone being out there who would do that.'

'True, but the show and the retailing of old records must go on, so here's those albums I told you about. Some early Doors and Love and the first Crabby Appleton record,' said Jeff.

'I'll get off then. Nice to see you after all these years, Matt,' said Nick.

'Yeah, you too, Nick.' Matt Little shook his hand firmly and smiled at him warmly. 'Great to see you again. You know, we should all go out for a drink, or a meal or something. Have a talk about old times at Ian Ramsey and Stockton Sixth Form College.'

Nick nodded, feeling that would be a depressing night out if that's all they talked about. Nostalgia wasn't what it used to be. It felt like a dead end on the road to nowhere. All we have is right here, right now.

'Yeah, let's go out sometime, or come round the house and we can just play records. If you give me your mobile number, I'll call you sometime.'

'Oh, I've lost my phone. I put it down somewhere the other week. I need to get a new one.'

'OK, well, Jeff's got all my contact details. Stay in touch, Matt.'

By the time he got in, Julie had put a chicken in to roast and taken a shower. She greeted him at the door in big baggy pair of linen pants and her grey hoodie.

'Hey missus,' he said, giving her a quick hug. 'You scrub up well for a rough lass.'

She slapped him playfully on the backside. 'Now then, are you're in the mood to have another go at making a baby? We've got half an hour before the chicken is done and I'm even wearing white underwear. Actually, I don't even know why I'm asking, you've never said no yet.' She gave him a playful look.

'And I'm not going to say no now.'

Ten minutes later they lay next to each other on the bed, naked and panting.

'Bloody hell Jules, that was short and very sweet. We really went for that. I bloody loved it.'

She let out a low moan and wriggled her legs. 'Ooh I could have another one if I tried, I feel all tingly.'

'I think that's actually the smell of roast chicken in the house. It's enough to make anyone orgasmic,' he said.

She giggled in a girlish way she reserved for post-coital situations, took a tissue from a box on her bedside table and cleaned herself up.

'Feel lucky?' she said as he got up to do likewise.

'I've just had it off with you, I always feel lucky after that,' he shouted from the bathroom.

'I mean there's a two percent chance of that shag getting me up the duff - if I'm not already preggers, like. Two in a hundred isn't a very good bet, but people win the lottery with far worse odds than that, don't they?'

He came back in with a towel in his hand.

'Don't wipe your cock on the clean towels, there's a good lad,' she said, just as he was about to.

'Sorry.' He used the corner of the bed sheet instead. She laughed and threw a pillow at him.

'Eeee what are you, like? Come here.'

He got back onto the bed and pulled her into him in an embrace, kissing her as he did so.

'Two in a hundred doesn't sound that unlikely really. But we don't know if it is two percent, I might be shooting blanks. We don't know.'

'True,' she smiled at him and ran her fingers over his chest hair, looking him in the eyes.

'Do you mind?'

'Mind?'

'If I don't get pregnant?'

'Err...well, I'd like it if it happened...'

'...and if it doesn't?'

'...if it doesn't, it doesn't. There's nothing we can do, is there?'

'Well, I could have fertility treatment.'

He paused to think about that.

'Would you do that?'

'Yeah. I would if you really wanted kids. I'd give it a go anyway.'

'Nah. If it's not going to happen naturally, then it's not meant to be. We're old buggers. Nature is trying to tell us something.'

'That's what I think, but I don't want you to get upset about it. About not having kids.'

'Are you alright about it?'

'I'm fine. It doesn't bother me at all. Maybe it will in the future, but it doesn't now. I've never felt broody. I'm just happy to do some unprotected shagging and if we had a kid it'd be amazing, it really would, but there's no point in getting our hopes up unrealistically.'

'It's funny isn't it? All those years we were so scared of getting pregnant or getting someone pregnant...it doesn't seem right that it's almost impossible to do it now.'

'That's because it's hard to come to terms with being older. In our heads we're still horny 20 year olds, but our bodies are in their 40s. Still, think of all the money we're saving on contraception.'

The alarm on the cooker went off.

'I'll get that,' he said, putting on a dressing gown. 'You might not have a bun in the oven, but at least we've got a chicken in instead,' Julie laughed and grabbed hold of his arm as he got up.

'Just a minute,' she said.

'What?'

'I was just about to tell you something.'

'What?'

'Don't get excited, but I should have got my period on Monday. It's Thursday and I've still not. I'm not saying...'

'...really? Bloody hell, Jules...it could...'

'...it could, but it probably isn't. I'm just getting older. You get less regular as you get older.' His heart was beating fast, but she was right and, as always, practically minded. 'I just had to tell you though, didn't I?'

'Aye of course. Well, err...keep me informed about your...err...menses,' he said, feeling a bit embarrassed.

She laughed and slapped at him. 'You're so cute when you go all shy. Now go and get my chicken out, I've got a right shagger's hunger on us.'

He made some gravy with the juices and put some broccoli on, then nipped back upstairs and put some clothes on. Julie had dressed and was combing her hair.

'That smells bloody fantastic. It actually smells of roast chicken crisps, you know what I mean?'

'Aye, well, one way or another, I love to service you with juicy meat,' he said, pulling his jeans on.

She chuckled her rolling laugh. 'One way or another, I'm a lucky woman, me.'

As he got cutlery out and laid the table, Julie carved the chicken.

'See, this is another man's thing, isn't it?' she said.

'Carving a chicken?'

'Yeah. Carving meat is always a man's thing. That's what my mother would say. She'd invite any man to carve meat before asking me. Every time. Why? Why is carving meat a male thing?'

'You're right, but I have no idea why. For some reason, meat is sort of masculine, it's the dog of the food world to the vegetable's cat. But it makes no sense at all. None of these things do as soon as you give them even a cursory bit of scrutiny. They're pointless gender demarcations. Does ownership of a penis allow you to slice meat better? My dad did the carving and he was rubbish at it. He even bought an electric carving knife to try and stop savaging joints, but it just made things worse. Sunday dinner was like a slasher movie at our house. But every week he'd stand there and do it and mam never did, even though I bet she'd have been better at it.'

She cut a leg off for herself along with both wings and then carved off half the breast for him.

'Due to coitus-themed distractions, I haven't had a chance to tell you something odd,' said Nick.

'Oh yeah? Oh god, this is delicious.'

'Fantastic, yeah. You know I went to Jeff's and picked up that single, as I was leaving this bloke we used to go to school with came in. Jeff had put some records to one side for him. Matt Little. I remembered the name. Anyway, as I walked out I bumped right into him and though I didn't know it was him until he said, I did actually recognize him. He was the driver of the Lexus that dropped that glamorous Deirdre woman off. Weird eh?'

'Yeah, that's funny. Sometimes I feel like Teesside is a very small place and if I saw any stranger in town, I'd only be one or two degrees away from knowing them. You know what I mean? My mam is a good case in point. Between her, her sister and her mates, they're connected to hundreds of people, thousands probably. If you sat in the pub on the estate, no-one who came in would be unknown to one of them, one way or another.'

'Yeah, that is true. I get amazed when I'm at the Boro how many people I know there. Some to speak to, some I've just seen there for literally decades, but never spoken to. Inevitable when it's a small club in a small town, I suppose. Anyway, he's divorced, got two grown-up kids and lives in Easingwold.'

'Easingwold? Where's that?'

'It's half way between York and Thirsk. One of those posh little North Yorkshire market towns.'

'Oh yeah, it's on the A19, isn't it? I don't like those sorts of places. I mean, I know they're nice to look at, but a lot of the time they're full of those strange countryside types aren't they? People in pink trousers and green quilted gilets. What are they all about?'

'God knows, but that's North Yorkshire to a tee.'

'I don't know why, but I always feel you get a higher proportion of old school reactionary types in the countryside, especially in North Yorkshire. I'm a townie lass, I have no interest in wearing jodhpurs and wielding a riding crop unless it is for normal, healthy, sexy perving reasons, naturally.'

'Rightly so. I'd actually quite fancy shooting and fishing and eating the catch, but have no interest in doing it with a lot of horse-faced braying toffs or rich business blokes who are half cut on whisky, yomping across a grouse moor pretending they're big men.'

'God no. We're more poacher than gamekeeper us though, I reckon.'

He spent the next morning writing a couple of columns then went into town to see Jeff, while Julie went up to Durham University for a couple of lectures on her History MA course. It was nice having Jeff local to drop in on, just like their days in Harrogate. Not that they ever did much except drink tea and talk about records, but then they didn't really want to do much else.

'Aye aye, fella. Seen any ghosts yet?' he said as he walked in. Jeff was slotting a UK copy of the first Mothers Of Invention album, *Freak Out*, into a plastic sleeve on the wall.

'I thought I saw a ghostly presence earlier, but it turned out to be my own reflection in the window. Hard morning at the keyboard?'

'Exhausting. It's like working down a pit.'

Jeff laughed. 'I've got to go and see Hair Bear in a minute.'

'Oh aye, exactly why is he called Hair Bear?'

'Probably because if anyone could actually ride an invisible bike with two other bears, it'd be him. He's taken so much acid that would be a piece of piss for him. And he's got massive hair as well, obviously.'

'What are you buying?'

'Just a bag of grass. Trying to cut down on me drinking. If you're stoned you don't want to get boozed up so much. Thought I'd have a smoke and then go out the Black Bull tonight.'

'Yeah, but you end up eating all the food in the house instead. Less booze, more snacking.'

'Ah, but only Monster Munch. It's been medically proven that's the only food that satisfies the stoner's munchies.'

'Where does yer man Hair Bear live now, then?'

'Still on Hartington Road.'

'Still? That was were all the dopers and acid heads lived when we were teenagers.'

'Aye. He's keeping a great Stockton tradition going.'

After a cup of tea they crossed over the High Street, walked down Dovecot Street, taking a left onto Hartington Road. It seemed a bit nicer than how Nick remembered. The houses were smarter and in better condition. The only one that wasn't was a small terraced house that, at some point 40 years ago, had been covered in greying plaster. It was now crumbling off. That was, inevitably, where Hair Bear lived.

Jeff knocked on the old blue painted door. A face appeared behind a dirty old net curtain that hung in a decayed bay window. Jeff waved.

The door opened to reveal a stick thin man who appeared to be about 50 percent hair and 50 percent unwashed laundry. Somewhere underneath it was Hair Bear, or Harry Underhill as he was known to his mother. In his early 40s, he'd lived a life dedicated to consumption of narcotics, funded largely by the retailing of said narcotics.

He squinted at the sunny sky. 'Ironically, I've never found light very illuminating,' he said and gestured them to come in. The house smelled damp and of things that were decomposing, including, quite possibly, Hair Bear himself.

'I like what you've done with the décor in here Hair, man,' said Jeff as they went into the front room. 'You've gone for that organic look.'

'Yeah man, I like nature inside the house, not outside. It's no good to me outside.' He pointed at some dark, fluffy mould growing on a wall.

'And a textured carpet too,' said Nick. 'Some would say, crunchy.'

'You can lose your soul to a vacuum,' he said, enigmatically. Nick laughed.

'How much are you after, Jeff?'

'Whatever 50 quid will buy me,' said Jeff, squatting down and looking at a pile of records stacked against a wall.

'Anything good?' said Nick, as Hair Bear left the room.

'Hawkwind, Gong, Tangs, John Martyn, Bob Marley. All your 70s classics for weed smokers. All of them battered and embedded with cannabis resin. If you smoked the sleeves, you'd get high.'

'The coppers must know about this place. Why don't they bust him?'

'I've always wondered that. He doesn't cause any bother. Maybe they like his low-key dealing ways. Could be someone much worse. Also he doesn't sell any class A's, does he? So he's hardly a big catch.'

'Coppers probably score their dope here too,' said Nick. 'Though I can't imagine Colin Harcombe sucking on some spliff.'

Jeff laughed. 'Bad business Nick, we've run out of Rizlas.'

Nick sat down after clearing a space on an old sofa and looked at the TV. The local news was on, but with the sound muted. Hair Bear came back with a plastic bag tightly packed with cannabis.

'There's your key to the cosmic highway,' he said, taking Jeff's money.

'What do you do all day here, Hair?' said Jeff, sitting down on an exhausted armchair, peppered with fag burns and covered in crumbs of snack food.

'I contemplate existence and do time in the universal mind. It's a big place to explore, man.' He spoke in an accent that was somewhere between a Greenwich Village hipster and a Teesside steelworker. It was an odd combination; as though Allen Ginsburg had been born in Eston. He wasn't American at all, but the drawl he had once affected, just be a cool druggie, had stuck as a permanent mode of expression.

'Don't you ever just want to go out for a walk and enjoy the sunshine?' said Nick.

'Life is bigger on the inside than the outside, man.'

'Is life a Tardis, like?' said Nick, laughing again.

'That is wiser than you know, my friend,' said Hair Bear, taking out a pack of Rizlas and beginning to stick them together. He looked up at the TV. It was showing a preview of a programme due to be on later that evening called *The Urban Renewal Revolution.*

Hair Bear pointed at the screen in a way that was so languid it looked as though he was underwater.

'That dude man...' He paused, but the moment seemed to drift away from him. Nick looked at the TV. Davey James from the Urban Renewal Organisation was saying something. The small screen filled with his big bearded face. 'That dude has two kids,' he said, resuming his sentence as though no time had passed. Nick grinned at Jeff who made a stoned face back at him. 'They score dope off me. Nice kids. Fucked up. But nice.'

'Are you sure, Hair?' said Jeff. 'How do you know that?'

'They told me. Both cats look like him too.' He took out a pouch of tobacco and sprinkled it into the Rizlas.

'How old are they then?'

He hunched and made a sort of shrug. ' Urghh...what is age anyway? And why are we counting in 12s? Why have an Imperial system for months? Why not decimal? Crazy. Who got to say about that, man? Time is an illusion. Lunchtime doubly so.'

'That's from *Hitchhikers Guide to The Galaxy*,' said Nick, pointing at him. 'I love Douglas Adams.'

'Yeah man. I once thought I'd found the restaurant at the end of the universe. Turned out to be Oxbridge chippy. Man, I was trippin' off me tits.' He wrenched a rasping laugh out of his over-smoked lungs. 'Counting in the traditional 12s mode, they're late teens. They buy a lot of grass with the old man's money. They pay over the odds like it's a rebellion trip. I dig that, man. The kids have got class and man, do they love the smoke? Want the strongest stuff too. Started asking me for other gear a while ago - coke and speed, but I said, no way man, that bus doesn't stop here.' He nodded approval at himself and took out a small block of cannabis resin and began to shave it into the joint with a pen-knife.

'Well kids still love the auld wacky baccy, don't they?' said Jeff. 'Mind, it's much stronger than it was. This isn't your mind-bending skunk is it, Hair?' He pointed at the bag.

'No man. It's retro grass. It's cool.'

He looked back at the TV. Davey James was walking around a new housing estate.

'Yeah man, they were sitting right where you are just the other day saying how all the dude's whole gig is corrupt. I said, tell me something I don't know. I mean, it's all corporate bullshit. Today's hero is...like...y'know maaaan...like...yeah...whatever...' His brain seemed to have slid sideways for a few seconds.

'Come on then, Jeff. Let's go and get something to eat,' said Nick standing up. He really didn't want to sit around smoking dope, not least because he wasn't sure what it would do to his psychological condition and also because even mild grass was just way too strong these days. It was more like an anaesthetic than the stuff he'd smoked as a student.

'...tomorrow's fish and chip paper...yeah man,' said Hair Bear, finishing his sentence long after he'd started it.

'Nope, that still doesn't make any sense Hair, old boy,' said Jeff. 'We'll have to leave you and rejoin straight society for the afternoon.'

'I pity you man, I really do. There ain't nuthin' out there for me. I ain't trading in my black feathers for a crown. That's for sure. It's all in here.' He tapped his head with a nicotine-stained forefinger.

'I don't blame you, Hair, dude and I'm not, y'know...err...trading in my plumage for a rainbow,' said Jeff, shrugging at Nick and rolling his eyes up into his head.

CHAPTER 6

That evening, when Julie got in, she was in a hurry to change and go out with the TW women.

'What should I wear for a night out on the drink with a bunch of women?' she said, looking at the rail of clothes that hung behind a curtain in an alcove as a makeshift wardrobe.

'Where are you going?'

'It's only in the Penny Black.'

'Ah, estate pub. Just t-shirt and jeans then.'

'You reckon?'

'Safe bet, isn't it?'

She took off her work pants, pulled on her black Armani jeans, a black t-shirt and fastened a fine silver necklace that he'd given her for her last birthday.

'There...any good?' she said, turning to him.

'You can see your white bra through the black t-shirt. I dunno if this matters in the world of high fashion and haute couture at the Penny Black, though.'

She turned and looked at herself in the mirror. 'Oh bugger, you're right. Trust you to notice white underwear. Perv. Are you sure you can't see my white knickers through the jeans as well?' She gave him a cheeky look.

He squinted his eyes as though looking really hard. 'Sadly, no.'

'You absolute total perv,' she said again with a short laugh. 'What is it with you and white underwear?

'A man needs a hobby,' he said innocently.

She found a black bra and changed as he sat and watched, then put on a smart, loosely-tailored Nicole Farhi jacket. She stood in the front of the full length mirror again. 'Too smart?'

'Yeah too smart and too posh.'

'Me? Too posh? Yer jokin', aren't ya?'

He took her white denim jacket off the hanger. 'Wear this instead. Black and white. It's classic isn't it?'

She took off the black jacket. 'When did you become a fashionista?'

'I know nothing about clothes, but I do know what you look good in. Or what I think looks good, anyway.'

She turned to look at her self side-on in the white jacket and pulled at it. 'Y'know. I think you're right. This is much better. I can't believe it. You don't normally take much notice of what I wear.'

'Looks good with your hair, doesn't it? Now you've made it more blonde.'

He picked a strand off the jacket and brushed her shoulders down. 'Are you going to get ratted?'

'I'll try not to get too wankered.'

'I don't mind if you do, not least 'cos you tend to get randy when you're drunk.'

'Drink does go straight to my crotch. I'm weirdly wired like that. That's got me into so much trouble over the years.' She pulled a face and stuck her tongue out and wiggled it at him.

He laughed.

'What are you and Jeff doing tonight?' she said.

'He's going to smoke a joint out the back and then get a cab to the Black Bull. I'm staying in. Sitting in a pub for four hours just drinking water while everyone else gets fuck-faced is a bit tedious. I'll get some more writing done instead.'

'Aw. I wish you could have a drink or a bit of Jeff's weed, just to take the edge off, like.'

'I could, but I like not being so down or depressed more than I like being drunk or stoned. It's no massive sacrifice. I've had a bloody good drinking career and enough drugs to last me for a while yet.'

She put her hands on his chest. 'Yeah and let's face it, you can't get old Big Pink up properly when you're drunk and I may need you to do that for me later if my crotch gets legless.'

'A legless crotch? That sounds like a hell of a messy night out.'

After she'd gone out and Jeff had left for the pub, he lay down on the sofa to watch TV. The Tyne Tees local news programme that had been trailed earlier in the day started, focusing on a new public housing project just off Darlington Back Lane which had been funded by the Urban Renewal Organisation. In a unique arrangement, it was leased back to the council at zero percent interest over a 30-year period, allowing the much-needed expansion of affordable social housing at no upfront cost to the cash-strapped council, who would then pay for them out of the ongoing rents, but end up paying well over the market value for them, thus providing URO with a lot of profit.

The boss of URO, Davey James was interviewed. He was a big guy who put Nick in mind of Led Zeppelin's old manager, Peter Grant. Tall, with a cropped black beard and a bulky 22-stone frame, he was quite a presence. With ice blue eyes and a passionate, articulate, but still very much working class Teesside voice stretching out his vowels in a classic Middlesbrough fashion, he was a really charismatic bloke. That came across on screen really clearly as he spoke with eloquence about the project.

'In this country, we're too addicted to the idea of owning property. Prices go up and up and up, but wages don't. Everyone who gets on the housing ladder wants to pull it up after them, because no-one wants prices to go down and devalue their asset. It's an addiction we must break. We need more social housing that regular working people can rent for a price they can easily afford. Those people will spend their wages in the local economy and that's what we want. We don't want most of their money going to private landlords offshore accounts, do we? What most people really want is a nice place to live, somewhere that is secure and they can call their own. That's what this project is all about. I'd love people to move in and spend the rest of their lives here. There's nothing down-market here about renting or being a tenant, in fact, we want to see renting redefined as a socially responsible investment. I'm convinced a happier society is one that isn't so obsessed with their housing investment and is more concerned with living well. I like to call it socialist capitalism. Everyone makes a profit from the building project, but it is effectively owned by the people, for the people, in perpetuity.'

An articulate, intelligent, but working class voice is always the most powerful, being both educated and informed and yet not aloof. Davey James had that in spades. Every time he was on TV he made himself more popular. A recent live debate he'd had with three local politicians had only inflated his reputation. Here was a successful local man fighting to make his area better. The elected officials seemed weak, pusillanimous and arse-covering by comparison. Having a clear vision and being able to express it simply and without nuance worked well in the modern media, not least because so many politicians were more concerned to talk loud, but say nothing. He'd also mastered sound-bites of easily understood information which anyone could grasp.

There was no doubt URO was making good money on the back of these building projects and as the TV programme showed, everyone was now falling over themselves to get some of the reflected glow from their success. The council was keen to acquire more land for the URO to build more houses on, green belt legislation was being over-turned to free up building sites, while other organisations wanted him to rebuild or renovate run-down housing in other parts of Teesside.

Even if it was for the greater good, what Davey James had done, by framing the URO in this "socialist capitalism" light was to create an awful lot of work, an awful lot of houses and a lot of profits for his company, while turning himself into a local hero. And he made it seem as though it was all done altruistically for the community. It was very clever and you had to admire him for it. Even if he did hugely benefit, there was no doubt that the area very much needed the housing.

There was a short profile of James, highlighting his work in Spain, then a couple of shots of his kids, Zak and Toni, who were described as teenagers. Just as Hair Bear had said, they did look very like him. There was a photo from the family album of him with his wife and kids, smiling dutifully.

By the end of the show, Nick found himself warming to James and his ideas. They were an interesting political hybrid, driven through by James' sheer force of personality and will to succeed.

Jeff came in at 11.30 and eventually a cab dropped Julie off at 12.30. He could never sleep until she was home. She appeared at the bedroom door, obviously really drunk and did a big goofy wave.

'Yes. I am pissed,' she said, before he could say anything. 'Turns out those women can't half bloody drink,' she said, sitting down on the edge of the bed and pulling off her socks.

'Northern women? Drinkers? Never,' he said, sitting up with his hands behind his head.

'Shocking innit. Throw my pyjamas over. Hey, I'll tell you what, you'd have been proud of me, I picked the most obscure rock song on the karaoke machine to sing, like...class it was...'

'I thought I could hear a howling noise in the distance. What did you sing?'

'Crazy On You,' by Heart. "Bloody hell, it's a right lung buster, that. Impossible amount of words and then a huge chorus. I just shouted it. 'Lemme go crazy, crazy on you. Ha ha...the women didn't know it. I said, "where's your inner rock chick?" I'm all for non-sexist trousers, but there's got to be room for some rock...err...trousers...or whatever, in your life as well."

He laughed. She was slurring her words. 'Not sure that actually makes any sense, Jules.'

'Doesn't it? It sounded alright. Brain and mouth not working together any more.' She pulled off her clothes and burped loudly. 'I mean, I was just farting around, wasn't I? Not everything has to be a big political thing, does it. Or does it?'

'Life is political; non-sexist trousers especially so.'

'I suppose that's right, smart arse. What about farting, is that political?' she said, staggering sideways as she aimed a leg at her pyjamas.

'Farting is an oppressive tool, I'm afraid.'

'Bugger.   I'm   a   terrible   tool   then   or   an ohpressure...oppenpress...oh-press-or, then.'

She got changed and went for a wash, returning a little unsteadily. 'What did you end up doing?'

'There was a big Davey James interview on telly. He was really good. Talked about that new estate on Darlo Back Lane.'

'Oh I know. He's dead impressive, him.'

'He was going on about socialist capitalism. It all sounded just right for this area.'

'Yeah. I like the sound of that. Showshillist Cappything or whatever. Fuck. I sound like Paul Merson trying to pronounce a foreign name.' She lay down and let out a slow long breath. 'I'm so knackered. I'm such an old sod. It's not even one in the morning.'

'I thought you were going to be an inebriated love machine.'

'Oh god no. I might puke if you start humping me.'

'You're not the first woman to say that.'

She fell to sleep immediately. Eventually he dozed off too, waking up when it was getting light. Julie was turning uneasily beside him. Then she groaned.

'I think I'm going to be sick. Feel terrible,' she said.

He leaped out of bed and ran to the bathroom, picked up a big white and blue enamel bowl and ran back.

'Here...use this...'

'Oh fuck...' she sat up, retched and released a thick stream of what looked like vegetable soup, once, then twice and then with a loud, final barking retch, a third of mostly stomach bile.

Nick got a wet flannel and gave it to her to wipe her mouth.

'All done?'

She was pale and sweaty now.

'Yeah. Oh god...'

He took the bowl of stinking puke and flushed it down the toilet and cleaned it out. As he was coming out the toilet, Jeff emerged from his room at the far end of the hall.

'Did, I hear the distant, but strangely familiar sounds of puke-age? Everything cool?'

'Aye. Jules is a bit worse for wear.'

'Is she alright?'

'She will be, aye. Thanks, Jeff.'

He put a thumb up.

'Here, have some toothpaste,' he said, throwing the tube onto the bed. 'Freshen your mouth up a bit. And drink some water.'

She groaned a little and sat up to drink.

'Feeling better?'

'Yeah. I like a good vom. Afterwards, anyway. Feel a bit better now.'

'It releases relaxing endorphins. Clever thing the human body. Likes to make you feel nice when it can.'

'Yeah. Maybe I shouldn't be abusing it so much then. Poor bloody thing.'

'What had you been drinking?'

'White wine.'

'Did you have a lot?'

'You never think you've had that much, but I must've had six or seven big glasses. I'd say never again if I hadn't said it about a thousand times before.'

'Drink some more water so you're not dehydrated.'

'Me taking sober tips from you doesn't seem right. You were such a huge drinker.'

'That's why I'm an expert in surviving boozing sessions.'

'Thanks for looking after me.' She patted at him.

'S'alright. Can't be doing with puke on the bed.'

'Nothing less sexy than a woman being sick is there?'

'Not much. I once almost puked up in a girl's mouth when I was 16. We were kissing, she had a long tongue...disaster. Out came four pints of Harp lager and lime.'

'You lady killer, you. I love you so much I could puke. At least I wasn't that bad.'

The morning was grey and damp as Nick made breakfast. Jeff emerged again at the first whiff of bacon and sausages.

'You want tomatoes, eggs, black pudding as well?'

'I'll take it all, my good man.'

'I can do you some liver as well if you like, and kidneys. The full old school mixed grill.'

'Liver for breakfast? Are you insane, man? It's...it's a liver.'

'I bloody love liver. It's got more vitamin C than oranges, you know.'

'Has it? Bloody hell, doctor. We used to have it at school, remember?'

'I loved school liver. No-one else did, so you could get stacks of it.'

'But it was like eating rubber.'

'I'm weird, I know.'

'Liver for brekky is a step too far for me.'

'Wuss.'

'Jules OK?'

'Headache, but that's it.'

'Hammered, was she?'

'I've seen her worse, but she just felt sick. Caught it in time.'

'I've had 21 years now without being sick. It's a good run. Last time I was sick was at the 1988 Reading Festival. Such a terrible line up that I got fuck-faced, threw up during Deacon Blue and then passed out to thankfully miss Hothouse fucking Flowers and Squeeze. Squeeze headlining Reading! Disgrace. Only went to see Heep on the second day. Ah ha. Here she is. What a hero.'

Julie appeared at the door in a dressing gown.

'Morning. I hope my lower oesophagus reflex didn't wake you up, Jeff.'

'I love a woman who can drink till she's sick.' he said, amused. 'It's an important social asset in the north of England.'

'I feel a bit icky again actually, but there's nowt in me to puke up.'

'Have some eggs. You need something in you,' said Nick, putting some scrambled eggs on a plate.

She sat down, looked at it doubtfully, ate two mouthfuls and immediately had to run for the bathroom to be sick again. When she returned, she looked washed out.

'Dunno what's wrong with me. Waves of nausea. Must be the thought of going the football.'

But an hour later, after tea and a bit of bacon her stomach seemed to settle down a bit.

'Are you actually up to coming to the Boro?' said Nick as she dressed in baggy pants and a loose sweatshirt and baseball cap.

'Yeah. I'll be fine by then.'

'Cool. We've been invited to a press thing before the game. A bit of food and drink...'

'...don't mention drink...or food for that matter.'

'...there might be a chance to meet a couple of Boro legends and talk football to the great and good of Teesside cultural life.'

'That shouldn't take long then. Does that mean I have to look smart or, more importantly, put a bra on?'

'Nah, it's the Boro. Bras are always optional at the Boro, you know that, on women anyway.'

'When I was a bra-less 14 year old I once got felt up on the Holgate End. Copped a handful just as Mickey Burns scored. Cheeky sod. I could probably sue him for that now.'

'Ah, romance is never far away on Teesside. But no, we don't have to be smart.'

'Good. I'm in the mood for big knickers and loose clothing today.'

They drove into Middlesbrough and Nick parked in his usual spot in town, a ten-minute walk from the Riverside Stadium. Julie took his hand as they walked.

'I know what you're thinking, y'know,' she said.

'What?'

'That it was morning sickness and that maybe your tadpoles sniffed out one of the last of my decent eggs.'

'I do like eggs, if that helps,' he said.

'I don't think that counts and I'm not a hen.'

'I dunno Jules, you've got decent plumage. Mind, if you were, you'd do all of your business out of the same vent.'

'Ha, yeah. I'd actually like that. Nice and tidy. Women have got too many holes and flaps if you ask me.'

'I've always thought it's very complicated down there. I keep a map handy at all times, in case I get lost.'

'That explains a lot. Sometimes I've wondered where you're going and what on earth you think you're doing.'

'It's like a jungle down there, man. Geography was never my strong point and certainly not biology. I need a torch and possibly a St. Bernard to help me.' He put his arm around her. 'Come on then, mother.'

The media event was being held in one of the lounges. His name was on a list at the door. As soon as they were inside, it was clear who was the focus of attention. There at the far end with a semi-circle of about 20 people around him, Davey James was holding court. Nick saw a lad he knew who helped the press out on match days.

'Hey, Harry.'

'Nick. Now then. Can I get you owt?'

'Two black coffees would be good.'

'There's free beer.'

'No thanks, man. I see the big man is the centre of attention,' he said, nodding toward the property developer. The lad lowered his voice.

'There's talk of him being Boro's sponsor next season, so he's being wined and dined, or as much as the Boro wine and dine anyone. An afternoon here should bring him to his senses. He doesn't normally watch us, like, so I wouldn't say he's actually a fan.'

'Oh right. I was wondering what this little get together was about.'

'Club also wants to get some good press don't they? There's rebellion in the ranks 'cos our form is so terrible. They've got Big Chief Bullshit in because everything he does is good news, innit? Sun shines out of his arse, probably pisses gold an' all.'

Nick grinned. 'Are you not a fan then?'

'You could say that. There's a carvery in about half an hour.

Should be a decent feed. I'll get that coffee for youse.'

'Full bellies and free booze is as good a way as any to get the press on your side, I suppose,' said Julie.

'A decent win would help more. C'mon, let's see what the big man is saying over there. He's got quite a crowd around him. You'd think he was campaigning for election or something the way everyone in here is looking at him. It's supposed to be about the Boro, not about him.'

'Well he's the man of the moment isn't he? Everyone loves a winner. Look at them all - it's all blokes as well - hanging on his every word like he's a fat Moses.'

'Fat Moses sounds like a great 70s band.'

They stood to one side of him and listened to what he was saying.

'...the problem with local government is that it's run by amateurs. Councillors mean well, but they're often just not up to speed. I've met some of them who don't even have email. Yet businessmen have to deal with these people all the time in relation to local planning and administration.' He nodded as he spoke, as though cajoling the circle of people who listened to him into his viewpoint. This provoked mumbles of agreement. 'A businessman needs decisions and answers quickly. He has to act quickly. He can't do everything by committee. That's the problem.'

'...and business*women* too, presumably...' said Julie her voice raised about the murmuring. Everyone, literally everyone, turned to look at her. Davey James focused his diamond blue eyes on her.

'...businesswomen are as frustrated by red tape as businessmen,' she added by way of clarity, her arms folded.

Davey James roared a big laugh, as though someone had told an especially good joke. That seemed an odd response, but it encouraged other people to equally force a laugh. Julie set her jaw against him as soon as he did that. Nick had seen that jaw a thousand times. The jaw of defiance. The jaw of "who-the-fuck-do-you-think-you-are-talking-to?"

'Yes, of course I mean businessmen and businesswomen. That

really goes without saying, I hope.'

Julie walked around to his side. Nick followed.

'Yes, but the correct words are there to be used correctly. So if you mean people in business, you say business people, if you mean men you say businessmen and if you mean women you say businesswomen. It's not difficult that, is it?'

Someone groaned. Nick clocked him. A solid chunk of middle-aged man, balding, ruddy cheeks. He looked like someone who'd normally be on a pheasant shoot, wore a green tweed coat and had a high blood pressure, impatient look on his face.

'No no, you're right. I agree,' James said, with a well practised emollient tone. 'As you probably know, the chairman of URO is a woman.' But he said it in the self-conscious way that men do who think they're being progressive, but who really aren't.

'I think you'll find she's your Chairwoman then. A Chairman would be male,' said Julie, arms still folded across her chest.

'That's just political correctness gone mad,' said the balding man, who had now an iridescent flush in his cheek. 'It's just a waste of everyone's time. Feminist PC rubbish!' He shook his head and looked so angry that a man in his late 20s stepped away from him in the way you do when you think you've accidentally stood next to a crazy person.

'No no, she's right,' said James, but with a tone that suggested it was his judgement which should prevail on this matter. 'I'm a big believer in equal opportunities and equal pay. The URO is all about community, men and women coming together to create a better society.'

It was a nice line, but it did sound like a line. In fact much of what he said seemed like public relations and was too smooth. It was OK in the edited medium of TV, but here in real life it felt fake. But it was a way of talking which would easily impress a lot of people, just because it was self-assured and confident. It wasn't hard to imagine him convincing some people that black was white. The gathered crowd here were obviously fans.

A few drifted away and some more people arrived, most of them local journalists.

'Here's your coffees,' said Harry bringing Nick and Julie a white porcelain mug each.

Nick thanked him and took them. 'Full of shite, if you ask me,' said Harry quietly in Nick's ear. He grinned at him and handed Julie a mug.

'Here you go, Ms Pankhurst,' he said. She rolled her eyes at him and mouth the words "very annoying" at him and walked away across the room. The red-faced man was pleased to see her go, turning to look at her with a sneer that Nick found really sodding annoying. It raised his hackles. Prick.

'I think my blood sugar has dropped. I need food. I feel really narky,' she said, sipping at the coffee.

'Take it easy, man.'

'Don't tell me to take it easy. You don't need to tell me that. What do you think, I'm going kick him in the balls or something? Though he deserves it. That was so much bullshit. Phoney get.' Her accent had slipped back into broad Teesside as her anger had risen.

Nick held a hand up in surrender.

'I was just saying...'

'...well don't.' She scowled at him and went over to a table which was laid out with sandwiches and biscuits. She took three digestives and a ham sandwich.

It was unlike her to get as narky as this. It wasn't some sort of sign of pregnancy, was it?

James soon began holding forth again, waving his arms around like he was orating for the masses. It seemed inappropriate in this context, but it was probably how he behaved everywhere he went.

'Yeah, the Darlo Back Lane estate is just the start. We have community projects in the pipeline all over the region. Small estates with local facilities to service them. Shops where the housewife can pick up something for dinner without having to go to some big hypermarket on the edge of town. Somewhere for hard-working families to live. Your typical politician is just not good enough. He's just going to follow the party line and not do what needs doing. It's time for the people to rebuild the place with their own hands. I just want the council and the politicians to get out of our way and let us do what needs doing.'

That made Julie furious. She spun around and marched back over to his little gathering.

'Housewife? Housewife?! What are you saying housewife for? What about men who want to buy food? What about women who are not married? What about women who are single? Why does wife and house go together? Why say housewife? That's just sexist. Little woman at home doing the cooking while men go out to work? Is that it? It's so outmoded, man. That's not how we live now, thank Christ. And hard-working families? What about people without families? Why are you excluding them? What about those who would like to be hard-working but can't get a job? Oh and by the way, there are women who are politicians as well. We're everywhere these days, you know. Haven't you noticed? Yeah, they even let us out the kitchen!'

She jabbed a finger at him, jaw set at a defiant angle. But this didn't go down at all well in the room.

'Aye, more's the bloody pity. Do shut it Germaine bloody Greer,' said the bald, red-faced man in the flat vowels of North Yorkshire; an accent perfectly designed to express misery, disgruntlement and annoyance. Some openly laughed at this. Nick's hackles went up again, feeling really defensive on her behalf. He looked around at those who were smirking.

'Very witty, you fat-faced fuck!' shouted Julie, raised up on her toes as though to volley the words more powerfully at him. Nick put a hand on her arm in attempt to calm her down, but she was raging now.

'Oh, very lady-like,' he retorted. 'Who died and made you Queen?'

'Oh, do piss off, you sexist pig. Come back and talk to me when you've lost your virginity and entered the 21st century.' She said it with the same witheringly sarcastic tone she used with her mother.

'You want to watch her, mate,' said another man in response to her words. 'She'll have your balls in a vice, that one.'

'You what, son?' said Nick, hot blood suddenly rising in his veins, taking a big stride towards him and getting in his face. He was balding, unshaven and tanned. Maybe 55. He stank of beer.

'I'm just saying, like...' he said, taking a pace backwards, seeing Nick hadn't taken his quip well.

Nick stood in front of him. He was an inch shorter and pudgy.

'No no, say what you said again. You think you're a funny man, don't you? Come on then...' He pushed the man in the chest, ready to twat him now.

'Alright, alright, we don't want any trouble here,' said a voice from somewhere, but Nick didn't take his eyes off his opponent. 'Come on then, what are you waiting for? Say it again.'

'Come on, I was just having laugh. I didn't mean anything mate.'

'Yes, you did. You were being a sexist fuck-wit. That's what you were doing. You were trying to put her down because she can stand up for herself against idiots like your pink-faced retard mate here.' He pushed him again.

'It was just a joke.'

'Not funny. Apologize to her. And you too fat boy...' he pointed at the other man, 'or you'll get yours as well...' He'd fucking have them both...who the hell were these people to behave like this? There had to be consequences. You couldn't just let them get away with it.

'Come on now...everyone calm down,' someone else said.

'Under. The. Thumb,' said the red-faced man in his designed-to-induce-fury accent.

Nick took a step towards him and leaned into his face. He was four inches shorter, but built like a water tank. Gently and repeatedly, Nick tapped him on the right cheek, one slap between each word. 'Now, now, darlin' are you on the rag or something?' Then he grabbed the man's face, pinching his cheeks together with an iron grip. The man tried to pull away, protesting as he did so. Nick pushed him hard, making him stumble and fall onto his backside, then swung around to the man who had made the 'balls in a vice' comment. 'I still haven't heard you apologize yet...'

'No. And you're not going to, either. Why don't you both fuck off home and leave the football to the real men. Fucking bed wetter.'

That was it. He was just the right distance away to knee him in the balls with sufficient power to knock them up into his pelvis. But he was too late. Julie got there before him. She kicked him in the back of the knee, giving him a dead leg and then pushed him with a double-handed shove, so that he fell over backwards alongside the other man.

'Come on, Nick, let's get out of here and leave the real men to wank themselves off.' He followed her out of the suite. The remaining men looked on with rather pathetic, impotent looks on their faces, unsure who to side with and unsure how to behave in the face of raw aggression like this.

'Yeah, go on, do as you're told', the red-faced man said from the floor.

Nick stopped, turned around and leant over him and pulled his arm back as though to belt him in the face. No-one tried to stop him. The man flinched and put his arms up to protect himself.

'Don't worry son, I wouldn't waste my knuckle skin on shit like you,' he said, pulling up short of actually hitting him.

Two security men had arrived to sort them out.

'It's OK, we're going to our seats,' said Julie to the fluorescent jacketed blokes who looked about as dumb as a brick wall and twice as dense. 'There'll be no more trouble.'

'Well, that was fun,' he said as they sat down in their seats and looked out at the bright green sward. He tugged at his armpits, wet with the adrenalin sweat.

She was quiet. Clearly upset. Then she shook her head. 'Sorry, that was all my fault. I provoked all of that. I don't know what got into me. I was so furious and wanted to pull their sexist tongues right out of their mouths.'

'It wasn't your fault. They were being bastards.'

'I know, but fighting doesn't get us anywhere, does it? It's just the old macho thing again. It's their thing. Fighting or being horrible is their game. So we're as bad as them, really. I was so wound up. I just hate all that housewife thing so much that I wanted to provoke a reaction. I wanted to have it out with them and show them up. But why? It's no way to go on. What did I think I'd achieve there?'

'But you were in the right.'

'I was right, but I was also wrong. You can't fight abuse with more abuse. It's just making everything worse. I should know that by now. Being a better, nicer person is the biggest revenge and the best way to change things.'

He sat back and folded his arms across his chest, feeling the adrenalin dropping out of his bloodstream.

'Aye, maybe. But sometimes you need to fight your corner. Sometimes backing down gets you into more trouble.'

'Yes, but not literally fight. We made a right show of ourselves there and all because we thought we had the moral high ground. Or that's what I thought anyway.' She grimaced at the thought of it.

'I noticed that big Davey backed away as soon as it looked like we were going to kick off. He went to the far end of the room and turned his back on it all, like it was nothing to do with him.'

'Yes, I spotted that. Coward.' She took out a hanky and blew her nose.

They went quiet as the ground filled up, both still upset by the confrontation.

'Can someone be a twat and still do public good?' said Nick. 'It's like when you hear about a musician being evil, but you love their music. The two things feel like they should be incompatible, but they're not always. I totally agree with what Davey James says about so many things.'

'His sexist language shows what he's really like, if you ask me.'

'But maybe it's like you say - words are just words. You can say the right thing and behave badly, so maybe it can also work vice versa. You can say the wrong thing and behave well. I think you can compartmentalize bits of your life. That's why people who are arrested for some terrible crime are often said to be a lovely co-worker or son. We like to think the evil people are evil in all areas of their life, but that isn't true. Even murderers can be nice to their kids or whatever.'

She chewed on her cheek. 'I just hate the idea of Davey James being a big asset to Teesside, but a total git.'

'I think he'll bully anyone he feels is beneath him or is weaker than him,' Nick said. 'The way he talks, he definitely thinks his view is the most important one in the room. That's a bully's mindset. He'll also try and co-opt anyone he thinks could be an enemy or a rival. That's how it always used to work at school.'

'When you had the fat bloke's face in your hand, I noticed Davey was looking on and checking you out. I think he liked what he saw,' said Julie, standing up to let someone past to their seat.

'Checking me out? What, sexually? He's not my type, Jules. You know the only man I'd have sex with is Fabio Cannavaro.'

She laughed a bit at that. 'I'd let you have it off with Cannavaro an' all. I'd deffo give you a free pass on that one as long as you'd let me have a go on him after. No I mean, he was seeing what sort of man he was dealing with. Weighing you up, like. Maybe he'll want you on board as some sort of enforcer.'

He snorted. 'I'm not scary enough for that.'

She looked doubtful. 'I dunno. You were all over those two blokes.' She took hold of his hand and bounced it up and down on her leg. 'Trouble is, right. I actually sort of like you like that in such a situation: being aggressive and defending me...it's sort of flattering and exciting...but...and this is dead important, right...but that's because of my upbringing and conditioning. In some part of my retarded brain, real men protect their women with their fists. And that's exactly what the women at TW are working against. In a way, I condoned your behaviour there. I should've stopped you. Do you understand?'

He nodded. 'But, I'm not like that, am I? Not some macho thug?

110

I've never been like that.'

'No. Not usually, but you've got it in your locker, haven't you? You just showed that. Most men wouldn't have taken two blokes on like that. And we both know you would have beaten the shit out of both of them.'

'I can't help but think they deserved it, though. I was defending you and me as well, really. I just felt like they shouldn't get away with this sort of crap. That there had to be consequences.'

'That bloke was being a twat, but it was only words, and I know words are powerful, but you punching someone in the face would be on a whole different level. You would have mashed the snot out of them. I've been reading a lot of about this sort of thing recently, about how to modify your behaviour and not get co-opted into other people's...you know...into their way of thinking and behaving.' She kept on chewing at her cheek as she spoke, fretting.

The players ran out.

'Bloody hell, I never thought I'd get a lecture in sociology while watching the Boro.'

All his life he'd never wanted to be a blokey bloke and always felt he was more sensitive than that, but maybe it was all a lie he'd been telling himself. Maybe he was just as bad as the knuckle-headed thugs. It was just so much easier to default to that concept of being a man. It was a role written for men to play and one which they often got a sort of grudging respect for, sometimes respect from women too. But he hated the thought of that. Intellectually, he wanted to put spirituality above physicality, but when push came to shove, he shoved back and physicality won.

'Sorry Jules.' He squeezed her hand. 'I just feel really defensive when it comes to you. Brings out the caveman in me, I think.'

She smiled at him. 'I know where you're coming from and I know you're basically a really lovely fella. We're all trying to escape our upbringing or conditioning and trying to be better, but sometimes it drags us back in. We've just got to try and learn from stuff like this. We can't go around punching people in the face or knocking them over just because we think they're not very nice or because they've been rude. Mind, I wish the Boro were trying to be better, though. We're bloody awful. Can't retain possession, no creativity. We're making Wigan look good here.'

She was right. Middlesbrough were poor. At half time it was 0 – 0. He went to get them some coffee. On the way back he saw the red-faced man approaching, but ignored him as he walked past. 'Wanker,' the bloke said, as soon as he was out of reach. Nick laughed. Yeah, really brave, mate.

He sat back down and handed Julie the hot, tasteless liquid and told her what had happened.

'Funny thing is, laughing at that, rather than lashing out at him, or even just swearing back, feels much better. Rising above it, like. Christ, I'm sounding like some sort of Buddhist.'

She smiled. 'You're a bloody big puff, you, like.'

The game didn't get any better. As the final whistle went after two minutes of injury time, finishing 0 – 0, Julie took out her camera. 'Come on, let's have our post-match photo.'

She'd been taking a shot of them after each game for a year. It was a nice way to document how much or little they changed week to week. She held it at arm's length as he leaned into her, and took a couple of photos. They sat and let people drift away before making a move.

As they walked towards the exit, a voice called out his name. 'Nick, Julie. Can I have a quick word?' They turned around. It was Davey James. What the hell did he want now? He held his arms out wide to them.

'I just wanted to apologize to you both for earlier. It was all of my making. My careless language. You were right to take me task for it, y'know. It's a bad habit I've got, always thinking of generalized roles as male. I totally understand why you were annoyed and those two blokes' comments were well out of order. Just wanted to say sorry.'

Nick shrugged. 'Fair enough, mate. I'm sorry for kicking off. Powerful things though, words. You've got to be careful which ones you use and when and where. If we don't use them properly we all get misunderstood.'

'True. Very true,' he nodded at him and then at Julie, who had her arms folded across her chest, looking him up and down.

'I'd like to apologize as well. I shouldn't have been so...so aggressive,' she said, her lips pursed together.

'OK. We'll leave it at that, then,' said Nick.

'Mind, you can handle yourself, can't you Nick?' said James, with a quick, sharp grin.

'Eh?'

'You can handle yourself. Fearless, like. '

Nick shrugged.

'Can be a useful quality, that.'

'And a destructive one,' said Julie, but James didn't look at her now. Instead, he handed Nick a card.

'My contact details, just in case you need them. Maybe for a column or whatever. I'm always here to help.'

He nodded in turn to them, turned and walked away.

'Slimy git,' said Julie as they walked on.

'That was weird, wasn't it?'

'I told you. He was checking you out,' she said.

'He was checking you out, more like. I know that look in a bloke's eye.'

'Eh, what look?'

'The, I'd-like-to-get-in-your-knickers-look. Didn't you notice?'

'Not really. I found it hard to look him in the eye, actually, He's quite intimidating.'

'Anyway, I'm not a head-breaker. That's not me at all...I can look after myself if I need to, but I'm a bit of a hippy at heart.'

'You're tough. You are. Tougher than you know. You've got a physical presence to you these days. Back when we lived in Harrogate, you went to seed. You were all podgy and stodgy. Now you're lean and muscular. If you twat someone, they'll stay twatted. That's why that bloke backed off after he'd said about me having your balls in a vice. He was scared you'd really hurt him.'

'But that sort of sounds like a compliment doesn't it? I feel sort of proud when you say that. And that's just that male, macho thing again isn't it?'

She nodded. 'We're both so fucked up, aren't we?'

He put his arm around her shoulder. 'Whoever said life would be easy though, eh? No-one.'

'Not when you're a Boro supporter, anyway. What's that? Nine games, three points and only one goal? We're stinking the place up. We've got the West Ham replay in the cup next and then, God help us, Liverpool. We're toast, man. I wish the Boro had a bit of your fight in them."

'Yeah, callers to the show will be raging again.' He looked at his watch. 'Talking of which, I need to be at Tees Digital in half an hour. Will you pick me up later? Say about nine?'

'Sure.' She unlocked the car, put her hand on his waist and kissed him. 'Have a good show. Don't swear at anyone or get into any fights eh, Mister Muscle.'

'I might say the same to you.'

'I'll put a curry on, like a good housewife, eh.'

'Aye, football, a hot curry and then Saturday night on the nest. The classic macho triple.'

'You forgot the ten pints of lager.'

'I'll leave the heavy drinking to you, Jules.' He gave her hand a squeeze and walked off to the studio.

CHAPTER 7

Malcolm Pallister was just walking out of the radio station as Nick walked in.

'Ah, Nick. Amy is ready and waiting for you. It'll all be fine. She'll keep you on the straight and narrow.'

'OK.'

'Heard any news about Alan's killer yet?'

He shook his head. 'No. I've not heard anything.'

'I'd like to have faith in the police, but it's a bit hard sometimes, when you meet them. Thick as pig shit half of them. I wouldn't like them to have to find out who had killed me, not that I'd care I suppose, as I'd be dead, wouldn't I? Have a good show. I'll be listening on the way home.'

That was a bit off-colour.

'Hi Amy,' he said. She looked up and pushed her fringe off her forehead.

'Ah, hiya. I'm glad you got here early. I wanted to run through the desk with you while the news is on. We'll handle the calls, of course. You just need to check the screen so you know who is coming through next.'

'Yeah, I've seen Alan do it many times. I think it'll be OK.'

She sucked her lower lip in. 'I'm still so shocked about Al. I'm on auto pilot emotionally. I just can't believe he's not alive. I think I'm pretending he's just on holiday. To think he was killed while we were all there. I feel like we should have done something to stop it.'

'I know. It is so horrible. Have the police been here yet?'

She nodded. 'They've taken statements from everyone, me included. They took away some recordings of the last month's shows as well, though I find it hard to believe his killer would have called the show. Or maybe I just don't want to think that.'

She shuddered and pulled her cardigan around her.

The syndicated news reports on the hour kicked in so he walked around the other side of the glass, put on the big padded headphones and sat at the big microphone. A computer screen had a list of callers building up. Mike from Ormsby - sack Southgate; Hunter from Dormanstown - sack Southgate; Brenda from Roseworth - get Mowbray in; Johnny from Fairfield - thinks Gibson is right.

It was surprisingly easy to talk to people about football. All you had to do was let them go on for a minute, question them a couple of times and then cut them off if they went on too long or were simply unable to cohere a sentence, which was more common than it ought to have been.

'Hello. My name's Nick Guymer. You're listening to the Alan Armstrong Football Hour.'

The theme tune music faded out.

'Before we get into tonight's calls, I just want to say a word about my old friend and colleague, Alan. I'm sure you're all aware of this week's events. It's been a shocking time for all of us. We wondered if we should really do a show this week, but I know Al would have wanted the show to go on and for us to talk about the Boro. So here I am, flying solo this week and I'm sure AA is out there somewhere still hoping for a Boro win, which of course we didn't get today. Another goal-less game. Call and tell me what you thinking and what Boro can do to avoid seemingly inevitable relegation.'

Amy put her thumbs up at him as they went to an ad break before the first call.

'Good stuff, Nick. You're a natural. A lot of angry punters on the phone tonight. I'll keep my finger on the swear button.'

'Yeah for me as much as them.' She smiled.

The reaction was predictable enough; football fans were nothing if not predictable. There were a lot of calls for the manager to be sacked, followed by a back lash against that back lash. It was the usual course of events. Nick had often wondered what the people ringing in gained from the process. Didn't they have anyone else to talk to? Was this their only outlet for football talk? Did they think airing it in public would influence the club, or the chairman, or the manager? If so, they were sadly mistaken. The day anyone in football takes notice of someone raging on a phone-in, or on a message board, would be the day they let the lunatics take over the asylum. That's how it'd be viewed, not least because football fans are so fickle, every hero is soon a zero, every zero soon a hero.

'Dave from Wolviston is up next. Dave. You want to talk about the upcoming Liverpool game.'

'Aye...but first can I ask what exactly happened to Alan, do you know Nick?'

'Well, there's a police investigation ongoing...so we can't say much.' He looked through the glass. Amy put her thumbs up.

'You were there when it happened though, is that right?'

'Yeah. Sadly, I was. But like I say, the police investigation is ongoing...'

'Who'd want to kill Alan though? I just don't understand it.'

'No. Me neither. It's a cruel world Mike. We're all really upset here. But nothing we say will make him come back.' Amy was making her throat cutting sign to say he had to go to an ad break. 'We've got to play some adverts Dave...'

'...I'd watch out if I was you, son. You might be next,' the caller said, his tone changing to a more threatening one.

'You reckon?'

'...oh yeah. I reckon it was a case of mistaken identity. I reckon they meant to get you. You'd better watch your back.'

The line went dead. Nick grasped for words, but couldn't find any. Amy hit the adverts button.

'Have you got that last caller's number?' he said. The station called everyone back, so you always had to leave your number.

'Yeah. It's a mobile. Was he being threatening, do you think?' said Amy. 'He didn't sound that threatening to me when we called him up.'

'Yeah. I think he was. I think. I'm not sure. Maybe he wasn't. I'm just a bit paranoid.'

The rest of the show passed without incident. Afterwards he picked up a note of the man from Wolviston's number and then gave Jules a call. She was on her way in.

'Where you listening?' he said, as she drove them back to Yarm.

'Yup. You were smooth. Was it easy to do?'

'Yeah. It was over so quickly. Did you hear that bloke from Wolviston saying I should watch my back?'

'Yeah.'

'Do you think he was threatening me?'

'Threatening? No. He was just trying to be clever. Playing at detective, like.'

'Yeah. Alright. I took his number though.'

When they got home, the house smelled of curry.

'Coming home to a meal is still one of life's simple pleasures,' he said.

'It'll be about half an hour. Just want to get the beef really tender. It was a real old piece of scraggy boot leather,' she said, sitting on the sofa and taking the SD card out of her camera. 'I'll just upload today's photo to the diary file. It's funny that you don't realise how much you change over a month or three or six. Now, when I look at me a year ago, with my hair shorter and more like its natural colour, I look really different, but in my head, I've not really changed.'

'I've often wondered why I don't notice the lines on my face until they're more like scars. It must take years for them to get like that.'

'Aw that's a good one,' she said and turned the lap top screen to him. 'We both look quite human in that.'

'Unlike most photos where I look gormless or alien,' he said, taking a look. 'Oh yeah. For a quick snap that's rather good, Jules.'

'Just lucky. I really should try and learn how to use Photoshop to tidy these up.'

'Give us a look at the other one you took...oh dear, I'm half-blinking on that. Dopey looking sod.' As he spoke he noticed something in the bottom right corner of the photo. Numbers. 4.42.

21*2*09. He pointed at them. 'Is that the time and date?'

She squinted. 'Yup. It happens automatically. That's how I knew the time that the photos in Jeff's shop were taken.'

He stared, breaking into a heart-racing sweat as he did and swallowed.

'Jules man, that time is wrong. The camera's internal clock, or whatever it is, is set wrong.'

She stared dumbly at him. 'Eh?'

'You took that right after the game ended. There were two minutes of added time, so the game ended at 4.52, not 4.42. No game ends at 4.42. It's ten minutes slow. You know what that means, don't you?'

She yelped and put her hand over her mouth.

'The timings for the shop photos were wrong and we've based everything on those timings. Everything. And so have the police, too. That means there are ten minutes missing. Anything could have happened in those ten minutes. Any number of people could have come and gone from the room and killed Alan. Bloody hell.'
She let out moan and looked at him with worried eyes.

Nick looked back through some notes he'd made.

'OK so when we thought it was 5.43, the time of that first photo, it was really 5.33. Your last photo we thought was 5.46, but it was really 5.36. Jeff came out at that time. But we know when you went in the back room and met us it was definitely about 5.52 because you looked at your watch and thought about getting your mam a cab.'

She looked around her, focusing her thoughts and put her hands out, palms down.

'Alan must have gone to the toilet at around 5.28 or so. We found him dead at 5.52. If he was killed after Jeff and Rita had left at 5.36 or 5.37, which he had to have been, where had Alan gone from when he left you? He can't have gone to the toilet as we thought and he wasn't in the room during the photos, so he must have gone outside and then, unnoticed by us, come back in to use the toilet.'

'He might have gone outside to speak to someone. People did hang around outside. There were quite a few there when I came back from the car.'

'But if he was outside, he wasn't at the front or you'd have seen him.'

'Would I? I wonder. I might not have. I've not really thought about it before because we thought everything happened in a different time frame. I was wrapped up in my own thoughts. He could have been there or he could've been round the corner out of view between the shop and Stockton Parish church. Maybe he met his killer round the back, was followed in and killed.'

'What's actually behind the shop?' said Julie.

'I don't know. We should take a look tomorrow...presumably the police have already searched the area.'

As he spoke, Jeff's van pulled up and he soon came in.

'Oh man, that smells like my idea of heaven,' he yelled out as he came in, a shoulder bag of records under his arm. 'Why hasn't someone made a curry perfume called 'bhuna' or 'jalfrazi'? I would splash it all over.'

Nick ran the new timings and ideas past him while Julie served them up the curry and some wild rice, poured Jeff a gin and tonic and put a big wedge of lime in it and took the food into the living room on a tray.

'I just love living here and getting my dinners cooked. It's like being back home with my mam only you're not always pissed out of your brains. You're an angel. Seriously, you really are,' said Jeff, taking it from her eagerly.

She pulled a face. 'The only thing with wings in this house are feminine hygiene-based and I might not need them any more,'

'Eh?' He frowned at her.

'Nowt. Ignore me.'

'Ah, right, well this is all very interesting. I can tell you what is behind the shop. Trees and a bit of overgrown grass. Behind that is the churchyard grass and the path that leads across it. I went and had a look around when I first got the keys. Someone could easily hide there, or stand there and not be seen. Easily. I mean stand there and chat to someone. Nothing sinister.'

'When you came out of the back room, you said that you went around topping up glasses...'

'...yup. Like I said originally, I had thought it was for longer than a couple of minutes. It's hard accurately remembering time passing though, isn't it?'

Nick nodded. 'You recall two like it's five minutes and five seems pretty much the same length as ten when you think back.'

'Could Al have walked past you and gone into the back while you were topping up and chatting? Would you have noticed?' said Julie.

'Yeah of course he could. You were there as well, with your mother. I could ask you the same question. You don't notice every person all the time, do you? My mind was on other things anyway, such as my infidelity, so I was totally distracted. He could have walked behind my back while I was topping up drinks and gone in there and I'd never have seen him. It's not a massive shop, but it's not tiny either, and it was packed.'

'Well that's what must have happened then,' said Julie, putting her feet up on a pouffe, as she rested on the sofa after eating. '5.38 you come out, Al goes in sometime between 5.39 and about 5.49 - probably after being outside - because you go in and find him around 5.51 then go and get Nick and by the time you're both in and I arrive, it's 5.52.'

Jeff shovelled food into his bearded face as she talked. 'Yup. That makes total sense. Better give Col Harcombe a ring and let him know.'

'It still doesn't help identify who might have done it though, does it?' said Nick.

'My money is totally on Jimmy Butcher,' said Jeff. 'Now we know there was time for him to do it – before, we thought he couldn't have had time. But now...it'll be him. He's a known knifer.'

'Why would he look at me funnily though?'

'He thought you were Alan.'

'Harcombe said that. I don't look like Alan though.'

'You don't look massively unlike him. It's not as if you're black and he's white, or he was bald and you're hairy.'

'I'm not having that. If you've been paid to be a killer you'd have a damn good idea who it was you'd be killing, if only because you'd not get your money if you knifed the wrong man,' said Nick.

Jeff put down the cutlery, having finished his food. 'Bloody delicious that, Jules. Thank you so much. I'll cook us a Sunday dinner tomorrow, right?'

'Nice one,' she said, smiling.

He held a finger aloft. 'But think about it. You and him do a radio show. It'd be easy to get you mixed up. Maybe he saw you, thinks, ah ha, there's my man. Waits for his moment, but sees Alan going in the back, thinks it's you and goes in and does it.'

He got his laptop out and went online. 'Let's have a look at the Tees Digital web site. See how like you AA was, hopefully they'll not have updated it to remove him.' He loaded the 'Our Presenters' page and sat, pointing, mouth open.

'What?' said Nick.

'Does he look like Nick on there?' said Julie.

'No. No he doesn't. Not really.' He spun the computer around and pointed to the pictures of Nick and of Alan under the Saturday Football Phone-In page. Nick was more gaunt and lean. Alan more flushed and slightly older looking. They were not alike at all really, apart from similar-ish hair.

'Well, Butcher can't have thought I was him,' said Nick and Julie agreed.

No. No you're not getting it,' said Jeff, jabbing his finger at the screen. 'Look at the names...they've listed your name under him and his name under you. They've got the names the wrong way around! He must have thought Alan was you.'

'Fucking hell!' shouted Nick. The logic of what he was saying all flooded into his brain at once. 'Butcher looked at this, used it as a reference and knifed the wrong man. Shit, shit, shit. He *was* after me.'

They all sat and looked at each other in shock.

'Well...we...we...we...don't know that for sure, do we? We've put one and one together there and assumed we've made two, but it could be 11. We don't know,' said Julie, but the worry in her eyes betrayed her fears.

'Yup. You might be right. But it makes the whole thing work,' said Jeff.

Nick sat back and groaned and put his head in his hands. 'Why does someone want to knife me? I've done nowt.'

Jeff raised his finger, 'Ah. Good question. A pissed-off football fan? Some sort of stalker, maybe?'

'Jeff man, I'm on Tees Digital, not Fox News. About ten thousand people listen at most. And if Butcher was the man that did it, he's a hired killer. That's his gig, by all accounts. No-one hires someone like him to stab a football radio show presenter. They might jump me in a fit of anger, but paying someone to do it is too calculated and rational.'

Julie pick up the phone. 'I'd better call Colin Harcombe and bring him up to date with all this.' She found his card, dialled his mobile number and left a message.

Jeff finished his gin. 'Let's just calm down. We don't know if the killer identified their target from this, do we? We're just speculating. He might have known exactly who he wanted and he just looked at you funny because he's a mad bastard.'

Nick let out a tense breath. 'Yeah. Yeah, that makes sense.'

'For all we know, the killer actually got their man. OK, the police can't find a motivation for that, but that doesn't mean it isn't what happened,' said Jeff.

'Alternatively, it was still mistaken identity,' pitched in Julie, tucking her feet up under her, '...and they thought Alan was someone else, but it was still nothing to do with you at all. There's no evidence it's anything to do with you at all, luv. None. These names being wrong doesn't prove anything. We're getting carried away and paranoid.' She shook her head as though to dismiss the idea.

Her phone rang.

'Colin? Hi.' She went over the issues they'd been discussing. He said he'd come around.

Nick turned to Jeff. 'Are you away to Harrogate tomorrow?'

'Yeah, I'm going to run the Stockton shop until I can get a manager in that I trust and can actually afford to pay. Which isn't yet. I can travel up each morning. It's only an hour.'

'You really don't have to do that. You can stay here for as long as you want,' said Julie, 'or until the shop takes off. You can't do a two or two and half hour commute every day. That's just mad.'

'...and I'd quite like some added muscle around the place until all this knifing business is sorted out,' said Nick. 'I know that sounds mad but...'

'Yeah. No problem. Well thanks, kids. I'll take you up on the offer. I'm happy to fend off knife-wielding crazies for you. Especially when you're making curry that good, Jules. Any more gin?'

'Help yourself, it's on the fridge. I'll have one too. Just a small one.'

'Two gins coming right up. You want anything, Nick?'

'I'd like not to be stabbed in the guts with a big sodding hunting knife.'

'I can arrange that too. You want lime with that?'

Half an hour later they heard a car coming down the narrow country lane to the house. Their ears were now tuned to any engine dropping revs up on the main road.

'That must be Colin,' said Julie getting up and looking out of the window. But it wasn't.

'It's Ricky and Kev,' she said.

'Your brothers?' said Jeff.

'Yeah. What do they want at this time?'

She opened the door. 'Now then youse two. To what do we owe this pleasure?'

'Alright Jules,' said Kev, coming in. They were two big blokes.

Heavy and thick set, fair hair cut short and going grey. They both just wore t-shirts, even though it was cold.

'Now then, Nick,' said Ricky, 'Alright Jeff.'

Kev reached into a bag he was carrying, pulled out a large knife and held it up at him.

'You know what that is?'

Jeff took it off him and looked at it. 'That is a big fuck off knife, that's what that is,' he said.

Kev and Ricky both laughed. 'Aye it is that, like. It's a Bowie knife.'

'...like the one that killed Alan Armstrong?' said Nick

'That'd be my guess, aye.'

'How do you know that?' said Julie

'Because the bloke we got this from was asked for two knives the other week, but he didn't have any in stock,' said Ricky.

'Was it Jimmy Butcher asking?' said Nick. 'He was at the party.'

'Was he? Oh well, case fucking closed son, he's your killer then,' said Kev, firmly. 'He's a fucking nut job is Butch. He was in Durham with me for about a month once. Fucking terrifying bloke, even by Durham jail standards. They sent him for psychiatric tests or summat. I'm sure he's mental. If he was there and someone was stabbed, chances are Butch did it.'

'So where did you get this from?' said Jeff.

'A hunting and field sports shop up in Teesdale. When you said that it was a big knife with a big handle that'd killed him, we said, didn't we Kev, that it'd have been a Bowie bought out in the country. So we made a few calls. Not many places sell these things...'

'...'cos no-one has to gut a fucking wild bear on Teesside,' said Kev with a snort of laughter. 'Not unless they're drinking in the Garrick anyway.'

'...but this blokey up in Reeth sometimes has them.'

'What did the bloke who bought it look like?' said Nick.

'Bloke? It was a woman,' said Ricky.

'A woman?' said Julie. 'What did she look like?'

'All he said was she was a country type. Wore tweed and a headscarf.'

'Old or young?' she said.

'He never said. Just said she was posh,' said Ricky.

'To be honest, right, that fella is a shifty get. He won't look you in the eye,' said Kev.

'That's probably because he was shit scared of you, man,' said Julie with a shake of her head. 'You do look menacing. Look at youse two...big sodding arms bulging out of t-shirts that used to fit before you bloated up on the beer. And in the middle of winter as well. You don't not look like trouble.'

'Hey, that's bit harsh our Jules. Ricky's lost four pounds today, haven't you, Rick?'

'...aye had a massive shit after a curry,' said Ricky and hi-fived his brother. It must have been something they said regularly.

'I hope you haven't broken the law getting hold of this weapon,' admonished Julie. 'I don't want you going around beating people up, right? I've had e-bloody-nough of all that with you two.'

'We never hit him, did we Kev? He was alright. Wilf Anderson in Reeth. That's his name. I just took a borrow of this for a few days. I'll take it back to him soon.'

''Took a borrow,' is not an innocent phrase Ricky. I know what it means. So take a telling off us, right?' said Julie, eyebrows furrowed, jabbing a finger at him.

Her brother looked a bit sheepish and looked at the floor and nodded. 'Alright Jules. Alright.'

Jeff laughed loudly. 'You've got a nice line in euphemism though, Kev.'

'I've got what, like?'

'Where else sells Bowie knives then?' said Nick. 'Anywhere local?'

'Nah. Nowhere round here. Nearest is up Alston way and there's a place down near York - where's that, Rick?'

'Easingwold. That's the only other stockist,' said Ricky, brushing his thumb across the blade. 'Mind, someone might have got it off the internet.'

Nick sat up. 'Easingwold eh? Hear that, Jeff?'

'Aye. Where Matt Little has his house. So what, like?'

'Dunno. Seems an odd coincidence.'

'Matt hasn't killed anyone though, has he? He wouldn't say boo to a goose, much less savage one with a blade like this.' He took it off Ricky and let the weight of it rest in his hand. 'It's a beast, isn't it? Feels powerful.'

'Magic, isn't it?' said Kev. 'I'd have one meself if I was going on a killing spree...or had to go into Dormanstown after dark, like.'

Julie interrupted him. 'You two better get out of here, Colin Harcombe is coming round. Thanks for finding this out for us lads, but take the knife with you...I don't want it here...it's horrible.'

'That's actually why we came over man. Just to make sure you're all tooled up, like,' said Ricky. 'Any muscle, weapons, guns...y'know...just give us a shout, Jules.'

'Aye. Don't mess around, Jules. If Butch comes anywhere near you, call us and we'll be right over to fucking cunt him up, proper like.'

'Hey hey, watch your language. I don't want you c-ing in here. This is our home, not Durham sodding jail. Now get on your way. We'll be fine.' Julie waved them off.

'Funny two, them,' said Jeff after they'd gone. 'They still make me shit me pants. Terrifying. Easily the hardest men I've ever met in my life.' He pulled at his beard. 'I sort of admire it. Menacing is an art form.'

'How they're not both inside, I really don't know. I expect to get a call about them every day,' said Julie.

'Good mates to have in a fight, though,' said Nick. 'Totally fearless. They are, aren't they, Jules?'

'Well, they certainly don't seem to care what happens to themselves, which is a good starting point if you're going to be a lunatic who likes to fight.'

They'd only just gone when Harcombe called Julie again and

said he'd be at their house in ten minutes.

As soon as he arrived, they went over everything, including the details of the Reeth shop which had sold the knife, as well as the revised timings.

Harcombe sat back, making quick notes, his dark, sharply defined eyebrows flicking up and then down with each detail. He tapped at his notepad with a pen.

'I couldn't work out when Butcher had done this because he was in the photos and there didn't seem to be a time window for him. But these revised timings give him a good chance to do it after you'd taken photos, Julie, and after you had vacated the stock room, Jeff. I feel sure that's when it was done. Whether Alan was the intended victim or not remains to be seen. We'll pull him in and see what he says. It will be a pleasure to get a violent psycho like Butcher behind bars again. I regret the day a man like him is ever allowed back on the streets. He's a real bad one. I'm sure he's committed crimes like this before, but getting evidence on him has been difficult. We've interviewed him half a dozen times over the years. Last time he went down for GBH, but we felt he was up to his neck in another murder. From the first minute I knew he was there, I thought the odds were on him being involved. Good work all. Thank your brothers for me, Julie. Very good. We shall make good citizens of those lads yet. I wish all members of the public were as helpful - though you,' he pointed at Jeff, 'you deserve a dressing down for lying to my men, initially. Shocking stuff, Jeff. Do not hide anything from us again, right? This isn't a game. It's not about you and your shenanigans with women. It's about a dead man. That is far more important.'

Jeff nodded. 'Sorry Colin. It won't happen again.'

'I should think not. Bad business. You're lucky I'm too busy to take further action.'

The policeman was like a stern parent or a teacher who was firm but fair. Authority is a strange thing. Some people don't have it, no matter how they speak or what they say, others seem to exude it naturally. Colin Harcombe was very much in the latter camp.

He got up to leave, but stopped and turned around. Nick stood opposite him.

'Be warned, though. Butcher may well be our killer, but he was paid to do this. That much is almost certain. So our next task is to find out who paid him and why. I don't expect he will be forthcoming with that information. Scum like him never is. If you'd like to apply your three not inconsiderable minds to that problem and find me a solution, I would be most grateful.'

He smiled as though this was a rather good joke.

'Do you have any leads on that at all?' said Nick.

'Not so much leads, as lines of thought.'

'Do you still think it could be mistaken identity? And that they were, for some reason, trying to kill me or someone else?'

'Hmm. Personally, despite my previous ideas, I think this mis-labelling of names on the web site is an unhappy coincidence. If I learn anything to the contrary I'll let you know. Don't worry, Nick.'

After he'd gone, Nick felt a weight lift from him with the policeman's reassurance.

He woke the next morning to the sounds of Julie throwing up again. This time she'd made it to the bathroom. After ten minutes, she returned and flopped back into bed.

'Are you OK?'

She panted a little, looking sweaty. 'Not really.'

'Aw, you poor thing. I'll make you some tea.'

He got up.

'Nick?'

'Yeah?'

'I know this sounds mad, but I've got a feeling it's happened.'

'What?'

She coughed a little. 'I think I might be pregnant. I've just got a feeling. Hormones or something.'

He stood and looked at her feeling a rising sense of panic and yet joy.

'Wow. Should we get some sort of test done? I mean, you might just have a stomach bug or something.'

'Don't laugh, but my nipples feel funny. Tingling, like. They feel weird and I feel odd. Not normal. That's one of the signs I've read about.'

'I tend to have that effect of women.'

'Stop making a joke of it man, this is serious. I'm scared. I didn't think it'd happen did I? I'm an old bag. There might be something wrong with the poor bairn. It's much more likely at my age.'

'Woah man, let's not get ahead of ourselves.' He sat down on the edge of the bed and pushed her blonde hair off her forehead. She was clammy. 'Let's give it a couple of days, see how you feel. Then get one of those pregnancy testing kits.'

'I've already got one, man. It's in the bathroom cabinet. Didn't you notice it?'

'I don't know what's in there. I never look. You could keep a diesel-powered, kick-start vibrator in there and I'd not know.'

'I do. But if I'm up the duff I can't be more than three of four weeks gone. I'll wait before I do the test. I don't know if I'm ready to know yet, either way. I need to let it sink in a bit.'

He nodded. 'A bit of colour is coming back to your cheeks.'

'Aye, I feel a bit better now. Bloody hell, what a week this has been, eh?'

CHAPTER 8

The news came mid-morning that Butcher had been arrested at someone's house on the Roseworth estate. Harcombe did a brief media interview saying he had been arrested as part of the investigation into the murder of Alan Armstrong. Julie received a text from him a little later. 'We have our man. Thanks for your help again.'

Nick and Julie had bought a big new stand-alone bath to replace the old plastic thing they'd inherited in the farm house. It could fit both of them easily, so they often took long soaks together. As Jeff prepared Sunday dinner it seemed like as good a time as any to relax and let the tension go that had built up in both of them.

Julie stripped off and sat on the edge of the bath with a hand mirror plucking out errant eyebrows hairs. She stood up and pointed at her belly.

'Funny isn't it? Thinking what might be growing in there?'

He looked at her flat, white tummy and rubbed his hand over it.

'Weird to think there's an animal in there...'

'...hopefully a human animal. It's amazing though, isn't it? That white stuff comes out of you and swims up me and burrows into an egg.'

'It's both totally commonplace and totally incredible. Of all the vast billions of sperm I've produced over the years...

'...rivers of the stuff since you where what, 14?'

'Aye. 13 and three quarters actually. I remember vividly when it first happened and thinking, bloody hell, what is this stuff? Within a week I had such bad blisters I couldn't touch the thing.'

She laughed. 'Hadn't anyone told you about it?'

'Only in biology class, but that doesn't prepare you for it. Now over 34 years later, finally, one of them gets to do what it was designed to do.'

He knelt down and put his ear to her abdomen. 'It sounds noisy. Gloopy.'

'That's just my usual wind, man. I'm such a lady, aren't I?' She pulled a face at him.

'I really dislike the word lady. It's like when they call women footballers, ladies teams. We don't call male footballers gentlemen do we? So where did this ladies thing come from? There's a moral dimension to the word ladies that seems oppressive to me,' he said.

'Is this you doing your feminist bit again, Guymer?'

'I suppose so. It's not right though, is it? Ladies. Urgh.'

'Nope. It's the thin end of a massive wedge, but I wish that's all women had to worry about.'

'Aye. True,' he said, getting undressed.

'Give us a look at you,' she said.

'Why?'

'Because I haven't seen you naked in bright light for ages and I like to inspect you from time to time. Your body is really changing, y'know.' She stroked his protruding abdominal muscles. 'Eeee, you're all muscle and no fat you, eh.' She squeezed his arms. 'You've got quite big and muscular without me really even realising.'

'It's doing the weights. I'm lifting 40 kilos now. More than Jeff, but I didn't like to say. Hate the macho showing off thing about stuff like that.'

She stroked the muscles on his shoulder and the top of his arms.

'You can tell...it's all put muscle on your shoulders and pecs. You look like a boxer, lad.' She picked at the skin above his hips. 'And you've not even got a little bit of a love handle left. You're not doing this body-building to impress me, are you?'

'It's not body-building as such, is it? It's just resistance training.'

'Whatever. If you are, you don't need to. I loved you when you were a chubbster, remember?'

'Yeah, but I didn't. To be honest, I'm doing it for myself, to feel like I'm not going to seed and becoming a middle-aged slob. And the exercise endorphins are probably good for my head.'

She nodded, stood up, hugged him tightly and held on to him, running her hands up and down his back and shoulders.

'Well you do look good, mister. Not bad for an old bloke.'

'What's this about?' he said nuzzling into her neck.

'We don't hug enough do we, daddy?'

'Daddy. Gawd. No, we don't. We have it off, but we don't just hug. Funny that, really. But it is nice. Especially naked.'

'Don't get horny, though. I just want a hug.'

He knew what she meant, but that wasn't really possible.

She put a hand between his legs. 'I told you not to get horny didn't I?'

He laughed. 'Jules, we're naked and you're pressed up against me. Feeling a bit horny is just a natural response for me, but it's not like we have to do anything. The hard-on does not always needs servicing. There's too much worship of the almighty cock if you ask me, all the way through society up to and including that Gherkin building.'

'More bloody feminism. Have you been reading my Gloria Steinem books?' She kissed him on the lips, gave a quick, playful tug on his erection and got into the bath. 'Well, I'm sure it looks very healthy and…err...very...what's the posh word for it...?'

'Priapic?'

'Aye, that's it...very priapic, but I'm just not in the mood, so you'll have to use all that blood in some other part of you instead. Sod it, look at that, I've got a big nipple hair and it's a black nipple hair. Where did that come from and why is it black? How did that happen? All my other pubic hair is light brown, so why have I got a thick curly black nipple hair? She looked down at her breasts and her pink nipples. 'It doesn't even match.' A black hair protruded from the edge of the areola. 'Pass us the tweezers...there, oww, that hurt, but in a nice way. No you can't rub it better. Ha ha.'

'Chapel hat peg alert,' said Nick, pointing at the stiffening nipple and laughing. 'Plenty for the little 'un to suckle on there, Jules. Our kid won't go hungry.'

'Do bigger breasts actually fill up with more milk?'

He shrugged. 'I have no idea. I don't think they actually fill up, do they? It's not like they're two empty bags, are they?'

'I have no idea either. My body is a mystery to me at times. I don't even know what these really are, even though they've been hanging off me since I was 14 or 15.' She shook her breasts. 'I wonder if anyone ever has actually been able to hang a coat on their nipples in the chapel hat peg-style?' She hoisted them up and pushed them at him. 'Can you imagine? It'd be impossible. They'd have to be very big, rock hard nips to hang a coat off them.'

'It's a figure of speech, isn't it? It's the same thing about hanging coffee cups off your cock. No-one can really do that.'

She laughed loudly and splashed around a bit as he got in the opposite side, so that they were side by side and face to face.

'What about trying these?' She emptied the dregs from the white china mugs they'd been using.

'You're not serious?'

'We need to put the theory to the test. On your knees mister.'

He knelt in front of her. 'Now what?'

'Get yourself hard again then.'

'Julie, man. This is actually embarrassing.'

She grabbed him, laughing as she did it.

'I can't help feel my priapic response is being abused here somehow. I am not a piece of meat for your entertainment.'

'Of course you are.' She got hold of a mug. 'Think of it as just another weight-lifting routine. Now, that's one mug over...oh yes...can it stand the weight? Yes, it's on. Ha ha...hold on, ha ha, steel yourself, here's the second...nearly...ooh there's a bit of drooping...yes...it's on. What a hero!'

He stood, arms aloft, in the manner of a footballer who had scored a goal.

'This is a talent I did not know I possessed. Sadly, it isn't a skill I can monetise,' he said, carefully unhooking them and sitting back down.

Julie was weeping with laughter. 'Oh dear me...ha ha... that was so funny...you looked ridiculous and so proud too. Way to stay rigid, lad.' She hi-fived him.

'All it takes is a lovely naked woman, a bit of friction and good blood pressure.'

She wiped tears from her eyes. 'That is one of the funniest things I've seen in ages. I should take a photo and put it on my Facebook page. I might get some work for you. Oh god.'

They topped up the hot water and settled in for a soak.

'I'm going to do a full week at TW this week,' she said, eyes closed.

'OK. Are you up to speed with your MA work?'

'Yeah. I'm well on top of that.'

'Think you'll pass?'

"Yeah. I'll get a pass with merit, I reckon. A distinction is probably pushing it a bit.'

'Cool. Julie Wells BA Hons, MA. Classy. Should you be a Master of Arts though? Shouldn't it be a Mistress Of Arts, or a Madam of Arts?'

'God yeah. I never thought of that. I want to be a Madam not a Master.'

'Your mam always says you were a proper little madam.'

'Takes one to know one. The old rat bag.'

'So what next? After the MA?'

'Get a job, I suppose.'

'What do you fancy doing?'

'I think I'd like to do more work in the TW organisation or maybe in Women's Aid. I'd have to do training though. And the pay is rubbish.'

'It's taking the piss, that.'

'Would you mind? We'd have no money.'

'We've got sod all as it is and of course I wouldn't. I'd be proud of you and I reckon you'd be great at it. Seems to me in that sort of work you need a mixture of hard-faced pragmatism and limitless compassion. That's totally your gig, Jules, even if you do lose your rag, give strangers a dead leg and have terrible wind.'

'Thanks, luv. I just feel like I want to do something really useful.

I mean, the scale of domestic violence in this country is frightening. Some Women's Aid stats estimate over a million women suffered it last year, and that one in four women will suffer it in their lifetime. A couple of women are killed by a current or ex-partner every bloody week. It's like it's an invisible plague attacking half the population, man.'

He lay back and closed his eyes. 'It's like society pretends it doesn't happen somehow, but when you think about it, most women you meet have had some experience of it one way or another...I mean, you have, haven't you?'

'Yeah. I've had two blokes hit me. Another bloke nearly kicked in my door because he thought I was with another bloke. I've had a men go weird on me during sex and get aggressive. I've been stalked by an ex-boyfriend. And it's not like I'm unusual. In fact, if anything, I've had it easy compared to a lot of women. And then there's all the unwanted male attention, groping of tits, pinching your backside, being whistled at and all of that, which I've always just thought of as part of every day life, but shouldn't have to put up with.'

'I once groped a lass called Mandy at a party when I was 16, uninvited like. She just pushed me off. After that I felt so embarrassed at myself that I never did it again.'

'You probably grew up thinking you had the right to do that.'

'I did. I blame Benny Hill. Seriously, I do.'

'At least you didn't carry that into adulthood, though. You actually learned it was wrong.'

'The look on her face told me it was wrong. I can still see it now.' He shuddered.

She stroked his leg with her foot. 'Well, let's not dwell on it all. If I can get a job helping women who are having a bad time, I will. Still got to get my degree, though. Hey, it's nice of Jeff to make us dinner,' she said, taking a bar of soap and washing herself.

'Aye. I think he's going to dump Janice on the phone tonight so he can go out with Rita Walker with a clear conscience.'

'Funny that...he's gone so long without any relationship and now he's got two on the go. He should do that, though. It's just dishonest otherwise.'

'Yeah, I think he feels bad about it.'

'So he should.'

'Yeah, but men are weak when it comes to sex, Jules, you know that, especially someone like Jeff who frankly, has been celibate for about 20 years to my knowledge. He just wants to fill his boots at every opportunity.'

'I know...and women can be like that too. She seemed nice. And she'd been messed about by her ex-husband. I hope she doesn't take rejection badly.'

'Yeah. Relationships, huh? But he cooks a good roast though, so we should be in for a decent feed. That rib of beef he got looked awesome.'

'I bloody love rib of beef, me. I'm starving as well. My belly is touching my spine.'

'Well you're eating for two now, mam.'

'Don't say that. Not yet.'

'Sorry.'

'And don't tell anyone, either. Not even Jeff.'

'Of course not.'

But it was in his mind all day. How could it not be? The thought of becoming a parent was frightening, that was the first emotion, followed swiftly by joy. The responsibility of it was overwhelming. First, a little baby to nurture and then a small child, then a bigger child, a teenager and an adult and you'd never stop caring about them, or loving them, or being concerned for them. It would be a life-altering thing way, way beyond anything he had ever experienced and something unique that he and Julie had created between them. Other people, most people, went through this a lot earlier in life, in their 20s or 30s, but he was nearly 50. How would he cope? How would Jules cope? They were older people and this was a revolution about to happen. Would it keep them close or would it drive them apart?

It seemed that it had to be the ultimate in intimate experiences to create a human life together and yet you met people all the time who had done this, once or twice, or more with someone, and then got divorced or split up, subsequently disliking, or even hating each other afterwards. So it clearly wasn't as profound a thing for many people as it might appear from the outside. Having children together appeared, for some, to be no more binding than if you'd bought a sofa together. But he loved Julie with every ounce of his soul. He was as sure about that as about anything and he cared much more about her than he did about himself. If he was going to be a father, he'd be the best father he damn well could be.

It was a great dinner; lots of roast meat and thick gravy.

'That was superb, thanks mate,' said Nick, cleaning his plate of the last of the beef and licking the gravy.

'No problemo. Thanks for youse two giving me bed and board while I get this shop going - murders not withstanding. Talking of which, I wonder if Jimmy Butcher has 'fessed up as to who paid him to do the knifing.'

'I doubt he'll do that,' said Julie. 'It's part of the life to keep schtum. Ricky and Kev are just the same. Funny really because our Terry is the opposite. Never could keep a secret about anything. Not even to keep himself out of jail. But the other two would never grass anyone up to the police as a matter of principle, not even if they'd been crossed, not for any reason at all. They just won't ever say anything to the authorities. It's mad but it's how it's always been. Butcher will go down in silence.'

'Plus he might get the old knife-ola in jail if he did confess,' said Jeff. 'Courtesy of someone paid by the same party.'

Nick cleared away the plates. 'But I still don't see why Alan was targeted.'

'They'll find something. My money is still on him having some sort of severe drug habit. You can never tell. Blokes can live two lives concurrently, as I've found out a bit myself. You don't have to let one side touch the other. Not much anyway. It's like these men who have two wives and two families on the go for years, just a few miles from each other and no-one finds out. Talking of double lives, I'd better give Janice a call. Not looking forward to this at all. I'll do it out in the garden under the darkening late winter skies of Teesside.'

Nick patted him on the back. 'Good luck, big man.'

He and Julie loaded up the dishwasher.

'How are you feeling?' he said.

'Fine now. Just normal now.' She made an excited 'argh' face at him and laughed. 'Not sure I can actually wait any longer to do the test, though. It's all I can think about now: am I, or am I not, up the duff.'

'I thought you said you weren't ready to know yet.'

'I know. I'm not, really. But if I am then we might as well know, mightn't we?'

'There's no reason not to know, if you feel you want to do the test.'

'Shall I go and do it?' She bit her bottom lip nervously and scrunched up eyes, emphasising the crows feet in the corners.

'I really, really, really want to know.'

She let out a quick breath. 'Right. I need a wee anyway. Here goes. I am *bricking* myself. It's even worse than the last minute of the League Cup final against Bolton, when I was sure we'd let in an equalizer.'

He hadn't ever been so nervous about anything, as he listened to her walk upstairs. His hands were sweating and butterflies were in his stomach. How long did it take? He heard the door close and then, 30 seconds later, the cistern flushed. She'd done it. His mouth was dry now as he rubbed his head with his hand. She was in there waiting, waiting, waiting. Oh Jesus. He climbed the stairs slowly, one at a time, stopping on each step to pause, then stood outside the bathroom door. 'Jules. Any news?'

He heard her walk to the door. It opened. She stood, her turquoise blue eyes wide, gazing back at him. Her mouth open.

'Well?'

'It's positive.'

'It's not.'

'It bloody is. I am well and truly up the stick.'

She held up the device. A blue strip confirming it showed in the window.

'Bloody hell, shit and fuck.' He went all tingly and light headed. 'You were right.'

She put her arms around him. 'I told you, my nipples don't lie. We did it! We bloody did it!'

They began laughing and jumped up and down, hugging each other. It was unbelievable. Just a two percent chance, but they had beaten the odds.

'Well, what do we do now?' he said, feeling a bit tearful.

'I suppose we wait for nine months and then I ruin my vagina by heaving a small animal out of it. I'll have to go to the doctor and get it all confirmed and that. It's still really early though...and y'know...'

'Yeah, I know...it's harder to carry it to term at your age.'

'Exactly, so we won't tell anyone yet. OK? Not for another month or so. Just in case like...I'll make sure I don't do any trampolining or any more drinking. Oh god, that's a bit of a lifestyle change.'

'Ha ha, yeah you'll have to give those up along with the cage fighting and caber tossing.'

They stood for a moment just grinning at each other. In that moment he was filled with a degree of happiness that was quite alien to him.

Jeff came in as they went downstairs.

'What was all that noise about?' he said. ' I hope you were not engaged in perverse sexual practices while I was out of the house.'

'Ha ha...nothing big man. We were just messing around. How was the phone call?'

'Alright. It was a bit of "It's not you, it's me". Not the most fun to do, but this is what I get for being a glamour model of great allure.'

That evening Nick and Julie went out for a meal to celebrate. The Lamb House was a new restaurant in Hartburn Village dedicated to serving lamb and nothing but lamb. It was a casual place with old church pews being used as seating in little wooden booths, making it appear that the customers were in a church to worship the meat. That was a religion Nick could understand. A bright-eyed and bushy-tailed middle-class girl came up to give them menus, full of youthful energy, with restlessly moving legs and a happy smile.

'The special today is a long-cooked lamb stew. It's like totally delish,' she said with more joy than was normal in a British restaurant.

'Nice to see someone who is cheerful,' said Julie.

'Being happy to serve someone is not a natural instinct for the British.'

'I never understood that. There's a snootiness about people who work in shops and restaurants here in a way there never is in America. Like as though it's not worthwhile.'

'All labour should be valued, whatever you do,' he said.

'Amen, brother. Come the revolution we shall free the working class from their shackles.'

'Aye, well, we'll have to sober most of them up first.'

He looked down the menu. It was relief to see there were just three starters, three mains and four desserts. Big menus with dozens of dishes always seemed like the restaurant didn't believe in their own food and were trying to offer something for everyone, instead of just doing two or three things so well that almost everyone would love them.

'I think I'll go for the special - the slow-cooked stew,' said Julie.

'Yeah, I fancy that. Funny, isn't it? It's exactly the sort of food we were raised on; stewed meat and vegetables and yet now it's sold in nice places like this as wholesome, rustic food.'

She nodded. 'Sometimes, it feels like we've gone through the looking glass about food. In the 70s we all wanted shop-bought stuff.'

'I was addicted to Vesta Chow Mein.'

'Oh god, aye. I loved Goblin meat puddings. Remember them? You boiled them in a tin. Boiled in a tin! Fantastic. But now we don't eat any processed food and have reverted to our mam's cooking of the 1960s, frying everything in lard and butter.'

They ordered a charcuterie meat, cheese and pickle plate to share for a starter.

'Are you supposed to avoid soft cheese now - as a preggers wifey?' said Nick, pointing at a circle of cream cheese.

'Yeah, I think so. I'd better swot up on it all. I had liver the other day and I think I'm supposed to avoid that as well.'

'Are you scared?'

She shook her head from side to side. 'Not of liver, no. Ha. No, I'm intimidated, but not scared. It's natural isn't it? Just pushing the thing out is the only bit that seems gross, really. But I've got nine months to get used to it, hopefully.'

'When do we tell people then?'

'Let's wait until I'm three months gone...that's...y'know...the most dangerous period as far as I can gather. I really don't want to have to tell everyone I'm preggo and then have to tell them, oops actually I'm not. I don't want people's sympathy and cooing if that happens. Urgh no.'

He nodded. She was always so sensible, even about something like this. His head was in the clouds half the time, while her feet were on the ground. Maybe that's why they were such a good mix.

Half way through eating the excellent stew, a large man backed into the restaurant, pushing the door open with his backside. He was talking to two teenagers, a boy and a girl. They walked past their booth and took one across and down from them.

Nick leaned forward and quietly said, 'Davey James has just come in, and with his two kids by the look of it.'

Sitting on a bench facing him, he could see just how similar they were to their father. Toni was dressed all in black, in a Gothic-style. Her hair long with dark eye shadow. She was tall and broad. Her smaller younger brother, also dark-haired, looked sulky and petulant with a big, soft, red bottom lip. He was dressed in a hoodie with, inevitably, the hood pulled up. His father leaned forward and pulled it back, but the kid responded by pulling it up again immediately.

'They don't look like they're playing at happy families,' said Nick. 'If looks could kill, there'd be blood on the table.'

'No-one is happy when they have to eat out with their parents, especially at that age.'

'Christ, that is true. A trip to the Berni Inn with my mam and dad for an over-cooked steak and chips was emotionally scarring. I just wanted it to be over before it even started.'

'It was always supposed to be a treat but my mam always got drunk and made a show of us, usually by making advances at the waiter.' She shuddered.

'The girl, Toni, she's a big lass. Not fat, I mean she's strapping. Tall like her dad, with swimmer's shoulders. She does look like a stoner though. I'd have guessed that even if Hair Bear hadn't said. She's got that demeanour. Davey James is very charismatic-looking though, isn't he? I was thinking that when I saw him on telly.'

'Well he's confident, isn't he? Confidence makes people attractive. That and power. And money. I maintain he's a slimy twat though.'

'I don't know where you get confidence from. If I try to be confident, I quickly end up being arrogant and arrogance is worse than being unconfident, I reckon.'

'You say that...but...when you're healthy, in the head like, you're very confident and sure of yourself. It's just that the times you're not, you feel *so* unconfident that it dominates how you define yourself. Hey, that was a good bit of cod psychology wasn't it?' She grinned.

'Lamb psychology, surely, not cod,' he said pointing to their meal.

'Ho ho. Shall I start slagging James off again? Take him to task for his sexist language.'

'I'm sure the kids would be delighted if you made a show of him in public. Man, they're really sullen and are giving their dad some proper stick. There's a lot of pointing and jabbing of fingers and that suppressed, but very angry whispering going on.'

'Oh dear. Rowing with parents in public. Never a good thing. Trying to keep your voice down while losing your rag is an impossible combo.'

As she spoke, there was a crashing noise as Davey James' daughter banged the table, sending cutlery and a plate onto the floor, where it shattered. Staff scurried over and began clearing up as the father apologized and the kids scowled at him, as though the embarrassment was all his fault.

Nick gave Julie a running commentary. 'The girl looks like she's going to hit the old man. She's spoiling for a fight. The lad is now trying to calm her down. He's got her arm and is patting it...she needs to smoke some of Hair Bear's strong stuff to calm her down.'

'Maybe she's already on it. I was reading an article in the Guardian about how skunk makes some people psychotic. Really messes with their brains.'

'Yeah, it's dead powerful stuff. I had some at Jeff's a few years ago and I was just zoned out for 48 hours. Even the morning after I just sat there, staring, feeling no pain. It wasn't good. It was as though I'd had some sort of general anaesthetic. It stopped me feeling anything. I suppose sometimes that's quite a useful thing.'

'It just makes me feel dizzy and then sleepy. Don't see the point in that. Booze has always been my drug of choice.'

'Yeah, me too. I've had a go of everything else, but I only wanted to stay with drink long term. The first love is the deepest, maybe.'

'Babycham was my first booze. I genuinely hated wine until I was about 30. It tasted rancid to me, then somehow I got into it.'

'Our generation, from our backgrounds, just never even saw a bottle of wine, let alone tasted it. It always seemed really expensive to me. You got a lot more lager for the same money and more is always better when you're skint.'

'I bloody loved lager, me. Remember having my first bottle of Sol in the late 80s with a lime wedge in it. I thought I was the coolest chick on earth. Just tastes like slightly sweet, fizzy water to me now. Funny how your palette changes.'

Nick finished his meal and cast another glance over at him right at the same time Davey James was looking around. He nodded at him.

'We've been spotted,' he said. 'Well, that was superb. We'll come here again, eh. Lovely juicy lamb.'

'Mmm plenty of it as well, as I'm eating for two...well...one and a tiny bit anyway.'

He grinned and shook his head.

'I still can't believe it, you know. It is genuinely amazing. The odds were so against it. Maybe your eggs are super fertile. Hadn't you ever had a scare before? Missed a period or anything?'

She shook her head firmly. 'I was always really careful. I mean, I was on the pill from the age of 16 until just before I met you in my late 30s when I got tired of how it was knackering my hormones. Never forgot to take it, not once. In fact, I was paranoid about it.'

'When I was 19, a girl I was going out with skipped a period and we thought it was the big P, but it was just a false alarm. She'd probably counted the days wrong. I remember thinking, if she's pregnant this is going to ruin my life, but I'll just have to support her if she wants to keep it. Stupid really, because it wouldn't have ruined my life at all. I can see that now. It'd have just changed it.'

'Yeah. I was the same. I was terrified it would keep me in Hardwick with mam. But it probably wouldn't have. I'd have moved out and got on with life, one way or another, even with a small army of sprogs in tow. Nowt would have stopped me.'

'If that lass had had a kid. It'd have been 30 this year. 30!'

'And they'd only have been a kid for a few short years. We don't think that, do we? It seems like they'll be little forever, but in ten years they're small people and in 20 they're fully grown adults.' She smiled a big smile at him.

'What?' he said, smiling back.

'I just realised how excited I am about it, y'know, bringing a new life into the world: a new Teessider, a new Boro fan!' She grabbed his hand and squeezed it tightly, raising her eyebrows excitedly. 'We might have to have a few more kids before we've enough to fill all the empty seats at the Riverside, mind.'

As she spoke, out of the corner of his right eye, Nick saw Davey James getting up and taking a few paces over to their table. He was so big that as soon as he was alongside, it was like someone walking in front of the sun. The shadow he cast was huge. His deep, resonant voice had every vowel invested with a strong taste of Teesside.

'Hello Nick, hello Julie. I hope you don't mind me coming over. Just a quick word, if I may.'

Nick shifted along the bench and gestured to the space alongside him. 'Sit down, Davey.'

As he did so, his kids got up and stormed past him without so much as a glance in his direction. He watched them go and raised his eyebrows, but made no comment.

'Great food here, isn't it?' he said looking from him to her.

'It's our first time, but it's really nice so we'll come again,' said Julie, dabbing at her lips with a serviette. 'Are they your kids?' she said, gesturing in the direction they'd left.

'Yes. I'm afraid they are not in the best of moods. The amount of money I pay for their education you'd think they'd instil some better manners into them. If I had spoken to my dad the way they speak to me, I'd soon have been black and blue.'

'Yeah, but that's progress, isn't it?' said Julie. 'Not beating children up, like. It's a good thing.'

Davey James gave an amused snort. 'Yeah, well, you'd think so. Sometimes I wonder with those two. I just came over because I wanted to apologize again for the trouble at the Wigan game and to make it right with you guys.'

'Well, I'm sorry too. I could have made my point less confrontationally and I didn't have to give that bloke a dead leg

146

either,' said Julie.

'And I probably didn't have to threaten to beat the crap out of those two...though frankly, they were being obnoxious,' said Nick.

Davey James wheezed a little laugh. 'Well, that is true too. But since then I've looked into your work, Nick, and I'm really impressed; your books, your pieces, that TV documentary you worked on, it's a good body of work and I need people of that quality in my organisation. Would you consider working for me doing copyrighting, writing some speeches and working on URO media stuff? I can put you on my payroll. I'm sure it'd be something you'd be good at.'

Nick was surprised. He always needed more paying gigs. Things had been so tight recently.

'Thanks for the offer. I tend to work freelance though. I like the independence.'

'I thought you might say that. You seem to have worked for yourself since the 80s.'

Nick took a sip of coffee. It was always uncomfortable when someone had been researching you. It never felt like a good thing.

'Yeah. Well, I'm an ornery bugger, aren't I?'

'No-one is good enough to be his boss,' said Julie, pointing at him. 'That's how you've always felt, isn't it?'

'Listen, I understand. This region needs good, bright minds and not more corporate drones who toe whichever party line it is. That's certainly what URO needs. I don't employ people who are just going to say what I want to hear. Freelance is fine by me. If you give me an email address, I shall be in touch with more details.' He held out a bear-sized paw to Nick. 'Good. Which brings me to you, Julie Wells.' He turned and smiled at her with his sparkling eyes. 'You were a rising legal PA star as I hear it?'

'Rising? Drowning, more like. It wasn't me really, though I did it for ten years, nearly. I quit a couple of years back to do my MA in history. Never regretted it and I won't be going back into that sort of work.'

'That was a brave move.'

'You've gotta do what you've gotta do. Like I say, I don't regret it for a minute. Education is often wasted on the young. Lifelong learning should be everyone's aim.'

'Well said. Yes, I agree. We've overlooked that for far too long. The working man has for too long thought that his education was done at 16.'

Julie held up a finger and cocked an arched eyebrow at him. 'The working man and the working woman, Davey. You forgot women. Again. Tut tut.'

He put his hand over his mouth and feigned shock.

'Me and my sexist mouth. I'm so sorry. Well, that's what I wanted to speak to you about. The URO is a growing organisation. We employ 115 people and within 18 to 24 months that will be 300. I have a position in mind for you as a diversity officer for us.'

'A diversity officer? Me? Why me?' She was genuinely surprised, her arched eyebrows raised.

'The way you spoke in public, in front of a largely hostile group of men, that is a rare quality. It showed firmness of mind, principle, a strong moral compass and an ability to articulate yourself under pressure. All essential. You obviously care and you can't fake that.' He took hold of her hand. 'I think you're exceptional, Julie,' he said, patted the hand, let go and sat back. '£40k a year. That's what I'd pay you. Do consider it. You'll have your degree at Durham by the summer and will need work, I'm sure.'

Nick's bullshit alarm was going off in his head. This was part of some ploy. James got up, saluted them both. 'Nice to meet you again, in less confrontational circumstances. Think about what I've said. I shall be in touch.' He paid his bill and left to find his children..

Once he was out of the door, Julie stuck her finger down her throat, mimed being sick and wiped the hand he'd held on a serviette as though to cleanse it.

'Bloody hell, that was nauseating.' She looked at the bill. '35 quid. I'll leave 40. The lass serving us was nice. Hopefully she'll get to keep the tip.'

'I hate tips all going into one big pool of money. Never seems fair,' said Nick, putting his leather jacket on. As he pushed the door open and went outside, he was immediately aware of raised voices. Toni James was shouting at her father, 15 yards away in Hartburn Village, as her brother stood and looked on.

'More trouble in paradise?' said Julie, coming up behind him and looking at the scene.

'She's not happy about something.'

Suddenly, she screamed a high volume, piercing yelp and lunged at her father, grabbing him around the neck with her right hand while clawing at his face with her left, her face a mask of wild fury.

Nick sprinted over to them. 'Hey, hey...that's enough...' He pulled her hand off his throat and pushed her away a little. She didn't even look in his direction though, instead she spat a large dollop of foamy sputum in her father's face and marched off in the opposite direction with her brother running to catch her up.

Davey James looked a bit shaken and had a scratch on his cheek from Toni's nails, his neck red from where she'd grabbed it.

'Thanks Nick...a tad embarrassing. She's...she's a wild one, that girl.' He looked shaken and shocked by her aggression and wiped the spit from his cheek with a tissue.

'No worries.' It was awkward. He didn't know what to say, so he just nodded and went back to Julie, took her hand and led them in the opposite direction back to the car.

She drove them home in the Peugeot. 'Firstly,' she said, 'I don't like anyone holding my hand like that. Not a stranger. It's an invasion of your personal space and anyone with an ounce of sensitivity would know that. Secondly, I never said I was at Durham, or when my degree would be concluded. Thirdly, he knew about my old job. That means he's looked into me. He's done research. Fourth, he has no idea at all if I'd be any good as a diversity officer. I've no qualifications for that job, so he's just offering it to me because he wants to flatter me. And lastly, he just totally sets my rapey alarm off. He's so creepy. Charismatic, yes, but just fundamentally untrustworthy. I mean, I've been wrong about people in the past, but this bloke, no, I'm not having it...I don't trust him at all.'

'I'm glad you said that,' said Nick as they turned off Oxbridge Lane onto Hartburn Avenue. 'At first I thought he was being OK. And offering me some work isn't such a dumb idea because I could do that shit easily...'

'...but he was greasing you up from the start...'

'...oh yeah, I know. Obviously so. And all this gazing in your eyes business and 40 grand wages. It looked more like he was a pimp looking for fresh meat. He must be more stupid than I thought to think we'd find any of that in any way acceptable.'

She shuddered. 'Urgh. Horrible. His daughter is no fan, either, clearly.'

'That was just a little bit astonishing, don't you think? Grabbing his neck and scratching at his face.'

'Yeah. I mean, I've felt like doing that to mam plenty of times, but I've never actually grabbed her by the throat. I punched her once when I was about 14. She gave me a right bloody hiding. Never did it again.'

'Even more freaky was the way she just didn't look at me. Like I wasn't even there.'

'Yeah she was a bit blank-eyed wasn't she? He was mortified, I thought.'

'Totally, aye.'

'Anyway, apart from him being a slimy sod and having a crazy kid, I don't want to start a new job only to have to give it up to drop the bairn do I?'

Nick looked out at the Stockton suburbs he'd grown up around

'Actually, we've not even talked about that - about going to work afterwards.'

'I'm not going to work for a bit. I'm going to stay at home and look after the little 'un, aren't I?'

'I don't know. I thought you'd be keen to get back out to work.'

She licked her lips and cocked her head to one side in contemplation. 'Obviously I will if we're totally skint, but I think kids need their mam around, don't they? I know it's a radical and old-fashioned notion. I don't want to be a housewife, mind, don't get me wrong and you can do all the nappy stuff.'

'I'll be home working a lot of the time, so if you want to go out to work, you can. I'll be fine with the whole nappy and feeding thing. Having watched the Boro since the early 70s, staring at shit all day long doesn't bother me. Mind, I'll have to leave the suckling to your fine, pert nipples.' She barked out a surprised laugh.

'Well I've had you hanging off them three nights a week for the last few years, so it won't be much of a change. Let's just see how we feel later. It's early yet, but one thing's for sure, I'm not going to take any job that big creep offers me.'

'Nope, me neither and I think that'll really piss him off. I get the feeling he's not used to people saying no to him.'

'When he gets in touch we just make excuses though...be polite...don't just say, sorry pal, you're a creepy fat git,' she said.

'Damn, and that was the line I was going to use.'

CHAPTER 9

The next morning an email appeared from Davey James office outlining the roles he had in mind for both of them, along with details of the wages and contract terms. Nick decided not to reply right away. Instead he started to do some research. There were literally hundreds of news stories about him and the Urban Renewal Organisation and plenty of newspaper interviews too. He'd come from a one-parent family in Middlesbrough. His father had left one day never to return and had been a drinker, 'probably an alcoholic.' That sounded pretty much like Julie's dad. 'That's why I have always put aside money every year for women's charities.' He had said in an interview with *The Guardian*. 'I totally support the work Women's Aid and other charities do.'

A quick cross reference with the URO web site showed three women's charities in their 'Organisations We Support' list. Most interviews he did he talked about how hard his mother had worked to bring him up right and how he'd rejected later approaches from his father.

Interestingly, Zak and Toni were both featured in a big spread in the new year lifestyle section of the *Evening Gazette*. They were 16 and 18. They looked out of the photo with dark sullen eyes.

The interviews and features all uniformly gave the impression of a man who had risen to the top and made his fortune by pulling himself up by his bootstraps and working really hard. It was an irresistible, feel-good story and one which, with the growth and success of the URO, looked set to continue.

But it was the very last interview he came across that really made Nick sit up in surprise. It had been given to the *Stockton and Darlington Times*, an old local newspaper that he didn't even realise was still in existence. There, looking back at him, was a photo of Davey James alongside a photo of Matt Little. The headline read 'Stockton man to invest in URO project.' It dated from 18 months ago. Scanning the story it seemed as though Matt had invested what was described as 'a significant six figure sum' in URO. He was described as a 'successful local businessman'. Davey James was quoted as saying, 'we are always looking for serious investors in order to expand at a quicker rate. There is so much work to do in bringing life back to Northern towns and we want to get down to business right away. Matt's investment helps that happen.'

Jeff had said Matt had invested in companies in the area. He must have some serious money to spare. He shut his laptop; it was already noon and he had to visit his mother for an hour. A long-time paranoid schizophrenic, she'd been in North Tees psychiatric ward for years, but recently she had been moved out to a nursing home. Her drug regime seemed to have finally, after so long, stabilized her and though it seemed she would never recover properly, she was more cogent.

It was only a ten minute drive to the village of Sadberge; a lovely little place just off the A66 in the countryside. The nursing home was set next to a village green. As he walked in, he saw her sitting in a high-backed chair. She was knitting. A rotund, big-faced receptionist smiled at him.

'Hello Nick. How are you?' she said

'Great. Thanks. Nice day. How's mam doing?'

'She's good as gold. She's in the lounge if you want to go through.'

She looked up at him as he walked in.

'Hello our Nick.' That was a good start. She'd recognized him straight away. It hadn't always been the case.

'Hi mam. Isn't it a nice day?'

'It is, aye,' she said, her watery blue eyes, glassy and distant. 'It's lovely here. Your dad used to drive us out here, do you remember?'

'Yeah. That was about 40 years ago just after we first moved to Stockton. It seemed like it was right out in the country didn't it?'

'Aye it did. It still does. Well, it's all fields out the back of here. So how are you? How is that Julie of yours?'

'We're both fine, mam.' He wanted to tell her about the baby, but he'd sworn to secrecy. They talked for a bit about something and nothing. 'Mam? Do you think I'd make a good dad?'

She looked at him, but kept on knitting an Arran cardigan in cream wool, her fingers seemingly operating independently of the rest of her as she wove ends of yarn in and out, pearled stitches and did cabling. It looked so complex, but she made it appear easy to do. The fact she was once again capable of such a thing spoke volumes of her improved mental acuity.

'A dad? You? Why are you asking that?'

'Just wondered.'

'Well, you've always been a bit of a kid yourself, haven't you?'

'I suppose so.'

'When you were little you were always being silly and making up stories.' She gazed into the middle distance, as though hearing something quiet and far away. 'You used to sit up in your pram and just giggle to yourself. You were always laughing. I used to think you were telling yourself jokes.'

'When I was a teenager I used to laugh to stop myself crying.' Shit. That was out of his mouth before he'd had time to think. She looked at him, but through him.

'I'm sorry, I never knew that. I always think of you with a smile on your face. You've always had a nice smile, our Nick,' she said, now distant again...almost as though he was a stranger. Then a memory came to her and she caught hold of it like it was passing piece of paper, blowing in the wind.

'You used to look after that little lad from next door. Ian, I think he was called.'

'Oh yeah, that's right. That was when I was 16. I do quite fancy being a dad y'know.'

'Well, it's never too late. You never know.' She seemed to refocus and return to the room.

'You don't think I'm too old? It's just we thought we might...'

'...you're never too old to do anything, our Nick. Not these days. It was different when I was your age. How old is Julie then?'

154

'She's 44, mam.'

'That's no age. 44. Not these days. That's like 22 these days. 44 really was 44 when I was 44, but a lass like her isn't 44, not these days, like.'

Even though she could mangle a sentence spectacularly, he knew what she meant.

'I'm a bit scared though. If we had a baby, the responsibility of it seems so massive.'

'Oh you just get on with it, Nick. You always did think too much about things. There's no point in doing that. Life just happens to you anyway.'

He smiled to himself. That was exactly what Jules always said.

She looked at him, again with unfocused eyes, her skin papery and washed of all colour except the palest of flesh tones, her hair a fine silver grey. She seemed almost impossibly old, yet she was only in her late 60s. All the ECT and drugs had aged her to the point she seemed to be a ghost and little more than a bag of bones held together by loose-fitting skin. Yet she had, after a fashion, come back to life and for perhaps the first time since he was a boy, he felt like he could interact with her, felt a kinship, even though her ill-health and mental condition had blighted much of his teenage years and caused a lot of problems that he'd yet to exorcise. It felt like she'd been away on a long holiday, one that had lasted since he was about ten.

'Would you like it if we had kids, mam? Would you like a grandchild?'

She glanced down at her knitting and then up at him. 'I'm not fussed. You do what you want, our Nick. It's not about what anyone else thinks. Its your life. If you two want kiddies, you have them. I'm easy either way. Having a family should be nice though. Make sure things are nice. That's all I'd say.'

'Yeah, we'd make sure things were nice.'

'Nice is nice. You can't beat a bit of nice,' she managed a light smile at him.

They chatted about the food in the home - good. The other

residents - some nice, some not. The weather – sunny but cold. She managed to get through the whole conversation without once mentioning omelettes. For years she had been obsessed with the omelettes in the hospital being poisoned. It was a mental tick she couldn't seem to shake off, but now it was gone, at least for a while.

'Eeee, it's been lovely to see you,' she said, as he got up to go.

'I'm glad you're feeling a bit brighter, mam.'

'Aye. But are you alright, our Nick?' She put a cold hand on his arm.

'Me mam? Yeah, I'm alright.'

'I'm sorry I've not asked before now.'

He didn't know what to say.

'It's alright mam, you've not been well.'

'Hmm. I just can't understand what got into me.'

'What do you mean?'

She sighed a light, almost imperceptible breath. Then it seemed like she was talking to someone else. 'It just seems one minute since our Nick was little and we moved into that house in Palm Grove and we had all those years ahead of us. I thought it was all going to be alright, but it wasn't and now I'm here and all that time has gone and our Nick is middle-aged and I just don't know where all the time has gone to...it's just all gone.' It was unnerving that she had slipped into referring to him in the third person, as though he wasn't there. He looked at her. It was as though the movie of her life was playing in front of her eyes.

'Oh well, who said life would be easy mam? No-one.'

He held her hand. She'd lost three decades or more to her illness. The drugs zonked her out for a lot of them. The ECT had removed a lot of the anxiety she'd suffered, but took most of what was her with it, rubbing out her old self and her past and leaving her adrift in the now, without much idea of how she got there. It wasn't just sad, it was upsetting. Tears glazed his eyes.

'I'll come again next week, mam.'

She looked back to her knitting and nodded. 'That'll be nice.

You tell Julie to just lie back and think of England and let nature take its course. Tell her not to worry. It'll all be alright. You'll be alright. It might even be the making of you. You always were daft as a brush. Had your head in the clouds and your feet an' all for that matter. A family would be nice for you both.'

He laughed a little to hear her talk like that. As he walked back to the car, his emotions got the better of him. He stood by the BMW and let a couple of tears roll down his cheek. Her life had been destroyed by mental illness and it didn't seem fair at all, not on him and certainly not on her.

That afternoon Julie came home from the doctors as he was finishing off his *Yorkshire Post* column.

'What did she have to say?' he said, swinging around in his chair as she came into the living room.

'That I'm in good shape basically, but nothing more other than what we've read online. Makes me wonder what doctors are there for these days, if you've not got something hanging out of your arse or need a nipple re-attaching. She said there's a good chance I might miscarry...but then she'd said it was almost impossible for me to get pregnant, so I don't know what that's worth. She means well, but I really think I know as much as she does and what I don't know, I can find out.'

'Well, we already knew all that and the chances of other...y'know...issues. Are you alright about it?'

She shrugged and flapped her arms in the air. 'There's nothing I can do really, is there? Not within reason. I'm supposed to get lots of sleep and rest and reduce stress, but beyond that it's sort of out of my control so...whatever happens, happens. As long as I do everything I can do for it to work out well, that's all I'm bothered about. But I don't want you tiptoeing around me like I'm an invalid, right?'

'Righto missus. I'll get some dinner on in a minute. Jeff's working at the shop till about seven.'

'That's a long working day.'

'Yeah, but he reckons the evenings will be good for sales. He's still talking about opening till ten, but I think he'll just end up getting piss heads in, especially at weekends.'

'Fair play to him for putting the graft in.' She took off her coat and put on her slippers and sank onto the sofa, putting her feet up.

Nick told her about his research on James and about Matt Little's investment.

'That's weird, isn't it? Giving money to women's charities like that but still using sexist language all the time.'

'Actions, not words...that's what you said, Jules. Judge people by their actions, not their words.'

She sneered. 'Alright, clever clogs, it might not be a watertight philosophy. I can't work out if he's a lot nicer than he seems, or a lot worse, and not for the first time when it comes to blokes, mind.'

He got up and began to prepare a roast chicken by stuffing it with onions, carrots and celery, rubbing some mixed herbs and butter into the skin and sprinkling it with sea salt. Julie had dozed off to sleep by the time he was done, lying there with her hands crossed on her belly, breathing slowly and deeply, eyes closed. As he sat down opposite her quietly, he smiled, feeling oddly changed by the baby news. The early hours of fear now replaced by an irrepressible contentment. Even talking to his mother had helped ease his worries and the better than even chance of Julie having a miscarriage hadn't dented it. Maybe it was simply having achieved a pregnancy that felt so good. At least it had happened between them, whatever the outcome. They'd made a life. He'd almost immediately started feeling really protective of her. His instinct was absolutely to wrap her in his arms and not let her go, but knew that protection and smothering lived right next door to each other.

He noticed there was an email from Jeff.

'Going out for a burger and a drink with Big Fish. Back 11-11.30. Got some interesting news.'

Big Fish, or Stevie Salmon, was his brother, a local and highly successful stand-up comedian. Jeff had been meeting up with him from time to time and despite initially being a bit wary of each other, having only learned of their common parentage in the last two years or so, they seemed to get on quite well now. Nick didn't like him and found him too boorish, but Jeff seemed to have a greater tolerance of that aspect of his character. As he was a multi-millionaire, he was a good friend to have and Nick had wondered if he was cultivating the friendship for that reason.

There was also a Google alert for a news story that had just been published in the *Northern Echo*. He'd set the alert up for anything that mentioned Colin Harcombe and Jimmy Butcher. The headline read 'DJ Tees Murder: Man Charged.'

He scanned the piece. 'DI Colin Harcombe said today that investigations were making "significant progress" in the Alan Armstrong murder case. Roseworth man James Butcher was arrested on Sunday and has this morning been charged with the murder of the popular local Tees Digital presenter, often known as DJ Tees. Police consider he was acting on someone's instructions in return for financial reward. Focus of the investigation is thought to now have centred on the radio station owned and run by Malcolm Pallister. The police have made no comment on newspaper speculation that Armstrong had extensive debts and had recently been trying to borrow money, nor on other speculation that Armstrong was having an affair. DI Harcombe said at this afternoon's press conference that his next task was to find out who had paid James Butcher to commit the murder. "We will not rest until this matter is resolved and all miscreants concerned are behind bars".'

It was a very Harcombe-esque line. Very Dixon Of Dock Green. Very moral. Miscreants, indeed. The rumours mentioned were new to him. Maybe they were just press talk to fill a few lines.

'Have I been asleep long?' Julie sat up and rubbed her eyes.

'Not too long...'

'That chicken smells brill. As I'm pregnant I'll have it with a spoon of coal.'

'I'll get the pickled eggs and strawberry jam.' He told her what he'd been reading.

'If he did have debts and was having an affair, it would all start to make a bit more sense, wouldn't it?' she said.

'I don't see AA having either of those though. He didn't have a flash lifestyle. He was semi-detached suburban Mister Armstrong.'

'Mam always says, still waters run deep.'

'Yeah, but Alan Armstrong wasn't like that.'

'But you'd have said Jeff wasn't the sort of bloke to cheat on his girlfriend with another woman in the next room. You said it yourself, when it comes to sex, men are weak. Might as well add money into that too.'

'Well it must be a bad man he's crossed if that's the case.'

'A bad man or a bad woman.' She pointed at him and raised her eyebrows. 'Women are killers too.'

'Aye, but it's almost always a bloke, isn't it?'

'Yeah, it is. But think about it, they just had to pay Butcher the money. They didn't have to actually do any killing. That'd open it out to a lot more people, both male or female. It's a different psychology, isn't it?'

'It is, aye. Sounds like the police have got some strong leads, though.'

She got up. 'Colin will solve it. I'm sure he will. How was your mam, anyway?'

'She's doing much better. She said you've got to lie back and think of England and let nature take its course.'

'You told her about the baby?'

He shook his head. 'I said we were thinking of having kids.'

'Huh. Well the lying back bit was the easy bit. It's the legs in stirrups and pushing a human out of me while strangers look up me doo-dah bit, that's what is most worrying.'

'That does sound like it'll make you eyes water. I don't know how you'll...y'know...stretch that wide.'

'*You* don't? I bloody don't. It doesn't actually seem possible, but unless I'm anatomically different to every other woman who has dropped a kid, it must be able to stretch wide enough. I presume they have butter and some sort of shoehorn available.'

'Well, that was how we conceived it, so I should hope so.'

Julie had gone to bed by the time Jeff got home at 11.20pm. Nick was sorting out vinyl records in the music room, a downstairs space which housed his 10,000 vinyl records and CDs. He had bought 78 albums at a record fair a couple of weeks ago and had yet to file them away alphabetically. Just picking up each one, inspecting it and finding its place on the shelves was relaxing, almost meditative.

Jeff put his head around the door and pulled a crazy face. 'Now then, young man,' he said in an imitation of Brian Clough's voice.

'Hey big boy. Good night out?'

'Aye, had a double cheese burger with Big Fish at that place next to Green Dragon Yard. Highly tasty amalgam of eyes and arseholes. They do a low carb version y'know?'

'Gettaway. That's bit radical for Stockton. What was it?'

'The burgers came wrapped in lettuce leaves.'

'Well I never. Is that what you had?'

'Yup. BF thought I was on a health kick until I told him about all the butter and lard I'm eating. He reckons he can't lose weight because it'd be bad for his image, as what he likes to call, a "Funny Fat Fucker".'

'Charming.'

He sat down on the big padded leather armchair that was Nick's favourite writing seat, picked up a battered copy of Free's second album and slid the record from its sleeve.

'Nice. A pink Island copy. Gatefold sleeve. First pressing. Bloody great record this an' all. How much did you pay for that?'

'One whole pound. It's shagged though, probably unplayable.'

Jeff held it to the light and squinted at it. 'Aye, nice rare thing to have though. £150 for a mint copy. Not that there are any mint copies. Where does it go?' He got up and looked along the shelves. 'After Peter Frampton, I'm guessing and before...' he picked through the records, '...and before the interesting acoustic, country-ish band Free Beer on the Buddah label. Interesting label

Buddah. Some bubblegum pop and art rock. Beefheart's *Safe As Milk*' album came out on Buddah originally, y'know.'

'Aye, didn't it spring out of Kama Sutra? All my Lovin' Spoonful records are on Kama Sutra.'

'You are correct-a-mundo, my snake-hipped friend. So you're doing a bit of late night sorting, eh?'

'Yeah, I'm not tired. Jules has gone to bed, but I'll not sleep if I go now. You seem surprisingly sober.'

Jeff grunted. 'Whisper it quietly, but I've been getting a bit tired of being pissed. It bloody takes it out of you and since I lost the weight, I can't take it like I once did. So I had two gin and tonics while Big Fish went through six pints of Stella. Not for the first time recently I thought I could give up boozing and not miss it.'

'Jeff man, you can't give up drinking. If you do that the western economy will collapse. Millions will be thrown into poverty.'

'I dunno what's wrong with me. It's like I'm turning into someone else. I'll be eating bean sprouts and quinoa next. Oh hey, El Fisho told me a couple of interesting things. You know he's doing one of his arena tours soon? Well, he's doing warm-up gigs in small clubs, one of which is called The GC. Have you heard of it?'

'Nope. Is it on Teesside?'

'Aye, it's in the Boro, off Corporation Road. GC stands for 'Gentleman's Club' and you know what that means don't you?'

'Strip club?'

'Pole dancing and topless waitresses, the BF says. They put comedians on in between the dancing.'

'Honestly? Good god.'

'What?'

'It's the 21st century, man. Do we really have to have clubs where women get their tits out to serve men lager? How can anyone sit there and think that's acceptable? I just don't get it. It's...it's awful, that is.'

'Awful? Naked breasts, awful?' he said, in disbelief.

'Yeah. Totally awful.'

'They don't have to do it, do they?' said Jeff with a dismissive wave.

'You don't know that. Maybe they do have to. You don't know. I'm willing to bet no woman actually wants to walk around half-naked for the pleasure of men, not unless she absolutely has no other option in life.'

'Alright, alright, it's too late for you to give me a gender politics lecture, Right-On Rodger. I'm only telling you because El Fisho says Davey James actually owns it. He got told by the manager. He keeps it quiet like and it's all done through a holding company to keep it at arm's length. Got fingers in a lot of pies that man...as it were, like.'

'Huh. Very interesting indeed. Not exactly progressive and somewhat at odds with his professed support of women's charities and such. Hey, you know Matt Little?'

'Uh huh.'

'I just found out he's actually an investor in URO.'

Jeff's eyebrows raised. 'Is he now? Well, here's another bit of gossip from Brother Fish for you about Davey James. Him and Matt are both sleeping partners in Tees Digital with Pally,' said Jeff.

'With Malcolm Pallister? Really? I mean, Matt mentioned something about that last week, but I didn't know James was involved as well.'

'They both put money in and left it all to Pally to run, but according to Big Fish, the company is crashing and burning. It's losing money hand over fist and both Matt and Davey want their money out, but Malcolm can't raise it. He reckons it's causing a lot of aggro.'

'It's hardly a big station though, is it? It can't be a big earner. The amounts involved must be quite small.'

Jeff shook his head and continued looking through the records. 'That's what I thought, but apparently Tees Digital is just one of 15 small local digital stations that they set up...'

'...Pally's never mentioned that...'

'Aye, from Inverness to Exeter, apparently. So between them all, there's a lot of wedge at stake. The BF only knew about it because Pally had come to him to invest some cash to keep it all afloat; a request the fat sod turned down.'

'He didn't fancy it?'

'Nah. He doesn't like Malcolm. Says he's a devious two-faced bastard who he wouldn't trust as far as he could spit him. He's also a tight wad is The Fishy Boy, so I don't think he'd have put money in, regardless.'

Nick pursed his lips together. 'Well we thought Matt was loaded, but he seems to be involved in a lot of things. If he's got investments in those two companies, presumably he's got some others as well.'

'And where there's money there is often trouble,' said Jeff.

'There was also a news report in the *Echo* saying there were rumours that Alan Armstrong had been trying to borrow money y'know...'

'Linking that in to why he was knifed?'

Nick shrugged. 'Could that be something to do with Malcolm actually needing the money?'

'Maybe Al was trying to raise some for him, aye. He was the station's biggest asset, I'd have thought. The most popular broadcaster they had, so maybe Pally sent him out to try and generate some funds. He'd have been more trusted, wouldn't he? Everyone liked AA. Still, why would anyone kill him for that? Lend us some money, no, sod you mate, taste my knifey-knifey. That's not how it goes, is it?'

'No. No-one is stabbed for asking for money. More traditionally, you get stabbed for not paying money back.'

'Raped more like, if you've borrowed money from a bank,' said Jeff, filing a record onto the shelves.

'Hey, leave them for me to do, man. I like to look them up as I'm putting them away.'

'You can come to the shop and do some of that if you want. I've still got a dozen of those big plastic boxes to put into the racks. It's taking forever on me own.'

'Aye OK. I'll come in with you in the morning for a couple of hours. I'm up to date with all my work.'

'Cool. Thanks man. How's Jules?'

'Jules?'

'I heard her throwing up again this morning. Has she got some sort of bug?'

'Yeah, something like that. Poor lass. Feels pukey early doors.'

Jeff raised his bushy eyebrows quizzically at him and pointed. 'Maybe you have fertilized her with your demon seed.'

'Doesn't seem likely, does it?'

Jeff shrugged.

'Would you want kids, Jeff? If the opportunity arose, like?'

'Me? Yeah. I'd bloody love it. It'd be funkier than a mosquito's tweeter.'

'It'd be what?'

'Come on Nick. You're the big Joe Bonamassa fan. It's a track on the *John Henry* album. Just got a vinyl copy of that in if you want it...'

'I want it...of course...great record, that.'

'Thought you would. But aye, I'd have liked kids, but it's not going to happen now, not unless I hook up with some nubile young wench, which isn't likely. I was talking to Rita about this actually. She had a son in her early 30s. Wasn't sure she was going to have kids, didn't fancy it really, but then she thought she'd probably regret it if she didn't and she's glad she did, obviously.'

Nick nodded. It was hard keeping his news from Jeff. He really wanted to share it.

'So is it not going to happen for you and Jules? Nil by kiddie?'

'You never know. Stranger things have happened.'

'She'd be a great mother, her,' he said, sitting down on the floor and looking at a copy of Lynyrd Skynyrd's début album. 'Hard but fair, I reckon.'

'You reckon?'

'Totally. Jules is like one of those teachers at school that you were scared of, but really liked.'

'Are you scared of her like?'

'Well...not scared like I'd be scared of Jimmy Butcher, but she is intimidating isn't she? In a good way, like. I'm making this sound bad aren't I?'

'Aye, you are. Just a bit.'

'I just mean, when she fixes you with one of her looks...'

'...nope, that's still sounding bad...'

'I'll shut up then. But you know what I mean. It's what you love about her. She's her own woman and she'd be a great mam.'

'What about me?'

'You'd be a rubbish mother. Yer tits aren't big enough.'

'Are you sayin' I've got nowt, like?' said Nick, in a thick Teesside accent.

'If you want man boobs, come to daddy,' he said, shaking his chest.

Nick laughed. 'Do you think I'd be any good as a father though? With my moods and that...'

'Well, you never know, do you? I reckon you'd be odds on to go all soppy and be really soft with them. Jules would be the hard one. You'd be all "wait till your mother gets home".' He wagged a finger.

Nick laughed again. Jeff was totally right. He knew him all too well.

After filing a few more albums, he yawned. 'I think I'll go to bed.'

'Aye, me too. Shall we get an early start on that record sorting? I really want it done and out of the way. '

'OK. How early is early?'

'Up at seven, out at eight? I'll make breakfast.'

'Sure. Bloody hell Jeff, you never used to even know there was a 7am on the clock.'

'I know. That was when I was a massive booze hound though. I like waking up early here in the countryside. Listen to the birds singing.'

'Hey I was always Harry Hippy, you're giving that a go now, are you?'

'Being more sober more often changes you, doesn't it?'

'It changed me a lot, aye.'

Jeff nodded. 'Right, let's go up the wooden hill to hear the Confessions of Doctor Dream and Other Stories.'

'Kevin Ayers album, 1974, right? For some reason, I used to get him and Kevin Coyne mixed up...' he said, turning out the lights.

'I was like that with Randy California and Randy Bachman.'

'A touch of Randy confusion?'

'You're not kidding.'

Nick slept quite well by his standards, waking at 6.30 as light began to come in around the curtains. Soon the smell of frying smoked bacon began to waft through the house. Jeff had obviously got up early. It was odd him being more healthy and sober. He'd been a pedal-to-the-metal party guy since his teens. Things seemed to be changing all around. Life was moving on. The things he'd thought were permanent were turning out to just be phases. That's what life was, just one phase after another. Permanence was an illusion. As he lay on his back contemplating things, Julie rolled onto her side and lifted her right leg over his left.

'Morning, you,' she said.

'Morning. I didn't know you were awake.'

She nuzzled into his neck and ran her hand up and down his thigh. 'I've woken up with a bad case of the horn. I had the dirtiest dream about you...'

'Oh aye, was I any good?'

'You had two huge penises. One came out of the end of the other like the alien in the movie. It flipped back and sort of poked out.'

'Bloody hell. That's not sexy, is it?'

'You wouldn't think so, but I bloody loved it. You had to stand at the end of the bed to get it in me, it was that long. It kept on going in and in and in.'

She rolled onto her back and pulled off her pyjamas. 'Come here you. The real thing is much nicer than a dream even if it is about eight foot shorter.'

But as soon as they had started to make love he knew something was wrong.

'What's up?' he said, stopping and looking down into her eyes.

'Oh god, I feel so sick. Get off us...quickly, man, gerroff.'

She rushed to the toilet naked and threw up.

Nick took her pyjamas in to find her on her knees over the toilet, her backside in the air. Her whole body heaved. Poor kid. He squatted beside her and stroked her back. She turned and looked at him wearily, with a long string of thick, glistening slaver hanging from her slack mouth.

'You and that bloody dick of yours, you did this,' she said, contemptuously.

CHAPTER 10

'Help yourself Nick...there's about a million albums that need putting out.' Jeff pointed at a pile of transparent plastic boxes full of records, stacked up in the back room of the shop. It did feel odd being in that room with the toilet at the back where Alan had been killed. It was hard to mentally grasp it. Nick found himself flinching from even thinking about it.

'It does feel weird in here, doesn't it?' he said.

'See, I told you. Luke wasn't bothered. But there's a vibe I reckon. But I can't move out, can I? I've just signed a two-year lease. I'm just hoping it passes with time. I don't think I'll ever use that toilet. I just can't step in there. I've been going in the Royal Oak instead.'

'I don't blame you. I wouldn't.' A fanciful notion crossed Nick's mind. 'Maybe it's his spirit. Maybe until his murder is properly solved, he won't rest and that's what we're picking up on.'

Jeff looked at him horrified and shivered and looked around. 'Oweee Alan, give it a rest eh, son.'

Nick took a box through to the shop and began to pull out records to go out into the racks. Jeff and Luke had priced them, but they needed putting in the right racks. Jeff didn't bother with genres because it was too difficult to know where some of them should go, so he just put everything in alphabetical order. It wasn't perfect, but no way of filing records was.

He'd just put a pristine copy of The Peanut Butter Conspiracy album *The Great Conspiracy* out when a familiar face looked into the shop.

'Alright lads.' A face looked in the door. It was Matt Little. 'Are you open this early?'

Jeff's face registered surprise at seeing him again so soon.

'Yeah, yeah, come in Matt. We've got an early start today. What can I do you for?' said Jeff.

'I saw your lights on so I thought, even though it's early, I'd get a good look through your stock.'

'Browse away, my good man,' said Jeff, taking out a copy of the Grateful Dead's *Wake Of The Flood* album and putting it on the turntable.

'So how come you're in town so early?' said Nick.

Matt smiled nicely at him and pushed his messy hair behind his ears.

'Oh, I'm just picking someone up in a bit. She's going to go shopping in Middlesbrough while I nip in and see Malcolm Pallister. A bit of business, 'y'know?'

'Pally? I know him from my phone-in show,' said Nick. 'You're an investor in Tees Digital, didn't you say?'

He nodded. 'I am, for what it's worth, which is the square root of sod all right now. Still, what's a chap to do? Investments can go down as well as up and sometimes they evaporate all together.'

'Is it having troubles?' said Nick. 'I heard it was.'

'Big time, yeah. I've got to sort it all out with Malcolm today actually. Push has come to shove, you might say. Not looking forward to it really, but it's got to be done. Oh hey, I heard they arrested Jimmy Butcher for the DJ Tees murder. He's always scared me.'

'You'd be stupid not to be scared of him,' said Jeff. 'I'm just glad I didn't know he was here or I might have stained my nice clean floor!'

'He looked me in the eye,' said Nick. Matt opened his eyes wide.

'Really? Did he say anything to you?'

'No. But he had a peculiar look about him.'

'Yeah, I thought so as well. I mean. I always did. Looked a bit crazy, if you ask me,' said Matt, fiddling with a tight curl in his hair.

'I didn't actually recognize him. I only recalled his name, not what he looked like. 30-odd years is a long time. Is this of interest Matt?' said Nick taking out the Peanut Butter Conspiracy album he'd just filed and passing it to him. 'Late 60s LA psychedelic folk rock sort of thing. Rare as hen's teeth.'

An expression, common to all record collectors spread across Matt's broad face; a mixture of delight and pain, he made an oooh noise and scrunched up his face.

'Nice, nice, nice. This, I like. I've got the début album called *The Peanut Butter Conspiracy is Spreading*, a US copy on Columbia. Is this a UK copy?'

'Yeah, remarkably it is,' said Jeff. 'It came in an old dead hippy collection I bought down in Harrogate. I love a dead hippy collection...I mean, y'know...from a record perspective...poor bloke etcetera.'

'Cool. I'll have that. How much? 20? No worries. Now let's see what else there is...'

They all went quiet as records were looked through, filed away and inspected. It wasn't something you could multi-task whilst doing, at least not for blokes and probably not for women either, though not that many women spent a lot of time in Jeff's shops.

After half an hour, Jeff put the kettle on. Over coffee he went through some of the records Matt had pulled out, mostly late 60s, west coast stuff. It came to £120.00.

'We'll call that a hundred Matt, if that's OK,' said Jeff, bagging up the records. 'These will go nicely with those Doors and Love albums you got the other day.'

'Lovely. Thanks Jeff. I'll enjoy playing these tonight.' He handed over ten tenners. As he did so a glamorous, middle-aged woman in a black wool coat came in the shop. It was Deirdre from the TW Centre.

'I thought I might find you here,' she said with a nice smile.

'He's been getting his vinyl fix,' said Jeff, pointing at the bags.

'Haven't you got enough records? You'll never play them all,' she said.

This caused all three men to groan loudly. 'It's not playing them that counts, it's owning them,' said Matt with his warm smile. 'Aren't I right, lads?'

'Totally. You just committed one of the greatest insults in the record collector's world. Thinking we play records. We don't. We play about 50 in a year. The rest are there as a sort of sucky blanket; a defence against the travails of the world,' said Nick.

'Sorry about him,' said Jeff, pointing at Nick. 'He thinks he's a bit of a philosopher. Want a coffee?'

'No thanks. We must be going,' she said, putting her hand affectionately on Matt's arm.

'Always a pleasure chaps,' said Matt with a wave. 'I'll pop in in a week or so and see what new stock you've got.' He thanked them again and waved goodbye, happy with his vinyl purchases.

When they had gone Nick said, 'He's just like he was when he was 16, isn't he?'

'Totally, aye. Some people change massively, Matt looks a bit different, but he's as laid back as he ever was.'

'I actually saw him drop that woman off at the TW centre where Julie works, y'know. They call her Deirdre.'

'She works there as well?'

'No, she's a customer, or user, or whatever they call them.'

'Interesting. Given that women go there who are getting knocked around, I wonder what the problem is? They seem really happy together,' said Jeff

'They do. She was all smiles, wasn't she? Maybe it's a front she puts on. Maybe Matt is really a bastard to her. Doesn't seem likely though, does it? I'll see if Jules can find out something about the girlfriend.'

'You can't be anyone's girlfriend when you're in your late 40s though, can you? Sounds wrong.'

'I know. I've started to call Jules 'the missus' to some people. I can't say girlfriend or lover, can I? Not at our age? Partner sounds like it's a same sex job. Wife isn't right and even if we were married, she's just not a wife conceptually or politically.'

'I would hate to be called a husband. The word reeks of tartan slippers and shower-proof blousons,' said Jeff.

They ploughed on filing away records. At 10.30 after a couple of strange-smelling old men in dubious overcoats had spent fifteen minutes looking through a box of hundreds of old 45s that Jeff had bought for £5 at a car boot, their old friend Paul Trent came in.

'Now then, Paul. We've just put another brew on, do you want one?' said Jeff, fetching another mug from the sink at the back. This was just what his shop in Harrogate was like; a kind of home for waifs and strays who were socially disaffected and semi-dysfunctional. The sort of men, and it was always men, who didn't really fit in anywhere else, but who, in the environs of some old records, found a place to be who they were without harsh judgement. He'd often said it was more of a social service than a retail store and now, within a few days of opening this new place, the same sort of people were already gravitating towards it, like moths to a flame.

'Oh yes please. Never turn down a tea, me. Just got my cup replay ticket for the West Ham game tomorrow.' He waved it at them. 'Just came to look at those singles you said you had, Jeff. 'ave you put them out yet?'

'Aye, they're over on that table,' said Jeff, pointing to several boxes.

A Boro obsessive who pretty much only lived to see them play football and to collect punk and new wave singles, Paul spoke in a broad Stockton accent and despite being in his late 40s he seemed ageless because he'd been exactly the same since he was 15. They both knew him from school, often running into him at Alan Fearnley's record shop on Linthorpe Road in Middlesbrough back in the day, they'd all drank in the Stockton Arms as teenagers, sitting for hours talking about rock music over pints of Stones Bitter or Carling Black Label. Now going a bit bald and sporting a large beer gut, he was the sort of man who had never known the love of a woman and was likely to die a virgin. In some ways it was sad, but in others he was very self-contained and rather enjoyed his narrow life. He wasn't the brightest of blokes and he'd been in all the remedial classes where they'd called him simple and even retarded, but that was unfair. Nick had often thought he was just tuned into a different frequency or wavelength to most people.

Nick smiled at him and nodded at him. 'Aye aye, Paul.'

'Now then, Nick. I saw you and Julie at the Wigan game,' he said, rubbing his nose with an unpleasant tissue, 'I was going to say hello, but you were in a bit of bother in one of the lounges with some journos and that Davey James...'

'Oh yeah, we had a bit of a contretemps I'm afraid. You saw all that, did you?'

'You're a hooligan you, Guymer,' joked Jeff.

Paul laughed in an unusually squeaky manner. 'I fucking hate that Davey James gadgee, me. He thinks he's it, him.'

'Well he is *it* if *it* is being a bit of a git,' said Nick.

This made Paul explode in high volume tittering.

'What was it all about, like? I thought you were gonna smash someone in the face.' He said face in a very specifically Teesside way, extending the short word by elongating the 'a' so that he pronounced it "faaaysis"

'Oh it was just something James said that Julie took offence to and then someone insulted her and I lost my temper.'

'I came past that lounge like and I stood there watching youse. Why'd they say owt about your Julie? She bought us tea once y'know. We were playing Watford. She was on her own an' all and she saw us and said 'ere Paul 'ave some tea and I love tea, me, so she's give us some. 'ow nice is that? Didn't have to, like.'

'That's just our Jules, man. You know what she's like. Very generous with tea,' said Nick.

'If someone had been giving her trouble I'd 'ave 'elped you smash their 'ed in, but they'd take away me season ticket if I got into a bit of a ruck in the ground, like and I'd be lost without me Boro.'

'Thanks Paul. I didn't need your muscle though. I shouldn't have kicked off really. Doesn't help anything.'

'I knew some of that lot in there. All Davey James' hangers on. Greasy gets, them lot. Yes Davey, no Davey, three bags full

Davey.' He sneered and feigned being sick. 'I met his kids once y'know. They were alright, like.'

'Did you? How come?' said Nick

'I worked at Sanderson's last year. Just for a few months, like. They laid us off.'

'The builders' merchants on Portrack?' said Jeff

'Aye. I was using the forklift...brrmmm...great job that.'

'Did you supply James' company then?'

'Aye. He used to come in with some of his lot. Once his kids came with him. Dunno why.'

'What were they like then?' said Jeff.

'Not stuck up or nowt. They were taking the piss out of him, like. Saying he was so fat they should use him to knock buildings down. Ha ha. He is a massive fat shite, like.'

'Me and Jules saw him with them in a restaurant in Hartburn. The lass grabbed him round the neck and scratched his face,' said Nick.

'Really? Beauty. Good lass,' said Paul, approvingly. 'I wouldn't fucking take a shit in one of his 'ouses, me, like.'

'Hey, did the coppers take a statement off you, Paul? After the murder here?' said Jeff

'Aye they did, like. I made a joke and I said I was outside killing someone else so I couldn't have killed Alan. They kicked off about that, like.' He looked like an embarrassed boy and went a pink colour. 'Didn't mean owt by it, did I?' He put on a deeper voice, imitating the police. "Don't be disrespectful. No joking matter. Think about what you say, Paul". Bloody bollocks. Just 'cos I knew Alan they were really giving us a hard time.'

'Did they?' said Nick

'Aye they bloody took us down the station and asked us loads of questions.'

'Why did they do that? They didn't do that for everyone, did they?'

'Dunno, but I never liked him, me. I know he was your mate Nick, fair enough, like, but he wasn't a Boro fan, not really. He was a York City fan. That's where he was born and he was just taking a lend of the Boro, if you ask me. Best thing Tees Digital did was get you on the show. Proper Boro fan, norra a fake one. Class, you being on there, like.' It was like he was a sulky 15 year old, sometimes.

Nick knew this was actually true. Alan's allegiance to the Boro was from years of living in the area, but his first love had been to his home town team. This wasn't an issue to anyone except a die-hard Boro fan like Paul whose self-identity was completely tied up with the club.

'Did you hear who've they've charged with the murder?' said Jeff, handing Paul his tea.

'It was Jimmy, wasn't it? They nicked him. He's a vicious get. Remember at school he punched that French teacher in the face and she ran off crying? He was only 14 then. Mad bastard him, like. He could gerra job beheading people on the internet, him.'

Nick and Jeff burst out laughing. This was typical Paul, every now and again he'd come up with a funny, off-beat idea or expression. Paul looked pleased with himself.

'Aye, the cops reckon Butcher did it, but someone put him up to it,' said Jeff.

'I saw Jimmy at your do. Shit meself when I did. Up to no good, him, I thought. Always was. I 'ate it when he comes out of jail. Scares us. Fuckin' looks at you funny, like he's gonna do something mad.'

'Yeah he looked at me funny. Does he do that all the time?' said Nick.

'Yeah, gives you the stink eye.'

'The stink eye, eh? I walked right past him when I came into the shop, but I didn't recognise him,' said Nick.

'Was he in the shop, like?'

'Yeah. I thought you said you saw him?' said Jeff.

'Aye, but not in the shop. I saw him outside the church next door, like. I'd been in the Castle and Anchor and when I came past, there he was with this bloke...'

'...he was with a bloke?' said Nick.

'Aye. Balding fat-faced bloke. Had a big fucking tomato head like Phil Stamp's. I didn't know him. But I saw him again at the Wigan game...'

'At the Boro? Where did you see him?'

'He was in that lounge with youse lot when I looked in. You had hold of his face. Thought you were going to burst the fat get. Brilliant, that. I bet you could really fucking twat someone, you Nick. Big fucking lad, you, like.' He mimed punching someone as though to emphasise the point.

Nick cast his mind back, wondering if Paul had the right man. It was an odd coincidence if so.

'Was he short-ish, big cheeks, red-faced, not much hair? Dressed like he was from the country.'

'That's him, aye. Like I said he'd got a big old Phil Stamp tomato head on him.'

That certainly sounded like it could have been the same man. Was it possible that he had asked or paid Butcher to kill Alan for him? To answer that, he'd need to find out who that bloke was.

'Are you sure you didn't know him?' said Nick as Paul began looking through Jeff's box of new wave singles.

'He must be a mate of Davey James, mustn't he?' said Paul, pulling out an early Ramones single on Sire. 'Aw man, look at this!' he held it up like a trophy.

'It was mostly journalists and media types, I think. Or that's why I was invited, anyway. The club was supposed to be giving us a bit of free food and drink so we might all stop being so critical of the club.'

'They need to start winning, then everyone would lay off 'em,' said Paul, excitedly finding a picture sleeve version of Richard Hell And The Voidoid's 'Blank Generation'. He held it up.' Bloody hell Jeff, I've wanted that since 1976. I never see it. It's a Belgium copy. How much?'

'To you Paul, a quid.'

'Eh? Are you sure. It's worth a lot more.'

177

'Aye, go on. Pick out some more stuff if you like, I'll do you a good deal.' Jeff winked at Nick. Paul had almost no money and went from one minimum wage, short-term contract to another, mostly stacking shelves and shifting boxes.

'If you want to know who was there, why don't you ask Tracy Collins in the office to give you a list,' said Paul, moving onto another box. 'She'll know 'cos she'll have had to put all the names on the door. That's 'ow it works, like. Then when you've got the names you can look 'em up on the internet like a stalker does on Facebook and Twitter an' that. That's what I do with lasses from school. See who they married. See 'ow fat they got. Eventually you'll find him. Everyone is on the internet somewhere.'

'Good thinking Paul. Excellent work,' said Nick, patting him on the back. That was Paul all over; always thinking, but on an unusual frequency.

After Paul had left clutching his haul of seven records for five pounds, Nick looked up the Boro office phone number, called it and asked for Tracy Collins. He was put through to a woman with a husky smoker's voice that sounded like broken glass and sawdust.

'Tracy, it's Nick Guymer. '

She recognized his name.

'Hello Nick. How are you?'

'Good, thanks. You sound like you've got that cold that's going 'round.'

'No. No, I'm fine. I always talk like this. Ha ha...take your foot out of the bucket, Nick. Ha ha.' She rasped a laugh. He cringed at his social faux pas. What next? Asking fat women when the baby was due?

'Sorry Tracy. Listen, you remember at the last game we had that little do which I was invited to?'

'Yes. I heard you had a disagreement or two. Word got around. You might find it difficult to get another invite this season now.'

That was no hardship.

'Fair enough. I actually wanted to find out the names of some of

178

the people I was arguing with. Just to get in touch and apologize. Could you email me a list of who was there?'

'Yes. I'll fire that over. I said it didn't sound like you. You're never usually any trouble.'

'No. I'm a good lad, really. I just lost my temper. Stupid of me.'

He rang off and waited for her email. When it arrived he sat at Jeff's counter on his laptop and began to go through the 28 names on the list, 12 of which he already knew were local writers and journalists, four more were from the TV media. Searching the remaining dozen names soon produced some interesting detail. The guy who had said Julie had his balls in a vice was Frank Carter. He owned a nightclub in Middlesbrough. There were photos of him in news reports opening it. He was married to Marion. A brassy-looking woman. All whitened teeth and Dubai tan. The other names he looked up were similar sorts of men; self-made working class blokes from the Middlesbrough and Stockton area.

Sometimes names leap out at you. Sometimes people look like their name. As soon as Nick saw the name Mick Root, he knew that he was the fat-faced man. He looked like a Mick Root. A search soon found his Facebook page and most of it was set to public for viewing. He scanned his photos.

'I've found him, Jeff.'

'Give us a look. Oh, he's got a face like a blind cobblers thumb. What's he do?'

'Shit. Now here's something interesting. He owns and runs a country store in North Yorkshire. In Easingwold to be exact.'

'Easingwold? Remember what Kev and Ricky said? The other shop that stocked Bowie knives is in Easingwold. That must be his store and it's where Matt Little lives too, remember?'

'Yeah yeah. What an odd thing. Does he know Root, do you reckon?'

'I'd be surprised if he didn't at least know of him. It's a small place, Easingwold, isn't it? All pink trousers and head scarves out there,' said Jeff. 'The other day he said he'd seen a Bowie knife, didn't he? He said a shop in Easingwold has them, so he must know him or know of him.'

'Aye, that's right. He did.'

Nick did a search for the shop. 'The North Yorkshireman.' No Yorkshire women allowed, presumably.

'Here we go. It's all tweed jackets, quilted body warmers and walking sticks. And surprise surprise...hunting, shooting and fishing gear.'

'Ah ha. It really should have a spiky red handle, a Bowie knife, and a flash across it.'

Nick looked through the inventory. 'Yes! He's got two different ones. So, this is interesting, isn't it? This bloke had easy access to knives and Paul just said he saw him with Jimmy Butcher minutes before Alan was killed. He must be involved. I bet he's given Butcher the knife. I bet he has. He was a right nasty twat, Jeff. A real bastard.'

Jeff sat down and opened his lap top to look up a record on Discogs. 'Being obnoxious isn't illegal, luckily for me, but what could Root have had against Alan? Why did he want him killed?'

'We'll have to look into him a bit more to find that out, won't we?'

Jeff looked up at him and let out a cry.

'Shit. Listen to this! Malcolm Pallister was found dead this morning in the URO offices in Middlesbrough. Unofficial reports suggest he was the victim of a knife crime. More details to follow. It's on the *Gazette* web site.'

'Pally! Pally's dead?! Jesus H fucking Christ. What the hell...what's going on? Butcher is in jail so he can't have killed him...so who did? Matt was going to see him. Maybe Matt found him. Maybe Matt killed him!'

Jeff shook his head slowly, his face stripped of colour. He pulled on his beard, distracted. 'This has to be about money, doesn't it? It's something to do with Tees Digital going bust. Pally the boss, AA the star. Both dead.'

'Shit. I didn't know Pally that well, in fact I didn't really like him...but poor sod, he didn't deserve that. Oh god.' He paced around the store, pushing his hair off his forehead, distressed, heart racing. 'Hang on man, Matt wouldn't have told us he was going to see Malcolm if he was going to kill him, would he?'

Jeff raised his conspiracy index finger right away. 'Not unless it's an elaborate double bluff. Right so here's an idea - both Malcolm Pallister and Alan Armstrong were involved in some dodgy scheme to raise money for the station. They've pissed off someone important who has, via two different hired assassins, killed them both.'

'Alright. But why? Why do they need to be killed?'

'Big Fish said the company was going down. Pallister was trying to raise cash. Maybe he couldn't pay off someone big and bad who had said, cough up, or we whack you. He couldn't come up with it so he gets Bowied. These money lending sorts have a reputation to keep. They have to whack people in order to keep up pressure on other borrowers. And who do we know had money in the company?'

'Matt Little and Davey James.'

'Exactly and of those two, James is the powerful one.'

'Is he really going to have people murdered? He's a bit of a git, but murder...that's something else. He's a lot to lose.'

'I agree, actually, when you think about it, it looks bad for Matt. The coppers will be all over him like a disease. He's owed money by the bloke who's dead and he must have been at the scene of the crime.'

'I don't like this, Jeff. I mean, the bloke I worked with and the bloke I worked for are both dead. How long before they come for me?'

Jeff blew out air.

'Don't be so paranoid. You're not alone there. I mean, several people could say exactly the same thing, producers, admin staff and other presenters or DJs.'

'True. Well look, I'd better send this info on Mick Root to Colin Harcombe along with the fact Matt said he was going to the Tees

Digital offices this morning.'

He took out the policeman's card on which was a private email address. There was no point in calling him as he'd be busy with this latest murder. After writing out everything as clearly as possible, he sent the email and then called Julie.

'Hiya mister,' she said.

'Jules. Have you heard the news about Malcolm Pallister?'

'What news?'

'He's been found dead in his office. Knifed.'

'Good god. What on earth...'

'I don't know. It's really weird.'

She breathed heavily into the phone. 'Have you any ideas?'

'A few. Listen, do you remember that bloke whose face I grabbed at the Boro?'

'The sexist pig?'

'Yeah. He's called Mick Root.'

'Root? He's called Root? Sounds like something from the middle ages, appropriately enough.'

'I've found out he owns a country shop in Easingwold and you know Paul Trent...?'

'Daft Paul?'

'Yeah. He says he saw Root with Jimmy Butcher just before Jeff's party outside the church.'

'Really? I don't remember seeing him there.'

'No, me neither, but that's not saying much, because we didn't know who he was then, did we? Have we checked the photos you took to see if Root is in them?'

'No. We haven't looked at them since before the Wigan game, so he might be on there as just another anonymous face. Eeee fizzin' hell...do you think he might have done it and not Butcher?'

'He might have killed Pally and given the knife to Butcher. He had access to knives in his shop. We'll look at the photos again later. There's one other thing...you know the Deirdre woman that we saw Matt Little drop off, would you be able to find out anything about her?'

'I don't know. Why?'

He explained about Matt being in the shop and Deirdre collecting him.

'I was wondering if she was going to the TW Centre because of something he was doing to her?'

'Maybe. You might think he'd not be dropping her off if that was the case, but he could just be really controlling, wanting to know where she was going. Then again, she could have a husband or partner who has been giving her trouble and Matt is the new boyfriend. OK, I'll see what I can find on Deirdre.'

'OK. Great. How are you feeling?' he said.

'Oh, I'm fine, man.' She said it with quick exasperation. 'You don't have to ask how I am all the time. You wouldn't normally.' She lowered her voice. 'I'm just pregnant, not ill.'

'Yeah, of course, sorry Jules.'

She sighed. 'Alright. I'll see you a bit later.'

They had just finished sorting out the last box of records and putting them into the racks by four in the afternoon, when a car pulled up right outside the store. Colin Harcombe came into the shop at pace with an officer in tow. His face was set in a tense grimace.

'Jeff, Nick. Thanks for your email. Busy day. Obviously, you heard about Pallister. What have you two been doing all day?'

'We've been here sorting records since just after eight this morning,' said Jeff. 'Do we need an alibi, like?'

'Everyone involved in this needs an alibi. And you've had customers in and out all day?'

'Yes, it's been quite busy really, hasn't it, Nick?'

Nick nodded. 'Yeah, since Matt came in at half eight.'

'...Matt?' queried Harcombe.

'Matt Little is a big record collector. Like I said in my email, he said he was going to see Malcolm at ten o'clock, Col, so he must have been around and about at the time of the murder.'

'He was definitely here this morning?' Harcombe pointed at the floor.

'Yeah until about 9.15. He bought a dozen records. A woman came in and picked him up; the thing is, I've seen him drop her off at the Teesside Women Centre that Julie works at...I don't know if that's significant,' said Nick.

Harcombe raised his dark eyebrows and nodded at the officer with him who immediately left the shop.

'Is that important?' said Nick.

'Can't say.'

'Can't or won't?' said Jeff

'The latter,' said Harcombe without emotion. This Mick Root character...'

'...is Root someone of interest to you?' interrupted Nick

Harcombe pulled his chin in contemplation. 'There are concerns about him, yes. The North Yorkshire boys have been in touch. A bit of an odd bod. He was once pulled in by them for horse-whipping a man he suspected was a poacher. '

'Get out of here. Horse-whipping? Who horse whips someone?' said Jeff with a bitter laugh.

'Well. Exactly. No charges were brought. He was cautioned though.'

Jeff told him what Big Fish had told him about Pallister touting around for investors. The policeman listened intently and made some notes, nodding, but making no comment. He never gave much away.

'What about the rumours about Alan owing money and having an affair?' said Jeff.

'Nothing in them at all. Someone just made them up in the press.' He extended a firm handshake to each of them. 'Thanks for your ongoing efforts, chaps. We will get our man.'

'...or woman,' interjected Nick.

Harcombe cocked his head and nodded. 'Indeed...man or woman.'

'Are you going to interview Matt?' said Nick.

'Interview him? I think we may be arresting him.'

Nick and Jeff looked at each other in surprise.

Once the policeman had gone Jeff made Nick some green tea and some Tetley's for himself.

'Matt isn't a bad bloke, is he? He's not done anything wrong here, has he?' said Jeff. 'Harcombe is obviously suspicious of him. But I suppose that's his gig, isn't it? Suspicion.'

'He's always seemed nice enough, going right back to school. We said how nice he was when he left here this morning, didn't we? But Julie's been saying for a while now that you can't always tell. Someone can say all the right things, but act totally differently.'

'I know what she means, but, no offence like, she's working amongst a lot of women who have seen the worse side of blokes, so they're bound to be a bit anti-man. Professional feminists, like.'

'Bollocks, it's not about being anti-men or pro-men, it's about what's right or wrong. And so what if they're feminists? It's not a bad thing. They've had loads of experience of how abuse works, much more than we have. There are blokes out there who are conniving, violent twats and others who are specialists in psychological torture. I'm not kidding man, don't look so cynical. There are women there who get kicked around by blokes who everyone else thinks are bloody wonderful. They're like night and day. They reserve being a bastard for their wife or girlfriend. I mean, the stories Jules has told me...it's just horrible, man. I never knew it was so widespread and commonplace. I'm not just saying this for effect...it's real...maybe even for the majority of women at one time or another.'

'Is it really, though? I mean, if someone called me a fat bastard in the pub, that's abuse, but it's not the same as being hit in the face, is it? It might all get reported as abuse, but there's abuse and abuse. Men get abused all the time.'

'No. It's just all abuse. And it affects millions of women one way or another. The fact that men get abused as well doesn't invalidate what women go through. It's not a competition between men and women for who is most abused, is it? The point is a lot of this happens to women behind closed doors and it's not just the occasional insult, it's much more extreme than that and a part of their every day life and it affects kids as well, obviously. They get conditioned into thinking it's normal.'

Jeff was clearly cynical, thinking that it wasn't that big an issue and that was really bloody annoying. Did he think women were just making this up to annoy blokes? God, it couldn't be further from the truth; the vast majority of abuse almost certainly went unreported. Julie had opened his eyes to it, but then maybe without her, he'd have been equally as cynical.

He sipped his tea and wondered, why were some men like this? As if it wasn't bad enough that they inflicted so much misery on the women in their lives, it seemed like society had ganged together to pretend it didn't even happen that much. Not for the first time he wondered if the male of the species was, by and large, just no good. Jeff wasn't a bad bloke by any means, but then maybe he was just putting a veneer on his true nature. Maybe that's what all men did. It wasn't a happy thought and it was one he kept returning to as he drove home, leaving Jeff to run the store on his own in the evening.

Julie was already home when he got in and he sat down at the kitchen table while she prepared some venison liver for their tea.

'I've been a clever girl,' she said, 'I sneaked a look at the list of people who attended the last Freedom Programme class and then cross-referred them to the case files on the computer. I found out who that Deirdre woman is.'

'Good stuff. Who is she?'

She dusted the liver in a bit of seasoned flour. 'I'll tell you who she is mister, she's actually called Deirdre James...'

'Oh yeah?'

'Yeah, and she is Deirdre James because she's actually Davey James' wife!' She nodded at him with wide turquoise eyes. 'Yes, that Davey James. There now, that's shocked you, hasn't it? It shocked me.'

'Really? Wow. Are you sure?'

'Positive.'

Nick sat with his arms folded and watched her prepare the slices of the bloody organ. 'Christ. That's a bit of a story right there, you know.'

'I know. It means he's an abusive man y'know, and that's not just a little thing. The fact she's coming to the Freedom Programme could mean she's getting ready to leave him, or has just left him. They're really good at supporting women through all of that. I should be able to get a bit more info about him tomorrow, if I do a bit more snooping. Think about it, though. If the story comes out, it's going to make him look bad, isn't it?'

'I wonder if anyone will want to actually run a negative story in the media about him? He's the big local hero. It'd be like throwing a blanket over the sun.'

'Very poetic.'

'Hold on though, Jules, Matt is having an affair with her and he's an investor in URO and both him and Davey are investors in Tees Digital. That's probably how Matt and Deirdre met. I can't see a man like Davey James taking this lying down. Matt's invaded his territory, that's how he'll see it.'

'No. My thoughts exactly. He's the sort of fizzin' git who would take it very badly, which makes me wonder if he wouldn't want to get at Matt somehow - presuming he knows about the affair, that is.'

'Or the other way around - Matt might want to get at Davey James for what he's done to his wife.'

'Well, there's no doubt now that she's been going through hell with him, probably for years. So he might well be angry at him.' She began frying the liver in some butter.

'The thing is Matt came into the shop this morning to look through some stock while he waited for a woman to pick him up. It was Deirdre. He said he was going to the Tees Digital offices this morning to meet Malcolm and then we heard that Malcolm was dead.' Nick sat back and closed his eyes to remember what he'd said. 'He had a ten o'clock appointment. He said he wasn't looking forward to it.'

'He hasn't...y'know...he hasn't killed him, has he?'

'You wouldn't say you had an appointment with the person you were going to kill though, would you?'

'Maybe he didn't mean to kill him, but lost his rag. Most murders are done in the heat of the moment, not planned out. Maybe they argued about money...'

'...and then he pulls out a knife? No. That's not right, is it?' He sighed and rubbed his eyes. 'I need to put this on my sub-conscious back burner and let it cook for a while. All these people are inter-related. There's the Matt, Davey and Deirdre triangle. They both have money in Pally's company and Matt is a URO investor as well. Matt lives in Easingwold, the same place as Mick Root, who has a shop there which stocks Bowie knives, the sort of knife that Butcher killed Alan with, and now Pally has been knifed as well. Root is a fan boy of Davey James and a bit of a prick. Paul Trent says he saw Root talking to Butcher outside of Jeff's party.' He drummed on the table with his knife and fork. 'What does it all mean, Jules?'

'God knows. They're obviously all pieces in the same jigsaw, but I have no idea what the picture is.'

It was giving him a headache. 'Oh god, let's just talk about something else. Did you have a good day at work?'

'Yeah, I did. I *really* like working there y'know. My karaoke session seems to have gone down well. Apparently, I was throwing all sorts of rock chick shapes in the Penny Black. I don't remember that, like. I didn't even know I had any rock chick shapes to throw.'

'You must have been channelling your inner Pat Benatar from the 80s.'

'Well, I do love her. Have I showed you the photos of me in the mid 80s? I used to have my hair like hers on the cover of the *Best Shots* album. That shortish, shaggy, wet look.'

'Oh yeah, I've seen that. It made you look really different. All pouty and posey.'

'Then by about 88, I grew it out and had it like she was on the cover of *Wide Awake In Dreamland*. I had that exact hat, white top and jeans with neckerchief thing she wore in the inside sleeve of that record, as well. I was all about the Benatar, me.' She pursed her lips and slung her weight onto her right hip, holding the spatula up to her mouth "C'mon hit me with your best shot." Actually, that sounds like she's asking for a slap. Bit dodgy, that.'

'A lot of rock 'n' roll would fail basic gender politics analysis, I reckon. Almost all of Whitesnake's catalogue especially.'

She held up a finger and then looked at it quizzically, 'I'm getting Jeff's finger habit. That's bad. What I was going to say is, I love Whitesnake and I reckon most of those songs are just about having a broken heart or about having it off, which isn't in itself necessarily sexist, is it?'

He looked doubtfully at her.

'Take Me With You' has the line, "I know what love is and what it means, it's a skinny little girl in tight ass jeans." That's a case for the prosecution, surely.'

'Yeah alright, not ideal, but it's still about sex, really. That's what he fancies and we all fancy something, don't we? He's not asserting that as a universal standard. It's just his preference. There's also a line in that about spreading someone's pretty legs, isn't there? See, that's just sex again, isn't it? It's all about sex with Coverdale. And anyone that can sing 'Ain't No Love In The Heart Of The City' like he does on the live album is pretty much going to get me sitting on their face in a heartbeat. I love that song so much.'

'I like your argument here. It means I can listen to them with a guilt-free conscience. Mind, the videos, Jules...they were heinous.'

'The Whitesnake videos are bloody terrible on every level. That is true. The big hair is probably the very worst thing about them. Who was the woman in them? Tawny Kitaen? Yeah good luck with that name on the Hardwick estate, darlin'.'

'I can only imagine the amount of pussy jokes told by the Whitesnake road crew.'

'Ha ha. God, yeah.'

'Actually, her real name was Julie.'

'Gettaway.'

'True fact.'

'I like her better already. Maybe we can re-define all her lolling around and pouting on cars, as an empowering feminist statement?'

'Right on, sister,' said Nick, holding a fist aloft.

'Hey, someone at work said something good today. They said whatever you want to call it, feminism, gender politics, whatever, it's really just about good manners. Asking before you do something, thinking about your actions' effect on another person, it's all just about manners: about being polite. That takes the pompous politics out of it. Labels can put people off, but everyone knows what good manners are. Even David Coverdale would ask nicely before removing your knickers and writing a song about how your fanny makes him feel. Ha ha, y'know...or whatever.'

Nick laughed. 'You're a rude woman, you are.' She poked a tongue out at him, put a handful of rocket on their plates, chopped a tomato in half and served up the meat and vegetables.

'This looks beautiful, Jules. It's a middle class mixed grill.'

'I bloody love liver, me. Annoying how offal has become artisanal, middle-class food these days. Nothing was more working class than liver, tripe and brawn when we were kids.'

'True, but we didn't eat venison, liver did we? Never saw venison until the 90s. So we must be going upmarket.'

They ate their food in silence. Nick finished the plate, wiped his mouth. 'Delicious. You're getting better at the cooking thing, almost as good as me.'

'I've got a way to go yet. I've over-cooked the liver a bit. It's like school liver.'

'Talking of school, do you actually remember Matt Little at Ian Ramsey? He was in our year.'

'No. But then I don't remember you either, even though I went out with lads in your year.'

'Yeah, but you were in the second year, when we were in the fifth. That was too big a gap for anyone, except those odd, emotionally retarded boys...'

'...or exceptionally mature girls. But no, I don't remember him. Why?'

'I was just wondering if me and Jeff's memories of him were accurate. He was always such a steady, laid back sort of lad and he still seems exactly like that, but after what you've been telling me about abusive husbands and partners, I know that might not mean anything. He seemed such a gentle soul today. I liked just chatting about records and stuff. I got on really easily with him and that almost never happens to me. A very different sort of bird to Davey James. Deirdre has taken a 180 degree turn by hooking up with him, or that's how it looks.'

'I know the Freedom Programme is partly about learning how to spot Mr Right and Mr Wrong. So maybe that's why she's made a better choice. Then again, some victims of abuse keep walking back into the same type of dysfunctional relationships.'

They loaded the dishwasher and made some tea.

'No booze for me now. I'm going to have to join you in the land of the sober,' said Julie as they sat on the sofa and put the TV on. 'Y'know, I've never been sober for more than a week or two since I was 17.'

'You don't think about it after a bit. Being drunk seems weird to me now, after not drinking for nearly two years.'

She was about to reply when her phone rang. Nick got up, took it from the table and threw it to her.

'It's Martha at Teesside Women,' he said, looking at the display.

'Hi Martha. How are you? Good...fine thanks, yeah. Not much. Me and Nick have just eaten and we were just going to watch some TV.' She played with a long strand of hair as she listened, nodding and making approving noises, wrinkling her nose up at something. 'That is odd. Hmm. Nick was just talking about her actually, well, about the new fella actually. He knows him from school. OK. If you think I should, I'm happy to do that. Is it OK?

191

Yeah. OK just give me the address.' She wrote it down on a newspaper. 'Uh huh. I'll do that now. I'll let you know. No, it's no problem at all, I'm happy to help.'

'What's that all about?' said Nick, as she put the phone down.

'Well that's funny. Fancy a trip to Middleton St. George?

'Out into the countryside at this time of night? Why?'

'It seems that TW has given a house to Deirdre Jones. They have houses and flats for women to escape to who are being abused at home y'see and apparently they'd given her one a few weeks ago. It's just a small one-up, one-down, old terraced house in Middleton St. George, but there's a problem.'

'Has Davey James been hassling her?'

'No, it's not that. She's suspected of breaking the rules. When you sign up for one of these things, there are things you can and can't do in the home. Stuff like taking drugs and having wild parties.'

'She didn't look like a party animal. I can't imagine her skinning up a big one and listening to some Tangerine Dream. She seemed the epitome of lower middle-class respectability'

'Apparently, they're not allowed to have male visitors after nine in the evening.'

'Seems a bit draconian for grown-ups. I presume she's had Matt Little around.'

'Yes it does, but TW are really strict about such things. They see their role as trying to help the woman create a new way of life and to protect them from making rash relationship decisions. I mean, you can see what they mean. If you've left an abusive relationship, you'd be emotionally very vulnerable and probably badly in need of a little bit of TLC. And there are some blokes who are on the sniff for the slightest whiff of vulnerability who will pounce on you.'

'Rotten sods. Not sure Matt is like that though, but then again, I'm beginning to wonder if I can judge anything about anyone.'

'All she wants me to do is just drive by for half an hour a couple of nights this week and see if anyone comes and goes after nine.

Deirdre doesn't know me and I've not spoken to her, so even if she sees me she shouldn't get suspicious.'

'Is this how they police it? Seems weird.'

'How else are they going to do it? They can't ask the police. They have to do it themselves and keep everything in house with people they trust to respect privacy and security. Some of the other women there will take a look as well. It's all quite informal in some ways. The fact she's asked me is a good sign.'

'Of what?'

'Of their trust. It might mean that if I can get trained up, I can work full time there and not just as a volunteer.'

'OK, cool. Do we have to go now?'

'Yeah we don't have to do anything. Just sit there.'

'I thought they'd relocate women miles away from the bloke they wanted to escape. Middleton St George is only ten miles or so from her husband.'

'Yeah they sometimes do. But not always. There'll be a reason. Perhaps Deirdre requested it or maybe he's not been violent, so they don't see him as a threat as regards coming round the house and assaulting her. It should be a secret anyway.'

She stood up and yawned. 'It's already well after eight, so if we get off now, we can park up until half nine.'

'OK we'll go in the BMW. I'll drive if you like.'

'Cool.' She got her Duffel coat and a woolly hat. 'I feel like we're doing some spying!'

'Well, we are really. Do you have to take any photos?'

'I'll take my camera just in case...oh, we haven't looked on the photos for Mick Root. Let's just do that before we go...we've got 20 minutes spare.'

She loaded the card into her lap top and plugged it into the TV.

They sat together and watched each photo tick over in a slide show.

'Nope, he's not in these first ones...here I am coming in...'

'...still looking gormless...'

'He's still not there. Woah. Stop. There he is Jules! There. He.

Is.'

She paused the image on the screen.

'He's gone right in front of me. That's a good shot of him there, a side-on close up. He's really a repulsive slob isn't he and he's built like our old immersion boiler. I took no notice of him on the day. Funny how you just don't register strangers in a crowd.'

She leaned forward and pointed at a shadow on the lower right hand part of the picture.

'What's that there? It's a bulge in his Crombie. He's got something heavy in there which is making the fabric sag out,' she said.

'Roll it on...stop. Hmm, could it be a knife? Those Bowie knives are big heavy-ish things.'

They looked at the remainder of the photos.

'He doesn't seem to be talking to anyone, does he?' said Nick. 'In the last one, as Jeff comes out of the back room, he's looking directly at him...or at the door to the back room. Hard to read anything from that, though. He doesn't seem to have acknowledged Jimmy Butcher in any of these, but Jeff obviously didn't invite him and since Paul saw them together outside, there must be some sort of conspiracy going on between them. He's got access to the sort of knife Alan was killed with. Are we putting two and two together and making five there? I don't think so. I think he at least provided the knife. The fact Root was at the party has to be massively significant. He's not there for no reason. He's not come from Easingwold for no reason. Colin said Root was odd. I bet they pull him in tomorrow when they've done sorting out Malcolm's death. We'll text him later to tell him we've spotted Root in the pictures. Root's up to his fat neck in all of this.'

CHAPTER 11

It was a damp, drizzly evening as they drove into Eaglescliffe and then went west through open countryside on the A67 to Middleton St George, alongside the railway line, passing the airport along the way. They took a left at a roundabout into the village along Yarm Road.

'It's just down here on the right,' said Julie as they entered the village. 'One of these terraced houses.' She counted numbers. 'This one here. The one painted pale blue.'

'OK, let's park down the street from it so we're not right outside.'

He swung into a space about 20 yards away. They had a clear view of the front door of the house. Lights were on downstairs and up in the bedroom. He looked at his watch. Ten past nine.

'If some bloke comes in or out, what do we do?'

'Nothing. She's not allowed male visitors now, so either is technically breaking her contract with TW.'

'Would they chuck her out for that?'

'I imagine there's a warning procedure of some sort. Three strikes and you're out, that sort of thing. It feels very sneaky just sitting here though, doesn't it?'

'Totally. Aye. Look here comes someone.' He nodded at a Mini that pulled up ahead of them. A small woman got out, fastened her coat, walked down the street past the TW house and into the one next door. 'Ah, false alarm.'

The rain got a bit heavier.

'Of course, if she's already shacked up in there with someone and he doesn't come out till morning then we'll never know,' she said, pulling on a pair of woollen gloves.

'I love that expression, "shacked up", it's so 1970s. That and "living in sin".'

'I like "over the brush". I'd much rather live over a brush than get married.'

'Brush-based relationships seem more romantic, somehow.

195

Actually, talking of that...'

'...you're not going to propose to me, are you?' she said, rubbing her cold nose.

'Well...' It was something he'd actually given some thought to.

'You're not, are you?' she turned to him with a look of bemusement.

'No. Not as such. But we need, at some point, to think about what our kid's surname is going to be, don't we? Wells-Guymer, Guymer-Wells? I mean, that sounds like some sort of aristocratic, inbred old fart. That or a retired Home Counties colonel from the 1950s.'

She laughed a little. 'Yeah, it does. Well it'll have to be mine or yours, won't it? Do you mind which?'

'No. I don't mind at all. Do you think getting married is totally out of the question though? Just for the kid, like?'

She tutted. 'Don't be so old school. You don't really want to get married, do you? Everyone knows we're a couple, we don't need a legal contract to endorse it, do we? We know how much we love each other. We don't have to say it in public.'

'Totally not, no. I was just saying to Jeff that I sometimes refer to you as my missus these days because I don't know what to call us.'

'Julie and Nick. That's our names.'

'Aye, I know, but if we were married do you think it'd give our kid something? Make them feel snug and secure? Like they'd know we wouldn't abandon them?'

'Did the fact your mam and dad were married give you that feeling?'

'No. Not at all. I'd have rather they'd split up and been happy than stayed together in a miserable house.'

'Well, there you go then. It's about us and how we behave, not about the legal status of our relationship.'

He went quiet for a bit. No-one came or went from the house.

'Where's all this come from anyway?' she said.

'What?'

'Marriage talk.'

'Just thinking, that's all. Maybe it was talking to my mam. I dunno. Having children changes things, doesn't it?'

They went quiet again. A tortoiseshell cat emerged from a cat flap, wandered across the road and into a hedge beyond.

'We *can* get married if you want,' she said, 'I don't mind at all, as long as I don't become a Guymer. Apart from that, I'm sort of neutral on it. I don't see how it changes anything.'

'No, I don't either. But...'

'...what?'

'...but for some reason, some part of me wants to be married to you, now you're pregnant. Just so we can say we're husband and wife in front of the youngster. It doesn't make any sense, I know. I'm being old fashioned.'

'How weird. You've *never* wanted to be married before.' She leaned forward and looked at him with a little amazement.

'Maybe I just want to prove to myself that we can be happily married parents unlike my parents...unlike yours, too.'

She hummed a little. 'Maybe psychologically you now see that as a greater degree of rebellion than not getting married.'

That sounded about right. 'I am an ornery sod. Now that marriage is optional and not obligatory, it's probably changed my mind. But I can't make an argument for it on any rational grounds. So, y'know...let's just forget about it.'

'My mam would like it. She's always going on about us getting wed. "Make an honest woman of our Jules, Nick".' She could do her mother's voice exactly right.

'Yeah that's a good reason not to do it, obviously.'

'I'll think on. It's early yet. We don't know what's going to happen. You know it might all go bleurggh.' She made a gesture with her hands to suggest something gushing out of her.

'I know that, but I might want to get married regardless of the little 'un though. Sorry.'

'Don't be sorry...' She put her gloved hand on his,'...but you're a funny bugger, you.' She cleared her throat. 'Mind I'm not wearing a white dress, or a dress at all in fact. I've got a Nicole Farhi cream suit, I could wear that with my burgundy velvet waistcoat. I've no shoes though. Maybe I could do it in trainers? That'd be quite cool.'

'Very cool, yeah. I note you're already coming round to the idea.'

'Ha ha...maybe. I like to make you happy, just as long as it doesn't involve wearing uncomfortable underwear or masks.'

He grinned at her. 'We'll just see, eh. It would be quite a change for us.'

'It would, like.'

Nick looked out the back window and over the road. Cars were parked up, but no-one seemed to be around. Unsurprising really, it was a quiet little place.

'Aye, aye...look...we have lift off. Get your camera ready, Jules. Here's Matt's car. The Lexus.'

She took it out of her bag and tipped it up, looking at the settings, cursing at how fiddly it was in the dark. The door to the TW house opened. Deirdre James stood framed in the doorway with a phone to her ear. Yellow light flooded out onto the pavement. She looked up and down the street a couple of times. A Lexus stopped some distance in front of them and reversed backwards. Matt Little got out and strode over to her at the open door, giving her a quick embrace. The door closed behind them.

'Did you get any of that?' he said, turning to Julie.

'Yeah. I think I filmed it...hold on...yeah, look, it's a bit blurry to start with and it's a bit grainy, but you can see him.' She showed him the footage. It was dark, but it was proof of the visit. 'Let's just wait a bit and see if he comes out,' she said.

'She's just having someone around. It really doesn't seem like a big crime,' said Nick. 'She's probably lonely. They might not even be having sex. Matt might just be a good friend.'

'Might be. But I bet he's more than that. She could go to his, or even to a hotel, rather than here to the TW house though. It does seem harsh, but there have to be rules.'

They sat in silence for five minutes without any further action at all.

'I wonder if Colin Harcombe knows Matt is here?' said Nick. 'Maybe I should text him or something. He must need to interview him now that we've told him he had an appointment with Malcolm. He said he might even arrest him. Feels wrong though. Like I'd be grassing him up or something.'

They were just thinking of going when an old Land Rover stopped right in front of them and out stepped a distinctive squat man dressed in a cap, dark hacking jacket, dark trousers and big leather boots.

'Oh bloody hell...bloody hell...Jules, get down, get down, man...look who that is!' Nick hissed in a whisper, sliding down in his seat. 'That's Mick bloody Root. What's he doing here? Get down. Don't let him see us.'

She slid right down in her seat, set the camera going and put it on the dashboard pointing at the house door.

'I don't understand. Why is he here?' whispered Julie. 'Maybe he's after Deirdre for Davey James. Spying on her or something.'

'Yeah, well he obviously knows who lives there.'

Nick's mouth went dry as he watched Root stride up to Deirdre James' house and knock on the door. He looked up and down the street, wobbling his right leg as he did so, agitated. He had on the same jacket he'd worn at the party, again the inside pocket sagged with the weight of something. There was no reply. He knocked again. Still no reply. He looked from side to side again. The street was quiet. No-one around. He took two steps backwards and ran at the door, shoulder-charging it, once, then twice, but it was solid and didn't budge.

'Good grief. We've got to stop him,' said Julie, but Nick was already out of the car, not thinking, just acting on pure instinct.

'Well, well, well...who do we have here?' he said. 'I know you, don't I mate?'

Root looked up at him with wide, shocked eyes. He pulled his tweed cap down a little, as though he might disguise himself.

'Doing a bit of breaking and entering, are you?'

'What? How are you here?'

'Me? I'm like the wind, I'm everywhere, Rooty, lad,' he said, looking from side to side.

'Eh? How do you even know my name?'

'We know a lot about you, son and so do the police,' said Nick, sucking air in and sticking out his chest to make himself look as big and broad as possible in front of the squat man.

Julie got out of the car and stood, hands on hips, looking at Root. 'I think you've got some explaining to do for the police, don't you? I've called them. They're on their way.' She said it matter-of-factly, trying not to be angry or indignant.

'I might've have fucking known she'd be here...fucking stuck-up bitch...why don't you go and bust someone else's balls, darlin'? Let the men sort this out.'

Julie gave him a sardonic grin and flicked him the V's with both hands.

'Well you're just a lovely man, aren't you?' said Nick.

'Fuck you. You're a fucking pussy, you are. Under her bloody thumb. Embarrassing.' Root pushed him hard in the chest with big strong hands, knocking Nick back a step.

'Oh, don't start trying to be the big man with me Root, you know and I know that I could beat the fucking snot out of you with one hand tied behind my back,' said Nick, feigning a leap at him.

Root jumped back, bristling, sneering at him under the orange sodium street lights, panting through his nose from the exertion of trying to knock the door down. He looked from Nick to Julie and then back to Nick. Nick bristled with adrenalin.

'What's going on, Root? Why are you doing this? Did you kill Alan Armstrong and Pally? Why were you at Jeff's party? You weren't invited. Why? Come on, if you really want to be the big man, tell me. You'll have to tell the police soon enough. We've told them all about you. What are you going to do, eh? Are you going to horsewhip me? I'd like to see you bloody well try.' He laughed at even saying horsewhip. It seemed so ludicrous. He gestured at Root with his hands, standing on his tip-toes, like a football thug ready for a fight.

But Root said nothing. He was expressionless now, just staring at Nick, his fists clenching and unclenching, rolling on the balls of his feet, as though plucking up the courage to do something.

'You're pathetic you know that? You're so full of yourself. You talk a big game and play the big man, but you're nowt, son,' said Nick. 'You come on like you're this fearless warrior, but you daren't even have a pop at me, even though you obviously want to. Oweee, come and have a go if you think you're hard enough.' He was pretty sure now that Root wouldn't have a go. If he'd wanted to, he would have done it by now.

Root shook his head, sucking on his lips. The expression on his face was unreadable; perhaps somewhere between anger and bemusement.

'Well, we'll just stand here looking a bit awkward until the police come then,' said Nick. 'I normally like weird blokes, but I don't like you. Something's badly wrong with you. Why are you so angry all the time? Are you here to hurt Deirdre James? Is that it?'

As he spoke, quickly, in one fast, smooth move, Root drew a large, heavy Bowie knife from his inside pocket and lunged at Nick. There was just a brief flash of orange as the blade reflected the lamp light above. He slashed at him in an over-arm bowling motion, trying to bring the blade down into Nick's neck. Julie screamed, but Nick was too hyped up and too quick for Root. Seeing the movement, he made an agile leap backwards, causing Root's lunge to miss and him to stumble forward; he'd put too much energy into it and had overbalanced.

Seeing his chance, Nick put all of his weight onto his left leg and launched a right-footed volley into Root's face, his brown leather boot instep connecting full onto the bridge of his nose. He let out a low groan and whelping sound, raising his left hand to his nose, still holding the knife in his right. Bam! Nick kicked him in the face again, this time with all the power he had; right from his thigh, right through the ball, right on the sweet spot.

Root's head flung back with the force of it this time and he sank to his knees, the knife skidding out of his grasp. Julie leaped forward to grab it, but Root saw what she was doing and made a grab towards her leg from his prone position, pulling on her ankle. She spun around, pulling her foot out of his grasp and stamped on his hand hard.

'You fucking bitch!' he screamed, almost hysterically furious now. Driven on by his madness, he got to his feet, nose bleeding and lunged at her, grabbing her neck as she bent down to pick up the knife. As soon as he touched her, Nick felt a surge of electric energy, the like of which had never flooded his muscles before.

He ran around to Root's right-hand side, pulled his arm back at speed and, with a laser-like aim and absolute fury, he hit Root on the right side of his face and hit him so hard that his whole arm shuddered with the vibration of the impact on his cheekbone. But he was solid bastard who wouldn't go down easily, so Nick hit the fucker again, with another crashing right hander to his cheek and neck. And then hit him again, this time a big swinger to his guts. The powerful blows made him release his grip on Julie in order to swing a defensive punch at Nick, once and then twice, with short powerful arms, grunting and panting as he did so.

The second one hit Nick in the kidneys and hurt like fuck, making him let out an involuntary yell and go down on one knee. Root, bleeding from the nose and somewhere beyond angry, advanced on him to knee him in the face. Seeing it coming, Nick fell forward and rugby tackled Root, grabbing his legs and hauling him down. The squat, powerful man fell like a solid piece of timber, kicking and bucking like a powerful little mule as he did so. Nick got on top of him and pressed down on the fat, solid bulk of flesh with every ounce of power he had in his frame, pinning him to the pavement.

'Dear me, ass kicked by a couple of feminists, how will you live this down, Root?' he said, leaning over him, shouting into his face. Root, panting, still crazed, spat in his face once, twice, three times.

'You dirty bastard,' shouted Julie. She leaned over him and slapped him in the face hard with the palm of her hand, took two steps back and kicked him hard in the balls.

'Argh...argh...fucking hell...you fucking whore!'

She slapped him hard again. That must've really hurt him because he didn't utter another curse and just lay there prone under Nick's fierce grip. The kicking and bucking now subsided from his furious body.

'You're a lunatic, Root. I should break your fucking head. You ever hurt her and you don't ever recover. Got that? I don't make idle threats. Hurt her and I will break you beyond repair.'

Sirens in the distance were quickly getting closer.

'I'll ask you again, what the hell are you doing here?'

'What are *you* doing here?' yelled Root. He seemed impossible to intimidate because his anger was just too dominant an emotion.

'I get to ask the questions, because I'm the one who can really fucking hurt you, and trust me, I'll fucking make mince of your fucking face if you don't talk. So one last time Root, what are you doing here? You'll go to jail for this, you do know that, don't you? You just tried to murder me, you fucking idiot.'

That seemed to re-energize him and he began to thrash his head from side to side, still trying to get free, even though he had to be in excruciating pain, one way or another. He'd taken two kicks in the face, three of the hardest punches Nick could throw and a severe kicking to the balls. Was he on crack? He didn't seem to feel pain like a normal person. Nick raised a fist and held it to his face. 'This is going to break your face, Root. You've got three seconds. One, two.' He raised his fist to shoulder ready to bury it deep into the gross little man's face.

'Alright, alright...I'm here for Davey. I'm helping out Davey James. His wife's in there with that Matt Little bloke. He hates them...I was going scare them into not seeing each other.'

'Davey James sent you?' said Nick, licking the dried spit off his lips.

'I never said that. Did I? Prick.'

Nick looked down the road and saw the blue lights approaching and took his weight off his opponent. As he did so, he jammed his knee into Root's bollocks, making him howl out in pain again. 'Ooops, sorry Rooty, lad.'

Blue lights flashed against the terraced walls. People were looking out from behind net curtains. Soon a uniformed officer was alongside him.

'Tell your gaffer, Colin Harcombe, it's Nick Guymer and Julie Wells and this thing on the ground is Mick Root. He had a Bowie knife, it's over there by the car.'

'He was going to kill Matt Little and Deirdre James and he tried to kill Nick,' added Julie. Root began shouting on hearing that, only to be told to be quiet by the officers.

Root continued to somewhat pointlessly protest his innocence of any crime and was soon handcuffed and put into the back of the squad car, while Julie and Nick gave a detailed account. The policemen knocked on Deirdre's house, but no-one replied. They must have left out of the back door as soon as Matt had arrived. There was a back alleyway which they could have taken to the end of the street and from there disappeared into the night. Maybe they'd seen Root at the door.

After the statements and collection of the knife as evidence, Nick and Julie were allowed to leave and go home. The officers, having spoke to their boss, told them he'd be in touch later. By now it was nearly 1am.

Jeff was eating a large battered piece of haddock at the kitchen table as they got in.

'Ah, there you are. Been out for the night?' he said.

'Sort of,' said Nick, immediately going into detail about what had happened. Jeff let out a bellow of shock when he described Root trying to stab him and the ensuing fight.

'Right, that's it. Root was the hired killer in my shop, not Butcher and I reckon he's done Pallister as well,' said Jeff. 'And now he's after Matt or this Deirdre woman. They must have known he was on the warpath though and they legged it before he arrived. Root is a nutter, even more of a nutter than Butch and he's a woo-woo heed-the-ball. He's also got access to as many knives as he needs.'

'Yeah, he is totally crazed. I could barely subdue him,' said Nick. 'And I battered the shit out of him.'

'I've never kicked anyone in the balls as hard as that, but it didn't seem to make much difference to him,' said Julie. 'Maybe he doesn't have any balls. Maybe that's why he's so angry.'

Car headlights came down the track and briefly shone through a gap in the curtains. Julie looked out. 'Christ, it's Colin, he's never away from here these days. Y'know, I'm getting getting pissed off with all this. Can't we just have a peaceful life? I'm so knackered and I really don't need all this stress.'

Harcombe strode in wearing a dark wool coat and tight black leather gloves. His side-parting was sharp and immaculately defined, despite the late hour, but it didn't disguise the exhaustion in his eyes.

'We meet again and what a day it's been. Murders, attempted murders, it's all a bad, bad business.' The poor bloke was shattered.

Jeff put the kettle on. 'Brew, Col?'

'Please. Yes, Jeff. Thank you.' He sat down heavily and ran his hands over his eyes. 'Never known a day like it. You've had quite a shock too, by the sounds of what my men have told me.'

'You could say that, aye,' said Nick, his knuckles still sore from hitting Root. 'Can you tell us anything about Malcolm's death yet? Was he killed with a knife like it said on the *Gazette* web site? said Nick.

'Yes. Same as Alan. Exactly the same.'

'So it's the same person? Not Jimmy Butcher, obviously, as he's in jail.' said Nick.

'My fear now is that when we charged Jimmy Butcher, we charged the wrong man.'

'Didn't he actually confess?' said Nick. 'I assumed he must have done.'

'No. He said he hadn't done anything at all. Says he was just there to blag free drink. We found ten thousand pounds in used notes on him, though. Clearly payment for something. He wouldn't say where it was from. He refused to cooperate at all. But crucially, we found his thumb print on the knife handle that was used to murder Alan Armstrong. There are another set of prints on it, but we've not matched them to anyone on our records. Could well be from whoever sold him the knife. He said he had no knowledge of the weapon, but that print and your photos were enough to give us the go-ahead to charge him. He offered no alibi, no defence of any sort. He's just clammed shut.'

'Why would he do that if he was innocent?' said Jeff

'Because if he didn't do it, he probably knows who did kill Alan and he fears he'll suffer the same fate if he says anything.'

'So he won't even confirm knowing Mick Root?'

'Not yet. He won't say anything other than to say he didn't do it and was just trying to get free drinks.'

'Root seems an even better candidate for the murders to me. He's a very angry man. He exudes it from every pore. It's like he's angry at everyone and everything and he's bloody powerful little unit as well,' said Nick. 'When he came at me with the knife, he took some knocking down. I had to really clout him.'

'He'd have killed Nick, Colin. He would have if Nick wasn't quick on his feet,' said Julie.

'As long as Butcher keeps quiet and keeps his head down, he'll likely get 25 years, out in ten or 12. That's what he'll be hoping. He sees that as better than the alternative. Plus you've got to remember, he's an old hand at doing time. Someone like Butcher probably prefers inside to outside, anyway. He's spent most of his adult life behind bars,' said the DI. 'Tell me this, were there any other witnesses to this fight with Root, either looking out of their windows, or maybe in another car?'

'Not that we noticed. Not until it was all over. It was really quiet,' said Nick.

'Oh, hold on...I took some footage of Matt Little arriving at the house and I left it running to film Root too. I'll just check that to see if it shows anyone,' said Julie, getting her camera and laptop.

'Hmm, the one of Matt is only 35 seconds long,' she said, clicking the play button. It was very gloomy-looking footage, illuminated only by the orange street lights and showed the Lexus arrive, park, Little get out and knock on the door, the door open, a brief embrace and then the door close behind them.

She replayed it twice. Jeff leaned into the laptop screen and pointed to something at the very start of the recording. 'You're obviously just getting the settings sorted out at the start here, but it's started to record anyway. It's all messy for a few seconds, then you've raised it and filmed the door of the house...but if you go to the very start when you turn it on, it's filming out of the door window. See? There's a car across the road and down a bit. And someone is in it.'

Harcombe asked her to replay it frame by frame.

'Well spotted, Jeff,' he said. 'It's a Mercedes and someone is in the driver's seat...damn it...it's too blurred and happens too quick to tell who it is. It just looks like a smudge of light. Someone is there though.'

Jeff pointed at the screen again. 'Aye, but look down at the bottom there, you've got a partial number plate. DJ 6 something. That's obviously a personalized number plate. Did you see it drive away at any point?'

'It wasn't there when the police arrived and nothing went past us until Root turned up. We got a bit fizzin' distracted after that, so it must have driven off at some point during the fight,' said Julie.

Harcombe got on the phone right away and requested an identification of the plate on the Merc. As he did that, Julie played the video the camera had taken from the dashboard of Root charging down the door. The flash of orange light off the knife blade and Root's lunge at Nick was clearly captured, along with the subsequent fight. It looked more frightening on film: more violent and crazed.

Jeff let out a big 'woah' when he saw Nick swing the three big punches. 'Fuck me. You really gave it to him, brother.' Jeff leaned over and hi-fived him. 'You've got to hand it to the twat, he didn't go down easily and he caught you with a good one. Didn't that hurt?'

'At the time, but I feel OK now.'

'That'd have floored a bloody horse those three right handers. Fuck me. Where did you pull those from? I'm not getting on your wrong side, son. Never seen the like. Bam.'

'I was scared he'd hurt Julie. Lucky I didn't hurt myself badly, really.'

'I was alright, man,' she said, dismissively. 'But lord knows what he'd have done with that knife. He'd have killed both of us if you hadn't battered seven shades out of him.'

'Self-defence would be my definition of that situation. No charges to be brought,' said Harcombe, who reduced every human activity down to police language, if at all possible. 'Tremendous work though, Nick. Full admiration due, I feel. Three magnificent punches. Right from the shoulder.' Men loved a man who could fight. It was another of those awful default male things.

'I thought you'd have pulled Matt in by now,' said Nick.

'The North Yorkshire boys had paid his house a visit this afternoon, but he wasn't there. We'd have got him sooner or later.'

Five minutes later Harcombe got a call.

'DJ 61 is registered to the Urban Renewal Organisation,' said Colin. 'That's the only plate it could be.'

They all looked at each other in the night silence.

'DJ. Davey James. 61 is probably his year of birth. Davey James was spying on his wife,' said Julie. 'That sounds about right. The toe rag. All part of his control freak behaviour.'

'Not just that. He's watching Root go about his business for him. Root said he was there for Davey,' said Julie

'No he didn't, actually. In fact he specifically didn't want to say that when I challenged him,' said Nick.

'So what are you thinking. Nick?' said the DI.

'I'm just wondering if Root didn't do this off his own bat as a favour to James? To get in his good books, perhaps. Why would he lie about it at that moment of maximum stress? He must have already known he'd go down for attempted murder on me, if nothing else. He had no reason to protest unless it wasn't true.'

'But James is there in the car. That suggests he's working under his instruction,' said Harcombe.

'I know. I can't work that out. Maybe its not him in there.'

Harcombe nodded and pinched at his lips. 'I have to say, I don't see him putting his empire at risk for the sake of revenge on his wife. That makes no sense to me.'

'It makes total sense to me,' said Julie. 'He's being driven mental by the removal of his power over his wife. He lives to control people and he controlled her for years and now he can't, so by killing Matt, or having him killed, he's still exerting power over her. That's *exactly* what a man like him would do.'

'That is a convincing theory...' said Harcombe, getting to his feet. '...and one I like, but it is just a theory. I need evidence to prove it and I have no evidence of Davey James even getting so much as a parking ticket, let alone conspiring to have someone killed.'

They'd had just over four hours sleep when Nick awoke to the sounds of Julie being sick again.

As she got back into bed, he reached out for her.

'Only the one puke today. It's an improvement. Hope it doesn't go on much longer, I'll be stripping the enamel off my teeth at this rate and my stomach muscles are sore from the retching.'

He lay for half an hour, but couldn't sleep any more so got up to make tea.

As he waited for the kettle to boil, he put the TV on the BBC news channel. It was the usual litany of intolerance, poverty and violence. Sometimes it was overwhelming. Every day, every month, every year. It was the same shit over and over again. After the goings-on of the previous night, it was hard not to feel that humans were destined to be a cul-de-sac of evolution. Too hell bent on a toxic and contradictory mix of self-destruction in pursuit of self-preservation.

It wasn't so much survival of the fittest, but survival of the richest, to the benefit of almost no-one else. Those with the power were not about to surrender it and it seemed they had successfully managed to turn the people against each other to distract them from greater crimes. What sort of world was this to bring a child into? Was it even responsible to do that? Was it not just massively self-indulgent?

He let out a big sigh and sank down onto the sofa feeling suddenly and profoundly miserable. An innocent, beautiful child, untainted by the dirt of existence would have to grow up and feel this pain and misery. Wasn't it just out-and-out cruelty? Could any amount of love ever counterbalance the evil?

There was no mistaking it. He was sinking into himself, into a depressive state. When it came on him, it felt like going down hill on a slide. You couldn't stop until you had hit the bottom. He took the tea up to Julie and put it on her bedside table.

'Ta. Hey, are you alright?' she said as he turned to go back downstairs.

'Yeah, I'm a bit down, I'll be alright,' he said, not looking at her, knowing she could read his moods in an instant by his body language. The last time he'd felt really low, he'd gone for a long drive. Being preoccupied by the process had seemed to stop his mind from turning inward quite so much. The worst thing to do was give in to the instinct to hunker down and hide away, because it just made him dwell on it even more and get into a circle of loathing and depression, even though, ironically enough, that was exactly what he felt like doing. So after Julie had left for the TW Centre, he got into the BMW, filled it up at a petrol station in Yarm and set off on a meander all over Teesside.

He drove south to the A19 and then took it north, heading to-wards the steel core of the Teesside conurbation, going nowhere in particular. On a whim he took the A1130, a right into Acklam and began to meander around the suburb of Middlesbrough, passing by seemingly endless numbers of plain semi-detached houses on Acklam Road, passing by the crematorium where they had set fire to his father three years earlier. Acklam looked exactly as it had looked 30 years ago, only busier and with bigger, less rusty cars.

Crossing over the A174 Parkway dual carriageway, he drove into Coulby Newham, a small maze of new housing estates, mostly built in the last 20 years to expand the southern suburbs of Middlesbrough. It was all so neat, well organized and tidy, with wide grass verges alongside the road and stands of trees and bushes; not the sort of place that people from outside the region associated with the word Middlesbrough at all. To the outside world, Middlesbrough meant decay, destruction and post-industrial wasteland, if it meant anything at all. And yet here was Coulby Newham, a regular, out-of-the-box gathering of perfectly decent housing estates which could have been located anywhere in Britain.

He got onto Stainton Way and drove at a steady 35mph through more of the southern suburbs of the Boro, taking a left onto Stokesley Road and heading north into well-to-do Marton, another area of the town that didn't match the idea of what Teesside was to the outside world. Leafy, green and prosperous, it stood against the easy cliché of Teesside's permanent decrepitude. He sat at some traffic lights alongside Stewart Park where you could find the cottage in which Captain James Cook was born, the Boro's most famous adventurer who, like the town's steel 100 years later, went all over the world. He ended up being killed in a fight in Hawaii - surely the only Teessider to meet their fate in such a location.

Driving along Marton Road to the A66 and heading west, he reconnected with Teesside's aorta, the A19, and headed north to Billingham, towards the giant, twisting digestive tracts of the chemical industry, driving east on Belasis Avenue on the B1275.

This was what really defined Teesside; bleak industrial waste-lands peppered with smoking chimneys and seemingly infinite metal piping taking god knows what, to god knows where. When he reached Haverton Hill, he headed back west through a mile or two of industrial devastation, but in Nick's state of mind, the bleakness was comforting somehow. Yes, it was ugly and horrible and almost hurt your eyes with the fractured brutality of years of decline and industrial devastation, but all the same, there was something about it that was impressive and almost noble. Tall cooling towers stood like sentries guarding the weave of iron fencing, weed-strewn verges and factory units. A single huge advertising hoarding, incongruously set amongst the industry, displayed a massive picture of a glass of lager, as though saying that the only way to survive all of this was to be drunk.

Tubes of metal piping ran alongside the road. It felt as if you were being digested by a massive industrial robot and these were its intestines. He pulled into a deserted bus stop on Haverton Hill Road, right beside the rectangular skyscraper concrete obelisk that he'd always known as ICI Wilton; still a featureless, almost detail-free icon of Teesside. A dark strip of rain clouds blew overhead on a gathering breeze. He jammed his hands in his pockets and looked around. Smoke poured from a chimney and a huge climbing frame of tubular gas piping was woven against the sky like a metallic tapestry.

It was good. Somehow it was good. It was sodding ugly and dirty and almost abused your eyes when you looked at it, but it was still good. This industry had to exist somewhere and it existed here and you might as well embrace it. It had a power and real presence. God knows, Teesside wasn't the Cotswolds and you wouldn't find vistas like these on any chocolate box - though if it did it'd surely be a best seller in the region. You could see why people had left it behind for prettier places, for nicer locations, for areas that didn't steam and smoke and belch industry. Yeah, you could totally understand that and Nick had done that himself with all his years in the leafy environs of Harrogate. But standing there, on a bleak late winter morning, with the hint of rain in the air and the whiff of noxious gases ever-present, there was something about Teesside that married with his state of mind. A gritty, run-down power that refused to be beaten. A filthy place, ignored or derided and certainly misunderstood, it simply stuck two fingers up at the nice places and the nice people and got on doing its not inconsiderable industrial thing.

He got back in the car feeling, perhaps ironically, that the melancholy had invigorated him a little. Heading west on Portrack Lane, travelling through Stockton town centre, he was soon back on Yarm Lane. Taking the A1027 he headed onto the A66 west and headed out towards Darlington. The local BBC news station went to a live report on the hour.

'Police were called this morning to the offices of the Urban Renewal Organisation. Vandals are said to have broken in, wrecked the office and sprayed graffiti on the walls. Reports from the scene, say a black Lexus was seen driving away from the offices at around 5am this morning. Police say they are following several lines of inquiry.'

A black Lexus. How many where there on Teesside? Not many. You could buy a house on Teesside for the price of a Lexus. That had to be Matt, didn't it? What the hell was he up to? It seemed an odd thing to do. What was the point in vandalizing URO's offices? Did he and Deirdre know Root was after them? They probably wouldn't even know he'd been arrested. It wasn't on the local news. Surely the police would pick him up soon.

Before reaching Darlington he took a turn off, went right around a roundabout and headed back east towards Stockton, taking Sandy Leas Lane onto Darlington Back Lane, now travelling through lovely open countryside. This was another Teesside that outsiders didn't know; a rolling rural landscape that was on the doorstep of so much of the industry for which the region was famous and yet separate and almost bucolic. It didn't last long, maybe a couple of miles at most before reaching the outskirts of Fairfield, but even so, it softened the harsher edges of urban Teesside and was nothing but a pleasure to drive through.

Drovers Lane joined the road from the left and for the first time he could see the new houses built by the Urban Renewal Organisation. A large estate, eventually it would join up with the Western and Northern fringes of Stockton. If you'd lived in some of the region's more dilapidated housing stock, the attraction of this new estate was easy to see. He took a left up an access road and onto the estate itself. They were all fairly generic red-brick modern houses, not especially high quality, but each with a patch of grass at the front and a small garden at the back. There were no shops or any community facilities at all and that made it seem more like a dormitory, but that was probably being churlish and perhaps those things would come in time. Affordable housing was, without doubt, really important and Davey James had made it happen here. People had already moved into some of the properties and had started to make their lives there with ornaments in the windows, curtains draped and pets sitting on doorsteps. It was hard to be cynical about it, really.

He drove around the whole estate and then took a left out onto Drovers Lane and headed back down to Darlington Back Lane. As he did so, a silver car pulled out of the estate road in front of him. It was only when rejoining the main road and he was travelling into Fairfield that he noticed the licence plate. DJ 61. A jab of adrenalin poked into his heart. Who was driving? Was it the same person who had witnessed the fight last night?

He was right behind it. On nothing but a whim, he decided to follow it, keeping a decent distance away so that he couldn't be seen behind the wheel. The Merc took a right down Rimswell Road, an area Nick knew so well from his childhood, when he's spent many summers wandering for miles around Stockton's suburbs in search of something to do. It was incredible how the place looked unchanged from those mid 1970s days. It was like going back in time. Almost by instinct, he knew his way around, the routes embedded into his sub-conscious in those formative days. He went left onto Bishopton Road West, a road he'd walked every day in the late 70s to his old sixth form college. This area had seen a huge expansion of new housing in the subsequent decades. Open fields, replaced by sprawling estates.

The Merc began indicating right. At first he thought the driver had just put the indicator on early for a turn onto Oxbridge Lane, but the Merc slowed and then pulled right into Stockton Sixth Form College, where he had attended 30 years ago. He followed it in, down a driveway to the car park. He pulled into a space in the corner and watched as the Mercedes came to a halt. No-one got out. Nick tried to see who was driving, but couldn't make them out from his angle. The shape of the head looked too small to be Davey James, though he couldn't be sure.

Man, there were some old ghosts here. The car park was much bigger now and there had been some extra buildings added to the college, but by and large it was the same glass and brick, faceless box that it always had been. He'd left in the summer of 1979 with four A levels, a drinking habit and more optimism than experience. It didn't feel that long ago; so close that he felt he could re-experience what it was actually like to live inside that 18-year-old kid's head. Maybe it was an illusion, but he wasn't sure he'd changed much. All the same predilections were already present at that age; all the same inclinations towards introspection and to deal with his depressions with drink and with humour. Still, at least he'd survived and there were times when he thought he might not. So that was a win of sorts. Whoever was in the car was obviously waiting for someone. Ten minutes passed and his windscreen began to get splattered with rain drops as a storm blew in from the west, bringing ink black low clouds scudding across the sky.

Eventually, two lads with hoods pulled up ran out of the college and across the car park, spotted the silver Mercedes and got in. They turned and drove out of the car park. In doing so, it briefly faced Nick. He saw the driver for the first time and he immediately recognized her as Toni James. Next to her was her brother, in the back, presumably a friend. She swung the car onto the college entrance road and headed out, taking a left, doubtless on the way back to their home on The Avenue, a mile away at most. He couldn't see any point in following her any more.

He wound down the window and sat for five more minutes, breathing in the air around his old school, reconnecting with his old self and the life he'd grown up living. Big wet splashes of rain fell onto his lap and across the dashboard. Was it possible that Toni had been behind the wheel outside of her mother's house last night? As he'd said to Colin Harcombe, it didn't have to be her father. In fact, anyone from the URO could have been driving the car.

Back at the farmhouse, he put on the kettle and made tea, feeling a bit less depressed. Before starting a column, he did a quick search for Mick Root on Google. It was a more common surname than he'd imagined, probably of medieval origin. He found his address in Easingwold easily enough. A picture search brought only two results though, both from the *Gazette* archive. He was pictured with several other men at a dinner function, in what was a classic local paper shot and probably of little interest to almost anyone. He squinted at the caption. "The URO Christmas Dinner 2008. Teesside International Hotel." There was a big list of names, but only Root's stood out. Davey James was not there, but it had to prove that Root had worked for, or was connected to his organisation in some capacity.

Julie got home at five, by which time he'd made soup with the leftover chicken carcass and the vegetables used to stuff it.

'Ooh, it's frosty out and that smells wonderful,' she said, giving him a peck on the cheek with cold lips, taking off a scarf. He dished out big steaming bowls of soup and put them onto the oak kitchen table, leaving some for Jeff.

'And how is my loony lover now?' she said, grinding some pepper into the soup. 'Give us a look at you. You look a bit better.'

'I'm alright. Not on top form. Just got to ride it out. This is when

I used to really get the urge to drink myself into a better place. Trouble is, it sort of worked in the short term. If I drank now I'd definitely feel better, but I'd probably get depressed again more quickly. Still, I sometimes still feel like giving it a go.'

'If it's any comfort, I feel like having a big drink, but I'm not going to either. Do you fancy going to the cup replay against West Ham tonight?'

'I don't really. You go with a mate if you want.'

'Nah. I don't care about the FA Cup any more. It's not like it used to be. There's only one thing more annoying than the actual FA Cup and that's people going on about how the FA Cup hasn't lost its magic, when it obviously has.'

'Its best days are well behind it. I actually like the league cup better.'

'Oh hey, I showed the footage of Deirdre to Martha today. She's very concerned. I got the impression she was going to get her to come in and explain herself. Now, I actually looked up the notes on Deirdre James today, which was a bit sneaky really and probably against the rules, but I felt justified given what's been happening and that we almost got killed by a crazy man last night. Honest, man, it's really shocking stuff.'

'Is it? What did it say?'

'That she was virtually a prisoner in the house for the last year or so. He'd always been very controlling and aggressive, but he got worse and worse and he wouldn't even let her have friends. He started to get so paranoid about what she was up to that he actually put CCTV all over the family home! Can you believe that?'

'He did what? To *watch* her? Bloody hell, that's insane.'

'I know. What sort of person would do that? He wanted to know who came and went from the house. I mean, OK we didn't like him, but you'd never for a moment imagine that he was that mad, would you?'

'It wouldn't have even occurred to me that he'd have CCTV in his own home to spy on his own wife. Isn't that illegal or something?'

'I don't know. The kids are at boarding school, but there was a note to say Deirdre hadn't seen them at Christmas because they'd preferred to stay at their schools during the holidays. So it must all have been really bad by then. He'd systematically destroyed Deirdre's self-confidence and undermined her self-worth over years. There was pages on it. Textbook stuff. He's a real wrong 'un. I'm sure she could bring charges against him, but I'm equally sure she won't because the court case would be a nightmare for her.'

'Did you hear the news about the URO offices being vandalized?'

'No. They have Radio 2 on in the office, so I've not heard any local news.'

He explained what he'd heard. There'd been no further update during the day.

'It's obviously Matt though, isn't it?' said Julie.

'Yeah. It must be.'

He explained about following the kids that afternoon. Julie looked at him with a furrowed brow,

'They're obviously going to be damaged very badly by all this. The TW women do classes to support kids and help them through domestic abuse situations. Maybe Deirdre could look into that.'

'The ripples are always going find their way back to shore in that type of situation, I imagine,' said Nick, with a slow shake of his head. 'Maybe they've actually taken against both parents. The dad for being a bully, the mother for having an affair with Matt.'

'Well James was jealous if she even spoke to any other man, going back years. That won't have gone away. Like I said to Colin, he's bound to be furious at her and at Matt. At one point he'd even threatened to harm himself and the kids if she got a job, or had any sort of life for herself. There was also sexual coercion, which we might as well call rape. The only thing he didn't do was hit her and I reckon that was because he couldn't afford to be seen in public with a bruised wife because people would put two and two together. Even when abusing his wife, he had an eye on his public image. But he did nasty things, like give her Chinese burns and pinch her and other things that would hurt, but wouldn't leave a mark.'

'What a bastard. Why is he like that? What's made him into this total monster?'

'More than likely he was abused as a kid by a parent or someone in the family. But that's still no excuse. He has a responsibility to address his problems and not hurt anyone else.'

Nick dwelt on it for a bit. It still shocked him what people got up to in their private lives. You assume all the people in those houses you drive past, are basically the same. Just people getting on with the basics of life. It was hard to grasp that actually, behind some of those doors, behind quite a lot of those doors, the most appalling things were happening and you just couldn't tell. It was all hidden, all covert, all kept under wraps.

'What's been depressing me all day is the idea that we're potentially bringing a little child into this stinking, cesspit of a world. A world which is full of beasts like Davey James and Mick Root and Jimmy Butcher. How do we protect them from that? It feels selfish, Jules. Like we're thinking of what we want and not what the child will have to endure.'

'Humanity would die out if people didn't have kids, man.'

'Hmm. Maybe that'd be for the best,' he said, stirring a spoon around his soup.

She pushed her hair behind her ears. 'Look man, there's no point in thinking life is anything other than a mix of love and hate or nice and horrible or ugly and beautiful. It's always all of those things for everyone. It's the nature of the...of the thing itself...of life, I mean. But look...if everything goes OK, we'll give the kiddie unlimited love and we'll make sure she or he is comfortable and warm and secure. We'll make sure they have fun and learn stuff...they'll have a quality of upbringing neither of us enjoyed. But we can't mollycoddle them or wrap them in cotton wool. They're going to get upset and they'll have their hearts broken. That's what life is.'

He nodded. 'It just seems so unfair though. You're born in a state of innocence and from the first breath you get corrupted by life.'

'Aye, but you also start feeling and experiencing the most amazing things as well. Just think of when you listen to some rock music you love; that feeling you get when all the hairs on the back of your neck stand up. They'll feel that. Or when you smell lavender, or go out on the first warm day of Spring or...well, you know...there's so much physical pleasure in life as well as spiritual and some, like an orgasm, are almost a blend of both those things. That's what being alive is about. You don't get the joy without the pain.'

'I don't want to be thinking of our offspring having orgasms, thank you very much. It's probably illegal.'

She laughed. 'That's more like the healthy you - making a joke of things. Do you know what I mean though? I understand you being worried and I hate what people do to each other as well, but I know that not everyone is like that. You're not like that.' She ruffled his hair.

He groaned. 'Yeah. Yeah I know. I just worry that any goodness is just a veneer, a top layer and underneath is something much less nice.'

She put her bowl on the drainer and filled the kettle.

'You think about things too much...'

'Mam said that the other day.'

'...well, there you go, you probably always have done, especially when you're not feeling so good. You won't solve the problems of mankind, nor of womankind, by sitting there getting upset about it. You'll achieve nowt like that.'

She was right. Of course.

'Come on...let's forget about all this URO and Mick Root business for a bit. Why don't we go to the sports club and play something? Exercise is good for depression. I'll kick your arse at badminton.'

'That's not fair, you're actually good at badminton and I'm terrible. How about table tennis, we're both rubbish at that?'

'Not strenuous enough. Let's play squash. We're about even at that.'

'OK. Yeah. I'm up for that. I can't even remember how to play squash though.'

'Doesn't matter. Basically you thrash the ball as hard as possible until one of us has a heart attack.'

He managed a laugh at that.

The sports club they went to was just off Yarm High Street, a short drive from their house. They got changed into shorts and sports shirts at home.

'These have shrunk,' said Julie as she pulled her black Lyrca shorts on. 'Or my thighs have got bigger.'

She looked at herself in the long bedroom mirror and tugged at them. 'I'm in danger of having a severe case of camel toe, look.' She turned to show him.

'Ow, that looks painful. I'll need a pair of tweezers to get those out of you.'

She pulled a silly face at him and pulled them down. 'I'm putting on my football shorts instead. I'll get arrested if I go out in these. "You come along with me, Ms Wells, we're nicking you for breaking the local labia laws".'

'Well, these things aren't much better, are they?' He said pulling on some sports leggings, designed to stop him tearing a muscle.

She laughed and pointed. 'I can see your willy. I can see your willy.' She chanted it like she was 11 years old. 'Eeee fizzin' hell, lad, put it away. Unless you're planning on touting for trade, I suggest you put your football shorts on as well.'

CHAPTER 12

By the time they got onto the squash court Nick's mood was lifting quite palpably. When he was very depressed, physical activity was almost impossible, it drained all the energy and life out of him. But now he was feeling quite sprightly as they got a game going, gently at first. He was powerful, but Julie was more nimble and kept doing drop shots which caught him out and sent him chasing around the court. She won the first game 11-9, he took the second and third 11-7 and 11-8. The fourth went her way 13-11. They stood panting, hands on hips, dripping with sweat before starting the deciding game.

'You're dead meat Guymer, you old man. There's a new chick in town, baby,' she said, wiping her forehead with the back of her hand and putting her cap back on.

'I'll start actually trying in a minute,' he said, taking a swig of water.

'Eeee, you bloody liar,' she said, swiping at him with her racket. 'Your serve.'

He hit the ball hard and she was at full stretch to make the return, but he was in the middle of the court now and hit a cute ball at half pace into the corner of the court. It was probably the best shot he'd played all night. Julie was fast-footed and lunged forward to return it, again at full stretch, but her touch wasn't powerful enough and he dispatched it on the other side of the court to win the point.

Turning around after his winning shot, Julie was squatting on her hunkers, getting her breath. 'Argh! Argh!' She clutched at her belly, collapsed onto her knees and bent double.

'Jules. Jules...what is it?...is it...is it...?' he couldn't bring himself to even say it. But he knew what it must be. He ran up to her, put his arm around her sweat-soaked back. 'Come on, lass. Can you stand? Come on, let's get you back to the changing room...' She was panting tight little bursts of air, her face contorted as she got to her feet.

'I'm alright. Leave off us. I'm OK. It's gone off. It's gone off...I think it was a cramp or a muscle pull.' She stood upright, stretched out her spine and breathed in deeply. 'Better stop though...' He patted her on the back.

'Are you sure? We can take you to A & E.'

'No. No, I'll be alright. It's not...it's not the baby...'

'Thank god for that.'

He helped her to her feet. They walked slowly out of the court, his arm draped around her shoulder.

'You gave us a right panic up there,' said Nick as they got into the car after showering.

'Sorry man, it hurt like hell.'

'Is it sore?'

She felt around her belly and a bit lower.

'No, but as I was on my own, I let out a big fart in the showers. Maybe it was trapped wind. A wind egg!'

'There's no...err...like...bleeding.'

'No. There's no err like bleeding. I'd have said wouldn't I?' She spoke with impatience. He nodded and said no more.

When they got home she checked on the Boro score.

'Bloody hell, we've won 2-0. Downing and Tuncay,' said Julie, sitting up in bed and looking at her computer. 'Maybe our luck has changed.'

'It's the Boro Jules, all hope exists in the shadow of imminent failure.'

She yawned and put the light out. 'Before that twang happened it was a great game of squash, that,' she said.

'Yeah, I'll be sore in the morning, you pushed me really hard. We've not had a game like that for years.'

She put her arm around his belly and snuggled into him. 'Fancy a bit of fun? Jeff's still out. We could have a quickie.'

'She rubbed up against him and kissed his neck.

'Aw, it's OK. I'm a bit knackered,' he said, knowing it wouldn't sound convincing.

She stopped, turned over and put the light on.

'You never turn the chance of some naughty down. You can usually do it on demand. You're a love machine, Guymer. It's one of your best qualities.' She gurgled a laugh and whispered in his ear. 'Do you want me to put some white undies on or something? Is that it? I don't mind, y'know.'

'No. Don't be daft. I'm just tired.'

She looked at him with narrowed eyes and pushed her hair behind her ears. 'I know what this is all about. You're scared it'll hurt the baby, aren't you? I won't miscarry because of that.'

'Well, yeah, I'm worried I'm too rough or something.'

'You? You couldn't be too rough if you tried. And you're not going to somehow knock the baby out the womb while we're doing it, that's not how it works. You do know that, don't you?'

He scrunched up and pulled a face. She turned out the light and rolled over onto her side. 'Eeee you're a funny lad, you. Well don't say I didn't wave you in. It might be the last chance you get for nine months. I might go right off it.'

'You're more likely to go the other way, knowing you.'

'Don't be so sure. My friend Diane went off it all together and has never got her appetite for it back after the baby was born. Then again, another lass I know was at her husband for it every few hours throughout the pregnancy.'

'That sounds more like your style, Jules. You've always had a bigger sex drive than me, ever since we first met.'

'Aye well, we're both high-performance engines that need a lot of revving to keep us well oiled, if you ask me.'

'Should I be making a witty fuel pump joke at this point?'

'Only if you intend to fill me up.'

'Oh alright. You talked me into it.' She laughed and turned back to him.

They had just finished when a car came down the track to the house and the front door opened. Jeff was late home. He must've gone for a late drink again. As they lay, getting their breath back, they heard him moving around downstairs, in the kitchen and then in the living room and then walking slowly up the stairs.

Something wasn't right. Nick sat up suddenly.

'What?' whispered Julie, quietly. 'Has he got a woman with him?'

He held up a hand to her face to stop her talking. The footsteps stopped at the top of the stairs. Nick leaned into Julie's ear and whispered as quietly as he could. 'It's not Jeff...footsteps are too light.' He put a finger on her lips, got out of bed slowly, pulled on his jeans and walked to the closed bedroom door. The steps outside started again, walking past their door and down the landing to Jeff's small room at the end, opened his door and went in for maybe five or six seconds. Then they came back and stood outside of their bedroom door. He clenched his fist ready to strike whoever it was the face. Should he confront them or let them go if he could? His instinct was to leap in and deal with it. Who was this fucker in their house, violating their sanctity? They'd fucking pay for it.

Julie was now sitting up and listening intently. He held a hand up to keep her back. He didn't want her getting involved in another fight. And that's what it was going to be. He sucked in a big snort of air through his nostrils and in a single move, yanked open the door to confront the form that stood there in the absolute dark of the countryside night, jumped on them and with adrenalin surging into his muscles, hauled them over his leg and threw them down the stairs.

They let out a yell as they tumbled down the steep old stairwell. They tried to get to their feet and escape at the bottom of the stairs. From the sixth stair he jumped onto their back and brought them down in the hallway.

The lights went on as Julie followed him out of the room.

'Alright, alright!' It was a man under him protesting as Nick grabbed his hair and pulled his head back.

'What the fuck are you doing in here? You trying to rob us, you fucker?! Call the cops, Jules!'

He held the man in a tight grip. From what he could see of him, face down on the hallway carpet, he was maybe in his 30s, with dark hair and smelled strongly of garlic. He didn't recognize him at all.

'Alright mate, let us go...come on, I wasn't doing nowt.' He yelled in a strong local accent.

'The fuck you weren't. You broke into our house!'

'The door was open...' he said protested as though this meant it wasn't breaking and entering.

'You've no fucking right...'

That was when a dam of anger burst into his veins again, just as it had when tackling Mick Root. It flooded his whole being with outrage and fierce loathing, so he pressed down hard on the man's neck. He'd fucking have him for this...coming into their lives...a no-good dirty piece of nothing. Just like the rest of the world. The world he wanted to keep from their love, from their child, from their existence. Dirty piece of shit. He stank. He was evil.

The intruder began making a choking noise.

'Aiyazz aiyazz ....you're killing me,' he squealed as Nick pressed down on his neck. Now, squeezing hard, cutting off the man's ability to breathe, a huge surge of adrenalin in his muscles gave him what felt like infinite strength. Nick leaned on him harder, harder...really wanting to hurt the fucker now...the greasy back of the intruder's neck was salmon pink and he began kicking his legs in air, unable to make any more noise as Nick pressed...harder, harder and harder. Full weight on him now, don't stop until he stops; every muscle straining to push air from the man's lungs. One final gasp of life escaped from the dying man's mouth; a horrible, throaty, belch of fear, a fear born from knowing that he wasn't far from the end of his life. Nick spat on him as he made the noise as though expelling evil from himself.

'Nick! Nick, let him up! Let go of him, for god's sake! Nick!' It was Julie. 'Nick! Let go!' She pulled at his shoulders with all her weight, hitting him on the arms to get him to release his fatal grip. 'You're fucking killing him! He's going to die!! Stop it!!!' She screamed it louder than he'd ever heard her scream; a cutting, icy rasp of fear to her voice.

Her storm of fury blew the red fog in his brain away, as her urgent voice permeated his consciousness. He eased up the pressure on the man's neck and with Julie pulling at his shoulders now, he stood up.

She squatted down beside the prone man, inspecting him for life signs and then stood up to confront him. 'What the hell, Nick?! What?! Stand back! Go on! Get back!' She walloped him on his bare chest with the palms of her hands and knocked him back two steps.

He wiped slaver from his mouth and the fear sweat from his brow. Panting, the intense, burning anger now dying down.

'Who is he?'

'Whoever he is, you nearly bloody killed him you stupid, stupid fool!' she yelled.

'He fucking broke in here...' he said, in his defence, pointing at him.

'Are you alright?' she said to the man who was panting arms out stretched.

'He nearly killed me...he nearly killed me...' the man gasped out, still not able to move from where he'd been felled, as he gratefully pulled air back into his lungs.

The man turned onto his side and tried to sit up, swearing as he did so, rubbing at his bruised neck. Julie stood up, hands on her hips, now that the man was obviously going to live, her compassion for his condition turned to indignation and anger.

'What the hell do you think you're doing coming in here like this? This is our home. How would you like someone coming into your house and creeping around in the dead of night?'

The bloke looked exhausted and was obviously in pain.

'I'll fucking sue you for GBH,' he said, almost in tears, jabbing a finger at Nick.

'Yeah, good luck with that,' said Nick. 'Now you're not just a robber, are you? If you are you're bloody shit at it.' From the moment he'd realised it wasn't Jeff, he'd had an idea that this was to do with something other than mere burglary. 'Who sent you here? What did they want? Was it Davey James?'

'Who? I don't know what you're talking about,' the man said, staring at the floor without much conviction. He looked exhausted. 'You're fucking mad, you. You can't just kill someone like that...'

'...oh shut it, if you don't want trouble, don't go breaking into houses,' said Nick, though even as he said it he knew he'd gone too far. In the seconds after he'd let him go, he knew he'd totally lost his mind and now, even though the intruder was still there, he felt bad, he felt guilty and he felt remorseful. What the hell had he been thinking? That was just it though, wasn't it? He hadn't been thinking at all. He'd let out his rage at the world by nearly strangling this man. Another act of malevolent male violence in a world already polluted by it.

'Well you can't have cased this place very well 'cos if you had, you'd have realised we've got sod all worth stealing, unless you want some old bloody records,' said Julie, her face set in a scowl at the both of them, but for very different reasons.

'He's after something, aren't you? What is it?' said Nick, modifying his tone to something less aggressive.

'Well, the police will find out, I'm sure,' said Julie. 'They won't be long.'

Nick stood over him as his enemy sat up, resting his weight on his hands on the floor.

'Look son, this isn't going to end well for you. You might as well help us. No-one even knows there's a house down the bottom of this track. You can't see it from the road. So who sent you here?' Nick said again, gently now.

He shook his head and felt his neck with both hands. 'You nearly killed me. I couldn't breathe. I nearly went...I was a goner, like.'

'Oh don't be a drama queen,' said Julie. 'You didn't even pass out and there's not a scratch on you.'

'You saved my life, you did. He'd have killed me.'

Two police cars came down the track with blue lights flashing.

Julie opened the door and showed two large, thick-set officers in. As soon as they saw the man on the floor they recognized him.

'Darren Harris. I might have known it'd be you,' said one in a Hartlepool accent, as soon as he saw the man sitting on the hallway floor.

'You know him?' said Nick.

'We know him alright,' said the other copper with an amused tone, as though finding this man in someone's house was part of a regular night's entertainment for them.

'He beat me up,' said Darren, pointing to Nick. 'He nearly bloody killed me. He was choking me. I want to make a complaint. He's an animal.'

'Darren, man, getting beaten up is an occupational hazard for you. It happens when people catch you breaking into their houses to nick their stuff,' said Hartlepool, with a lot of sarcasm and no sympathy. 'You look alright to me. There's no blood on you. Stop your moaning, will you?'

'Look at the marks on my neck. He was choking me. He'd have killed me if she hadn't stopped him.'

He pointed at the swollen red bruises on his neck.

'I just jumped on him to stop him...that's all,' said Nick, arms out-stretched, knowing full well that Darren Harris' account was more accurate.

The coppers made a gesture at him to suggest it wasn't a problem. More lights came down the track. This time, the familiar shape of DI Harcombe was at the wheel.

'Sorry to have to be here again. Are you two OK?' he said as he peered in the door.

'Aye go on, ask them how they are. He nearly broke my neck,' said Darren again, now sitting on the floor in handcuffs.

Harcombe took an officer outside for a brief word, came back in and stood over Harris. With a crisp and authoritative tone said, 'OK Darren. No messing around now. Who sent you here? Come on. Let's have it. What were you told to get hold of? I know you, you wouldn't come out here to steal from a place like this unless you'd been told to. This isn't your usual patch.'

But Harris wasn't saying anything. Harcombe let out a sigh of contempt. 'If you want to play games with me Darren, you'll find me extremely unsympathetic. This is important. You're not a bad lad, not really. Just spit it out. You know you're going to tell me sooner or later. Make it sooner, lad.'

Harris looked resigned to his fate and shrugged. 'It was just some bloke I met in the Garrick. I don't know who he was. Someone had told him about me.'

'He must have been new to the area because everyone here knows about you already Darren. They know you're possibly Teesside's worst thief. And what did he say?'

'He said he wanted some photos of a party that you'd taken,' he nodded at Julie. 'He said they'd be on a card in the camera and probably on a laptop as well. Told me to take both. That's it mate...honest.'

'Did you get them?'

'I got the card from the camera in there,' he pointed to the living room. 'Mind, I didn't even swipe the camera...I left it, I never took nothing...couldn't find the laptop though. I thought it'd be in a bedroom.'

'Did this mystery man say why?'

'No. He just came up to us, said someone had told him I was up for a bit of robbing, said he wanted the camera card and the laptop. That's it.'

'And what did he look like?'

Darren Harris looked around at Nick. 'He sort of looked like you, only a bit fatter. I swear I don't know his name, I don't know who he is. Looked well off, so I thought I'd have some of his dosh. He's paying us 500 so it was good money, like.'

'He looked like me?' said Nick. 'How like me?'

'Scruffy longish hair, about your height. Unshaven.'

'This man gave you our address?' said Julie.

'He told us where you lived, aye...'

'But you knew we were home didn't you?' said Julie, 'Why break in when we're here?'

'...especially as you are terrible at this sort of thing, Darren,' said Harcombe.

'He was in a hurry. Said he wanted them tonight. I was supposed to meet him in town when I'd got them. The front door was open...what do you expect if you leave your front door open? I thought my luck was in.'

Harcombe looked on with a shake of his head.

'Right Darren, I'd like you call this chap - you have his number I assume - and tell him you've got the card and laptop. Give me the number.'

'It's in my shirt pocket.'

Harcombe took out a piece of paper, copied down the number and handed it to his men then uncuffed Darren Harris and gave him his phone.

'Right. Do it,' he said. 'Arrange to meet him outside of Stockton Town Hall right away.'

They stood and watched while he dialled the number, looking quite sheepish.

'Alright mate...aye, I've got them.' He listened. '...how about outside the town hall? Half midnight? Bring the cash, yeah?'

'Well done. You're a better liar than you are a thief, Darren,' said Harcombe. His two officers laughed at that.

It was just after 11.30. They took Darren away.

'Right. Leave this with me,' said Harcombe to Nick and Julie in their kitchen. 'We shall see who turns up.'

'Who do you think it is?' said Julie

'I don't do guesswork unless I really have to, but I'm hopeful this is the break-through we needed.'

'Hey Col. What was that about the URO offices being vandalized this morning? Was that Matt Little? The Lexus...'

The policeman threw up his hands. 'As if we don't have enough on our plate. Truth is we don't know. We got an anonymous call reporting the break-in and the Lexus. We got there to find "Davey James - colon - Murderous Bastard, full stop", written on the walls in black paint. It's rare to get graffiti so well punctuated. Maybe the local scruffs are better educated these days.'

'Matt is well educated,' said Nick.

'Indeed. Trouble is, if it was him, I'm inclined to agree with his conclusion in some ways, if not his method of communication.'

'You think Davey is behind the two murders?' said Julie.

'That would not surprise me at all, but I have no evidence to back up this old copper's gut feeling.'

'What gut feeling is that then, Col?' said Julie.

'I won't trouble you with it now.'

'No. Go on. I'd like to know,' said Nick.

Harcombe waved the remaining officer away.

'Well, because you've been so crucial to all this, I'll share my thoughts. Now, this is mostly supposition, but I think James' financial investment in Tees Digital is crucial to this. I've got some men working on this angle...'

'...are they all men or are some women working on it as well? Sorry...it's just that...'

'Err...yes there are women too...yes, men and women.' Harcombe looked puzzled at her interjection, then continued. 'Somehow, I believe these deaths will financially benefit him.'

'What about his divorce?' said Julie. 'I'm sure that's in the mix, too.'

'Indeed. I'm working on that side too. Money and marriage. Two of the oldest motivations for criminality in the book. Plus, and I wouldn't say this to anyone else, I just don't like the man. Now, a word with you Nick.' Harcombe stood right in front of him for a moment and put his hand on his shoulder, looking into his eyes with a stare that wouldn't let him look away.

'Don't think I don't know what happened here tonight. I don't want to have to arrest you for assault or worse, even if it is on a toe-rag like Harris and you're lucky he's not the brightest of sparks, because if he really did want to bring charges...well...you understand?'

'...but I was just defending...'

Harcombe wagged a leather gloved finger at him and shook his head. 'No, no. Doesn't matter. Proportionate aggression, that's what you're allowed. The bruises on his neck, I know what they mean well enough, I've seen it plenty of times.' He pinched his forefinger and thumb together so there was a small gap between them. 'You were this far away from a serious problem. Right? No more of this. My tip? Understand your own strength, hmm? I can see all too clearly that you're a big, strong lad these days. More powerful than most. With power comes responsibility. Understand?'

Nick nodded and looked at the ground.

'Good lad,' said Harcombe, slapped him on the top of his arm and left.

As soon as they were alone, Nick turned to Julie.

'I'm so sorry, Jules.'

She looked warily at him and shook her head. 'That was *so* scary, man. You got carried away with yourself. What got into you?'

'I was angry and...and...and I was thinking of the baby and of you and of the fact we'd just been making love and how this was all like the opposite of all that...I just lost it...I can't really explain. I was furious at everything.'

She didn't say anything for a while, walking into the kitchen to put the kettle on while he went to put a shirt on. When he had returned she said,

'It was frightening someone being in the house, but you'd totally over-powered him and he couldn't move and you *were* going to kill him, Nick.'

He nodded. She was right. There was no defence to be made. He'd gone over the top and not just lost his temper, he'd briefly lost his mind. He walked away from her feeling ashamed. 'See what I was saying about what is under the nice veneer...'

She let out a big gasp of exasperated air. 'Well...there's nothing we can do about it now. We'll deal with it later,' she said, pushing her hair behind her ears in a no-nonsense fashion. 'I wonder where

Jeff has got to? He's later than usual.'

'I want to know who told that bloke to rob us, shall we go into town and watch what happens?'

She scrunched up her face. 'Colin would not be pleased.'

'He doesn't need to know. We can park on top of the Castlegate centre and watch what happens from up there. No-one will see us. Come on, man. I can't just go back to bed now, not after all of this.'

She sighed. 'Alright. I want to know as well. Just don't lose your rag again. Right? I won't visit you in jail. You're going to be a father, don't forget. You need to...'

'I know. I need to be a good example.'

'It's not just that. You need to be here and not banged up for breaking someone's head. You were lucky I was here, next time I might not be and that'll be that. You'll be inside for 25 years.'

He knew she was right and he knew he'd have to sort it out, somehow. Maybe more therapy was the answer. Trouble was when he thought of having to do some sort of anger management class, it just made him feel angry at himself.

It was quiet drive into Stockton town centre in Julie's car, the roads devoid of traffic, except for the occasional taxi. The town hall was a local landmark, sitting in the centre of the High Street, it had been the focus of attention since the 18th century, when it was built. The High Street had been built up and knocked down around it several times.

She parked on the roof top of the monstrous 1970s shopping centre. A wall surrounded the roof top, looking over it and down to the High Street below, it was the perfect place to watch what was going to happen.

At 12.25, Darren Harris walked up to the old building; presumably he'd been dropped off by the police. Nick looked up and down the length of the street, but couldn't see any police around yet knew they had to be somewhere.

It was a bizarre feeling to see the man who had so recently been in their house, the man he'd nearly choked the life out of just standing there looking around him then lighting up a cigarette. He kept rubbing his neck.

'I bet Colin is in that car down there,' said Julie, pointing to a mid-sized Ford parked up across the street from the town hall.

12.30 nothing. 12.35 still nothing. 12.40, a man crossed over from the other side of the High Street and looked to be walking up to Darren, but he passed him by without a glance. 12.43 and a Lexus pulled up in front of the town hall. It stopped. Even as it did so, Nick recognized who it was. His heart leaped into his mouth. The headlights went out as the driver took the keys out of the ignition and opened the door. Darren Harris turned to look at the person getting out. It was Matt Little, dressed in a suede coat.

'Jesus Christ. It's Matt. It's Matt! What the hell is he doing?' said Nick. 'He never sent that scumbag to our house to rob us, did he...or did he?'

'What on earth does he want my photos for? What's it to do with him? He wasn't even there, was he?'

'No. He couldn't make it. He was invited but he got held up. He told me and Jeff that himself. I just don't get it. The fucker. Fucking bastard sending a shit like that to our house. Christ, you think someone's alright and they turn out to be a total fucker. Oh God. Nothing would surprise me about him now, all the way up to murder. He probably did kill Pally. I give up on trying to know what anyone is like, he was so nice in the shop.'

They watched as Harris held up the SD card. Matt Little took it from his hand. As soon as he did so, four officers got out of cars parked within 20 yards and ran over to him. There was no time for him to make an escape and he didn't even try. Harcombe strode up after them, emerging from the black Ford, and led their man away without a struggle, droving off with him towards the police station.

As they walked back to the car, Julie leaned on the door. 'We need to look at those photos and see if we can see what it is that he's so worried about. If he was concerned enough to try and have them stolen, they must show something he doesn't want seen.'

Nick stopped and stood by the car, looking out across the orange glow of Stockton High Street.

'Hang on, hang on, you know what's weird? How did he know you'd even taken photos? Like you said, he wasn't even there, so how would he even know? Neither me, nor Jeff mentioned it.' He scratched at his stubble and rubbed his wrist which was throbbing after colliding with the bannister.

She scratched her eyebrow. 'Yeah. That's mad, isn't it? Who told him?'

It was one in the morning when they got home. Jeff was still out.

'He must have gone to a club,' said Nick as he made some tea. 'He'll be annoyed to be missing all the action. You know what he's like, he loves a bit of bother.'

Julie put the photos back on the TV screen and set them on slideshow. He joined her on the sofa and handed her a mug.

'I feel like I've seen these a hundred times,' said Nick as they ticked over one photo after another. She stopped it at the last one with Jeff emerging from the back room.

'I keep coming back to this one', she said, sipping at the tea. 'Since we first saw them I've felt like this is the most important one because it's really the only one to show anything different. The rest are the same group of people moved around a bit, photo after photo. The only exceptions are when Jeff comes out and before that when you walk in.'

He knelt in front of the TV and began counting the number of people in the room. 'There are 27 on this photo and 26 on all the others, was that right?'

'Yeah. Jeff was number 27.'

'No!' He yelled. She sat back, surprised. 'We're bloody stupid Jules, we've fucked up here. We've been so stupid. That can't be right, can it?'

'Why not? You've counted them yourself.'

'Yeah, but if there's 26 in all the others, someone must have left when I came in or there'd be 27 when I arrived, 28 here with Jeff. Go back to the start. We've made a mistake, Jules. Someone leaves at some point before I come in.'

The first six photos showed everyone, with the fish eye lens covering the room from doorway to counter and the back room door beyond. People stood at all angles, some were blurred as they were moving when the shutter fell. He sat and counted them again. Definitely 26.

'Right. Here I am for the first time,' he said pointing to himself entering the shop. 'I'm two maybe three strides in here. I'll just count again...' He put an index finger on each head including his own. '26. There's 26. There should be 27 now because Jeff is still behind the back room door with Rita.'

'OK, let's put the first one with you in it on screen and the last one without you, next to it.'

She arranged the photos and then sat back to look in detail and recounted 26 people.

'The fish-eye gives these the look of an album cover from the mid 60s,' said Nick. 'A bit like the Byrds', *Mr Tambourine Man'.*

'Let's tick each one off from one to the other. Start at the far right of the later photo. OK this guy here, the bald one...yup, he's in the earlier one. The fuzzy ginger here, definitely in the other shot, woman with long straight hair...'

'...yes, she's in...as is the blonde guy here.'

They went through each person and found them in both photos. Each was matched up. But by the time they'd identified over 20, it was clear one was missing. In the short space of time between photos, one had certainly left when Nick had arrived.

'This one in the foreground is the trickiest one,' said Julie, a Biro in her hand, pointing at a blur of brownish hair right in the foreground of the first picture. It was the back of someone's head without any detail of their clothes and they were on the move. It was just the back of the head. 'I thought this was him on the later one.' She pointed to a man who was now further away. Skipping from one photo to another, it just looked like he'd stepped forward a couple of paces.

'I can see why you thought that. Initially, I did as well...he looks similar, but it isn't and I'll tell you how I know. See here...the crown on his head in the first one is towards the back, but this later one is further forward. They're very similar, but it's not the same person. I think the later one is actually this bloke...' he pointed to the screen. 'Yes it is...he's got a blue shirt on...you can just see the collar edge on it here, but it's more clear in the later one.'

'So shaggy here is the missing man. According to the timer on the photo, there were eight seconds between these two photos for him to leave. But he must have walked past you as you came in and walked past at pace as well. Can't you remember anything?'

'I just can't. Someone did push past me. I guess it was him. But you know what I'm like, when I'm in my own head I don't notice anything.'

Julie folded her arms across her chest and sat on the floor right in front of the TV, just staring at the photo of the missing man. She went back to the computer and put the four pictures that preceded it on screen.

'Where is that man on these shots?' she said, waving her hand at the screen. There are 26 people on here, you're not in, so he must be on here. He's not right in front of the camera now. Let's match people up again with the later picture...c'mon, it won't take long. This is crucial.'

As they began to tick people off, looking at the picture in detail, it was clear which person it was. It was a man wearing a brown suede jacket. He had his back to the camera in all the shots, but it had to be him.

Nick chopped out the images they had of the man. There were three, all almost the same. As he arranged the edits on the screen, the sound of a car coming down the track made Julie jump to her feet and look out the window. 'It's Jeff in his van.'

The front door opened and Julie went to meet him. 'Man, you have missed one hell of a night. Where've you been?'

'Went out to Darlo with Big Fish. He's bought a restaurant out there and insisted on playing mein host. Got talking to a nice woman...and...one thing led to another...I went back to hers...what's been going on, like?'

'You've been shagging again?' said Nick.

'I believe culturally uncouth types refer to it like that, yes,' he said and pulled a face at him, then turned to look at the big TV screen.

'Why are you looking at pictures of Matt Little?'

Julie yelped and put her hand to her mouth. 'Fizzin' hell Jeff, is that Matt?'

'Yeah. Obviously it is. You didn't recognize him from behind?'

'I hardly know him. I only saw him at your shop for the first time in 30-odd years. I know him a bit from the front, but not from the back. I thought he had shorter hair than this. In fact I'm sure he does, doesn't he Jules?'

'He has now. Or he did tonight. He may have had it trimmed since I took these a week ago. I didn't recognize him because I've never even seen him close up. I've only seen him behind the wheel of that Lexus, in the dark at Middleton St George and then tonight at a distance when he was arrested.'

'When he was arrested! What?!'

They went over the events of the evening in detail. Jeff was slack-jawed at what had happened.

'This Darren Harris bloke, I think his dad is Charlie Harris. He was a couple of years above us at Ian Ramsey. His nickname was 'Chopper' after the Chelsea player and because he was also a violent sod. Him and that lunatic called Smezza. Remember?' said Jeff.

'Oh god, yeah. They were the sort of lads that had a full beard by 16 and a full prison record by 18.'

'Our Kev had a legendary fight with Smezza on the Hardwick estate. We could've sold tickets for it. Kicked seven shades of shite out of him,' said Julie. 'God knows what it was about, but they planned it well in advance. Mam even told Kev to go and sort him out and not to come back a loser.'

Jeff said. 'I'd liked to have seen that, mind.'

'It was horrible. Kev was a sod when it came to fighting. He'd take anyone on. He was an angry young man. Still a fairly angry middle-aged man, come to think of it. '

Nick instantly felt guilty for his behaviour that night, echoing those days.

'The thing is, right, Matt said he couldn't make it to the party, but he *was* there...this is him...' said Nick pointing to the screen. 'Why lie if he's nothing to hide? Why is evidence of him being there so important to hide that he tried to steal these images?'

'Well, I never saw him there and I would have recognized him because unlike you, I'd met him a few times to give him records. He'd come down to the Harrogate shop.'

'He left as I came back in with Alan's football programmes, didn't he? We don't know when he arrived, but I'm guessing he arrived when you were in the back with Rita and left before you came out. So you didn't see him. But this has to be why he sent Harris around here to get the photos. It must be. They reveal he lied and is trying to cover something up.'

'He's an idiot if he didn't realise you'd have copies and that the cops would have copies too. Hardly the work of master criminal, probably because Matt isn't a master criminal,' said Jeff. He stroked his beard thoughtfully for a minute and raised an index finger. 'I've got it. He actually came as planned to the party but when he got there, he's seen Jimmy Butcher. He knows Jimmy from school, just like we do. For some reason he takes fright at this. Maybe he knows or suspects someone is out to get him...'

'...someone like Davey James, whose wife he's having an affair with,' said Nick.

'Exactly. He thinks James has sent Butcher in there to get him, so he's legged it right away.'

Nick sucked on his lips, mulling over all the theories, chewing on his beard stubble.

'He was killed after the photos and when the back room was empty. I reckon Butcher looked at me, maybe wondering if I was the one he wanted, because me, Al and Matt all have longish straggly hair. Alan's been out of the room, he comes back in and is then spotted by Butcher who makes the mistake of his and Alan's life, thinking he's Matt. James has paid him to kill him for taking his wife. So he follows him in and does the job.'

'That's possible. Matt can't have killed Alan, because he left before that happened,' said Julie.

Jeff raised his finger. 'Before we *think* it happened. I'll tell you what though, Matt Little is not some sort of hard-nosed criminal. He'll 'fess up everything he knows to Colin. I just don't see him shouting "you'll never take me alive, copper", do you?'

'That's what I find weird, he's a regular bloke, not some toe-rag type. He seems too, for want of a better word, normal, to be mixed up in murder and criminality. He's nice to chat to, he's friendly, he's, like I say, just normal,' said Nick, hands in pockets, scuffing the pile on the carpet up with his toe.

'It's like I keep saying though, isn't it? Life is all about actions, not just words,' said Julie.

Nick brooded. What did that say about him? He'd just nearly killed a man. What sort of fucked up weirdo was he? He was full of nice, soft words, but look at what he'd done. Suddenly he felt utterly exhausted.

CHAPTER 13

They were all up late, but by 10am had demolished a breakfast of kippers and scrambled egg and the whole house smelled of smoked fish. Jeff went off to the shop. Nick loaded up the dishwasher. Julie wasn't due into TW until 11, so she made coffee and watched him clear up.

'It's bloody great not to throw up again,' she said, pressing the cafetiere plunger down.

'Any twinges from last night's game?'

'My legs are a bit sore and my shoulders. We should do that more. It was fun.'

'Yeah, it was.'

'Do you hurt?'

'Not from the squash.' His wrist was now bruised purple and still throbbed a bit. 'Jules...'

She looked up at him. 'Yeah?' He put in a dishwasher tablet, wiped down the sink and draining board. 'What is it?' she said.

'I still feel terrible...about last night...about choking him...y'know...I feel like I'm a monster. Like there's something bad inside of me that is just waiting, biding its time until it can show itself again. All this violence, first Root and then Harris...it's sucking all this horrible shit out of me and up to the surface.'

She exhaled through her nose and folded arms and bit her bottom lip and stared at the kitchen table.

'I mean, after everything you've talked about in these last few months, I feel like I'm part of the problem. Part of the macho bullshit that we talked about at the Boro. The evidence is in.'

She shook her head slowly.

'Alright, alright...I don't want to gloss over this, but let's not forget that last night you were under a lot of pressure. A man had broken into our house and you had no idea how dangerous or otherwise he was. You held onto his neck for, what, ten seconds longer than you should have? It's wrong. I'm not saying it isn't -

you had lost it and you need to work out why that is and deal with it. But it is, to a degree, understandable. He broke in here. He's the guilty one. I doubt any court would convict you for taking that sort of action against a burglar. Most people wouldn't have had the courage or strength to do what you did. Most people would think you were a bloody hero. Same at the Boro. Yes, you should've walked away and not been confrontational or physical, definitely, but those blokes were horrible. And it was me who gave the bloke a dead leg and pushed him over. You didn't actually hit anyone, you did show *some* restraint. But these were not innocent victims. It's not the same as someone like...like Davey James bullying his wife, for example. Not at all.' She shook her head again and wrapped a long strand of loosely curled blonde hair around her finger.

'It's just a matter of degree...I might be on the other end of the scale, but I'm still on the scale and I don't want to be. I want to be better than that and I think I should be. So much shit happens because of men's aggression and I'm just perpetuating that, aren't I?'

She cocked her head, raised an arched eyebrow and looked at him with an expression of exasperation.

'Well, I fail to see what the hell you could have done other than give Root a damn good hiding. That man is a beast. Seeing you kick him in the face was mag-bloody-nificent and I won't be told otherwise. He got hold of me and would have hurt me, probably badly, and you nearly knocked his head off his shoulders. Just standing there and asking him not to be so horrid would have been no damn good at all. He bloody deserved it in my book. You were defending yourself and me against a lunatic and you did it brilliantly.'

He obviously looked doubtfully at her because she looked away from him with an expression of total disdain.

'Oh for god's sake. Enough of this doe-eyed crap. You've got to see these things for what they are and not...I don't know...martyr yourself to some stupid, perceived notion of feminism or masculinity or...oh, I don't know, Nick...you're a man...a red-blooded man...all sweat and spunk and sodding muscle...for good and for bad. If you weren't then god help you, Root would have gutted you like a fish. You saved your life and probably mine as well. If you reserve your violent streak for people like him, I'll not be complaining. I'll try and stop you murdering someone innocent. And that's a bloody joke by the way. Seriously though, talk to Marc Lewis about it if you like, get it out at your next therapy session, but don't drag your guilt about it around our lives like a sorry-looking dog. You do my head in sometimes, you really do.'

She stood opposite him with her hands on her hips now, frowning.

'Get over yourself man. I'm not going to sit here all day and tell you how great you are, so stop pouting like a spoilt kid, pull your bottom lip in and deal with it. Neither you, me or life is perfect and no-one ever said they would be, did they? No, so suck it up and let's crack on, eh?'

He was beaten into submission by her remorseless logic.

'Right. I'm shutting up about it now then,' he said, doing the zipping mime that her mother so often deployed after being told off by her daughter.

'About bloody time.'

They tidied up the kitchen and Nick went to the toilet. When he came back he said, 'What a weird night though. We'd been having a nice session just before that all kicked off.'

'Ah ha. I've been trying to find the right time to tell you something about last night,' she began laughing loudly.

'What's so funny?'

'When I was chasing you down the stairs...' She paused to laugh again, throwing her head back, '...when I was chasing you down the stairs, I still had your love gravy in me...it was dribbling down me legs as I ran!' She hooted again '...I was trying to get you to stop choking him, while wiping at it with my pyjamas pants! It was all cold and sticky. Horrible.'

Nick bent double laughing at her. 'Love gravy? Good grief,

woman. I was so focused on killing him I never noticed that.'

'I was just hoping I wasn't going to have to sit on him, 'cos it'd have been a bit messy and he'd have sued us for some sort of act of abuse. And then the coppers came and I was worried I'd have big wet patches on display. Thank god they were dark pants or it'd have looked terrible. Oh bloody hell, you never see women have this sort of problem in films do you?' She rubbed tears from her eyes with a thumb. 'God, what a life. It's great if you don't weaken, eh.'

Julie had just left for work when Nick's phone rang. It was DI Harcombe, now sounding absolutely exhausted.

'Nick. Forgive me being brusque, I've been up all night so I'll get straight to the point. There have been significant developments and I need your help.'

'In what way?'

'I need you to help me.'

'Me? Why me?'

'Because I trust you and you are in the best position to move quickly on this.'

'Are you sure?'

'Very.'

'You arrested Matt, what did...'

'...how do you know that? Oh. I think I can guess. I might have known you'd be somewhere.'

'Sorry. I feel involved. I am involved. Hugely.'

'Yes, well. This is the problem. I am now under massive pressure.' He let out a sigh and seemed to be moving papers around on his desk. 'It absolutely looks to me and to my superiors that Matt Little is our man. He killed Alan Armstrong and Malcolm Pallister. I have as good proof as I need to charge him right now.'

Nick's stomach dropped.

'Bloody hell. Really?' He sat down, feeling a bit weak at the knees.

'I'm afraid so.'

'But he seems such a nice, regular guy. What about Root's attack on me and, potentially on him?'

'Forget about Root for now.'

'Are you holding him?'

'Oh yes. We're charging him with attempted murder later today. But I think you had it right about him. The bloody man is a public menace - a knife-wielding idiot. However, I'm not convinced he is anything other than a violent weirdo and a lone wolf. I think he's confusing our picture by trying to play the role of hero for Davey James, off his own bat. He's not been paid by anyone to do anything. In fact, he's on the verge of bankruptcy.'

'So what has Matt told you about why he wanted our photos?'

'That he went to Jeff's party as planned, was only there briefly and didn't know anyone. He couldn't find Jeff. Well, we know why that was. But he took off as soon as he saw Jimmy Butcher, who he knew worked for James as hired muscle. Don't forget he was, to some degree, on the inside of the URO as a major investor. So he knew, also to some degree, how James runs it.'

'Did he think Jimmy was going to kill him?'

'Deirdre had told him that Butcher "leaned on" people for Davey James. She knew what he was like and that he'd try and exact some sort of revenge on Matt once he knew they were together. Matt reckons it'd be someone like Butcher who would be sent to do that. We do know that James has a coterie of security people that seem to follow him around in one way or another. Butcher seems to have been one of those people. He worked as a security guard on various URO building sites along with a few other ex-convicts, all of whom have been inside for violent crimes. Matt says he didn't think Butcher would kill him, just intimidate him, but he didn't want a fight, so he left. Then he remembered Julie had taken the photos. He panicked and thought it would look bad that he'd lied about being there, especially after he found Pallister dead. Someone in the Garrick told him Darren Harris was always up for a bit of burglary, so Little told him where you lived. He says he didn't really think it through and had no idea Harris is such a loser.'

'That sounds like it could be true.'

'It could be, though it sounds a bit weak to me, but I know people panic and do silly things. However, there are a couple of important things to consider.'

'What's that?'

'Alan Armstrong owed Matt Little one hundred thousand pounds.'

'What?!'

'Alan was actually a partner in Tees Digital. He put in 200 thousand, 100K of which came as a loan from Matt. Pally took 500K off him. He was the network's major investor. Returns looked certain. The DAB revolution seemed to guarantee good advertising revenues, but it just hasn't transpired.'

'Has Matt told you this?'

'Well, we put it to him and he admitted it. We had all the proof in the paperwork, anyway.'

Nick ran his hand through his hair and pulled at a knot. 'That's amazing, Matt didn't even give us a hint of any of this when we met him. In fact, to all intents and purposes, he made out that Alan was a stranger to him. But that still doesn't make Matt a killer, does it?'

'No. It might give him motive. But there is now much more hard evidence against him. He might have left the party when Julie took the photos, but he had plenty of time to come back in and do the crime and then leave again. Both knives left in Alan and Pally were absolutely covered in his fingerprints. We've had the matches done. Those prints I told you about, they were all his.

'Christ almighty. Are you sure? I thought you said you got Butcher's print on the one in Jeff's back room?'

'We did. One thumb print. But as soon as we took Matt's last night, we made the match on both knives. He's held those knives.'

'How does he explain the prints?'

'He says Root once showed him some Bowie knives in his shop in Easingwold and suggested he pick them up to feel their weight, which he did. He says that's how the prints must have got on them.'

'But you don't believe that?'

'It's what someone in his position would say. It's certainly not provable, which is why a guilty man would offer it as a defence. Root denies it ever happened, but that man is as dishonest as they come. But there's more evidence against him. Pally's secretary had a call from someone saying not to go in that morning. We looked at that call and it was from Matt's phone.'

'Christ. How does he explain that?'

'He says he left it somewhere last week. Couldn't remember where.'

'That could be true. Actually, he told me that as well.'

'Did he? Interesting. It could be true then, but it is also exactly what every criminal I see would say. They're always losing phones. You wouldn't believe it. But the problem is, he *was* at Pally's office. He says he walked in and found him dead and then called us, but there's no evidence yet that anyone else was there that morning. If someone else did it, they did it purposefully to frame Matt. Only his prints are on the knife found in Pally.'

'God. That does look bad.'

'However, if he is telling the truth, as I say, it means someone has set him up and who would want to do that?'

'Davey James? Matt is having an affair with his wife, after all.'

Harcombe grunted loudly. 'Ah. Glad you said that name.'

'So why do you need me?'

He went quiet again.

'Something isn't quite right. Call it an old copper's instinct if you will. I've banged away killers all my life both up here and down in the Met. Matt Little isn't a killer, not to me. He's no history of violence and there's not a hint of any criminality. He also doesn't need the money he's owed. We know he's got a couple of million in UK accounts, probably more abroad. He's also been very co-operative, has had no run-ins with the police before and is suitably scared witless by being pulled in. I'm not naïve, I know men can be deceptive, but I'm not wrong often. Also, he's not a stupid man, why not wear gloves if you're going to kill two men? Why use a traceable mobile phone to make that call? Why call us from the office after you've killed him? Why go to the URO offices in such a distinctive car and vandalise the place? All of those could just be naïve mistakes made by a quietly angry man. One mistake, maybe, but not three big mistakes. Not for a clever man like Little.'

'Yeah. That is all woefully stupid.'

'Still, people do odd things and I've known men kill people and want to get caught. It's far from unlikely. But all the same, it just doesn't feel right to me and I'd like to rule out the possibility that he's being framed and if he is being framed, Davey James is the man who is in the best position to do so.'

'And that's where I come in?'

'Yes.'

'Is this going to be dangerous?'

He didn't pause for a moment. 'We will minimize all risks, but it might be, yes. I'll tell you why. James is inscrutable. He keeps his friends close and his enemies closer. We don't know which of those he considers you. You may have to spend some time in the lion's den, as it were.'

Before, he wouldn't have hesitated. Now, he felt differently.

'I don't know. I'll have to talk to Julie.'

'Fine. Then come and see me and I will brief you. Can you come to the station this evening, say seven?'

'I guess so.'

'I'll explain everything in full later.'

'OK, Col.'

'Good man.'

He called Julie to tell her this news.

'Listen, I'll come from work and I'll meet you there. I don't want you just agreeing to anything. You don't have to do the police's work for them, especially if it's dangerous. Why should you? He shouldn't even be asking you,' she said.

'Wouldn't it be the right thing to do?'

'You're just saying that because of yesterday. I know you, you're just trying to make amends. Don't agree to anything until I'm there. Right?'

'OK, Jules.'

He went into town and took coffee into Jeff. He was perched atop his stool, as ever, sifting through a large pile of records that someone had brought in.

'Ah ha. You must have read my mind. Is that a black Americano with an extra shot in it?'

'It is indeed. And is that a first pressing of *Disraeli Gears* on top of your pile?' He put the coffee down on the counter.

'Yup. Worth £100 if it's in decent condition...' He slid the record out of its psychedelic sleeve, '...and it isn't. It's knackered. Typical.'

'Give us a look...that'll play on my deck...'

'It looks like a hedgehog has been having sex with it, man,' Jeff said, holding the record to the light.

'Yeah, well so do I. I've not got a first pressing. How much do you want for it?'

'Here. Take it. I don't want anything.' He thrust it at Nick.

'Are you sure?'

'Yeah. Probably not worth as much as this coffee cost.'

'Cool. How's sales today?'

'Quiet apart from the two hundred quid I took for a nice original copies of' *My Generation* and *A Quick One...*'

'Amazing how The Who still sells so well.'

'Never hangs around long. Same with Bowie and The Beatles and Queen. People are mad for Queen. Don't understand it myself.'

'The first two albums are excellent.'

Jeff winced, 'It's all a bit sub-Zeppelin to me, but I'll happily sell them. Youngsters come in for them. Well, by youngsters I mean people in their early 20s.'

'Hey, I'm off down the cop shop at seven. Harcombe wants me to help him get some evidence.'

'Eh? Can't they do that themselves? They're the bloody police. I hope they're going to pay you to do their job for them.'

'Maybe I'll send in an invoice. But I've got news about Matt Little.'

'Yeah?'

He repeated what Harcombe had told him.

Jeff shook his head in disbelief. 'If he turns out to be the killer, I wonder if he'll let me have his album collection while he's in jail?'

'That's the important thing...all those early psychedelic west coast records will go to waste for 35 years.'

'I know. They need liberating back into the record collecting community. Still, honestly, that really is a shocker, that, isn't it? Just shows you, still waters run deep. Seems nice, but underneath he's a raging fire of murderous intent, like. His dabs were all over the knives - that's a bit incriminating, isn't it?'

'Dabs?! You've been watching too many 1970s cop shows.'

'Leave it out, you slag,' said Jeff, in a cockney accent.

'So who was this Darlo woman you were leaving your dabs on last night?'

He lifted his shoulder and shrugged. 'No-one you know.'

'Quite the lothario these days, you.'

'Aye. Making up for lost time. Amazing how losing some weight has worked for me like that. Let's face it, I'm no more charming than ever, but being less massive has given us more confidence. I reckon that's what it's all about. That and washing more often, like.'

'So what about Rita?"

'Oh this Darlo thing was a one off. I really like Rita. I'm seeing her later this week, actually. Going for dinner at The Parkwood Hotel.'

'It's years since I've been there. Didn't we used to drink Guinness in there when we were 17?'

'Yeah. A couple in the Stockton Arms, a couple in the Masham and last orders in the Parkwood. That was a nice little circuit.

Summer of '79 was the last time we did that, y'know. Seemed like it would last forever.'

'Bloody hell. That's so long ago. 30 years. Seems like just the other day. You know what album reminds me of that summer most?'

Jeff tugged at his beard. 'Summer of '79? Was it a Whitesnake record?'

'Nope. *Live In The Air Age* by Be Bop Deluxe.'

'Oh aye. Great album that. 'Adventures In A Yorkshire Landscape' - what a solo on that. I liked that album 'cos it came with an additional EP. Nice idea that. Like it's one and a quarter albums. Never caught on that sort of thing, more's the pity. Not that well-adjusted members of society, without a vinyl collecting habit, care one way or another.'

'Every time I hear it, it takes me back to that summer. I got it at Virgin in Newcastle. I went up there with the lass I was going out with at the time. Happy days, those.'

'It was a big day out, wasn't it? To us small-town kids, Newcastle seemed like the big city. Aye, we had all our lives ahead of us. Couldn't have guessed what it all held, could we?'

'No. I think I thought things would have turned out better, to be honest. When I hear that record, I still hear nervous optimism for the future. That summer was a good time. I knew I'd got into college and would be leaving home. I had a great girlfriend and enough money to go out drinking most nights of the week. After all the bad times, I really thought things were on the up.'

'Yeah. I didn't realise life would be so bloody hard or involve quite so many Boomtown bloody Rats albums.' He held up a copy of *The Fine Art Of Surfacing* and threw it in his big bin. 'Horrible cover, awful record and one absolutely no-one wants now. You couldn't pay people to take it away. Landfill is too good for it.'

Nick stared into space, thinking about 1979 and how damn long ago it was. Had he thought, aged 18, that he'd have kids by now? Yeah, he probably had, if only by accident after being too embarrassed to ask a girl if she was on the pill before having sex, or because he was useless at putting on condoms. That seemed much more likely than being deliberately childless in his late 40s.

'Earth to Nick, Earth to Nick, come in please,' said Jeff waving a hand in front of his face.

'Sorry man, I was miles away - in the late 70s, actually.'

'You're a bloody dreamer, you are. You can't live in the past, all we've got is right here, right now. That's what Sammy Hagar said and I'm always inclined to believe the Red Rocker rather than any of the more traditional religions or philosophers. There is, after all, only one way to rock.'

He held up his hand to hi-five him.

'Too fucking right man. Now as ever,' said Nick and slapped his hand.

'So, do you think I should help the cops get evidence to bang someone up?'

Jeff coughed and drank some coffee.

'Yeah. Fuck it. Take the bad guy down, be it Matt or anyone else. Whoever took AA's life in that room, if you can take that bastard down, you have to do it.'

'But what if it's dangerous...'

'Aye well, you and danger are no strangers to each other, are you? You've been to the edge before, man. Balls of fucking steel, you and you've got strangler's hands, by the sound of what you did to Darren Harris.' He made a two-handed gripping gesture. 'And those punches you laid on Mick Root, fuck me, that was worthy of an Ali-Forman fight. I still don't know how he didn't drop. You could see it shudder right through his body.'

'Yeah, luckily I didn't break my knuckles. Must have been his fat, pouchy cheeks that protected them. No, but it's all different now.' He scrunched up his face and pushed tangled strands of his hair back behind his ears

'How's it different? You've still got balls of steel. You're the most fearless lunatic I know. Certainly the most likely to kick a bad dude in the face, which, by the way, I consider a great compliment.'

He looked up at Jeff, who was making his crazy face at him. 'It's different because Jules is pregnant. I'm going be a dad.'

The look of disbelief on Jeff's face was absolute and total. He stared at him with mouth slack.

'You called it right. Jules has had morning sickness. She's only a few weeks gone. I'm not supposed to tell you or anyone...but, y'see where I'm coming from...if anything happens to me, it's not just Jules to think of.'

'Whoooo!! Yes!! Get in!! One nil!!' Jeff was shouting and running around the shop, arms aloft whooping. 'Ha ha...I think it's fucking brilliant, man. You old sod...you got one past the goalie. Well done, old son.'

He whacked him on the back. 'Oweee fella, this calls for a toast. Not actual toast - too many carbs - hold on, there's some of that knock off Cava left here...aye...this will strip the scum off your tonsils.' He popped the cork on it, found two tannin-stained mugs and poured him a splash. 'Here's to you both. Honest, I think it's fantastic. Let's just hope it comes out looking like her and not you, eh, you ugly get.'

'Cheers, Jeff. I never thought you'd be so happy about it.'

'C'mon man, it's brilliant, I can just see you and her with a bairn. Mind, I need to be its musical director. We're not having it growing up liking rubbish music. Get them into Uriah Heep early, like. Kids love early 70s heavy rock if you play it loud enough often enough, in the womb preferably.' He gripped his hand into a fist. 'Yes. Get in. Best. News. Ever.'

Nick took a sip of the wine. 'I'm pretty sure this is the shittest wine in the history of shit wine, Jeff. Can we toast the new baby with the coffee instead?'

'Aye, it has got notes of battery acid and stomach bile, hasn't it?'

'I hate to be a ponce, but this is corked and really, really corked at that. This is too vinegary to even actually be vinegar.'

Jeff sniffed at it. 'I thought it smelled like a nun's knickers the other day. I imagine that's a terrible smell, but I may be wrong and it's probably blasphemous to even think such a thing.'

He poured the Cava into the sink. 'That should keep it unblocked for a few weeks. Aye, well with that news, I can see why you're wondering what's your best course of action, like.'

'I mean, he said it might be dangerous, but that I was the man for the job. Whatever that means.'

'What's Jules say?'

'That I shouldn't feel obliged. They're paid to do this job. They should do it.'

'Aye, well, the lass isn't wrong, is she?'

'But you said I should just take the bad man down. Whoever it is.'

'Yeah...well...ah god, I can see the problem. For the first time in your life you've got an investment in the future that isn't vinyl and round or lets you do things to its downstairs bits.'

'Exactly, yeah. It makes me realise how little I used to care if I lived or died, now I've got to look after this little life and I already owe it everything because it was me and Julies who made it. I can't let it down.'

'I know nowt about being pregnant, despite looking as though I was carrying quintuplets for most of my life, but isn't Julie a bit...err...old, like? No offence, etcetera. Aren't there problems when you're getting on?'

'Yeah. A better than even chance that she'll miscarry...so maybe all of this contemplation will be irrelevant.'

'Ooof, bad odds those. Are you...y'know...prepared for that, like?'

'We've talked about it. We know the score...but...' Jeff pushed the tea across the counter. '....but if that happens it'll be really awful. Turns out I love the idea of being a dad and I think Julie is excited by being a mother, too.'

'Yeah?'

'Aye.'

Jeff nodded, not knowing what to say.

'Well, I'll just go and see Colin and see what he wants. It might be nothing heavy.'

'Well, he's not going to want you to wrestle a bear is he? Mind, I'd back you to beat the crap out of a bear if you've got a mood on. I reckon a bear would go down easier than that Root loon.'

'Fucking bears, coming over here, nicking our salmon. They'll get what's coming to them.' Nick held up a fist.

'Ha, yeah...big hairy bastards, you don't scare me. Actually, I once knew a bloke from Dormanstown who looked like a bear. Liked fish 'an all...only from the chippy though...'

'...well, he can't have been a bear then, not a proper one. You never see bears in chip shops.'

'Whatever happened to the Hoffmeister Bear? I liked him. He was a big drinker.'

'Turned to drugs after his TV career nose-dived.'

'Poor Hoffy. Him and Biffo both ended up unbearable.' He stamped his foot and put his arms out wide like a musical hall act asking for applause.

At just before seven, Nick walked out of the shop down the High Street, took a left on Bishop Street and made the short walk down to the police station. As he did so, Julie's car came past him. She tooted the horn and parked up next to a rank of white, blue and fluorescent yellow police cars.

She got out and smiled. 'Now then, big boy.'

'Hiya. Before we go in, I've just got to say that I just told Jeff about the baby...sorry...it just came out while talking about doing this. So he knows...'

She made a resigned face. 'Oh well...I'm sure he's not much bothered either way, is he?'

'No man, he was totally delighted. He was running around the shop cheering, in fact.'

'Gettaway. He wasn't, was he?'

'Aye. Said he thought we'd make great parents.'

'If it happens. Don't get ahead of yourself.' She wagged a finger at him.

'I said, if I was going to be a dad, I shouldn't be doing anything dangerous for the police, should I?'

'Exactly. I don't see why you're so indispensable.'

'We'll just see what they've got to say.'

She patted him on the backside as they went inside, as much to comfort her nerves as his.

'We've come to see DI Harcombe,' he said to a desk Sergeant who looked up at him with well-practised weariness and cynicism.

'Have you now? And why's that?'

'Because he asked me to. I'm Nick Guymer.'

This seemed to lift his fog of disbelief. He raised a hand and nodded. 'Ah yes. Come through, I'll tell him you're here.'

He unlocked a door and let them through. It was a horrible place, an awful 1960s, cheaply built block of brick and glass, its ugly insubstantiality at odds with the power it held. Something which belonged to the law enforcers should surely have had more architectural heft, in keeping with the profundity of being able to deprive citizens of their freedom.

He showed them into a two-tone blue interview room in which was a wooden table and four chairs. It was depressingly bleak; the walls scuffed with black smudges and exposed patches of broken white plaster presumably from newly nicked criminals raging at their treatment at the hands of the law. Then again, you didn't expect interior design to be an priority in a police station. The Sergeant closed the door behind them.

Nick looked around as they took seats on one side of the table. 'It's claustrophobic in here, isn't it? No windows, hot as hell, I'd confess to anything just to get out.' He gripped her arm in mock panic. 'Alright, I did it, guv, I'm banged to rights. Just don't hurt me face.'

'We're The Sweeney, son, and we 'aven't 'ad any dinner. Get your trousers on, you're nicked,' said Julie, in a gruff, Jack Regan-manner. 'I bloody hate this place. Reminds me of too many bad nights bailing out my brothers.'

Colin Harcombe strode in wearing a sharp, non-fashionable single breasted dark blue suit, pale blue shirt and navy tie. The scent of Imperial Leather soap followed him in.

'Thank you for coming down. Julie, too, I see. Good. Good.'

'Is it OK for me to be here?' she said.

The policeman held up his hands. 'Yes, that's fine, Julie.' He tossed a blue card folder onto the desk. 'Can I get you a drink?'

'No, we're fine,' said Julie. 'So what's this about? Why do you need Nick's help?'

He pulled out the chair opposite them and sat down heavily and with a groan. He had dark rings around his eyes and an ashen pallor to his skin. Opening the file, he took out a sheaf of papers which looked like statements and coughed.

'All of what I'm about to tell you must remain in this room. No telling Jeff or anyone else. OK? I think we're getting to the heart of the matter now.'

Nick found himself feeling sorry for Harcombe. The stress of his job was etched into his face all too clearly and for the first time, he realised just what pressure must come with being the people charged with sweeping up the criminal detritus that the dirty public left behind. Everyone looked to them to sort things out. Someone was dead, no-one wanted to put their hand up for it, no-one else was going to find out who had done it, it was all down to the police and ultimately to Harcombe himself. If humans were not so evil, none of this would be necessary and Colin Harcombe could sit back, relax and enjoy his life. Instead, every waking moment and probably most of his sleeping moments too, were taken up with trying to arrest and prosecute people who had, at the very least, been an utter bastard. What a weight to carry.

'I'm not sure how much you know about Davey James. I'm assuming you've done your research.'

'He offered us both a job so, yeah, I've done research,' said Nick.

'Did he now? In URO?'

Nick nodded. 'Didn't I tell you?'

'No. Very interesting. As I said to you on the phone, Nick. The evidence is stacked up against Matt Little and I can't really delay charging him with both murders much longer. I won't be allowed to. The top brass want an end to this. They think we've got the right man and we have absolutely no evidence of anyone else being guilty, with the exception of James Butcher, but frankly one thumb print and some cash doesn't beat two full sets of prints being at the scene of both crimes, trying to hide the fact by having evidence stolen and having a big financial motive.'

He wore a pained expression as he spoke, his face scrunched up, chewing at his cheek.

'But something isn't right to me. He is the least murderous man I have ever arrested. So let's just put his guilt on hold for a moment and think outside of the box the evidence is putting us in. It concerns me greatly that Davey James has Matt as an important investor in URO and that Matt is having a relationship with James' wife Deirdre, who in turn has moved out of the family home in the last month after some pretty damn heinous behaviour. I mean, we could bring charges against him if she chose to press charges, which doesn't seem likely right now.'

'I hope she does. He's wicked,' said Julie. 'But a lot of women just can't face being dragged through the courts and cross-examined, as though it's they who are the nasty, deceitful people. They'd rather try and get on with rebuilding their life.'

'Understandable enough. I've now also had confirmation that Malcolm Pallister had taken investment cash from Davey James as well as from Matt in the last year to help fund Tees Digital, cash he quite obviously was unable to pay back. "

"You're wondering if somehow James had Alan killed to scare Pallister into paying up and when he couldn't, he had Pally killed, but in both cases he has tried to frame Matt for the murders as an act of revenge for him "stealing" his wife?' said Nick.

'I'm not sure if that's exactly right Nick, but something like that. In fact I'd say that his wife is a bigger motive even than the money.'

There was a knock on the door and an officer looked in holding a piece of paper. He looked between them and apologized for the interruption. 'Thought you'd like to see this, sir.' He handed Harcombe the sheet. The DI scanned it, nodded and gestured for him to go away.

'As we suspected, Malcolm Pallister has a substantial life insurance policy. Two million pounds.'

'Would it pay out of he's murdered?' said Nick.

Harcombe kept reading. 'Yes. Only suicide would prevent a pay out.' He let out an exasperated noise. 'You know what this means?'

'It means the debts he owes, if they're personal debts and not company debts, would be paid out of the assets of the estate,' said Julie. 'Thus, everyone gets their money because of his death. Matt Little and Davey James will get their cash back eventually. I saw a few cases like this when I worked in the law firm. The policy will probably still pay out as long as there has been no collusion from the person who owed the debt. Obviously, if one of the beneficiaries has murdered him, that wouldn't apply.'

'Does anybody actually engineer their own murder to pay everyone off?' said Nick.

'Yes it has happened, for sure,' said Harcombe, thinking aloud. 'But in this case, I really do wonder if the man who stands most to benefit - Davey James - saw a way to both frame his love rival and get his money back from Pallister?'

'Doesn't explain why Alan was killed, though. I don't imagine he's got a big insurance policy...' said Nick, '...and surely, it's also as much of a reason for Matt to kill Pallister. He wanted his money as well.'

'Yes, that's obviously right. On the Armstrong killing, maybe we're back to a case of mistaken identity,' said the policeman.

'Has Matt told you about how James abused Deirdre?' said Julie. 'I mean, if he knows all about it, because Deirdre might not have told him. It's not the easiest of things to talk about.'

'Yes, he seems to know all about it. I mean, we knew most of it through what you told me, but he confirmed it. James is certainly used to getting his own way so I can see how Deirdre leaving would be such a profound thing for him.'

'He's a bastard,' said Julie, quietly.

'Well, quite. However, no-one else has a bad word to say for

James except his wife, of course. As it stands we have nothing we can pin on him at all, but...but...but...I'd really like to test him out. This is where I need your help, Nick, because without some sort of confession from James, we're not able to prove any involvement in these murders and frankly, that might be because he has no involvement. But I think he does. I think he's a wrong 'un and I think anyone who would do what he's done to his wife, would find it easy to pay men to kill a rival. I think he's one of those quiet but deadly sharks. However, as much as my radar is twitching about him, I can't charge him with anything because I have zero evidence of his connection to either of the murders. All I have is the DJ 61 Mercedes being present in Middleton St George. That, to me, is suspicious in the extreme. That wasn't a coincidence. To me, he was there to observe Root go about his business. Why would he do that? I'm asking you to do this for me on the off chance that it will bring something to the surface that he wants to hide from the world. But with Matt Little I already have both evidence and motive.'

'What about Butcher and Root? Still neither confessed to killing Alan and Malcolm?'

'They have not. Quite the reverse. Oh, Butch has got ten grand on him from some crime or other and he's put a thumb print on the knife used to kill Alan at some point. He now says he actually knows Root and at some point Root showed him a knife and he touched it then. He says he doesn't know what happened to it after that. Root says he had a break-in at his shop and had knives and other stuff stolen. He says the killer obviously got them on the black market or actually stole them. I can't prove any of that is lies. He even reported the break-in to the local coppers. So it stands up to some degree. He may have faked that, I suppose, to give himself a potential alibi. We will charge Root for your attempted murder in Middleton St George, but no, we cannot in any way pin the other two murders on either of them. Indeed, my bosses are keen we let Butch go asap with the Little evidence so strong.'

Nick was confused. 'But a confession, you say? James isn't going to confess to anything though, is he? Not to me, or anyone else. There's no reason for him to. He won't say, "Ah, yes I paid Butcher and Root to do the killings and I've tried to set up Matt Little". In what circumstances would he say that? None.'

'You may well be right. Even if Root and Butcher did say he paid them, a pound to a penny there will be no evidence to that effect. It'll all be untraceable cash. Even if *they* confessed to the crimes and said James had put them up to it, neither Butcher nor Root are reliable witnesses, anyway. A defence lawyer would just point to their records and behaviour and say, well, these men are criminal and both of them are unhinged. They'd seed doubt in any jurors' mind. If he did pay them, he picked good men for this, in that regard. James has tough London lawyers who will be all over us unless we have a watertight case. But this is where you specifically come in, Nick.'

'Go on...'

'One of the few things Root has told us, is that James is a bit of a fan of yours and has mentioned both of you two to several people in Root's presence. So, I'm not surprised he offered you work. Did you respond to the offer?'

'Not yet.'

There was another tap on the door and the officer returned with another sheet of paper which he handed to Harcombe. A thin smile washed across his face from left to right and his cheeks flushed a little. The officer grinned at him, nodded and left.

'I think Mr Root has a bit of a crush on you as well, Nick.' Julie snorted a surprised yelp. 'We're talking to him right now. He seems to admire how you'd tackled him in Middleton St George - he said it was...what are his words now..."expert physicalling" which isn't even a word, as far as I know.'

'That's bizarre. He liked how I hit him in the face?'

'Seemingly. He's one of these men who likes to think of himself as a survivalist and so any other men he encounters who seem like they could, I don't know, wrestle a wolf or something, he admires them. You must be one such man.'

'Survivalist? He'd be terrible at surviving anywhere outside of a pub,' said Julie. 'He's just a typical bar-room big man; he's all big words, wind and piss.'

Harcombe scanned the piece of paper and nodded. 'Yes, I'm sure you're right, Julie. But he is maintaining that he has had nothing to do with the two murders.' He put the sheet into a folder.

'So what was he doing in Middleton St George?' said Nick.

'He says he was acting alone and from his own initiative, just as you thought. Says he was just going to scare Matt Little off seeing James' wife. That was his intent. Not murder. So, the long and short of this is I will have to charge Matt Little with the murders within 48 hours, but that might actually make your job easier. If James thinks he's got away with this he may get more loose-lipped. That's what I need. I need some intimation that he paid for the murders. He probably won't out-and-out confess, but he may give us something which can take us to his door. If I get a reasonable suspicion of his guilt, I can hold off charging Matt. I have to give it a shot and I know it's a long shot and I may be wrong and it may indeed all be down to Little'.

'If he thinks I'm working for you, who knows what'll happen? He might get another psycho like Root in to whack me there and then. I'm sure it'd only take one call.'

Harcombe twitched his lips.

'Without wishing to scare you, he may have some of his security people at the house. We know he has meetings there with them. So you need to be aware of that possibility when conducting yourself. Do not put yourself in danger. If you're asking me if it's a perfect or foolproof idea, then the answer is no, but you're the only option I've got, Nick. He's a fan of yours and no-one who works for him will help us, for fear of losing their job or worse. His friends are all really loyal, his enemies too easily portrayed by a defence lawyer as having an axe to grind. Also, and I don't say this lightly or often, but I know you, Nick Guymer, and you're a damn good man. Usually cool in a crisis, good under fire and brave as a lion. I couldn't ask for better. If there is trouble, I know you can handle yourself until we get there.'

It was flattering to hear and gave Nick an electric trickle of pride almost because it was delivered as though Harcombe was living in a 1950s movie. But all the same, Nick was sceptical. Very sceptical.

'What do you reckon, Jules?' he said.

She drummed her fingers on the desk and turned to look at him with a hard stare.

'If you feel you can, you should do it. He's scum, we know that. He needs sorting out. If they can get him for this, all the rest of his horrible behaviour will all come out and we need that to happen to show how even the rich and powerful can be abusers. It might even inspire other women to leave abusive situations and save other people's lives too. A lot of good stuff could flow from this.'

She didn't leave any room for doubt.

'How would I go about it?'

'If we were in a TV show, I'd say you'll go and see him whilst wearing a wire.'

'A wire? An actual wire?'

'A recording device. We'll listen in and record it all. It may take a couple of meetings for us to get a proper idea of whether this line of enquiry is going to yield anything. I may be way off base. You'll need to get his trust. Play up to his way of thinking, ingratiate him, flatter him, make him think you're a big fan of his and are of the same mind. Get his trust. Don't forget, he's already approached you, so you've got an "in" with him.'

Nick blew out air, slapped the table with both hands.

'OK. I'll do it.'

'Good man. I knew I could rely on you,' said the DI, who held out his hand and gripped Nick's hand tightly.

'But you've got to keep him safe, Colin...' said Julie.

'We will.'

'...because he's going to be a dad.' She said it with a small smile and a nod.

His eyebrows shot up.

'Goodness me. Tremendous news. Congrats to you both. Well done...marvellous. When is it due...?'

'Oh it's early yet,' she said.

The policeman got up and kissed her on the cheek and shook Nick's hand again.

'Good luck to you both. I'm delighted for you. Genuinely delighted. We will be careful. Rest assured.'

As soon as they were at home, even though it was nearly 9.30pm, Nick called the mobile number on the card Davey James had given him. He answered after four rings.

'Davey. Nick Guymer. How are you?'

'Great. Thanks Nick. Good to hear from you. What can I do for you at this late hour?'

'I just wondered if we could meet up?'

'Sure. What's this about?'

'I wanted to discuss us working with you.'

'You and Julie?'

'Yes. If that's OK?'

'Very good. Julie is a fine figure of a woman isn't she? Absolute cracker.'

It was a weird thing to say so soon into a phone conversation with a man who was virtually a stranger. It was rude and intrusive and 'a fine figure of a woman' wasn't even an expression he'd heard since the 1970s.

'She is that...err...yeah.'

'I want you both on board, as I made clear. We can be very good for each other. Why don't you come to my house tomorrow, say 10.30am?'

'That'd be fine. What's your address?'

'The Oaks, The Avenue, Fairfield. Do you know where that is?'

'I grew up near there, actually, Palm Grove.'

'I know it well. OK, fine, 10.30 it is, I look forward to seeing you.'

That night Nick didn't sleep much, lying in the dark, wondering about Davey James and how he'd manage to befriend him for the purposes of revealing his criminality, if indeed there was any criminality. It just seemed highly unlikely that he'd let his guard slip with him, unless he could find his big weakness. Everyone has a hole in their armour, no matter who they are, no matter how rich or powerful they are. You just have to find it and James would be no different. He had an idea what it would be, a very good idea. It was most men's weakness.

As Julie snored next to him, her 'deeds not words' idea was all well and good, but words often gave you an insight into what the person would or wouldn't do and especially into what they really felt. For all Julie's insistence that you could mask your true self with carefully chosen vocabulary, he really wasn't 100 percent convinced that was true. In fact, though he hadn't argued the point with her, he was fairly sure she was wrong.

Words were a window into the soul even when the person who spoke them thought they were in control of the words and what story they told. He had to exploit that. To keep up a pretence every hour of every day was too hard. Eventually, what you were trying to hide, cover up or pretend didn't exist for any given audience, would show itself. It was like the times he'd gone out with women and he'd tried to hide the extent of his interest in rock music and vinyl records, fearing it made him seem a bit odd, nerdy and unattractive. Eventually he'd make a reference to something, or draw an analogy which would reveal knowledge of some obscure band. There was only so long you could ever hide who you really were, or who you thought you were, anyway. But if you felt you were with a sympathetic, like mind, then you could loosen your mental waistband, relax and let it all hang out. That was the position he had to get Davey James into. He had to make him feel that he understood why he might have paid for someone to kill the two men, so if there was anything for him to confess to, he could do so to Nick with complete confidence that he'd understand. It wouldn't be easy, but he felt confident about how he would go about it. Words and deeds. What you say *and* what you do. They were inseparable.

CHAPTER 14

They went down to the station in the morning and were shown into another anonymous room.

Nick lifted up his denim shirt and a policewoman taped a tiny wireless microphone to his chest under a black t-shirt. He could barely even feel it there.

'Just be aware enough of this to make sure you don't pull it off accidentally, say by scratching your arm pit or something,' she said.

He nodded, his mouth dry, his heart already racing.

Julie smiled at him encouragingly. 'You'll be fine, luv. You're a good liar, you always have been. All you need to do is be his mate, get him on side. You know how to do this. Be like every total douche bag dick head you've ever heard or met.'

'What is a douche bag, exactly?'

'I'm not really sure. I'm afraid to look it up on the internet. It's something to wash the lady cave out with, I think.'

'Not sure that's much of an insult then, really. It's like calling someone a flannel or a shower head. You big cleaning thing, you. Nah, it's silly.'

'Ha ha. You're getting distracted. Just remember he's a misogynist and a bully, so anything that suggests to him you're the same sort of bloke will make him relax.'

He nodded. 'Oh yeah. I can do it, I know I can. I grew up with it all around, so I can reach for it at any time, most blokes probably can.' He was working himself into a frame of mind to feel strong and resolute. Come on, do this. Just play the role. Play James' confidante. Be on his side. Get him to spew his guts. It would be revenge for good old Alan.

'And if you get into any bother, if anyone dangerous arrives, if there's even a suggestion that he's sending in any of his team, we'll be there right away,' said Harcombe. 'We'll be in a roadworks truck on the Avenue and we'll come in mob-handed, if needs be. If

268

you have to deploy violence, try not to actually kill anyone if you can avoid it.'

He grinned at Nick who nodded. 'No deaths from the deploying of violence. Right. Gotcha, Col.'

The WPC checked out the equipment. 'Just talk at your normal level, Nick,' she said, nodding, 'Yes that's fine. OK you're all good.'

'Now listen to me,' said Harcombe putting his hand on Nick's shoulder. 'As soon as he says anything to suggest he paid Jimmy Butcher and or Mick Root or anyone else to kill Alan and Pallister, you get yourself out of there as quickly as it's safe to do. We only need him to confess to one of those crimes. One will do. Two would be nice, but one is plenty. OK?'

'Yeah, Col.'

'And if he isn't forthcoming because he's not guilty, or he's just too guarded, then don't worry. Safety first at all times. This is just a shot in the dark that I'm asking you to make for me.'

'I know the score, Colin.' Nick's phone vibrated. It was Jeff.

'Hey man. Just calling to wish you luck.'

'Thanks, mate. '

Jeff clearly didn't really know what more to say other than that.

'What are you up to then?' said Nick, filling the void.

'Currently I'm filing an album called *In Blissful Company* by Quintessence under Q. I've got almost nothing in the Q's except Queen and Quicksilver Messenger Service.'

'No Suzi Quatro?'

'Sadly, no. Not so much 'Can The Can' as 'Can't The Can't.'

'Q-Tips?'

'Do me a favour. Never liked Paul Young.'

'Queens Of The Stone Age or Quiet Riot?'

'Nada. Oh, hang on, I've got *Operation Mind Control* by Queensryche.'

'I always liked that record. How about early 80s metal by Quo Vardis?'

'Quo Vardis bloody hell, that takes me back to the New Wave

Of British Heavy Metal days. I can still taste the Snakebite.'

'Lager and cider in the same glass, what were we thinking?'

'We were thinking, oh good, we're getting very pissed very quickly, that's what.'

'I know a Q you'll have. I bet you've got the first Quarterflash album there somewhere. You always see it in the 50p bins. It's the one with their big hit on...'

'Yeah, good call, that single was 'Harden My Heart'...yup, I've got that album waiting to be filed. Anyway, sorry, we're getting distracted.'

'And don't forget Quatermass. An original copy of their début album is worth good money...'

'Oh god, yeah, I sold a battered copy of that last year for 60 quid. I've got it on CD actually...it's good stuff.'

'...yeah, I like them. Don't remember them at the time. Was it 1970?'

'Yup, well they never sold any, did they?'

'No. Yeah, we're getting distracted. I don't think this is going to be a big deal anyway. It'll probably all come to nothing. It's a bit of a long shot by Colin.'

'Yeah, it is when you think about it. I still think you should ask for cash for your trouble though. The only thing I keep wondering about is the DJ 61 Merc being in Middleton that night. Was he driving that? It's such a distinctive car, if he'd paid Root to kill Matt or his wife, he just wouldn't sit outside his house in it for everyone to see. He's not stupid. Obviously, it wasn't Matt in the car, or Deirdre. So who?'

'I've seen Toni drive it. Maybe it was her. But where that takes us, I just don't know. Anyway, I've got to go. I'll catch you later big man.'

'Alright Fighting Boy. Take care, eh.'

He took Julie's hands and looked into her turquoise eyes and grinned.

'I'll probably have to be as bad as he is or worse, y'know, so if you hear what I'm saying, I'm just using the words, but you know it's not me, don't you? Well, I bloody hope it's not me. What are we anyway? Just a collection of assumed thoughts and ideas.'

'Oh gawd, do you ever stop being bloody philosophical? Just get in there and do whatever it takes.'

He hugged her to him and breathed in her soft scent; it was the place where his best self lived. He sucked it down deep into his lungs, as though to infect himself with it as an antidote.

At 10.30am, he was dropped off at the top of The Avenue and walked down to the house. The roadworks van in which the police and Julie were housed was just near the driveway. He went down the long gravel drive towards Davey James' house. It was a tall Victorian Gothic building which he'd walked past hundreds or even thousands of times in his youth. It had belonged to the family of a small dark-haired girl he'd fancied at school called Mandy. The same Mandy he'd groped at a party. What had happened to her? He'd passed this place on his way home from Stockton Sixth Form College. He'd even delivered football pools coupons to some of the houses on the street as part of his round. The Avenue was one of Stockton's relatively few nice, leafy streets and James' house one of the poshest. Strange how buildings had shifting roles to play in your life, often dormant or ignored for decades, but then suddenly and dramatically, really active and important.

The silver DJ 61 Merc was parked up outside. The house had an Addams Family quality about it. To the right hand side, around a bay window, was a path which led to a back garden. He wandered around and took a look. The grounds were surprisingly big, though totally hidden from the road. Mature trees stood tall, separating the grounds from the Bishopton Court estate beyond.

He walked back to the front, turned and looked down the narrow track. The road seemed a long way away and was invisible now. That life seemed a painfully long way away, suddenly.

Deep breath. Do this. Easy.

He pressed an intercom on the door frame and looked around. A camera mounted above the door was focused on him. He felt like he should wave at it, but that would just be silly.

'Hello Nick,' said a disembodied voice.

'Hey Davey.'

'I'll be right there.'

Half a minute later, the big man appeared at the door and welcomed him in. He was wearing a large black 5XL t-shirt, worn outside of black cargo pants. He seemed even larger in this setting.

'Thanks for inviting me over Davey,' he said, stepping inside the house onto a bouncy, plush taupe-coloured carpet. They shook hands.

'Not at all. Good to see you. I'm glad you called because I was really hoping you'd want to come on board. I was just reading your last piece in the Echo about the Boro being relegated this year not being such a bad thing. Interesting stuff. Everyone assumes it'll be a disaster if they drop out of the Premier League.' He looked at a large watch on his left wrist. 'The sun is over the yard arm. Can I get you a drink?' It was just 10.35am, a bit early to start drinking unless you were on holiday or an alcoholic. Then again, you didn't get to be Davey James' size without a dedication to consuming useless calories, most hours of the day.

'No, I'm fine, thanks.'

'Come on - have a drink. I'm having one.' He spoke with an insistent tone as he led him into a large Victorian living room with a big central rose in the ceiling. Nick looked out of the window. The mature hedges and trees meant it was still impossible to see the road where the police were listening to him. It was almost impossible to believe that they were there. James poured whisky from a crystal decanter. What the hell should he do? If he said he didn't drink would it make him think he was suspicious or weird? A lot of men were suspicious of men who didn't drink, in fact he'd been one of them back in his drinking days. But he hadn't had a drink for over two years and would have no tolerance for it at all. Best to try and turn it into an asset.

'I'm on tablets, Davey, for my blood pressure like and the doctor says I'm not supposed to drink, but sod that, I'll just have a small whisky. Make yourself seem like a rebel and an outsider. That's how he sees himself.

The big man nodded and smiled. 'Good lad. What do doctors know? My old man drank every day and smoked 60 fags as well and he lived till he was 92.'

'Exactly. It's all bloody guesswork.' He took the cut crystal glass from him and took a sip of the whisky. It tasted foul. How had he ever drank this stuff? It first burned, then numbed his mouth and can't have been a lot different from drinking petrol. But Davey didn't seem to have any such problems, knocking down a quick shot and then pouring himself a large one to settle down with.

'Lovely house this, how long have you lived here?' said Nick, looking around.

Flatter him about his lifestyle choices.

'We bought it 20 years ago, but we lived in Spain most of the time. Been living here pretty much full time for the last 6 or 7 years though.'

'Right. And do you live here alone?'

Pretend you don't know about his wife.

'Yeah. I do now that the kids are away at school most of the year.' He drew his top lip across his teeth, looked away from him and then turned back. They stood and chatted for ten or 15 or 20 minutes about football and Spain and growing up on Teesside. All inconsequential stuff.

'As I said in the restaurant, I've been very impressed with you both,' he gestured for him to sit down on a brown leather chesterfield sofa.

'That's good of you to say so, Davey. I really appreciate it and you know I'm a big fan of your work, too. I mean, Teesside has needed an inspirational man like you for years. You get nowhere trying to pull an area out of the economic clarts by committee. It takes vision and big balls and you've got that in spades.'

He was just feeding back to him what he'd heard him say, but by the look on his face it pleased him.

'Thanks. You're right, but then I am of the view that most normal people realise that. The people know what the people need, it's just the politicians that seem blind to it, or are not interested. '

It sounded exactly right, but also very like a sound-bite for the cameras. It probably was. In fact the line between his public and private persona seemed a bit blurred. If you live by sound-bites, perhaps they become the way you speak when not on camera too. However, what he said was also, perhaps unfortunately, true. You want your villains in life to be wrong about everything, not perceptive and clever and certainly not right about many things.

As James talked, Nick looked out of the window. Suddenly, he had a strong sense of being watched. Was it James' security guys? No-one was there. He looked at the door. Nothing and no-one there, either. Stupid. It was probably because he knew the police and Julie were listening to him. It was like they were in the room.

'Yeah, well, Julie is very much into all of that too. She thinks the URO is a great thing for the region. She's been a big supporter of low-cost housing for Teesside's working class.'

'Ah Julie. Yes. Lovely lass, her. Lovely. You're a lucky boy to have her.' He looked at him with one of those little sideways nods that men give each other to compliment them on their choice of girlfriend.

'I am. I know that. She gets a bit uppity, as you've seen, but I know how to handle her. She knows her place. I've got her well trained.'

'Really?' He took another drink, raised his eyebrows and nodded. 'Well, that's good to hear.'

'Oh yeah. I'm a big believer in that. Got to keep women in their place or they just cause a lot of trouble. The thing is, it's for their own good most of the time. That's what some of them don't understand.'

Give him all standard sexist banter. The sort of thing he'd heard all the time growing up in the north east in the 60s and 70s. Noticeably, these words seemed to almost physically comfort Davey James, like it was something he really wanted to hear. His body language, previously a bit stiff, almost awkward, seemed to ease and relax. He leaned forward and cocked his big, bearded head to one side and slapped Nick on the leg.

'Yes indeed, glad to hear you say that. We don't want the ladies worrying their pretty heads over business too much, do we? A bit of passion in a woman is good, too much can be a problem. You get me?'

'Oh yeah. Hey, we all want a cook in the kitchen, a maid in the living room and a whore in the bedroom, don't we?'

James laughed heartily at that, as though he had never heard the appalling cliché before. 'And which of those is Julie then, Nick?'

'She could be a better cook, she's very tidy, but there's none better in the bedroom. She knows what to do for me, if you know what I mean.'

'Likes to please her man, eh?'

Nick nodded and pursed his lips together, feeling a bit nauseous, either from the whisky or the words. It was amazing how powerful these few words were though; how they'd transformed this meeting already. It was as though he was speaking a secret code to James, the subtext of which was, don't worry, we're all real men here, no-one is going to giving you any grief. You can relax. It had a much bigger effect and much more quickly than he thought it would. The question was, how far could he push this and keep credibility? He'd seen him with Julie and he would have made a judgement about his relationship with her. Surely only so much misogyny coming from him was going to wash.

He coughed and scratched at his knee, distractedly. 'Well look, between you and me, she knows what'll happen if she doesn't keep me happy, Davey.'

He tried to say it with the sort of arrogant menace he'd heard men use in pubs since he was a teenager; the sort of men who would proudly declare they wore the trousers in their house and who would equally decry those who didn't, as not real or proper men. Even as a teenager, he'd thought it was a horrible sort of bragging. Hopefully Davey James wouldn't actually ask what would happen if she didn't please him because he didn't know what level of intimidation to pretend to employ. Should he suggest it would be imprisonment, violence or even rape? Whatever, it probably didn't matter. In this context you could pretty much say anything without attracting opprobrium. They were easy words to find.

James picked at a seam in the leather and looked out of the top of his eyes at Nick, clearly considering something.

'The thing is Nick, and don't get me wrong here, I'm not having a go at you. But your woman, Julie, she could be a problem for me.'

'She could?'

'She's attractive, very attractive. I mean, I don't blame you for hooking up with her. She's a stunner...'

Yeah mate, that's right, define women's worth by their appearance first and foremost.

'...but she knows people who can make things difficult for me. Maybe you can help me out on that?'

Nick didn't hesitate to exploit the opening he was being given. 'If I can help, I will, Davey.'

Davey James topped up his glass. Nick put his hand over his.

'I'm going through a divorce, Nick. My wife turned out to be a total, psycho bitch. She's trying to take me to the cleaners.'

'Oh really? I'm sorry to hear that. That sounds like a real drag.'

'Well, you know what they're like when they get a bee in their bonnet...'

Did he mean all women? All women, generalized from his experience with his wife, a wife he'd abused for years? Generalisations about women as a gender and not as individual people were common enough to hear; you can't live with them you can't live without them and all of that crap. *They* like shopping. *They* like getting their hair done. *They* are awful drivers. Nick let out an involuntary sigh of weary disgust at his words. It was out of him before he could stop it. Shit.

James looked up at him and nodded. 'Yeah, it's a real pain in the arse.'

He'd got away with it. He'd taken his expulsion of air as a critique of his wife and not of him. Then of course he would do that, wouldn't he? To men like Davey, life is all about themselves and no-one else.

'She's gone to one of these Women's Aid type of groups. It's run by a lot of lefty feminist lesbians who just hate men. They'll believe any old rubbish that a woman who arrives on their doorstep starts spouting. I mean, anything. And you can't defend yourself. Everyone just believes the woman and paints the man as a bastard.'

That's right mate, make out that it's actually you who are the victim here; it was a classic abuser mind-set.

'Terrible. I'm sorry to hear that, Davey. What's she been saying to them, like?'

'That I'm a total bastard. That I psychologically tortured her and tried to control her, even that I attacked her and all of this shit...it's like I'm the devil incarnate. All bollocks, of course. She can't point to a single bruise that I've put on her. She's not bothered to say how my money took her out of total poverty. House in Spain, a life of luxury. Oh no. No-one mentions that. She had nothing before she met me and now I get all this grief. When I think of everything I've done for her...'

Because money gives you the right to do anything. It was like she was a chattel he'd bought. Nick nodded, trying to look sympathetic,

'But you see, it's like this Nick, your Julie actually works at the place she's gone crying to.'

'The Teesside Women Centre? Oh yeah. But she's just a volunteer, Davey. Just does office work. Typing, that sort of thing. She's just doing it to get some office experience so when she's got her degree she'll be able to get a job again. It could be any office. She's not there because she's especially sympathetic. She doesn't really like it...the women are so shrill and whiny. They've got this victim mentality and are always shouting the odds and giving it all that.' He made a yapping dog hand gesture, easily one of the most patronizing, nasty gestures in the physical lexicon of misogyny, '...she moans on about them all the time.'

This was even easier than he thought, essentially all he had to do was to say the exact opposite of the truth.

'Does she, now? But your Julie is a bit of feminist herself though, isn't she? The way she goes on about businesswomen and all that about language. I mean, that's all standard feminist guff, isn't it?'

Nick shook his head. 'Oh god, no. She hates all that sort of thing. That's not her being feminist, it's just her being argumentative. She's from a mega-hard family, so she stands up for herself as you'd expect any Hardwick lass to do, but she's not fan of all the lefty, dungaree-wearing muff divers who work there.'

Where the hell did your brain pull this stuff from? Muff divers?! But importantly, Davey seemed to like it, grinning from ear-to-ear on hearing it.

'I see. I see. I get you. Good. Even better.' He seemed to be forming some idea in his mind, rolling his top lip over his teeth again. It gave his mouth a shark-like quality. 'So she has access to their administrative information, does she?'

'I assume so, yeah.'

'Would she be prepared to be...'

'...a spy for you?' It was all so obvious what he was going to say.

'For want of a better word, yes. I just need to know what the wife is up to. They've given her a house y'know, but they won't tell me where it is.'

Nick wondered if he could know that he and Julie had been there. Tricky. If he was in the DJ 61 car, he'd know that they knew this. Was he testing him? Trying to catch him out?' He looked into his eyes for any sign, but couldn't read any. Just avoid the question.

'Aye, I've heard they do that if the woman's got no money.'

'Hmm, well of course she's got no money. All the money is mine.

Women have it so easy. They get men to pay for everything then when they've had enough, a charity will give them a place to live. Try that on for size if you're a bloke. Yeah so I'd like to know where that house is and if they move her, I need to know where she goes. That sort of thing.'

Control. It was all about control. Deirdre was his. But if he was telling the truth it meant one thing, he wasn't in the DJ 61 car the other night. Someone else was.

'I'm sure Julie would like to help you, Davey. Like I said, she's a good girl.'

Suggest obedience to the male at all times. Say she's a girl, not a woman. Woman sounds too powerful. Girl is submissive and more childish.

'Good lad. That's what I like to hear. Ah yes, the delicious Julie. I envy you, I really do. There'll be good money in it for her.'

'She'd be grateful for that. She does like money. College costs a fortune.'

Nick had prepared for his bad attitude, but there was a greasy acidity to it that was hard to grasp, but felt very corrosive; it felt like he might rot your moral fabric.

He went onto a long rant about local government and how obstructive planning restrictions were. It was almost unendurably boring. Then he went quiet and tapped the side of his glass with his nail as though contemplating what to say next.

'Yes, as I say, I do like Julie. Like I say...she's a stunner.'

'Thanks. She is, like.'

Objectification, it was everything.

'If I can get you both on board with my team would there be a chance for me...'

'...a chance for what?'

The big man raised his eyebrows and cleared his throat. 'I'm just going to ask this, don't take it badly, take it as compliment...would there be a chance of a night with your Julie? Nothing extreme. All tasteful. It's a big ask, I know...no offence intended. It's your territory, I understand that...I'm just asking.'

He rested the glass on his lap and held his bear paws up in surrender. His sparky eyes flashed, the air whistling through his small, squat nose set into a big face.

Nick didn't get it at first. Didn't quite compute what was being said to him.

Sex?

Did he mean sex?

He did.

He was asking him for sex with Julie?

His angry heart rose into his throat on a tide of blood, heated by revulsion.

It was hard to resist the impulse to just punch him in the face with every last molecule of energy in his body. There was no level on which this wasn't wrong.

Suddenly, it was all getting worse, much worse.

James leaned forward. 'What does she like to do? I'm up for anything. Whatever it costs. Get me?' His eyes seemed to bulge out of his head a little, bloody shot in the corners. Nick sucked in air through his nose to calm himself. He could feel the fury building up in him. Adrenalin coursing back into his muscles, just as it had with Root and Harris.

But here it was. This was Davey James' weakness. The hole in his armour. This was his vulnerability: sex. Women reduced to an economic transaction. That's what he liked, that was something he could understand. It kept his power trip intact. When people wanted your money, you had power over them. You called the shots. But Nick felt so out of his depth, so shocked and so disgusted to his core. How could someone live like this with these sort of values? Where did you drag them up from? How was it acceptable to them?

His mouth was dry like sandpaper and he feared his eyes had registered every ounce of fucking outraged, contemptuous disgust. So he took a sip of the whisky - took a big sip this time. Nope, still horrible. What to say and do?

'Like I say, I don't want to offend you...we seem like we're on the same wavelength here...if it's not on, then I totally understand, but in my experience, if you don't ask, you don't get. So I'm asking.'

He'd thought Julie might be his weakness, but hadn't banked on it being this big a weakness. If he'd talk like this about her, he could get him to confess to conspiracy to murder. He took another sip of whisky, squinted at him through narrowed eyes to better obfuscate any expression. He had to conduct this on a basis James would understand. This was no ordinary request, though probably one he had made before. Seeing his hesitancy, the big man sat back and opened his arms wide.

'Again, I can make this worth your while for both of you. A nice, clean regular little thing. It'd set you up financially. She is special. A man like me doesn't get a lot of chance to...I'm sure you understand. Please don't take offence. She's a gorgeous woman.'

Nick cleared his throat and tried to be relaxed.

'Well, money makes things happen, doesn't it, Davey? She understands that as well as I do. Obviously, it'd have to be a high enough...'

The bigger the money you want, the more he'll think you're serious. The look of relief in James' eyes that he hadn't taken against him for suggesting this arrangement was easy to read.

'Oh yeah, yeah...high enough for sure...I'm thinking five figures and I don't mean 150 pounds and 20 pence.' He laughed at his own joke.

'50K?' said Nick, taking another drink.

James whistled and gave him a look which suggested he admired his balls in asking so much for one night with Julie. He roared a laugh.

'For 50 she'd have to be a very bad girl, but you are talking my language now...'

Of course I'm talking your language, you fucking idiot. I'm playing you like a fucking violin.

'We can probably do business, Davey. Yeah. 50 grand every now and again. That would work.'

His stomach made a violent flip, just saying the words. He made up his mind to only refer to her as Julie and not Jules. Jules was his love. Julie was the character in this façade. Keep some separation. What the hell would she be thinking listening to this? She'd probably be laughing. Yeah, she would. She was so much cooler than he was. Much better than him, really.

'See, I knew you were a good man. Good attitude. Both of you know which side your bread is buttered and I like that. We can do business together.' He grinned at him. Nick looked back. He wasn't good at reading people, but he felt sure James really believed him 100 percent.

'The key to a good relationship with a woman is to let them think they're doing what they want,' said Nick, brushing the arm of the sofa with the palm of his hand.

'See, that's where I went wrong with my wife. I can't even bring myself to say her name now. I loathe her for what she's trying to do to me. I wouldn't care, but I gave her so much and all I wanted in return was a bit of loyalty and support.'

'Wives are like puppies. You've got give them a hard time at the start, that way, further down the line, they won't give you any trouble. Lay down the rules hard and if they step out of line, slap them down. That way everyone knows where they stand,' said Nick, thumping his knee with a fist.

Push it harder. Let him think he can just say anything. He was weaker than he'd thought he would be. He'd already said things that would be thought totally unacceptable. Buying women for sex isn't looked kindly upon by most people. That alone would ruin him. He had him now and he didn't even realise. Go harder. Take him down.

'I tell you what though, Davey. If Julie ever, and I mean, ever so much as looked at another man, I'd have the fucker killed. I would. You and me, we can come to a little arrangement for her favours, if you get me? That's business and is just between us, but if she went out on a Friday night and a bloke kissed her, I'd have his fucking face cut off. If she was unfaithful to me...there'd be consequences, believe me.'

He tried to spit out the words angrily, letting himself be offended by himself in order to wind up his emotions. This was disgusting work, but it was piss easy, much easier than it really should have been. Easy because such words and emotions were so commonplace and familiar.

'Well she's your woman and to me, that's totally understandable. Frankly Nick, I wish I'd had my wife's cunt cut out and stuffed back down her whining throat just to spite her.' He said it quite casually as though this was a reasonable thing to think. Nick nodded. There was a noise somewhere in the house - a vibration of some sort. Something falling over, perhaps. He looked out of the window again, feeling paranoid that someone was there, but all was still clear.

'Yeah, well I hear you man. Fucking PC Nazi's are making all our lives much more difficult than they should be.'

Play the PC card, all these idiots hated anything PC. They used the acronym like a swear word.

Nick paused for a few seconds while James got more whisky.

'Actually, since we're talking frankly here, you might be able to help me...it's a bit of a delicate matter...' Nick looked around them as though checking to see if anyone was listening.

'Well, I'm happy to help you if I can, Nick.'

'Well. It's a bit difficult, Davey...I'm not sure I should...'

'Speak up. It all stays in this room.'

Nick sat back and composed himself. As he did so, for the first time he noticed a small CCTV camera in the top corner of the room. It had been obscured by the big candelabra before. Was it on? Was he being filmed by James? Was someone watching them? His hard men, maybe? Fucking hell. But he had to plough on now. He felt like he was close. If James had anything to confess, he could get it out of him and saw how to do it.

'Well there's a bloke she knows at college. I've had my suspicions about him. One of these college boys types. Rich. Fancies himself. He's sniffing around her. I really want to scare him and any others off. You know? Do you know anyone who could do that for me?'

He beat his fist into the plan of his hand to symbolize what he wanted to happen.

'I might do.'

'If I'm being honest, I'd prefer him to...to...disappear all together. Understand? I don't need some pretty student kid messing with my woman.'

Even as it came out of his mouth he thought this sounded over the top and totally lacking in credibility. Who spoke like this really? Whose words where these? James stared at his glass. He'd blown it. He'd over-played his hand. He'd got cocky and over-reached what he could reasonably pull off. That was it. He was going to clam up. He'd get suspicious. He must realise that this was all bullshit. So he expected James to get up and politely, but firmly usher him out, but he didn't. He just sat there looking at him implacably.

'Julie's got tough brothers, hasn't she? Notoriously so. Couldn't they do the job?' He'd researched her well. Now he had to think quickly.

'We're like that, me and the Wells brothers. They know the score.' He put his index and middle finger together. 'They've beat their fair share of heads in over the years. Vicious sods they are. They think violence is funny.'

'Yeah, I heard that about them. Even when I was kid in the Boro, we'd all heard about them.'

'I can't risk asking them though, Davey. They're nasty bastards and they'd kill anyone who they thought was fucking around with their sister, they're on my side Davey, but they're too extreme...do you know what I mean? Too crazy. They're irresponsible...' he paused and laughed a little. 'You know what, they remind me of that Mick Root bloke.'

'Oh him? He's away with the fairies, he is. Someone at work said the cops arrested him a couple of nights ago, you know...'

Careful. Was it a trap?

'...I don't know what went on...but it doesn't surprise me. Not with him.'

'Julie's brothers are too crazy. I need distance from them.'

James turned his mouth down and nodded in understanding.

'Err...well...you meet a lot of odd people in my game.'

'Crazy fuckers, you mean?'

'Oh yeah.' James had become noticeably reticent. Shit. He needed him to open up again. 'I keep people like him at arm's length. Doesn't do for me to dip my toe into those dirty waters. Not with the media all over me.'

The whisky was starting to make Nick feel dizzy and sick.

'Aye, well I can see that, like.'

Nick looked at the CCTV camera again and felt agitated and started to sweat. The pressure to get this over with began to feel overwhelming and intense. Fuck it. He didn't know what more to do. Getting on with people was hard enough for him at the best of times and this was fucking torture. Harcombe had said it might take several visits to build up trust. Screw that. He couldn't do this again. He just couldn't. He didn't have the social skills nor the psychological endurance. He'd only been there for a couple of hours at most, but it had felt like a whole day. It had to end one way or another. A win or a loss. A draw was no good. He hated draws. Always go for the win, in football and in life. Force the issue. There was only so long he could be around this slime ball without losing it and he could feel his temper boiling away somewhere in his subconscious, waiting to unleash itself with lethal force on Davey James. Push was coming to shove; with him, push always came to shove and James was going to need some really big fucking shoving. Like water rising inexorably with a full moon, he prepared himself for the brutality that he knew would end this.

'Come on, man,' he said it impatiently, flicking his head up the way aggressive football fans did at each other across a pub before a fight. He was challenging James. James looked at him askance.

'What?'

Nick exhaled, feeling dizzy again and once again feeling like someone's eyes were on him, like he was being watched. That bloody CCTV camera. He took a quick glance out the window and then rubbed a crust from his eye.

'Are you OK?' James said.

'I'm fine, yeah, but c'mon, we're pussying around aren't we?' Oddly he felt much more at ease being confrontational. At least if you got in someone's face you didn't need to worry about saying or doing the wrong thing. You'd already jumped off the cliff, it was just about finding a place to land safely.

'Are we?'

Nick raised his voice again.

'Yeah we are. You know we are. You know what I want.' He thrust a forefinger at him.

'Do I?'

He was still so cool. You had to admire him for that.

'And now I know what you want and how much you'll pay for it.'

'Go on.'

'So let's do a deal, Davey.'

'I love doing a deal.'

'OK so here's the deal. I'll let you fuck Julie for free, if you have this bloke killed for me. I'm happy, you're happy. Everyone's a winner. How's that sound? You can make that happen, I know you can.'

Davey James didn't change his expression at all. He just held out his big hand.

'Deal,' he said without emotion, as though agreeing the smallest, least consequential of things.

Nick gripped his hand as tightly as he could, pressing his fingers together hard. James' hand was damp and fleshy and felt like squeezing a freshly butchered joint of meat.

But was that enough?

Had he actually confessed to a crime yet? Was promising to have someone killed a crime? It had to be hadn't it? But it was just words, he could say he never meant it and it was nothing at all to do with the murders. He needed more out of him.

Nick let go of his hand and shook his head, thoughts coming out his mouth almost randomly now that he was drunk.

'But how do I know that you know what you're doing, though? No disrespect, but I don't want this fucking up, Davey. I don't want anything coming back to me. I mean, whoever did for Alan Armstrong fucked it up, didn't they? No way was Alan a target for that. He was a lovely bloke. They were after someone else. Big fuck up. Al was innocent, they got the wrong man there, whoever that was...I don't want some amateur fuck like that...I mean, they arrested Jimmy Butcher. He's mental. Someone wasted their fucking money. Must've been a fucking idiot to think he'd be any good. He always was a psycho even at school. That was some fucking shit-munching amateur that booked him for that gig, eh? Simple enough to get it right, he got it totally wrong.'

Nick felt sure James was guilty. He had to be, didn't he? He was a monster who would have a man killed in order to have sex with a woman. He'd paid for both murders, just as Harcombe had said. He had to have. He'd do that in a heartbeat. It'd be nothing to him. And he'd wanted Matt Little to take the rap for it. Perfect. It was probably better to have Matt in jail than dead. The torture would be all the greater for the man that had usurped him in his wife's life. This was what he was all about: power and abuse.

Come on, cough it out, you bastard. It felt good to vicariously insult him like this. It felt like he was jabbing, jabbing, jabbing at him using words as weapons. As he spoke he was sure there was some colour rising in James' cheek as he sipped whisky, but still said nothing.

But Nick was now emotionally exhausted and felt like he had to go for one massive punch. It was time to give him the full gun and if it didn't work, at least he'd thrown his full bollocks at it.

He knocked the last of his whisky down and coughed with the vicious kick. His head felt unsteady.

'I was told something on the grapevine...from a copper actually...you probably know them, but I'm not allowed to say who it is...' said Nick, lying through narrowed eyes, spinning a story out of nowhere.

'Oh yeah? What was that?' His face was expressionless because was used to not giving anything away.

'I was told by someone who fucking knows, Davey, that it was you.'

'Me? Me who did what?'

'Paid Butcher to kill Alan'

'Yeah?' He was still inexpressive.

'Yeah.'

'Are you trying to be clever with me Nick? Is this some sort of game?'

He didn't like the sound of that.

'I just want to know you won't make that bad a job for me. Not unreasonable. Do it right and you get Julie, do it wrong, I get jail. You can see why I'm twitchy.'

'I said it was a deal. It'll happen. Just give me the details.'

Nope, not good enough.

'But if you fucked that up, you might fuck this up for me. Did you fuck it up? Because if you fuck this up for me, you don't get to so much as touch Julie. Right? She's mine. Right? If you did it, be the big man and admit it, no harm in that...I just want to know where we stand.'

It was close now, surely. Davey James stared at him, still expressionless. Again, Nick looked around feeling like he was under scrutiny.

'Those mistakes won't be made again, I can assure you.' He said the sentence quietly. Nick was sure it was too quiet for the mic to pick up.

'Did you pay him upfront, Davey? I won't be paying you upfront with Julie. Right? You get her after it's done.'

James stood up, sucked in the last thin line of whisky from the bottom of the cut glass tumbler and poured himself another. Nick got to his feet, sensing the time was upon him now. An almost psychic understanding of what was about to unfold, held him in a frost-cold grip. He was calm, living utterly in the moment, but knowing the banks of the river of violence were about to flood.

'Yeah, should never have been paid before he'd done it. I didn't think either Butcher or Root would fuck it up so badly. Useless cunts. But like I say, it won't happen again. There are better men for the job. I'll sort it, not least because your Julie is a fucking magnificent prize to win. Well worth it. I'll fuck her every which way until she screams for mercy.' His tone was low, gruff and relishing in its own nastiness. The microphone better have caught that.

It was here.

Now.

A burning tide of hatred and anger poured into Nick Guymer's body from his soul. A stinking revulsion at the immorality of the world, of the evil that men do and of the man in front of him who seemed to embody all of it.

He was on him in a heartbeat. Super-human power and energy in every single one his muscles. No more words now. He swung a massive right hander into the fat man's face with such power that briefly both of Nick's feet left the ground. Not just from his shoulder this was pulled from somewhere deeper and more profound. As his fist travelled through the air towards its violent end point, for right or wrong, it felt beautiful, like the most perfect response to what James was and what he embodied.

His knuckles sank into James' face as though it was a cheap cushion, yielding and yielding through layers of fat until it reached bone and when it reached that bone, it cracked like deadwood underfoot. The transference of energy from his shoulder, down his arm, through his fist and into the red face was so powerful it knocked James, all 22 stone of him, backwards in a stagger, his face the very definition of stunned.

Nick loaded his shoulder again, took three steps forward, planted his right foot down and swung again with his right fist. As James was still moving, this punch connected with his neck; a neck so fat it looked like he was wearing a roll neck sweater of reddened flesh. This second assault seemed to waken James' senses and the big man roared and lashed back at him with more weight than Nick could ever muster. The blow hit him in the ribs and for a microsecond hurt like hell, but this was no time for pain. Let the adrenalin take care of that. The world was now all violence, nothing else existed or would ever exist; it was all encompassing.

Nick, fast on his feet, leaped over a big glass coffee table, got behind James and gripped him around the neck in a hold so tight and irresistible that he knew, as soon as he took it, he had him. He had the fucker now. This played to the core of Nick's strength. Resistance training had built his biceps, triceps and pecs. This was where all his power was and these were the muscles he needed now.

And so, quite consciously and deliberately, he began to choke him, dragging him backwards as he did so. The big man clawed at his throat, his face going purple as the pressure from Nick's arms denied his windpipe enough oxygen. He knew from the minute he took it, it was a death grip.

'You're. An. Evil. Piece. Of. Shit.' He yelled each word, yanking on his neck with every utterance. Something cracked inside of James' body. He felt its vibration run down his arm. It was like wrestling a giant bag of spluttering sand. But the struggle was soon dying from James' body. It was palpable, like a battery-operated toy running out of energy, he tried to resist, but then seemed to give up and accept that he had lost his battle for life.

The tension and fight soaked out of the huge mass and, as Nick gripped him tighter, he became heavier as his muscles lost the fight to stay conscious. Suddenly and without warning, James' knees buckled and the full 22 stone of his weight was left for Nick to bear; it was about three times as much as any weight he'd ever lifted and he just didn't have the strength to either hold him or push him away. The huge bulk pressed down and down and down on him, making Nick stagger back and back and then crash to the floor. There was an explosion - a bang and a shattering noise. For a split second, he thought a bomb had gone off and then a blinding white light and shard of intense pain spread from his head down throughout his whole body. There was no time to think, or appreciate, or understand what had happened. Suddenly and instantly his consciousness was gone.

CHAPTER 15

Noise. Some smears of light. Voices, lots of voices.

'Nick! Nick! Can you hear me? Nick, come on, lad. Come back to me. Come on.'

He opened his eyes. Everything was blurred and shifting from left to right. He shut them again and refocused his brain.

'Ah, there you are...come on lad, sit up, have a drink of water.'

It was the voice of Colin Harcombe.

For a minute he just lay there. There were so many voices and so much activity around him that it was scrambling his thoughts. Where was he? What had happened?

Harcombe was squatting alongside him holding out a glass of water. Nick sat up and took it, swallowing the cold, faintly chlorinated water and letting out a moan as he felt a stinging pain on the back of his head. He dabbed at it with his finger tips. His hair was wet with blood.

To his left the Chesterfield sofa had been pulled to one side and four paramedics were working on the prone body of Davey James. He was on his back, eyes closed, arms spread out in an unnatural shape. One of them shone a light in his eyes, another wiped blood from his face.

Nick's whole body hurt.

'Did he fall on top of me?' he said.

'No. He fell onto the glass table. You must have pushed him onto it.'

He stared at him. He wasn't moving. At first Nick didn't see it, didn't see what was sticking out of Davey James' body. It was transparent and almost invisible until the light caught it; a three foot long shard of glass from the coffee table had pierced him under his left rib cage, right up into his chest. The end which was sticking out tapered to a vicious-looking sharp point.

'What the fuck happened here?' he said, rubbing the blood off his fingers onto the carpet.

'By the look of it, he fell onto the glass table. You got lucky, your head got cut by some flying glass, but you'll be OK. The medics will deal with you in a minute.'

One of the paramedics turned and made a throat cutting sign at Harcombe.

Nick tried to get to his feet, felt dizzy and then, on his hands and knees, threw up a thin stream of whisky and bile onto the expensive carpet.

'Fuck. Where's Jules?'

'She's somewhere outside. Can't come in yet. Crime scene needed securing. We'll take you out as soon as you're more steady on your feet.'

It all began to form into a picture as Nick's synapses began to repair themselves. He knelt and rubbed his face. 'Did you get everything on tape that you needed? He confessed to conspiracy to murder, didn't he?'

'Yes, lad. We got it all.' But Harcombe's voice wasn't celebratory and Nick knew him well enough to know something was wrong. He looked at Davey James again lying there, dead. The final piece fell into place. He'd choked him to death. Just as he'd almost choked Darren Harris to death.

'I killed him, didn't I?'

Harcombe looked across at the paramedics preparing to take the body away and then back at Nick.

'That is what it looks like.'

Nick held his head in his hands, the enormity of what he had done flooding into his brain en masse in a hundred simultaneous thoughts and realisations. What the hell had he done? He'd taken away a man's life. He'd killed a human being. Why had he done that? Why?

'You're going to have to arrest me, aren't you?'

Harcombe patted him on the shoulder. 'Sorry lad. Who's your lawyer?'

He didn't have one. The only one he knew was his dad's old lawyer up in Teesdale, Leslie West.

'I'll get them to give him a call. See if he can come down to the station,' said Harcombe.

'I choked him, Col. I was pulling on his neck. It snapped, I heard it.'

'Don't say anything to me yet. Wait until you hear from Mr West.'

'Thanks, Col.'

Harcombe got to his feet and helped Nick to stand up. He shook his head.

'Bad business this, Nick. I warned you, didn't I? At your house. I warned you to know your own strength. I don't do this job to put good men like you in jail.' He sighed heavily.

'Sorry, Col.'

'Too late for that now, lad. Far too late.'

They took him down to Stockton police station in the back of a police car. He'd not even caught a glimpse of Julie as they'd led him out. She was everything to him. Everything. And he'd thrown it all away in a moment of red-hot blood. She'd saved his life with her love. And he'd repaid her like this. Their child was to be fatherless, their love now useless. Another man letting a woman down through violence. As the police door slammed shut, his freedom now evaporated, he cried dry tears and began wondering how he could end his life as soon as possible. He wasn't going to live a life behind bars. No way. This was going to end sooner than later.

They put him in a small cell. Outside, almost within shouting distance, was Jeff's record store. What a profound distance that was, though. The space between freedom and imprisonment. By the time all the paperwork was done and Leslie West called, it was nearly five o'clock.

Nick had sunk into himself, closing down to survive the quiet, motionless boredom of sitting on a hard bed in a small cell. He looked up at a rattle on the door. Colin Harcombe came in. He tried a smile, but realised it wasn't appropriate.

'Mr West will be here any minute. Just wanted to give you a

little bit of an idea of how all this is going to work. I wouldn't normally but...but this is obviously a special case - you being there to help us. That will help your case, Nick. A lot.'

'You mean I'm looking at 20 years instead of 25, then?' He chewed on his bottom lip, his emotions now almost totally evaporated. What point was there to having emotions? They only got you into trouble.

'Early days yet, lad. I shall be clear about your bravery. This was a moment of madness in the heat of the moment. When a court considers the nature of what you were doing and the degree of provocation, I'm confident you will get the lowest custodial sentence that it's possible to give...but we're already getting well ahead of ourselves.'

Nick nodded. 'Is Julie here?'

He stood up and turned his watch around on his wrist and then cleared his throat.

'No. No she's not, Nick. She just disappeared from the scene and was gone. Right now, I don't know where she is. There's talk, there's rumours about things happening, but I can't say anything right now. There is a huge media scrum outside, so you can't blame her for keeping her distance from here.'

He knew why she'd not come. She'd spent her life visiting her brothers in cells and in jail and here he was, just the same as the Wells brothers. Another thug. Another irresponsible, violent man. He didn't blame her. Better that she got on with her life now. Forget about him.

In such small moments life could change irrevocably. All that joy he'd felt at her being pregnant, all that happiness and love they'd shared, all of it was gone now. Everything altered. Sometimes it seemed actions just couldn't have such profound consequences. But they could. How often had she told him recently? Actions matter more than words. He'd listened, but he hadn't understood. Not until now. It seemed as if the consequences of what you did were isolated in the moment. You don't think of the longer, deeper, more widespread reverberations. The ripples kept on going and going and going from every action.

He heard Leslie West on the other side of the cell door as soon as he arrived. His breathing wasn't any better than it had been three years earlier when he'd handled the disposal of his dad's estate. At six feet five inches tall and well over 20 stone, he was a massive presence; a massive presence with a very purple complexion. It was amazing that he'd survived this long. He was the personification of a heart attack.

A firm-minded, bluff and unimpeachably respectable country lawyer in his late 60s, Nick was glad to see him as he was shown into an interview room. He held out his hand and Leslie shook with a grip as powerful as a much younger man's.

'Nick. Well, I'd say it's good to see you again, but these are far from ideal circumstances to renew our acquaintance. My, my. Well, life throws us some challenges, doesn't it?'

Nick didn't know what to say. So he said nothing.

Leslie took out some papers and looked through them. 'Now, I understand what has happened and why you have been arrested. They have not charged you yet, though, is that right?'

'No.'

'And you've not given an account of what happened to the police yet?'

'No. Colin said to speak to you first.'

'Good. I know Harcombe well. Good chap.'

'Yes, he is.'

'I don't expect them to charge you until they have the coroner's report tomorrow. You were there to work for the police and you got into a fight and Davey James died. What are your recollections, Nick. Take your time.'

He went over what had happened again, as he'd done so time and again in the hours since the fight. Leslie West breathed heavily through his nose, nodding and making affirmative noises as he took notes with an expensive fountain pen.

'Let me ask you this. Did you intend to kill him? By that I mean, did you stand there and think, "right Mister James, I shall kill you"?'

Nick sat for a full minute considering the question, whilst Leslie took a drink of water.

'No. I didn't think like that. But I am not going to lie about this Leslie. I knew what I was doing. I knew I was choking him to death. I knew if I kept pulling on him like I was, that he'd die.'

'Hmm. Well, I would suggest that firstly, your judgement was severely impaired by alcohol, secondly this man had just confessed to conspiracy to murder and he had also tried to procure your partner for sex. All the while, you were wearing a recording device and under instructions from the police. These are not normal circumstances, so I would urge you not to make such harsh judgements on yourself and certainly not to voice them to the police. Thinking you have done something and actually having done it are two very, very different things. Do you understand me?'

But Nick knew what he knew. He had to live with it. At least, for as long as he was going to be alive, which may not be very much longer.

'My view is, this is a very defendable case. We do not have conclusive proof that it was your choking him, that killed him. He had a shard of glass in him you said, we already know that.'

'I threw him onto that table. But he was already dead by then. I choked him or broke his neck, something went snap. I felt it. Even if I didn't, the glass went in him because of what I did. Either way, it's down to me.'

'No. You don't know that he was dead, nor that the glass killed him as you describe. You know nothing of the sort and my advice is that you never repeat those words. Do you hear me? These are testing hours. Do not talk yourself into guilt you do not know you should own, even if it is your predisposition to do so. I shall stay in town and I will return in the morning.' He put papers in to his briefcase. 'Has Julie visited you?'

'No.'

'Good.'

'Good? Why?'

'I don't want you to get more upset. I suggest you relax tonight, gather your thoughts and emotions and prepare to defend yourself with proper regard to the actual facts and not to your emotional reaction to what you *think* are the facts. You will, almost certainly, get bail because of your work for the police. You're not a flight risk and have a good personal relationship with Harcombe, whom I know is a big admirer of yours. So, there is much reason to have a lot of hope that we can overturn this and you will, not only not have to go to jail, but will walk away a free man, with your reputation intact.'

'Really? But even if the glass killed him, he wouldn't have fallen onto it if I hadn't been choking him. I initiated the whole thing.'

'My dear boy, that is nothing but speculation and has no place here. You either killed him or you did not. That is all there is to it.'

Leslie West never said anything he didn't mean. If you cut him open, 'my word is my bond' would run right through him. What he told you was the truth as he saw it. There was no doubting him.

He shook his hand in another iron grip. 'I will see you in the morning. Sleep well; hopefully, this will be your only night in jail.'

After the lawyer left, Nick lay down on his bed. It was like he had been in the presence of a proper grown up. He was 20 years younger, but it felt like a lot more. Leslie West was a solid, decent, reliable adult male, full of Yorkshire grit and resolution. Every time he'd met him he'd felt like that. Yet he was, by any standard, obese. Years of eating and drinking to excess had taken its toll on his body. Why had he done that to himself? Did it speak of emotional distress below the surface, a distress he kept at bay through over-consumption? It was so self-destructive and yet to talk to him, he was moderation itself without a hint of any inner turmoil. But no-one destroys their body in such a way for so long, unless something is wrong, surely. Somewhere, deep down, perhaps buried where no-one, not even Leslie West could find it any more, something was upset and causing him trouble.

Were they all messed up underneath? Men. Unable to really cope with life. Maybe that was commonly the male experience. Men were supposed to be strong and resolute and really they weren't. Really they were a mess. They were weak and were slaves to short-term physicality. They were assaulted by a million insecurities and distresses and were given no emotional tools to cope with them at all, so they swallowed them down with booze and food and tried to cover them up with misogyny, macho bluster, with aggression and displays of supposed strength. It was all a product of broken minds, but no more excusable for that. Why couldn't they help each other more? No man is an island unto himself; whoever said that was right, but also very wrong. Men were emotional islands, stranded from the shore, drifting in the seas of life with no direction home. It started from when you were small and it didn't ever let up; this crushing idea of what being a man was, what being a *real* man meant, it was always with you, whatever the social trends, cultures or mores of the day. Men needed liberating from themselves. Nick needed liberating from himself.

The darkness of the Teesside night seemed almost infinitely long. He didn't sleep; instead he seemed to drop into a vegetative state, somewhere between life and death, between consciousness and unconsciousness. Time without measure now. This could be death, or a sort of death. It was certainly no life. The station was quiet. Not even any drunks shouting the odds to break the monotony. Outside he could hear the diesel night bus engines grumbling down the High Street, taking the free people home. Then, just an occasional taxi.

He rubbed at his sore rib where James had punched him. It had been throbbing since he was arrested. As he fingered it gingerly, in one spot it delivered a sharp, jabbing pain. Probably cracked. Still, it felt like he deserved the pain. Same with his painfully swollen, bruised and grazed knuckles from the punches to James' face. That first punch was so hard, the hardest he had ever thrown, it was a wonder the bones in his hand were not shattered to dust. They were puffy and a shade of purple, but that was all.

At around two in the morning he got up and paced the length and breadth of the cell a 100 times and then did some sit-ups and push-ups. He was just resting after doing ten of each when there were voices somewhere towards the entrance to the station. He sat in the dark and listened. More voices, some raised now. Laughter. Probably one shift relieving another.

He began doing some squats, arms outstretched.

More noise outside. Then quiet again.

The exercise released enough endorphins into his bloodstream to give him a couple of hours of sleep. He was awakened by voices again. One was Harcombe's. It came closer. Then was at the door. A rattle of keys and it opened letting electric light flood in. Nick shaded his eyes.

'Ah, good, you're awake,' said the DI.

'I am now,' said Nick, sitting up. 'Don't tell me you've brought me breakfast at 4am.'

'Better than that. I thought you should know. There have been developments.'

'Developments?'

'Yes, serious developments. I've just come back from the coroner.'

'The coroner? In the middle of the night?'

'I asked him to start early as a favour to me. His early conclusions are that Davey James was killed by the shard of glass and not by you choking him. He was not suffocated, he died through the wound inflicted by that glass. It went under his rib cage and pierced his heart. He died almost instantly.'

'Are you sure?' said Nick, doubtful. 'I heard something break on him at some point. A loud, wooden snapping sound.'

'You damaged a vertebrae, but not his spine. He'd had had a sore neck but it wouldn't have killed him.'

Nick didn't know what it meant. He still felt like he'd killed him. The shard of glass wouldn't have killed him if he hadn't choked him so hard that he collapsed onto the table. He was still responsible for his death.

He turned to the officer alongside him.

'Has he had visitors?'

'Just his lawyer.'

He turned back to Nick. 'I can't go into details yet, but things are afoot.'

'Afoot? Who are you now Colin, Sherlock Holmes?' said Nick, eyes closed.

'Like I say, I can't go into details. Julie was in touch and we've pulled people in as a result. Bide your time, Nick. I'll get some food sorted out for you. I'll see you later.'

The door closed again. Freedom from those four walls would be nice, but you could never get freedom from yourself. Nick lay back down and put his hands behind his head. We come into the world alone, we leave it alone, really; whoever we share our space with, we're always alone. The one thing you can never escape is the loneliness of existence. That's what you have to deal with. Only you are inside your own head, only you know your inner voice, only you lives inside of you.

Half an hour later he was brought some fried eggs and bacon on a tray.

'I didn't reckon you'd do low carb breakfasts,' Nick said.

'Eh? Low what?' said the copper.

'Nowt. Ignore me,' he said, taking the food from him. Such things seemed a bourgeois self-indulgence now.

It was a sunny morning. A shaft of light from the south-easterly facing window only showed how filthy the cell was. How much longer was this going to go on?

At 9.15am he was called into an interview room to meet Leslie West again. He sat down opposite him. His big purple face had beads of sweat along his white hair line, but his mouth was set in a wide grin.

'Hello old boy, hello. Sit down, sit down.' He shuffled papers and tapped them into order on the desk.

'What a night, what a night indeed. Now, what did I say?'

'I don't know. I can't remember,' said Nick.

Leslie West bellowed a laugh which you'd have to call hearty.

'No, neither can I to be precise, but it was along the lines of don't give up hope.'

'What's been going on? Harcombe said something about developments.'

The lawyer put his thick, beef sausage fingers together and leaned forward. Nick was sure he could smell whisky on his breath. Had he been drinking already or was it residue from a big-late night session?

'A synopsis is in order.' He glanced down at some notes written in the style of a doctor who had lost the ability to actually write. Maybe it was his own version of shorthand. 'Cleveland Police are currently questioning Zak and Toni James about the murder of their father.'

'They're what?!' Nick stood up in shock. For the first time since he'd been arrested, he felt something other than suicidal misery.

'Sit down, old chap. There's more.'

'But how could they have killed him? They weren't even there.' He sat back down again.

Leslie West held up a hand to stop him talking and make him calm down.

'All will unfold, I'm sure. Mr James also appears to have confessed to crimes that he didn't commit. The kids went on the run yesterday...'

'....on the run? On the run?! On the run from where to where?'

'From The Avenue to, as it turned out, upper Teesdale. Reeth to be precise.'

'Reeth? I'm sorry, I don't understand any of this.' He shook his head. What madness was this? 'All I know is I pulled on James' throat until he was unconscious and he fell on to a glass table and that's all I know. Those kids were not there.'

'Ah, but they were. Unbeknown to you and to the Police. It was

Julie who spotted them leaving...'

'Julie?'

'And with her extensive, shall we say connections, in the network of err...shall we say underworld associates...what I believe is called The Word was put out. Yes indeed. They were found on the road approaching Middleton St George in the middle of the night and Harcombe's men have picked them up. They're being questioned in this very building as we speak.'

Nick listened to this with rising astonishment.

'How long was I unconscious for, do you know?'

'The police estimate it was about ten or 15 minutes, maybe longer. So, to recap, we now know you didn't kill Davey James. You are not a murderer. No sir. Not for a moment. The shard of glass only killed him because it was used deliberately as a murder weapon. The coroner has been working on this since the early hours and says it was impossible that it could have lodged itself in him as it did, without being shoved into him. It was a viciously sharp piece of hard glass and it had been thrust into him with some force. Jammed right up under his rib cage and there was a lot of bulk to get through. He didn't fall onto it. You were unconscious, he was unconscious, no-one else was there and yet the two children were seen by Julie, exiting the house from a back door, running across the garden to the silver Mercedes. The girl drove them out of there at speed and as all the police where in the house, they would have missed it had Julie not been there. Hopefully, they will do the decent thing now they've been arrested...'

Nick shook his head again in sheer disbelief.

'...in the meantime I have been told that you will be released on police bail today whilst the case is looked at and a decision come to on what, if anything, to charge you with. I doubt you will even be charged with assault, given the circumstances.'

He slapped at the table, leaned over and patted Nick on the shoulder. 'Your nightmare will soon be over, old boy. '

Would it though? Would it really? Didn't the nightmare actually just live inside of him?

'Where's Julie now?'

'I don't actually know. She was up most of the night with her brothers so I imagine she's getting some rest. I daresay she shall be along soon enough.'

'I don't understand what all this means, Leslie. I can't piece it together in my head.'

The big man cleared a considerable amount of phlegm from his throat and drummed the big, heavy fingers on the desk.

'I have read up on these murders. I think I see a common thread...'

As he spoke, there was a cheering sound, perhaps two or three rooms away, muffled but distinctive. Whoops and some applause. Someone shouted, 'Get in!' Leslie looked over his shoulder towards the sound. A door opened and DI Harcombe strode in with an expression on his face that looked suspiciously like joy. It didn't sit comfortably and it wasn't one he was going to hold for long, but here and now, in this instance, as he strode into the room and held his arms out wide to the two men, that was clearly his emotion.

'Good news, Detective Inspector?' said Leslie West, standing up.

Nick stood up and Harcombe patted them both on the back at the same time.

'The best news. The DJ Tees murders are case closed. Sorted.'

He drew a line in the air with his finger as though to symbolize the end of the investigation. He beamed from Nick to Leslie West.

'We couldn't have, no, strike that, we wouldn't have done it without your Julie's help. It was a magnificent effort above and beyond the call of duty. So you, Nick Guymer, you are free to go.'

He slapped him on the back as though he had done something to deserve congratulation, which was exactly the opposite of how he felt.

CHAPTER 16

Harcombe drove him home, after Nick was discharged on police bail to report back at a later date to see if any other charges would be brought. The way he talked it was as just as though a TV programme was over and the plot had been solved. It was as though it wasn't real life at all. Crimes existed in isolation to the policeman and once they were sorted out, he could draw a line under them and move on to other matters. But it didn't seem that easy to Nick. It was all one mass of heinous, awful criminality.

'You should've seen the relief on Matt Little's face when I told him he was free to go. Almost worth banging a chap up just to see that sort of relief. I jest, of course.'

'Must have been traumatic for him,' said Nick.

'We got a complete confession from the two kids. Both of them gave us the whole story. Same story from each of them. Not exactly hardened sorts. Just very, very distressed children. Psychiatric reports will be done, of course. Something is not right there, doubtless due to James' abuse. You'll hear all about it in due course,' said the DI as they headed south on Yarm Road.

'They killed their own father? Really? Are you sure they're not taking the piss, Col?'

'Oh we're sure alright. They're a strange pair. Damaged, of course. Began a campaign to terrorize the both of them last year and it escalated and escalated, especially as they smoked more and more of that dope they've been buying on Hartington Road.'

'And it was them who paid Butcher and Root to do the murders?'

'Not quite. They met Root when he worked on URO business and rightly saw how obsessed he was with their father. So they played up to him and got the knives from Root's store. Root was more than happy to buddy up with the kids of the man he was such a fan of.'

'They got the knives from the break in?'

'No, that never happened. Root made that up and told lies to the local plod. Root sold them the knives after, under their instruction, getting Matt Little's fingerprints on them. They sent Butcher the cash, he didn't know who had booked his services, so to speak. He got the money and a photo and was told where to go and when. Root met him outside and gave him one of the knives...'

'...when Paul Trent saw them?'

'....yes indeed. He was carrying the second knife on him, I reckon. You saw that bulge in his jacket. That'll have been it. They knew both their father and Matt had invested in Tees Digital and that Alan Armstrong was a partner with Malcolm Pallister and owed Matt the ten grand as part of that arrangement. Their intent was to frame Matt for the murders from the start, not to actually have him killed. Butcher did the job as instructed. The man knows his business. We shouldn't have doubted his ability to kill the right person once paid sufficiently well.'

'So he left s thumb print by accident?'

Harcombe nodded. 'We searched his cousin's flat in Roseworth, where we picked him up and found a leather glove with a hole in the right thumb. That's how he got his print on the knife. Sloppy work.'

'So why did he look at me strangely then? He can't have killed Alan at that moment. He must have done it when the coast was clear after Jeff and Rita had left the stockroom. He's followed Alan in there and knifed him in an instant and then fled.'

'Yes, that's exactly what he did do which is why, when we took names and addresses, he wasn't there. I think he recognized you from school and was worried that you'd recognize him. That's my reasoning.'

'But he knew it was Jeff's party, didn't he?'

'No. He was just told to go to there and kill Alan Armstrong and that's what he did. He wasn't to know that you didn't recognize him, or that Jeff would have known who he was if he'd seen him.'

Nick went quiet as they sat at some lights in Eaglescliffe.

'Really? All this was punishment for Matt's affair with their mother? Shit. That's a bit extreme isn't it, to understate it somewhat?'

'Ah, but you're seeing it in isolation. This was the final battle of a long war of attrition between them all and this wasn't going to be the end.'

'But Davey confessed on tape to paying for those murders. Why did he do that?'

'We'll never know for sure now, but my guess is to impress you. It sounded like what you wanted to hear, which it was, of course. He was very good at picking up on what people wanted to hear and feeding it back to them. He did that all the time in interviews. He thought, by doing so, he would get access to Julie. You suckered him into believing you. Ironically, you fed him what he wanted to hear. Brilliant work.'

They sat in traffic alongside the golf club where Nick had briefly been a young member before the discovery of drink and girls had made golf seem very sodding boring indeed.

'So what was Root doing out in Middleton that night?'

'He went out there to kill Matt, thinking in his twisted mind that he was doing a favour to Davey. My view is he's been on the verge of something like this for a long time. The North Yorkshire team have even had him on their watch list because he'd been pulled in for fights and other reckless behaviour a couple of times. But there was a twist there. It was Toni and Zak in the DJ 61 Merc. Earlier that day, playing him for a fool, they'd goaded him into the attack. They wound him up, told him their father would consider it a great thing if he did for Matt and that unspecified rewards would flow his way if he did. They told him where she lived, a fact they'd found out by spying on their own mother. They followed Root out there to watch him at work. They left once you made an appearance. They seemed to think it was hilarious. Fun, almost. By all accounts he didn't take a lot of winding up.'

'I can vouch for that. He was a ball of fury every time I've seen him.'

'Oh, he likes you and your, what was it now, 'expert physicalling'? He'd have killed you, but he'd have respected you. I'm sure that's a comfort, Nick.'

'Those kids are incredible. So young and yet so messed up.'

'They learned bullying, psychological manipulation and violence at their father's knee. Add in strong drugs and you've got a big problem.'

'Do you think they're psychotic?'

The policeman nodded as he drove. 'The girl certainly is, but I'll leave that to the appropriate people to properly diagnose. Put it this way, would anyone do what they have done if they were not psychotic? They found a like mind in that regard, when it came to Mick Root.'

'But he didn't kill Malcolm?'

'No he didn't. That was Toni James. The lad called the secretary, pretending to be Pally's brother and said he was ill and she wasn't to bother coming in for a couple of days. He'd used Matt's phone, which he'd stolen from the Lexus a couple of weeks earlier, while they were spying on their mother's new house. Matt had left the car unlocked. Toni went over to Tees Digital's office with Root's second knife, also covered in Matt's prints. She walked straight in and, by her own account, gutted him like a fish. Jammed it right up under his rib cage and into his heart.'

Nick went cold. Poor Pally. Jesus Christ, what a way for your life to be over.

'Was she fucked up on dope when she did that?'

'Oh yes. Both of them are on it the whole time. They had cocaine on them too when we got them. It had bent her mind. I don't think there's any doubt about that. And she isn't remorseful in the slightest. It's as though she lost the ability to see that these people are humans. We haven't yet uncovered any sexual abuse by her father against her, but it would not surprise me in the slightest if we did, because she has a vicious hatred of him, the like of which I've never encountered in 35 years in the force. That has really come out in the interviews which, unsurprisingly enough, she's treated a little like some sort of therapy. She was the one who spray-painted the office and then called in a false report of seeing the Lexus. Her computer has pages and pages of notes planning how to kill her father.'

'It's an amazing thing to even think of doing - jamming a big shard of glass into the heart of your own father. It's...it's appalling. There's no other word for it and that doesn't do it justice.'

'They were high at the time again of course, they'd been smoking while watching the CCTV, but all that hatred of their father for abusing their mother, all came to a head when they heard him talking in such a disgusting way about her. That business about cutting out her...well...you probably remember. That was what triggered it. That's why it happened as it happened. They wanted to hurt both parents, but only wanted to kill Davey.'

'I actually heard something when he was going on about Deirdre. A crash or noise in the house.'

'That was Toni throwing a lamp against the wall, in an absolute fury. Those words he spoke, they were, in effect, what got him killed.'

'Their poor mother. Years of torture at the hands of her husband and then being rejected by her kids and having her new boyfriend nearly killed and framed for murder. I mean, Jesus, she must be in a right state.'

'Yes. Well, indeed. It's not a happy outcome and there's no dressing it up. Lives torn apart, lives ruined, lives lost. That's the nature of my business, sadly. But at least it has ended.'

They drove down Yarm High Street.

'And so those kids drove that piece of glass into their dad whilst I was lying there spark out?'

'Yes. As I say, they saw the whole fight on the CCTV. They saw you wrestle big Davey over and onto the table. The damn thing went off like bomb. I mean, it was a big bit of furniture. You were both spark out, but we were still out on the Avenue, because we hadn't twigged what you were doing. We couldn't hear anything - the microphone was dislodged in your struggle. So they had a few minutes. Toni says she saw this three feet long "glass spear". She pulled on her leather gloves, picked it up and jammed it into him until she couldn't push it any more. After knifing poor Pally she knew where to put it for maximum effect. She'd researched it all long before. As I say, we were slow off the mark. We didn't realise what was happening. It wasn't obvious at first. But the kids were watching it all on a laptop from another room. Davey knew they were in the house, but they've said he hadn't a clue that they knew how to use the CCTV he'd set up. She saw her chance and did it. Mind, they had no idea we were around. Why would they? So when we came rushing up the driveway, they waited until we were all in the front and then left by the back door.'

'Really...wow...'

'I think Toni felt his abuse of her mother most acutely. Then to hear him talking about her to you and then the whole thing with Julie, well...as she said to me later, "he was sub-human scum who didn't deserve to live," and I have to say, I can see her point.'

'I do recall having the feeling that someone was watching me the whole time I was in there. But I couldn't see anyone.'

'Yes, well you were right. There were CCTV cameras all over the house - a legacy of his paranoia and desire to watch what his wife was doing. That house was virtually a prison for her. At times she was locked in and even if she did get out, he'd know right away.'

'That's so fucked up.'

'Well, we were absolutely astonished to hear how he talked to you. Shocking stuff. Not Julie though. She was calm as a mill pond. For what it's worth, I totally understood why you'd want to have a pop at him. Not that I approve of the public being violent to each other. Only creates paperwork for us.' He laughed stiffly at his own little joke.'

The car pulled up on the verge next to the dirt track that led down to Nick and Julie's old farmhouse. Harcombe got out and stood beside the car and gripped Nick's hand in a prolonged shake.

'Good luck. We shall be in touch with you soon, but off the record I wouldn't worry too much about any charges for assault and such...I shall have the appropriate word with the appropriate people in that regard.'

'Thanks, Colin.'

'Are you OK?'

'Not really. No. I'm left with the feeling that men are bastards. All of us. Bastards.'

'I can see why. Bound to be upsetting. Not true though. Lots of good people are out there, Nick.' He gestured into the Teesside sky. 'I've been sitting next to one. Get some help, perhaps. Yes? Good.'

It was time for Harcombe to move on to the next bad guy. There was always a new crime to investigate and a new evil-doer to take down in the ceaseless procession of wrong. It was all just work to him.

Nick watched him pull away. It was a quiet walk down the track. A robin hopped in front of him for a couple of yards and then jumped onto a hawthorn bush, singing loudly. Was it the same robin he saw on his morning walk? He smiled at it and, in his head, said hello to the smart little bird. Birds, they seemed nicer than humans. Much, much nicer.

As he got near the house, a familiar sound echoed off the trees that lined the path to the north of the house. The sound of someone chopping wood. As he rounded a shallow bend and saw the house, Julie was swinging a big axe, splitting logs and tossing them into their wood basket. She looked up as she saw him and made an extravagant waving gesture at him with the axe. Colin had let her know they were on their way. She took off her Boro baseball cap, wiped sweat from her forehead and pulled it back on.

'Now then, jailbird. How are you?' she said as he got close.

He didn't reply, just took her in his arms and hugged her close, breathing her in again. She patted him on the back. 'All done now, kidda. All over. What a 24 hours,' she said, guiding him inside with an arm on the small of his back. 'I couldn't face coming in to see you in there this morning, though...sorry. I just couldn't do it.'

'I don't blame you.'

'I've been in there way too much over the years with the brothers. When they told me you'd been arrested and what for, I just didn't believe it. By then I knew the kids were involved somehow, so I knew something else had to have happened other than you killing James.'

She put the kettle on.

'So you worked it all out? Colin's given me the low down about what went on,' said Nick.

'Yeah, as soon as I saw them leg it from the house, jump into the Merc and zoom off, it all began to fall into place quickly. After that it was just a matter of finding them, not that it was easy.'

'They could've gone anywhere. How come they went to Reeth?'

'To buy another Bowie knife. The fella had said he was getting some in, remember? Toni was the woman that the Sanderson bloke who runs the shop described to my brothers. Dark haired, wore tweed and a headscarf. We thought it was an older woman because of what she was wearing - bit narrow-minded of us, that - but it was Toni. Ricky and Kev told the bloke to ring them if anyone else came in for a knife. So he did. Blokes tend to do what Kev and Ricky have asked them to do, like. That was the break we needed because no-one could find them until we got that call. They'd changed cars to a less noticeable blue Ford Focus at the estate office. The police didn't even look for them to start with, because they thought you'd killed Davey James. By mid-afternoon when I'd enlightened them, the coppers had the Ford's registration plate, but finding a car like that was always going to take a lot of time. The bloke in the shop said it was two kids and described them to a tee, so we knew it was them. I reckon they were going to go after their mother. They weren't far from Middleton St George when the cops pulled them in. God knows what they'd have done. They'd just...just lost it, I think.'

As the kettle boiled she leaned against the sink.

'The lads, Kev and Ricky and Tez as well actually, to give them their due, were brilliant. They rang around and told people to look out for the kids and the car. Gave out the descriptions. Better than the police, really. Once we knew they'd been in Reeth, they called all their connections to keep an eye out for them.'

'Which connections?'

'God knows. Ricky and Kev have dodgy mates everywhere. Mostly working in pubs and garages or sitting outside of pubs and garages drinking, as far as I can tell. 30 years of criminality paid off.'

'Where were you?'

'At mam's. She thought it was brilliant. I've never seen her so excited. She was on the brandy. Pissed as a fart by midnight. She's still sleeping it off, I should think.'

'How did you know where they'd go after Reeth?'

'We didn't. Someone called, improbably enough, Purple Albert - something to do with an intimate piercing, I know, gross...anyway he called Kev and said they'd got fuel at his garage in Richmond. From there we didn't know if they'd head down the A1. I felt sure they would. About tea time, our Tez volunteered to go out on his motorbike and try to find them. I thought that was just stupid because they were too far away from him in Roseworth and you can't just randomly drive around looking for a car. Anyway, he said he fancied a ride out and so off he goes, but he never found them. We thought we'd lost them. I was sure they'd headed south. Someone reckoned they'd seen them at about six in Barnard Castle and someone else called to say they were at a Little Chef on the A1. Dunno if it was them, though. Then, just when it'd gone quiet for a few hours, at about 11, Kev gets call from his mate Fat Freddy who saw them parked up outside a chippy in Darlington. He took a photo of them and sent it to Kev. It was deffo them. I knew that they might be on their way to Middleton St George again. It's not far. So I rang Tez, who was on his way back home on the A67. He puts a bomb on and spots them as they're coming off the A66. I called Colin at that point and he sent out his men.

They pulled them over just outside of Middleton and took them in. Job was a good 'un.' She rubbed her hands together and looked pleased.

'That's just incredible, man. And I was just lying there while it all happened. I had no idea anything was going on until four in the morning when Harcombe had told me there were developments. We just never knew the kids were so embittered at their parents, though we might have guessed the way they behaved at the restaurant that day.'

She nodded. The kettle clicked off. 'We couldn't have known they were that mental. We just couldn't. Not even after the scene outside of the restaurant.'

Within an hour, Jeff arrived, bursting through the door singing Thin Lizzy's 'Killer On The Loose.'

'Here he is, public enemy number one. Now then son, how was life in the Big House?'

He hi-fived Nick and sat down grinning at him. 'Good to see you man. I thought you'd lost it and whacked old Davey boy. I was just weighing up whether to sell your records last night when her Ladyship here gets on the case. Amazing, it was. I was on the police scanner last night listening to it all go down.'

'She's been saying, like.'

'Fuck me, those kids were crazy. That shit Hair Bear was selling, messed them up good, eh? Just as well we never had any, maybe we'd have turned into Bonnie and Clyde as well.'

'Aye, maybe.' He didn't feel much like joking around. It was all too depressing.

'So what was a day in the cells like?' he said.

'Boring.'

'Well, you're out now,' said Jeff and began singing 'Freebird' and laughing.

'Did you hear everything Davey James said?' asked Nick, turning to Julie.

She nodded. 'We didn't realise what was happening quick enough, though. When you'd jumped on him, your microphone got dislodged so we couldn't hear much, except muffled rustling and a few noises. It didn't actually even sound like a fight, they thought you'd just knocked it down your shirt. Then there was a weird noise, a sort of hiss, which must have been the glass table breaking, but we still didn't twig what had happened and Harcombe was reluctant to send everyone in when you were still there. But then it went quiet. I think the microphone broken or was cut. After we'd not heard anything for seven or eight minutes, he decided he had to find you. They all piled up there, but I was told to stay back. I followed on behind, though, and that's when I saw the kids leg it. The police were all so preoccupied with what they found in the house. They were away and gone really quickly.'

'Brilliant work, that,' said Jeff, grinning and nodding. 'Hey, I went round to the station last night to see you when I heard you'd been nicked, but they'd not let me in. Saw Col briefly, by the look on his face, he thought he was going to have to send you down.'

'I thought he was as well, man. As far as I knew, I'd choked James or broken his neck.'

'Heavy shit. Literally in Davey James' case. He must have weighed 22 stone. Still, the world is a better place without a twat like him, if even half the things they've been saying about him were true.'

'I actually feel really bad about what I did to him. I lost my mind y'know...I did...and I tried to kill him, or at least I didn't care if I did kill him.'

'Save your pity for someone who deserves it,' said Julie. 'He was a disgusting monster.'

But the feeling of darkness was hard for Nick to shake off and he sulked around for the rest of day, silent and uncommunicative. By the time they were getting ready for bed, Julie was getting tired of his attitude.

'Come on, this is stupid. You're dwelling on it too much. I know it's upsetting, but you were the good guy in this whole thing.'

'I just feel infected by it all. Like James' shit has soaked into me. Like I had to live in his stinking world and it's sucked me into its evil. It's like he was a distillation of everything that's wrong. Then I compounded it by not trying to be the better man, as we'd talked about at the Boro, but instead, just choking the life out of him. I could have got out of there without doing that. I attacked him out of sheer fury.'

She let out a groan, cursed and began pacing around the room. He knew her temper was up.

'Look man, I understand, I really do. What you did wasn't clever...' She blew out air and groaned again. '...but...but, Jesus Christ man, you're taking this too far. You beat the crap out of an absolute ogre. He'd still be alive if he hadn't messed up his kids so much and everything Davey James said to you is not exceptional in any way at all. Right?' She waved a hand at him. 'You're being such a wuss about this. So he would pay to have sex with me, so what? For 50 grand there was times in my life I'd have bloody done it. So he said he wanted to fuck me till it hurt me.' She shrugged and held her arms out wide. 'Aw, diddums, you think that suddenly tells me some men see women as something to disrespect and to use and be violent towards? Well, duh? Where have you been since the dawn of time, son?! Eh?! You think it shows they see us as a body, not a person? You think I didn't already know that? Of course I knew that. All women know it, and know it their whole lives. We have to live with that every day.'

She drank from a glass of water, turned around and jabbed a finger at him.

'Y'know what? Not one woman would have been surprised to hear how he talked. Not one. Seriously. You think you feel bad after a couple of hours with him? Imagine if your life chances relied on him? Imagine what that's like. Imagine if you'd married him and got trapped into a destructive relationship with him, where he has all the money and power. Then when you've done thinking about that, imagine being put down and dismissed because of your gender. Imagine being told where you can and can't go, what you can and can't wear and what you can and can't do because of what men will do to you and not just that, imagine being warned that if you do any of those things wrong, you'll deserve every single bit of abuse that comes your way, up to and including rape and violent assault. Imagine that? At least when you've had a fight with a bloke, you know when it's over. It's never over for women.'

She banged her fist down on the dressing table, turned and leaned into him as he sat on the edge of the bed, pointing again. He tried to say something, but she shouted him down.

'No, shut up and listen for a minute! We grew up being told that if we wear the wrong skirt, in the wrong street, at the wrong time, it would be our fault if we got attacked. Even my mam told me that quite categorically. If I wore a short skirt and was raped, it would be my fault, *my* fault?! Thank you and good night. Women can't go where we want to go, or do what we want to do, when we want to do it, because of worrying about what some bloke might do to us and it's so ordinary, so everyday, that you'd think it doesn't really happen any more, but it does. And you're getting all weepy about some horrid words a man said. For god's sake, grow up!' She was shouting now, really angry.

'I know Jules. I see that totally. It's just having it right in front of you and someone you love being the object of it, that really brings it home.'

But she was still exasperated at him.

'Oh, man! It's always someone's daughter, it's always someone's friend, or partner or lover who is the object of it. Try being an articulate and aggressive woman and you'll be called strident, shrill or worse still, feisty. If we like sex, we're bitches and sluts, if we don't, we're uptight and frigid. If we're not Madonnas, we're whores. If I like fixing cars and football, I'm a Tom Boy. Not a girl. Not a woman. I'm a Tom *Boy*. You think that's fair? And that's just one issue, it's like that on *everything*.'

She kicked the leg of the bed in frustration and anger at him and at the world.

'It's only recently that anything has started to change and only because we fought like stink to make it change. An hour or two with a twat like Davey James is nothing, I've dated men who turned out to be like him, most women will have and you're sitting there all boo-hoo and down about it. Don't be so self-indulgent and pathetic!'

She went silent for a moment, but wasn't done yet.

'You're not like him, but I'm not going to tell you how great you are because you bloody well shouldn't be like him and there are plenty of good blokes around. Not perfect, or PC, or holy, or anything, just downright good. You're one of them and that's all we need - for people to be good. If you let all this shit beat you down, you let bastards like Davey James win. So be a real man, fight it with how you live your life, what you say and how you behave and never, ever, ever, bloody well give in to it, because it's wrong; it always has been wrong and it always will be very fucking wrong and the only way it will ever change is if all the good people stand together. So when you've done feeling sorry for yourself, get on with just being a decent man because, god knows, we need some decent men in the world. Right?! Right?! Good!'

She picked up a towel from the floor and threw it in the laundry basket and let out a bark of anger. He sat in silence, her words ringing in his ears.

Eventually he cleared his throat and checked his phone.

'Fucking hell, Jules.'

'What? What's happened now?'

'The Boro have beaten Liverpool 2-0.'

'Bloody hell. Get in!'

Two weeks later, despite the Middlesbrough's cup replay win against West Ham and the defeat of Liverpool in their performance of the season, normal service was soon resumed at Spurs with a 4-0 loss and then losing in the FA cup away to Everton.

Nick and Julie walked away from the Riverside, having seen a last-minute injury time goal from Marlon King rescue a point against Portsmouth, but knowing the Boro, firmly stuck in 19th position in the league, were doomed to go down. Calls for manager Gareth Southgate to resign were loud and vociferous.

'I'm glad Tees Digital have had to close down, y'know,' said Nick as they made their way back to the car. 'I don't think I could have tolerated doing phone-ins, with more people just getting on Southgate's or Gibson's back, like they've done something really terrible. I don't know why people care so much if we go down, I really don't. It's just football. As long as the club survives financially, which overspending puts in jeopardy, it doesn't seem to matter that much to me. It just means seeing them play some other teams and probably winning a bit more often. I like the second division, it feels like an old pair of jeans to me. I'm much more comfortable with it than top flight. I thought that back in the 74-75 season after we got promoted. It just wasn't as good in Div One.'

She zipped up her hoodie and jammed her hands into her jeans pockets. 'Some fans seem to see it as though it's a personal insult. There's too much sense of entitlement in football these days. Boro have spent more years in the second tier than anywhere else. It's just a return to the long-term norm. Still wish we'd built a ground which held 20,000 though and not 35,000. It's going to look very empty next year when 12,000 turn up to watch us play Barnsley, or whoever. There's ambition and then there's just silly. Boro have never had big fizzin' crowds, not even in the 40s and 50s, apart from the occasional game.'

'First game I ever saw at Ayresome in the early 70s there was 9,000 there to see us play Hull in the second division. We've been batting above average for years now. It's a small town and if the economics don't pick up, it's going to get smaller and poorer. It's not a recipe for 35,000 crowds unless you give away 25,000 tickets per game...and even then.'

They walked down Dock Street and stopped off in The Bridge, their regular match-day pub. Nick got Julie an alcohol-free beer and himself a fizzy water. They'd just got a seat under the TV when the local news came on.

'More developments in the DJ Tees murder case today.'

Nick looked up at the screen. It was strange how it had become almost a brand. The DJ Tees Murder. They had a story about Toni and Zak James being moved from where they were currently being held on remand.

'I wonder how long it'll be before the court case? Not looking forward to having to give evidence,' said Nick.

'Colin said he eventually expects them to cop a plea,' said Julie.

'Cop a plea? Who are you? Kojak?'

'I fancy being bald, me. It'd make life so much easier,' she said with a laugh, shaking her hair. 'I wonder what my head is like under all this mop?'

'I'll probably find out what mine is like in the next ten years.'

'Ah you're not going bald too quickly. Not yet. I'm looking forward to waxing your head like a massive bowling ball.'

'I'd like a proper big phone in the car like Kojak's, remember? Big thing on a curly wire it was. How did that work?'

'I don't know. It was the 1970s, so I expect nylon underpants were involved somehow,' said Julie with a silly shrug.

'Nylon underpants and Crimplene trousers. What a combo. The younger generation knows nothing about having static electricity in your pubes. They've not lived fully.'

' Ha ha...I used to have some properly electric knickers. They were mint.'

'What, you plugged them in, like? Bloody hell, you couldn't go far from home with them on, not without a huge extension cord,' he said.

She yelped a laugh.

'They had the days of the week embroidered on them so you always knew what day it was when you got up with a hang over. Useful really.'

'I love that. And you'd always know if you've forgot to change them.'

'Aye. But I'd put them on on the wrong days so I'd get all

confused anyway. I swear when I took them off, there'd be blue sparks everywhere. It was due to my bedroom carpet being nylon or something. I turned into a human Van der Graaf Generator. One time, I was about 16 and I was messing around with this lad on the bedroom floor. Dunno why we were on the floor, I think the bed was too sexual, the floor seemed safer somehow...and he was feeling me up top, right...'

'You've let other men touch you? I'm already jealous...'

'...and he's giving me a bit of breasty honk-honk through me acrylic sweater. All good teenage stuff.'

'My mouth's gone all dry. Breasty honk-honk, you say?'

She laughed '...and then he goes downstairs, as was traditional. He unzips my pants - which were some sort of acrylic - and slides his hand into my infamous jungle. Suddenly, there were a couple of big blue sparks of static electricity and he yelps and pulls his hand away from the offending area! Ha ha...somehow, between all the man-made fibres in the jumper, pants, knickers and carpet, my pubes had become electric and they gave him a painful blast. Poor lad.'

'I'm sure that's not the only time your fanny has given someone a painful shock, Jules,' he said.

She howled out laugh and punched him on the top of his arm.

'Shush, you, people are listening. I tell you what though, one fart and I'd have gone up like brandy on a Christmas pudding!'

A couple of people were looking at them oddly as they rocked back and forward laughing. When they'd calmed down a bit, Julie went on. 'But anyway, Colin said they'll plead guilty in return for some sort of reduction of the sentence.'

Nick nodded. 'Good. I hope so, then I won't have to go over it all again.'

She drained her bottle. 'Oh, that went down nicely. Think I'll have another.'

She got up and went to the bar. Nick gazed at the TV. It flashed up a picture of Davey James. It was odd to think of hitting him so hard in the face. It was as though that had happened in another reality and not this happy little world. Julie returned with a beer, grinning.

'See the lad at the bar in the Boro shirt?'

He turned and took a look. He was about 19, probably a student and sported wispy looking facial hair and some variety of black skinny jeans.

'That's what I call a 'my-first-beard' beard,' he said, turning back to her. 'What about him?'

'He tried to chat me up. Me. Eeee, an' I could be his mam. I'm over twice his age and he's giving it, what are you doing later, fancy going for a drink? And all that.' She chuckled to herself and lapsed back into her strongest Hardwick accent. 'I said, oweee son, yer jokin', aren't ya? I've gorra bairn in us, me, like so I'm going home for a bath with me old fella, kidda.'

'How frightfully common you are, Ms Wells,' said Nick, affecting a posh accent. 'What did he say to that?'

'He actually apologized really nicely and was embarrassed. I like nice manners, so I told him I was flattered that he'd asked and that he seemed like a nice chap. Told him to find a woman his own age and not to pick up strange auld bags like me. That seemed to make him happy. Shows not all blokes are bastards though. I like to remind myself of that after a week working at the TW Centre.

'Maybe. You don't know what was going on in his head, though. The male mind can be a cesspit of sexual fantasy.'

She took a drink. 'Ah, I don't mind even if he was thinking that. Sex makes the world go around. Thinking about having it off with someone isn't innately sexist. If it was, I'd have to hand in my feminist PC card. Oops, I just did it again. Ha ha. Don't worry, I was thinking about you naked, honest and not him at the bar. Well, not much.'

He put on a high-pitched voice. 'I feel so objectified.'

'You are nothing but a massive, powerful hunk of rutting meat to me, lad, you know that.'

He laughed. 'I should put that on my CV.'

She laughed loudly. 'Yeah, that'll get some paid work. It might mean hanging around some of the dodgy bits of town, though.'

'Just as well I brought my lippy and put on my best panties then, eh.'

They laughed loudly again.

'Oh dear. I'll wet myself in a minute. Ha ha. You're in a very good mood, considering the Boro are going down faster than my electric knickers. It's nice to see you so happy, luv.'

'Yeah, you know what it is?'

'My continuing successful up-the-duffness by any chance?' She held her hands away from her belly.

'Yeah, totally that...'

He drank some water and reflected for a moment,

'...and the fact we're going to have this little new kiddie has really made me focus on what is important in life. I'd been worrying about how easy it was for me to be an awful bloke when I was with Davey James and I was worried about the violent streak in me as well and I still am, I guess, but I've realised life is all a journey to somewhere, isn't it? I'm not perfect and I never will be. And when I got home after I'd been let out, you gave me such a bollocking that it's made me put it all in perspective.'

'Good, well it's time someone did. You dwell on everything so much. Far too much. Just get on with living life as best you can.'

'I think I've finally realised that. All you can do is keep trying to iron out the bad bits as you go: keep open minded, keep learning and don't be afraid to change or admit you screwed up. It's like you said the other week, it's about good manners and just treating people how you'd like yourself to be treated.'

'And we're all going to mess up at times. Look at me and mam and how we nag at each other. When I'm not there I always feel like I should be a better, nicer daughter for her, but as soon as I see her, I just can't do that and it's like I'm 14 again and she just annoys the hell out of me and she's bloody lucky I don't claw her sodding eyes out.'

'Ah, don't worry about it. You're flawed to perfection, baby.'

She squinted and thought for a moment. 'That's a Thunder song, isn't it?'

'Give a prize to the pregnant lady.'

She punched the air. 'Yay! But it's not men versus women, is it? It's just right versus wrong. That's all. It's not some sort of complex political theory. It's just being nice to each other. It shouldn't be that hard.'

'Totally, yeah, and that's what we'll tell our daughter or our son,' he said.

'And knowing the ornery Teesside genes they'll be inheriting from us, they'll probably reject that advice just to spite us...' said Julie, '...and I suppose, weirdly enough, I'd be disappointed if they didn't.'

'I'll drink to that,' he said and clinked his glass against her bottle. 'Here's to you and me and a new arsey little Teessider.'

THE END

324

About John Nicholson

John is a well-known football writer whose work is read by tens of thousands of people every week. He's a columnist for Football365.com and has worked for the Daily Record, The Mirror, Sky and many other publications over the last 14 years.

Other John Nicholson Books
published by Biteback Publishing

We Ate All The Pies -
How Football Swallowed Britain Whole (2010)

The Meat Fix -
How 26 Years Of Healthy Eating Nearly Killed Me (2012)

Books in the Nick Guymer Series
Published by HEAD PUBLISHING

1. Teesside Steal (2013)
2. Queen Of The Tees (2013)
3. Teesside Missed (2013)
4. DJ Tees (2014)

Kindle/Ebook/Paperback

http://www.johnnicholsonwriter.com